THE FAMILY

MANDASUE HELLER is a million-copy bestselling Queen of Manchester Gangland crime. She was born in Warrington, Cheshire and has worked as a professional singer and full-time writer, with various other jobs in between: TV extra, barmaid, waitress, pharmacy assistant, phone-line tarot card reader, to name just a few.

Connect with her here:

X @MandasueHeller
@mandasueheller
http://mandasueheller.com/

THE FAMILY
MANDASUE
HELLER

ORION

First published in Great Britain in 2024
by Orion Fiction
an imprint of The Orion Publishing Group Ltd,
Carmelite House, 50 Victoria Embankment
London EC4Y 0DZ

An Hachette UK company

1 3 5 7 9 10 8 6 4 2

A CIP catalogue record for this book
is available from the British Library.

ISBN (Hardback) 978 1 3987 1337 6
ISBN (eBook) 978 1 3987 1340 6

Typeset at The Spartan Press Ltd,
Lymington, Hants

Printed and bound in Great Britain by Clays Ltd,
Elcograf S.p.A.

www.orionbooks.co.uk

For my beautiful mum, with eternal love xx

Prologue

The air in the room was icy, but her body felt like it was on fire. She could hear her friend talking to the older woman who had arrived a few minutes earlier, but she was in too much pain to make sense of their words.

'Help her!' the girl's friend pleaded when she cried out. 'She's losing too much blood.'

'Stay here and keep an eye on her,' the woman ordered. 'I'll fetch the doctor.'

'That will take too long. The baby is coming already. Please . . . you have to help her.'

'Shut up before somebody hears you. I'll be back as soon as I can.'

Terrified when the older woman rushed from the room, the younger one hugged herself as she gazed down at her friend. Her skin was slick with sweat, but the colour had completely drained from her face, making the red stain on the sheet beneath her stand out all the more starkly. Her friend suddenly screamed and arched her back before flopping silently against the pillows, and she stared in horror at the bloody mess that had slithered out from between her legs. Realising that she needed to do something when she saw that the baby wasn't moving or making a sound, she ran to the bathroom and grabbed a towel and a pair of nail scissors before rushing back to the bed.

Her friend was still breathing, albeit weakly, so she concentrated on the baby, using the towel to ease it the rest of the way out before cutting the umbilical cord, as she'd seen the village midwife do when her mother had given birth to her baby brother. Tears scorched her cheeks when she gazed at its tiny face after wiping away the blood and the mucus, and her voice faltered as she whispered a prayer before wrapping it inside the towel and gently rocking it in her arms.

Chapter 1

It had been a busy day at The Bluebell Café, but the takings didn't reflect that when Cheryl Taylor cashed up after showing her last customer out. Most of her regulars were elderly, and she knew they came for the companionship and warmth; but them nursing a single cup of tea for hours on end wasn't good business, and the owner was already hinting that he might have to shut up shop if things didn't improve. A lot of the other units had already closed, and the once vibrant market hall was beginning to feel like a ghost town as customers deserted it in favour of the newly renovated Arndale Centre. But she hadn't lost her job yet, and she didn't want to add the worry of that to her existing list of woes, so she pushed it out of her mind and got on with cleaning up before heading home.

It was dark and bitterly cold when Cheryl stepped off the bus after a hellish ride through rush-hour traffic, and she kept her head down and her hand firmly on the strap of her bag as she hurried past the high-rise flats that lined the perimeter of the Langley estate. She'd lived there for ten years, but this particular part had too many hiding places where muggers were known to lie in wait, so she was always cautious about walking through there at night.

Relieved to reach her own road on the more well-lit side of

the estate, she glanced over at the derelict house on the corner when she noticed that the *For Sale* sign that had been standing in the jungle-like front garden was gone. The sole survivor of the privately owned Victorian villas that had once dominated the area, it had been left to rot following the death of its elderly owner three years earlier, and a gang of youths had been using it as a hang-out for the last few months, causing havoc for the residents as they raced around on stolen motorbikes at all hours – and threatening anyone who dared to confront them.

Hoping that someone had bought the place and the trouble-makers would be cleared out, Cheryl walked on to her next-door neighbour Bob Baker's house. His front door swung open as soon as she touched it and she shook her head in despair as she stepped inside. She was forever telling him to keep it locked, especially now it was getting dark so much earlier; but the stubborn old bugger seemed to think he was still young and fit enough to fight off potential intruders.

Bob was sitting in his battered armchair next to the blazing fire when she popped her head around the living room door. His mangy old cat, Cyril, was curled up on his lap, and the TV was blaring.

'Bloody hell, Bob!' She covered her ears with her hands. 'That's deafening!'

'Sorry, love.' He grabbed the remote and quickly muted the TV. 'A load of workmen have been in Edna's place making a racket, so I had to turn it up.'

'Yeah, I noticed the sign was gone. Has it been sold, then?'

'Looks like it, aye. A couple turned up this afternoon and took a look around.'

'What were they like?'

'No idea, but they had a lovely motor.'

'Trust you to notice the car but not the people.' Cheryl tutted. 'Typical man.'

'Couldn't help it; it was a beauty,' Bob chuckled. 'So, how's your day been?'

'Not great. But that's good for you, 'cos there were loads of butties left over.'

'Thanks, love. What do I owe you?'

It was the same question he asked every day, and Cheryl gave the same answer as always in return: 'Nothing. They'd only have gone in the bin if I hadn't brought them home.'

'There's more than usual,' Bob remarked, raking through the contents of the bag. 'It'll take me a week to get through this lot.'

'I'm sure Cyril will help you,' Cheryl said, watching as the cat sniffed the air before stiffly standing up.

'What would we do without you, eh?' Bob said, pulling a chunk of tuna out of one of the sandwiches and feeding it to Cyril.

'It's my pleasure,' Cheryl replied, patting his bony shoulder when she saw the gratitude in his eyes. He'd been an active man when she first moved in, always out and about doing odd jobs for the neighbours and looking in on the older ones. In his seventies now, with his health in decline, he rarely ventured past the doorstep, and she knew he probably wouldn't speak to another human for days on end if she didn't call in on him each evening. Making a snap decision to stay a little longer than usual, she said, 'Fancy a brew, Bob?'

'I'd love one,' he said. 'But I don't want to keep you if you need to get home to Chris.'

'We split up six months ago,' she reminded him as she slipped her coat off.

'Did you?' He frowned. 'I could have sworn I saw him going into yours earlier.'

'I doubt that, seeing as I took his keys off him when I kicked him out,' Cheryl muttered, her jaw clenching at the memory of the day she had arrived home early from work and caught her boyfriend of four years screwing one of her so-called friends. A lot more had come out after that, and she'd been shocked to learn that he had not only cheated several other times, but had also been helping himself to her money and taking out loans in her name – some of which she was paying off even now.

Still furious with herself for ignoring the red flags that she would have seen in a heartbeat if it had been one of her friends' boyfriends acting the way Chris had, Cheryl determinedly pushed him out of her mind and laid her coat over the back of the sofa before heading to the kitchen. It was the same layout as her own, with the same beige units and cheap council lino; but that was where any similarity ended, and she stared around in shock after switching the light on. The ledges were barely visible beneath mounds of rubbish, the dishes in the sink were immersed in a pool of slimy liquid, and there were so many bin bags piled up behind the back door, it would be impossible to escape if there was a fire at the front of the house.

Bob was a proud man and she didn't want to offend him by offering to clean up, but it was obvious he needed help, and she wondered if she ought to ring social services and ask them to send somebody over to check on him. Or, better still, she could track down his waste-of-space daughter and tell *her* to do something. The selfish cow lived nearby, but she only ever showed her face when she wanted a handout – and she was always in and out within seconds, so she never spent any quality time with him.

'You OK in there, love?' Bob called out from the living room, breaking into her thoughts.

'I'm fine,' Cheryl called back. 'Won't be a tick.'

Sighing, she swallowed her revulsion and gingerly plucked two cups out of the swamp.

Bob had been in a talkative mood and his voice was still ringing in Cheryl's head when she got home an hour later. Her house was freezing, but she was already dreading her next gas bill, so she decided to watch TV in bed rather than put the heating on.

The doorbell rang as she was about to make her way upstairs, and she was surprised to see her best friend, Anna Johnson, standing outside when she peeped through the spyhole.

'What are you doing here?' Cheryl asked, opening the door. 'I thought you were going out with Sean tonight?'

'He's dumped me,' Anna said, bringing a blast of icy air in with her when she stepped inside.

'Why?' Cheryl ushered her into the living room and switched the light on. 'I thought it was going well between you.'

'So did I, but he obviously thought different,' Anna said, flopping onto the sofa.

'What happened?' Cheryl perched beside her.

'He was supposed to meet me in town, but he didn't turn up,' Anna explained. 'His phone kept going to voicemail when I tried to ring him, and I started to get worried that he might have had a crash or something. But just as I was about to ring round the hospitals, he texted saying he wasn't coming 'cos everything's moving too fast and he thinks we need a break.'

'I'm sorry, babe,' Cheryl sympathised, reaching out to squeeze her hand. 'But at least he hasn't finished it completely, so there's still a chance he'll change his mind.'

'I just don't get what I did wrong,' Anna replied miserably. 'Why do the nice ones always end up ghosting me? I'm not that bad, am I?'

7

'Of course not,' Cheryl assured her. 'And Sean hasn't ghosted you, so don't write him off. I'm sure he'll get in touch when he's had a chance to think things over.'

'Well, he'd best not take too long about it, or he might find I've moved on,' Anna huffed. 'I could walk into any club in town right now and have at least ten guys' numbers by closing time.'

'But they're not the type of men you want,' said Cheryl. 'And if you went with someone to get back at Sean, I guarantee you'd regret it.'

'I know,' Anna conceded, sighing as she reached into her bag and pulled out a bottle of vodka. 'Oh well, there's nothing I can do about it tonight 'cos he's turned his phone off, so go get some glasses and let's get hammered.'

'I'll get one for you, but I'm having tea,' Cheryl said. 'I've got work in the morning.'

'One shot won't kill you,' Anna insisted. 'And you can't let me drink alone at a time like this.'

'OK, I'll have one,' Cheryl agreed. 'But then I'm going to bed.'

'We'll see,' Anna said, grinning as she twisted the lid off the bottle and raised it to her lips.

Chapter 2

Cheryl was woken by the piercing beeps of a reversing vehicle, followed by doors slamming and loud male voices. She groped for her phone on the bedside table and groaned when she saw that it was only 6.30 a.m.

'What's all the noise?' a voice croaked.

Shocked, Cheryl twisted her head round and stared at the lump on the other side of the bed. 'Bloody hell, Anna!' she gasped when her friend's bleary face emerged from under the quilt. 'You scared the life out of me.'

'Time is it?' Anna asked.

'Half six,' Cheryl said, dropping her feet to the floor and grabbing her dressing gown before heading to the window to see who was making all the noise.

In the dawn light, a group of men in overalls were unloading machinery from the back of a van parked outside the empty house across the road. Annoyed that they weren't even trying to be quiet about it, she was about to open the window and yell at them to keep it down, when a sleek BMW with tinted windows turned the corner and pulled in behind the van. She guessed that it must be the car Bob had mentioned, because no one on the Langley had the kind of money to afford a flashy motor like that.

Curious, she rested her elbows on the windowsill and watched as a dark-haired, middle-aged man climbed out of the driver's side door and walked over to the workmen. Unable to see his face when he stood with his back to her, she switched her gaze back to the car when the passenger door opened and a blonde woman wearing a full-length fur coat and high-heeled boots stepped out and looked around.

'Who's that?' Anna asked, coming up behind her and peering over her shoulder.

'I think they've bought the old house,' Cheryl said.

'They must have more money than sense,' Anna sneered. 'It's falling to bits.'

'Bob reckons it's huge inside, so it'll be worth a bomb if they do it up.'

'Not round here, it won't. No offence, babe, but you've got to admit it's a shithole.'

'Don't be cheeky.'

'Not my fault I've got higher standards than you,' Anna said, yawning loudly as she stretched her arms above her head. 'Anything to eat? I'm starving.'

'No.' Cheryl straightened up. 'But I'll make you something if you come to the café.'

'Nah, you're all right, I'll go to my mum's and get her to make me a spinach smoothie,' Anna said, patting her flat stomach. 'Need to shift this lard now I'm single again.'

'Behave,' Cheryl snorted. 'You'll disappear if you get any thi—'

'Oh my frickin' God!' Anna pushed past her and peered through the window. 'Who is *that*?'

Cheryl followed her gaze and saw a younger, more handsome version of the BMW's driver talking to the woman.

'Maybe their son?'

'Well, if he's your new neighbour, get ready for a lodger, 'cos he is fit as *fuck*.'

'Oh, so you'd leave your posh, *rent-free* flat to live in this shithole, would you?' Cheryl teased.

'If that was going to be my view every morning, you're dead right I would!' Anna gushed.

As if sensing that he was being watched, the man suddenly turned his head and scanned the windows on Cheryl's side of the road.

'Shit!' Anna ducked as if he'd aimed a gun at her. 'D'you think he saw me?'

'Doubt it, it's too dark in here,' Cheryl said, pulling the curtains shut and switching the light on. 'Hey!' she protested when Anna jumped up and rushed to the door. 'Don't be hogging the bathroom. I need to get ready for work.'

'Won't be long,' Anna called back over her shoulder. 'Put the kettle on while you're waiting.'

'You're a cheeky cow,' Cheryl muttered.

'Love you too,' Anna trilled, slamming the bathroom door shut.

The BMW was still parked outside when Cheryl and Anna left the house a short time later. It was fully light by then, and the fur-coated woman was sitting in the passenger seat of the car, with the window rolled down and her mobile phone pressed to her ear.

'Size of that rock,' Anna whispered, nudging Cheryl when a beam of sunlight glinted off a diamond ring on the woman's finger. 'Bet it cost more than the house and car put together.'

Cheryl glanced over, but immediately wished she hadn't when the woman glared at her.

Anna caught the look, but instead of averting her gaze,

as Cheryl had, she smiled and waggled her fingers, yelling: 'Morning!'

'Pack it in,' Cheryl hissed as the woman fired another eye-dagger in their direction.

'Only introducing myself to my future mother-in-law,' Anna quipped.

'Rather you than me,' Cheryl muttered. 'She looks like a right bitch.'

'A *rich* bitch,' Anna countered. 'Which means my new hubby will be too.'

'I see you've got over Sean, then?' Cheryl teased.

'Sean who?' Anna grinned, linking arms with her as they walked on.

In the back of the BMW, unaware that his mother, Sonia, had finished her call and was watching him in the vanity mirror as she reapplied her lipstick, Dale Moran twisted his head to watch the blonde and the redhead disappear around the corner.

'Stop ogling those girls and go get your father,' Sonia ordered.

'He's busy,' Dale said, nodding to the porch of the house, where his dad was talking to one of the workmen.

'Well, tell him to get a move on,' Sonia snapped. 'We've only got half an hour to get to the airport.'

'All right, keep your hair on,' Dale muttered, pushing his door open and wearily climbing out. He'd had a late night and could have done without being woken at 5 a.m. with the news that some relative he'd never heard of had died and his parents needed him to take them to the airport. Thankfully, his dad had insisted on driving there, giving him a chance to sober up before the return journey, but he couldn't wait to get home and go back to bed.

'About time!' Sonia said when her husband, Alfie, followed

Dale back to the car a few minutes later. 'I was starting to think you were deliberately trying to make us late.'

'Chill out,' he drawled, settling into the driver's seat. 'We've got plenty of time.'

'In whose universe is twenty-five minutes plenty of time?' Sonia argued. 'What if we hit traffic, or there's a delay checking in, or—'

Sighing, Dale stuffed his AirPods into his ears and turned up the volume of the music to drown out the sound of her voice.

Chapter 3

Exhausted after another long day at the café, Cheryl was looking forward to a bath and an early night, so she wasn't pleased to hear the whine of drills and the thudding of hammers coming from the old house when she got home that evening. Lights were blazing behind the windows, and she could see workmen moving around inside. As she was passing, one of them came outside and lit a cigarette, and she glowered at him when he raised his hand in greeting.

After dropping off the leftovers she'd brought back for Bob, she went home and scooped up the letters that were scattered on the mat behind the door. She skimmed through them as she made her way into the kitchen, but they all looked like bills, so she shoved them, unopened, into the drawer with the rest and then switched the kettle on.

Suddenly, there was the sound of pounding on the front door. Her heart leapt into her throat when the letter box flapped open and a man called: 'Open up! It's payment time!'

Stomach churning, Cheryl flipped the light off and crouched in the shadows at the side of the fridge.

A few seconds later, a different, more aggressive voice called: 'No point hiding, bitch; we saw you going in. Now get this door open or I'll kick it in. You've got ten seconds!'

Cheryl covered her ears with her hands, terrified when more heavy booms followed. A few seconds later, the banging suddenly stopped, and she heard raised voices outside, some of which sounded foreign.

Curious to know what was going on, she crept to the front door and peered through the spyhole. The loan shark whose voice she had recognised, and a younger, more muscular-looking man, were having a heated discussion with the workmen from across the road, but they were all shouting over each other, so she couldn't understand what they were saying.

As she watched, the BMW she'd seen that morning pulled up across the road, and a wave of shame washed over her when the man whom she presumed to be the new owners' son climbed out and looked over. It was bad enough that Anna had made a show of her in front of his mother that morning, but now her new neighbours would think she was the kind of person who borrowed money and didn't pay it back.

Dale had heard the commotion as he turned the corner, and he frowned when he saw that his dad's workmen were involved. Pretty sure that it was the house he'd seen the girls coming out of that morning, he walked over and asked the crew leader, Jakub, who was standing at the back of the group, what was going on.

'Alek went for smoke and saw girl go into house,' Jakub told him. 'Then two men came and start to kick door, so we come to make sure she is safe. They say they have warrant, but they refuse to show us, so—'

'We're court-appointed officials,' a voice bellowed from the other side of the group. 'And you boat-rats had better back the fuck off before I get you all deported!'

Dale narrowed his eyes and pushed his way past the workmen.

Smiling slyly when he came face to face with Kenny Doyle, he said, 'Thought I recognised that voice. Up to your old tricks again, are you, Ken?'

'Who the fuck are you?' the younger man demanded, squaring up to him.

'Your worst nightmare if you don't get out of my face,' Dale replied coolly.

'That supposed to be some kind of threat?' the man sneered.

'Why don't you test me and find out?' Dale challenged.

'Leave it!' Kenny hissed, eyeing Dale warily as he pushed the lad towards the gate. 'We'll come back another time.'

'No you won't,' Dale said, switching his gaze back to Kenny. 'This is our patch now, and there'll be trouble if I see you around here again. Understood?'

'Loud and clear,' Kenny mumbled.

'What the fuck?' The younger man stared at Kenny in disbelief. 'Don't tell me you're gonna let this ponce push you around? We might be outnumbered, but I'll take the whole lot of 'em on if I have to.'

'Shut your mouth and get back to the van,' Kenny barked. Then, turning to Dale, his tone deferential, he said, 'Sorry for the misunderstanding, son. Give my regards to your dad.'

'Will do,' Dale said. 'Oh, and I'll tell your *clients* the debt's wiped while I'm at it, shall I?'

'Absolutely,' Kenny agreed.

Dale watched as the man scuttled away and hopped into a small van that was parked a few doors down. He had no idea how much the girls owed, but he hoped it was a lot, because Kenny Doyle was a parasite who preyed on the weak and vulnerable, and he welcomed any chance to deprive the bastard of his ill-gotten gains.

After the van had gone, Dale sent the workmen back to the

house and then knocked on the door. When no answer came, he peered through the letter box. The house was in darkness and he couldn't hear anyone moving around, but Jakub reckoned at least one of the girls had gone inside before Kenny and his goon had turned up, so he figured she was probably hiding.

'If you can hear me, my name's Dale and I'm from the house across the road,' he called into the hallway. 'I just wanted to check you're OK and let you know that Kenny's gone and—'

The door creaked open before he could go on, and he straightened up when the red-headed girl he'd seen that morning peered out at him warily through the crack.

'Hi, I'm Dale from—'

'Across the road,' she finished for him as she looked out over his shoulder. 'Has he really gone?'

'Yeah, and he won't be coming back,' Dale assured her. 'He told me to tell you the debt's wiped.'

'What?' She looked confused. 'He's been hassling me for weeks, so why would he drop it just like that?'

'I guess his conscience got the better of him.' Dale shrugged.

'I find that hard to believe,' she said bitterly. 'I've told him the debt's my ex's not mine, but he doesn't care. He said it's attached to the house not the person, so I've got to pay it.'

'He's talking shit to scare you into paying. But you shouldn't have any more trouble from him now I've had a word.'

'I hope not.'

Dale could see that she was unconvinced and took one of his business cards out of his wallet. 'Here, take my number. You won't need it, because that clown knows better than to mess with me; but feel free to call me if you think you see him hanging around.'

'Thanks.' She slipped the card into her pocket. 'And can you thank the other men for me, as well? That thug would have kicked the door in if they hadn't come over.'

'No problem,' Dale said, glancing at his watch. 'I'm supposed to be somewhere, so I'd best get going. Are you sure you're OK?'

'Yeah, I'm fine. And I'm Cheryl, by the way.'

'Nice to meet you, Cheryl.' Dale winked at her. 'Catch you later.'

Cheeks on fire, Cheryl closed the door and watched through the spyhole as Dale crossed the road and climbed into his car. Releasing a tense breath when he'd gone, she rested her forehead against the cold wood. She hoped to God he was right about it being over with the loan shark, because she could barely afford her own bills, never mind being stuck with Chris's debts as well. If she'd had any idea where the bastard was living, she would happily have given his address to those men for landing her in the shit. But the last she'd heard he had moved down south to leech off some girl he'd met on a dating site, so it looked like he had got away with it.

Swallowing the bitter taste that always flooded her mouth at the thought of Chris, Cheryl went back to the kitchen. As she waited for the kettle to re-boil, she slid the card out of her pocket and gazed at the emblem of a black bird on a silver background. It read: *BLACK SWAN INC*, followed by Dale's name and mobile number, and she smiled to herself as she traced the embossed lettering with her fingertips. He was very handsome up close, with a lovely smile and twinkly eyes. His voice was nice too, with the hint of another, softer accent overlaying the Mancunian twang; and his suit had looked as expensive as his aftershave had smelled.

A thrill rippled through her stomach when she recalled the way he'd winked at her, but she quickly shook any notion that it had meant anything out of her head. Men like him didn't go for girls like her, not when there were beauties like Anna to choose from. In fact, it was probably Anna he'd been hoping to see when she opened the door, she guessed, and he had only been nice to her in the hopes that she would put in a good word for him.

Sure that she was right, Cheryl dropped the card into the drawer with the bills and finished making her brew.

Dale drove over to the family antiques shop in Didsbury. The shutters were down, but his older brother Stefan's car was sitting outside, so he parked up beside it and rapped on the door.

'You're late,' Stefan chided, giving him a disapproving look when he opened up.

'I got waylaid,' Dale said, handing over the package his father had asked him to drop off as he stepped inside. 'I called in at the new house and ran into Kenny Doyle and his muscle putting the frighteners on a girl across the road.'

'I thought he was dead,' Stefan said, carrying the package to the office at the rear of the shop.

'Not yet, but he will be if I catch him round there again,' Dale replied, weaving around a pile of dusty old furniture as he followed. 'Where's this shit from?'

'House clearance,' Stefan said over his shoulder as he opened the safe and placed the package inside. 'I know it looks like junk, but it'll fetch a fair price once I've cleaned it up.'

'If you say so,' Dale scoffed, pushing his cuff back to look at his watch. 'Hurry up, mate. I need to get moving before my date does a runner.'

'You've got a date?' Stefan raised an eyebrow as he took an envelope stuffed with money out of the safe and passed it to him. 'Does Caroline know?'

'What's it got to do with *her?*' Dale frowned.

'Aren't you back together?' Stefan asked. 'I'm sure Estelle said she saw you with her last week.'

Irritated to think that his sister-in-law had been spying on him and reporting back to his brother, Dale said, 'I wasn't *with* her. She turned up when I was at the gym – like the bunny boiler she is.'

'So who's the date?' Stefan asked, lifting his jacket off the back of the chair.

'No idea,' Dale admitted. 'She reckons I asked her out at the club after I split with Caz, but I must have been pissed, 'cos I'd totally forgotten about it till she messaged this afternoon asking where I wanted to meet up.'

'And you're still going? What if she's a freak?'

'She's actually pretty hot,' Dale said, taking out his phone to show his brother the photo attached to the WhatsApp message he'd received from the girl.

Stefan glanced at it and shrugged. 'She's OK, I suppose. But she's no Caroline.'

'What is it with you and my ex?' Dale scowled. 'Does Estelle know you've got a thing for her?'

'Don't be stupid,' Stefan protested. 'I only—'

'I'm out of here,' Dale said, cutting the conversation dead. 'See you later.'

'Are you still coming over for dinner next week?' Stefan called after him as he walked out through the shop. But Dale continued on his way without answering.

Chapter 4

A wailing alarm wormed its way into her dream and woke Cheryl, who had fallen asleep watching a film. Disorientated, she got up and stumbled over to the window, praying that it wasn't a fire, because if one house on the block went up in flames, the rest would quickly follow.

No smoke was coming from any of the neighbouring houses, but she noticed the alarm box on the wall of the house across the road flashing. Afraid that the gang might have broken back in after the workmen had left, she was contemplating whether to get Dale's card and give him a call, when the man himself rushed out of the front door and jogged across the road. Her stomach flipped when she realised he was heading to her house, and she quickly smoothed her hair and pulled on her dressing gown when the doorbell rang.

'Sorry if I woke you,' Dale said when she opened the door. 'But I saw a light on upstairs and hoped you might be up.'

'I was watching TV,' Cheryl lied, shivering in the icy air. 'Is everything OK?'

'I was on my way home and called in to check the house was secure, but I forgot the alarm had been turned back on,' he explained. 'I know it's a long shot, but I don't suppose you know the code, do you? I don't think it's been changed yet, so it should be the same one the last owner used.'

'Sorry, I don't,' Cheryl said. 'Edna was a bit reclusive, so I doubt she'd have given it to anyone.'

'Damn.' Dale raked a hand through his hair when lights started coming on in the surrounding houses. 'I was going to ring my dad to ask him for it, but I seem to have lost my phone.'

'You can use mine,' Cheryl offered. 'Come inside while I get it.'

'Probably best if I wait here,' Dale said. 'I don't want to disturb your friend.'

'My friend?' She gave him a questioning look. Then, realising who he meant, she said, 'Oh, you mean Anna? No, it's all right, she doesn't live here.'

Bob's door suddenly opened, and he stepped outside wearing baggy pyjama bottoms and a filthy vest that accentuated his wasted arm muscles and sunken chest. He shielded his eyes with his hand and looked around to pinpoint where the noise was coming from. Then, spotting Cheryl, he hobbled over to the fence dividing their front gardens.

'What's going on? Have them thugs got back into Edna's place?'

'No, it's not them,' Cheryl reassured him. 'This is the new owner, Dale. He came to check the house and forgot the alarm code.'

'Actually, my dad owns it,' Dale corrected her. 'But they've had to fly out for a family funeral, so I've been left in charge.'

'Well, hurry up and get that turned off if you're in charge,' Bob ordered. 'I've already had two days of racket, and I'm not putting up with it at night, an' all.'

'He's going to phone his dad to get the code, so it'll be off soon,' Cheryl said.

'Better had be,' Bob grumbled, heading back to his house.

'Don't worry about him,' Cheryl said, gesturing for Dale to come inside when Bob's front door slammed shut. 'He'll have forgotten about it by morning.'

'Hope so,' Dale said, stepping into the hallway and looking around. 'Nice place.'

'It's OK,' Cheryl murmured, quickly averting her gaze when she got her first clear look at his eyes and saw that they were hazel with tiny flecks of gold running through them. 'Go and sit down. I won't be a sec.'

She waved him into the living room, and then dashed upstairs to get her phone. Handing it to him when she came back, she backed out into the hall and pulled the door shut to let him make his call in private.

'Thanks for that,' Dale said, handing the phone to her when he came out a couple of minutes later. 'But you didn't have to leave.'

'I don't like listening in on other people's conversations,' she said, slipping the phone into her pocket. 'Did you get the code?'

'Yep.' Dale rolled his eyes. 'Would you believe it's one, two, three, four? Most obvious code in the world, and it didn't even occur to me to try it.'

'Ah, well, at least you won't forget it again.'

'Until they change it,' Dale said. 'Anyway, best go and turn it off before I get lynched by your neighbours. Thanks for the help. I really appreciate it.'

'Any time,' Cheryl said, smiling as she let him out.

She watched as he ran across the road and went into the house. Moments later, the alarm stopped and silence descended on the road. As the neighbours' lights started to go out, she closed the door and switched off the living-room light.

About to head back to bed, she heard a tap on the door and

quickly opened it when she looked through the spyhole and saw that it was Dale.

'Sorry for disturbing you again, but I wanted to apologise for getting you up unnecessarily,' he said, sheepishly holding up his phone. 'It was on the floor of the car; must have slipped out of my pocket when I got here.'

'Don't worry about it,' she smiled. 'I'm just glad you found it.'

'Me too,' he said. Then, looking awkward, he said, 'Actually, that wasn't my only reason for coming back.'

'Oh?' She gave him a questioning look.

'Feel free to say no if you're not interested,' he said. 'But I was wondering if I could take you out for dinner?'

'*Me?*' Her eyebrows shot up in surprise.

'Yeah, *you.*' He laughed. 'Unless you've got an invisible friend standing next to you; in which case, hi, friend.'

Amused when he waved at the empty space beside her, Cheryl said, 'If you're doing this because I let you use my phone, there's honestly no need.'

'No, I'm doing it because I like you and wouldn't mind getting to know you better,' Dale insisted. 'Unless you've already got a boyfriend?'

'No, I don't,' Cheryl said, casting a surreptitious glance at his hand to make sure he wasn't wearing a wedding ring before adding, 'And yes, I will go out for dinner with you.'

'Really?' Dale grinned. 'Wow. I wasn't expecting that. How about tomorrow? I could pick you up at eight, if that's OK for you?'

'Yes, that's fine,' Cheryl said, feeling suddenly shy.

'Great. I'll see you tomorrow then. Night.'

'Night.'

Heart pounding, Cheryl closed the door and hugged herself, wondering what the hell had just happened – and, more importantly, how she was going to tell Anna about it. If it had been any other man, it wouldn't have been a problem; but Anna had already set her sights on Dale and was bound to take this as a stab in the back. But there was always a chance that Anna would get back with Sean, so was there really any harm in it?

Telling herself that she was overthinking it, that Anna wouldn't have thought twice about accepting if the shoe was on the other foot, Cheryl rushed upstairs and rifled through her wardrobe in search of something suitable to wear. She hadn't dated anyone since Chris, and he'd never taken her anywhere fancy when they were together, so she'd had no reason to dress up. But Dale was a stylish man, so there was no way she could wear the jeans and T-shirts she usually opted for.

She selected an emerald-green smock-type dress that still looked fairly new and hung it on the back of her bedroom door to let the creases drop out, then switched off the TV and the lamp and climbed into bed with a smile on her lips.

Chapter 5

After the commotion with the alarm in the early hours, Bob had struggled to get back to sleep, so he was furious to be woken again by the noisy arrival of the workmen a few hours later. Tired and cranky, his muscles aching from tossing and turning, he muttered curses under his breath as he dragged himself down the stairs and into the kitchen. He felt like going over to Edna's place and giving the buggers an earful, but he'd heard them speaking to each other in a foreign language and doubted they would understand him, so he decided he would wait for the owner's son to turn up and give *him* what for instead.

As always, Cyril followed Bob downstairs and sat patiently beside his bowl. After feeding him, Bob switched the kettle on and was walking to the sink to fish out a cup when he stubbed his toe on something solid hidden beneath the rubbish. He instinctively reached down to rub it but lost his balance, flailing his arms as he fell. Stars exploded in front of his eyes when his head smashed into the corner of the table, and then darkness descended as he slithered to the floor.

Excited about her date, Cheryl rushed home from work that evening. Calling in at Bob's to drop off the leftovers she'd bagged for him, she was surprised to find his door locked for a change.

No answer came when she knocked, so she moved to the window and peered through the grimy net curtain, expecting to see him asleep in his chair – or to hear that the TV was turned up too loud for him to hear the door. When she saw that the room was empty and dark, she called his name through the letter box, but all that came back was a plaintive meow from the kitchen at the far end of the hall.

Sure that something must be wrong, because Bob never locked Cyril away, she ran to her own house and rushed out into the yard. Bob's back door was unlocked so she used her shoulder to force the bin bags out of the way and stepped inside. A foul stench rose from the bags, and she covered her nose with her hand and groped her way across the room to switch the light on. That was when she saw Bob, lying motionless on the floor in a pool of congealing blood, his face the colour of ash.

'Bob?' she cried, kneeling beside him and touching his arm. 'It's Cheryl. Can you hear me, love?'

He didn't respond, and his flesh felt like ice. Terrified that he might be dead, tears flooded her eyes as she rose shakily to her feet and fumbled her phone out of her pocket.

Dale was in a good mood as he drove over to Manchester to pick Cheryl up. His previous night's date had been an absolute disaster. Not only had the girl looked nothing like her photo, she also hadn't stopped talking from the moment they met; and he'd been seriously tempted to stuff his serviette into her mouth to shut her up as she banged on about all the famous footballers she reckoned she'd fucked.

Confident that he was going to have a much better time with Cheryl, he was smiling as he turned onto her road, but it quickly slipped when he saw an ambulance parked outside her house.

When he saw her coming out of her neighbour's place as he parked up, he jumped out and ran over to her.

'What's happened? Are you OK?'

'Bob's had a fall,' she told him, her hand shaking as she slotted her key into the front door. 'I found him on the kitchen floor when I got home from work. He's cut his head and they think he might have hypothermia, so he must have been there for hours.'

'Oh Christ, that's awful,' Dale said, following her inside. 'Is there anything I can do?'

'Not really,' she said, making her way into the kitchen to close and lock her back door. 'I'm sorry, but I'm going to have to cancel dinner. They've said I can go in the ambulance with him.'

'Hey, it's going to be OK,' Dale said, squeezing her shoulder when he saw the tears in her eyes. 'He's in good hands.'

'I know,' she sniffed. 'It was a shock, that's all. I meant to let you know earlier, so you didn't waste your time coming over, but the ambulance took ages to get here, and—'

'Don't worry about me, I'm fine,' Dale interrupted. 'Go and do what you need to do.'

Cheryl nodded and gave him a grateful smile, then grabbed her handbag and made her way out. The paramedics were already loading Bob into the back of the ambulance, so she pulled her door shut and said goodnight to Dale before rushing over to it.

Dale waved when Cheryl glanced out at him after taking a seat. Then, sighing, he pulled out his phone to cancel the restaurant reservation as he walked back to his car. His phone pinged before he'd had a chance to dial the number, and he frowned when he read the short message on the screen. He typed a quick reply, telling the sender that he would be there in ten minutes, then hopped into the car, fired the engine and drove off.

Chapter 6

It was almost midnight before Cheryl left the hospital, and she was exhausted as she set off for the bus stop. Bob's head injury hadn't been as bad as first suspected and she'd been relieved when he regained consciousness and felt able to sit up and drink a cup of tea. The nurse who was looking after him had told Cheryl that, as well as mild hypothermia, he was also anaemic and had a nasty water infection, so they were going to keep him in for a few days until he was stabilised. It had saddened Cheryl to realise that he must have been suffering for a while, but she'd been happy to hear that the hospital intended to contact social services to get a care package put in place before he was discharged.

As she neared the main road now, she heard a car driving slowly up behind her and quickened her step, conscious that no one was around to help if anything happened. Seconds later, the car pulled alongside her, and the hairs on the back of her neck stood on end when she heard her name being called. She glanced round and felt a wave of relief wash over her when she saw Dale smiling out at her through the open passenger-side window.

'What are you doing here?' she asked, leaning down to speak to him.

'I had to nip over to my dad's club to sort something out and cut myself on a broken glass,' he said, rolling his eyes as he held up his bandaged hand. 'It bled quite a lot, but there's no major damage, so they glued me back together and sent me on my way.'

'You're lucky,' Cheryl said, swiping her hair off her face when the wind whipped it into her eyes. 'One of my friends did that and sliced right through the tendon.'

'Well, thankfully it missed mine,' Dale replied. 'But never mind me; how's the old man?'

'Pretty weak. But they're keeping a close eye on him, so I think he'll be OK.'

'That's good,' Dale said, leaning across the seat to open the door. 'Hop in. I'll give you a lift home.'

'Are you sure?' Cheryl asked. 'I don't want to put you out.'

'You're not,' he assured her. 'I need to check the house before I go home, so I was heading over there anyway.'

'Thanks,' she said, gratefully climbing in and pulling the door shut.

'Have you eaten yet?' Dale asked as he set off. 'Only there's a great Indian restaurant not far from here that stays open till two, if you fancy it?'

Conscious that she was still wearing her work clothes and hadn't brushed her hair since that morning, Cheryl said, 'I'm not really dressed for it, but you can drop me at the bus stop if you want to go.'

'Absolutely not,' Dale replied firmly. 'I said I'd take you home, and that's what I'm going to do. Even if it *is* your fault I'm starving.'

'I'm sorry,' Cheryl apologised, feeling guilty that he'd missed out on dinner because of her drama.

'Hey, I'm joking,' he said when he saw her expression. 'But if you don't fancy an Indian, how about a burger? I know it's not the fancy meal you were probably expecting, but—'

'That would be perfect,' Cheryl cut in, happy that she wouldn't have to leave the car.

'You like burgers?'

'Love them.'

'Me too!' Dale grinned. 'Looks like you and me are going to get on really well.'

Shivering when he winked at her, Cheryl gazed out of the window and inhaled deeply to calm the butterflies in her stomach.

After a quick trip to a drive-through, where Dale insisted on paying for their burgers to make up for the missed meal, they headed back to Cheryl's house. Most of the estate was in darkness, but she saw a glow through the glass of Bob's front door and guessed that the paramedics must have left the kitchen light on when they'd taken him away that afternoon.

'Take these and let yourself in,' she said, handing her keys to Dale after climbing out of the car. 'I've just got to see to Cyril.'

'Cyril?' Dale gave her a questioning look.

'Bob's cat,' she explained. 'I promised I'd look after him, and he's been on his own all day, so he's probably starving by now.'

'OK, but don't be long,' Dale said, leaning back into the car and grabbing a bottle of wine off the back seat. 'Where do you keep your glasses?'

'First cupboard behind the kitchen door. Won't be a sec.'

Rushing to Bob's house as Dale walked to hers, Cheryl let herself in and almost tripped over Cyril, who was sitting behind the door.

'Hello, baby,' she cooed, gently picking him up when he

meowed. 'I know you're missing your daddy, but he'll be home soon, I promise.'

She carried him into the kitchen and shuddered when she saw the blood on the floor. With Bob out of the way for a while, she realised this would be the perfect opportunity to clean the place for him, using the excuse that she'd been worried about Cyril slipping on – or, God forbid, *eating* – the blood.

Decided, she fed Cyril and then made sure the place was secure before heading home, where Dale was waiting for her in the living room; burgers and chips plated, wine poured.

'Is the cat OK?' he asked, handing a glass to her when she sat beside him on the sofa.

'Yeah, he's fine,' she said, sinking into the cushions. 'I felt a bit sorry for him when he saw that it was me and not Bob, but he seemed happy enough when I left.'

'They're lucky to have you,' Dale said, clinking his glass against hers.

Smiling fondly at the memory of her neighbour calling round with a flask of tea on her first day on the estate, she said, 'Bob's been good to me, so it's the least I can do. You can't tell by looking at him now, but he was the go-to man if anyone needed anything doing when I moved in here.'

'How long ago was that?' Dale asked, sitting forward to take a bite of his burger.

'Ten years.'

'Wow. You must like it to have stayed so long.'

'Yeah, I do,' Cheryl said, reaching for her own burger. 'I know the Langley's got a reputation for being rough, but it's honestly not that bad on this side. You'll see what I mean when you move in.'

'We won't be living here,' Dale said, wiping sauce off his chin with the back of his hand. 'My dad'll be letting the house out.

He's already got tenants lined up, so we're trying to get it ready for them as fast as we can.'

'Oh, I see,' she murmured, hoping the disappointment at hearing that he wasn't going to be her neighbour wasn't visible on her face.

'He actually bought it by accident,' Dale went on. 'He had his eye on an old nursing home in Didsbury, but he got his auction numbers mixed up and bid on the wrong lot.'

'Couldn't he tell them he'd made a mistake?'

'Nah, it doesn't work like that. Once that hammer goes down, you're committed. I take it you've never been to one?'

'No.' Cheryl shook her head and quickly swallowed the food in her mouth. 'But I like watching that American show about people bidding for old storage units.'

'British auctions are nothing like that,' Dale laughed. 'I'll take you to one sometime, if you like?'

'Thanks, but I work all week,' Cheryl said. 'And you're probably too busy, so I wouldn't want to put you out.'

'What's with you always thinking you're putting me out?' Dale asked. 'If I didn't want to take you, I wouldn't have offered.'

'I know, but—'

Dale leaned forward and kissed her before she could go on, and Cheryl felt a rush of electricity course through her body. Unsure what to do when he pulled away after a moment, she grabbed her glass and gulped her wine down.

'Shit, that was too fast, wasn't it?' Dale asked, gazing at her flushed face. 'I didn't mean to rush things, but you look so beautiful, I couldn't help myself.'

'It's fine,' Cheryl said. 'I just wasn't expecting it.'

'Sorry,' Dale apologised, grinning as he added, 'I'll give you a two-second warning next time.'

Goosebumps sprang up all over Cheryl's arms when he peered

into her eyes, and she quickly dropped her gaze and put the rest of her burger onto the plate.

'I, um, think I'd best go to bed,' she said. 'I've got a lot to do tomorrow and I'm pretty tired.'

'Of course,' Dale said, putting what was left of his own burger down and reaching for his jacket. 'Thanks for tonight. I know it didn't work out quite the way we planned, but I've enjoyed spending time with you.'

'Me too,' Cheryl said, leading him into the hall.

'Are you sure you're OK?' Dale asked when they reached the front door. 'If I stepped out of line, I'm really sorry.'

'You didn't do anything wrong,' she assured him. 'I haven't been with anyone in a while, so it's all a bit weird for me. Please don't be offended.'

'I'm not.' He smiled. 'Take all the time you need. I'm not going anywhere.'

He politely kissed her cheek before letting himself out, and Cheryl locked the door and went back to the living room. His aftershave was still lingering in the air, and she closed her eyes and hugged herself when she recalled their short but very sweet kiss. She had no doubt that things would have gone a lot further if she hadn't pulled the plug, and she respected Dale for backing off when she told him she was tired. Chris would never have done that. If he was in the mood for sex, he'd push and push until she caved in – or go off in a huff and give her the silent treatment if she didn't. The contrast between them made her wonder what she had ever seen in her self-centred ex. But he was gone now, and she refused to spend any more time thinking about him, so she tipped the rest of the wine from the bottle into her glass and carried it upstairs.

In bed, she dug her phone out of her handbag when she remembered that she hadn't checked it since switching it to silent at the hospital. She had two missed calls and three text messages from Anna; the first asking why she wasn't answering her phone, the second *ordering* her to answer, and the third telling her that she'd spotted Sean in town with 'some skank' and was about to key his car. It was almost 2 a.m., but that last message had been sent only twenty minutes earlier, so Cheryl quickly rang her, hoping to catch her before she did something stupid and got herself arrested.

'Where have you *beeeeen*?' Anna yelled when she answered, her voice muffled by the sound of chatter and music in the background. 'I've been trying to get hold of you for ages!'

'Sorry, I had to go to hospital with Bob,' Cheryl told her. 'Where are you?'

'In the Gay Village,' Anna said. 'Club called Centre something.'

'Centre Stage,' another voice piped up.

'Yeah, that's it,' said Anna. 'Greta wanted to do karaoke, but she hooked up with some girl and took off, so the boys are looking after me.'

'Which boys?' Cheryl asked, annoyed that Greta had dragged her out and then abandoned her when she was clearly pissed.

'This lot,' Anna said, as if Cheryl could see who she was talking about. Then, to someone else, she said, 'Say hello to my bestie.'

'Hello, bestie!' a chorus of male voices yelled, followed by one saying: 'Come and join us!'

'Thanks, but it's a bit late for me,' Cheryl said, guessing that Anna had put her on loudspeaker.

'All right, Granny, you stay there and have your cocoa,' the man jeered, followed by raucous laughter.

'Awww, don't diss her like that,' Anna drunkenly berated him. 'She might be boring, but she's my girl.'

Offended as much by the backhanded compliment as the fresh burst of laughter it elicited, Cheryl tried to speak to Anna again, but it was obvious that her friend had forgotten about her when she heard her squeal: 'Oh my God, I love this song! Come and dance with me, boys!'

Cutting the call in disgust when she heard Anna slam her still-connected phone down on a tabletop, Cheryl switched hers to silent and then swallowed the wine and turned off her lamp.

Chapter 7

Despite the wine and the late night, Cheryl woke up bright and early the next morning. Dressed in leggings and an old T-shirt, she carried her cleaning equipment to Bob's house and fed Cyril before getting stuck in.

The kitchen was dirtier than it looked, and she spent the next few hours clearing out the rubbish before scrubbing the grease-embedded ledges. By lunchtime, she was exhausted, so she decided to head home for a sandwich and a cup of tea before tackling the rest.

As she let herself out, she saw a small white van parked outside her gate, and she hesitated when she spotted a man standing at her front door with his back to her. Scared that the loan shark might have ignored Dale's warning and sent somebody round to threaten her, she called, 'Can I help you?'

The man turned at the sound of her voice and she was surprised to see that he was holding a bouquet of roses wrapped in cellophane.

'Morning,' he said, smiling as he walked over to the fence. 'I don't suppose you could take these in for your neighbour, could you? I've rung the bell a couple of times, but no one's answering.'

'Actually, that's my house,' she said, reaching over to take the flowers from him. 'Who are they from?'

'No idea; I just deliver.' He shrugged. 'Have a nice day.'

As he walked back to his van and drove away, Cheryl plucked the small envelope out of its plastic holder in the middle of the blooms and smiled when she read the card inside.

Thanks for a lovely night. Here's hoping it's the first of many. D xxx

Heart swelling at the thought that Dale had gone to the trouble of ordering flowers for her on a Sunday, Cheryl was still smiling as she carried the bouquet to her front door.

'Are they for me?' a voice chirped.

Jumping, Cheryl looked over her shoulder and frowned when she saw a bedraggled-looking Anna walking up the path.

'What are you doing here?' she asked. 'Come to insult me again?'

'What?' Anna looked confused.

'Oh, we're playing that game, are we?' Cheryl tutted. 'Going to tell me you were so drunk you can't remember what you said last night?'

'I actually can't,' Anna said. 'But something obviously happened to get your knickers in a twist, so what is it?'

'Apparently I'm *boring*,' Cheryl reminded her. 'But it's OK, 'cos I'm *your girl*,' she added sarcastically. 'Ringing any bells yet?'

'None whatsoever,' replied Anna. 'I was really pissed and I genuinely don't remember anything past Greta dragging me out to the karaoke bar. And I *definitely* don't think you're boring, so I can't imagine I said that. Are you sure it was me?'

'Positive,' Cheryl said. 'But it's not worth falling out over, so forget it.'

'I'm really sorry if I upset you,' Anna apologised. 'I think someone might have spiked my drink, 'cos I didn't have a clue where I was when I woke up.'

'What do you mean?' Cheryl's frown deepened. 'Didn't you go home?'

'No. My bag got nicked and it had my keys and cards in it, so I ended up sleeping on some guy's couch. Luckily his place isn't far from here, and I remembered you've got my spare key, so I thought I might as well walk over and get it. And some money for a cab home, if you can spare it?' she added hopefully.

'I'll see what I can do,' Cheryl said. Then, remembering why she'd called Anna last night, she asked, 'What happened with Sean?'

'Sean?' Anna repeated. 'Nothing, why?'

'You messaged saying you'd seen him in town and were going to scratch his car,' Cheryl reminded her.

'Oh yeah,' Anna said, scowling when it came back to her. 'I saw him with some tart in that Italian restaurant he used to take me to. I wanted to go in and rip his cheating head off, but Greta told me to hit him where it hurts and fuck his car up instead. You know how much he loves the stupid thing.'

'So did you?' Cheryl asked, hoping she would say no, because Sean didn't deserve to have his property destroyed just because he'd dared to finish with her.

'Nah, it wasn't where he usually parks it, so he must have taken a cab into town,' Anna said. 'But fuck him. There's way better-looking men out there who'd treat me the way I deserve to be treated.'

'Give yourself time,' Cheryl counselled. 'I know how much you liked him, so don't rush into anything.'

A car pulled up across the road, and Anna's eyes widened when she glanced round and saw who it was. 'Shit, it's *him*!' she hissed, pushing Cheryl towards the door. 'Hurry up and let me in so I can brush my hair and put some lippy on.'

Cheryl turned to slot her key into the lock, but Dale was

already out of the car, and she grimaced when he called: 'I see they got here OK. Hope you like them?'

Anna gave Cheryl a questioning look. 'Is he talking to you?'

'I don't think so,' Cheryl lied, pushing the door open.

'Why you blushing then?' Anna asked, giving her a suspicious look. Then, mouth falling open, she said, 'Oh my God, those flowers are from him, aren't they?'

Before Cheryl could respond, Dale walked over, saying, 'Sorry for interrupting, but it just occurred to me that I should have asked if you're allergic to flowers before I went ahead and ordered them. You're not, are you?'

When Cheryl shook her head, he said, 'Thank God for that. It'd be just my luck to put you in hospital with your neighbour. How is he, by the way?'

'I'm not sure,' Cheryl said. 'I meant to ring the hospital this morning, but I've been busy, so I'll probably visit him later.'

'Well, I'm going to be at the house for a few hours, so let me know when you're going and I'll take you,' Dale offered.

'It's OK, I'll get the bus,' Cheryl murmured, acutely conscious of Anna glaring at her from behind his back.

'You're not still upset with me about last night, are you?' he asked.

Cheryl shook her head again. Then, changing the subject, she asked, 'How's your hand?'

'A lot better this morning, so I took the bandage off and put a plaster over it.' He showed her his handiwork.

'Boss?' a voice called from across the road.

Dale turned his head and waved his acknowledgement to the man who was standing by the gate of his dad's new house before turning back to Cheryl.

'Best go. We've got a load of furniture getting delivered and

I need to be there to sign it off. Call over when you're ready for the hospital.'

He leaned down and kissed her cheek before nodding goodbye to Anna and jogging across the road, and Cheryl dipped her face and moved to enter her house.

'What the fuck was *that*?' Anna demanded, stopping her in her tracks. 'And don't say nothing, 'cos your face is so hot, I could fry a fucking egg on it.'

'It's not what it looked like,' Cheryl said. 'I helped him out the other night and he invited me out for dinner to thank me. That's all it was.'

'Oh really?' Anna scowled. 'So what's with the flowers, and the kiss? You fucked him, didn't you?'

'No, of course not!'

'Then why didn't you tell me about it?'

'Because I know you like him and I didn't want you to think I'd made a play for him,' Cheryl said truthfully. 'I ran into him when I left Bob at the hospital. He'd cut his hand so he was there too, and he spotted me walking to the bus stop and offered me a lift.'

'If that's all it was, why did he kiss you just now?' Anna demanded. 'And why did he think he'd upset you last night if nothing else happened?'

Sighing, Cheryl said, 'OK, if you want the truth, it was late and neither of us had eaten, so we stopped off on the way back and got some burgers. He had a bottle of wine in the car, and I guess we both got a bit relaxed, because he kissed me. But it only lasted a few seconds, and he left straight after.'

Anna jerked her head back as if she'd been physically slapped. 'You are unbelievable,' she spat. 'You're supposed to be my best friend. How could you do that to me?'

'Oh, come on,' Cheryl groaned. 'It's not like you were seeing him and I went after him behind your back. You've only seen him once, and that was through a window. And *I* didn't ask him out, *he* asked *me*.'

'You should have said no,' Anna snapped. 'But you're so desperate, you probably threw yourself at him, even though we both know he'd have chosen *me* if he knew I liked him. Well, good luck keeping him now you've got him, 'cos I guarantee he'll dump you when he realises how boring you are. And yeah, I *did* say that this time, because it's *true!*'

She turned on her heel at that and stalked away, and Cheryl yelled, 'Anna, don't be so stupid. Come back and let's talk about this.'

Anna stuck two fingers up in reply and continued on her way without looking back.

Embarrassed when she noticed that some of her neighbours had come outside to watch the show, Cheryl scurried into the house and slammed the door shut. She'd known that Anna would react badly to the news that Dale had asked her out, but she hadn't expected her to be so vicious about it, and she blinked back the tears that were stinging her eyes as she carried the bouquet into the kitchen and placed it on the table.

The doorbell rang as Cheryl was looking for a vase. Half hoping that Anna had come back to sort things out, she rushed out into the hall and yanked the door open, only to find Dale on the step.

'Are you OK?' he asked, looking at her with concern. 'I know it's none of my business, but I heard you and your friend arguing and wanted to check you're all right.'

'I'm fine,' Cheryl lied. 'She's upset with me, but she'll get over it.'

'Was it about me?' Dale asked bluntly. 'Again, none of my

business, but she wasn't exactly being quiet about it, so I couldn't help overhearing.'

'Well, you obviously already know, so, yes, it was about you,' Cheryl admitted. 'I don't know if you saw her the other morning when you came over with your mum and dad, but she saw you and told me she liked you. That's why she got mad just now: because she reckons I broke the girl code by agreeing to go out for dinner with you.'

Dale tipped his head to one side and gave her a bemused smile. 'Broke the *what* now?'

'I know it sounds ridiculous, but that's how it is,' Cheryl said. 'So now you know she likes you, I won't hold it against you if you want to go after her.'

'Why would I do that?' Dale asked. Then, as if a light had gone on, he said, 'Hang on a minute, let me see if I've got this straight… She likes me, so you're not allowed to talk to me. Is that it?'

'Pretty much,' Cheryl admitted.

'Wow, that's hilarious.' Dale laughed. 'And what about what *I* want? Because I'll tell you now, it's not her.'

'Really?' Cheryl was surprised.

'*Really*,' he insisted. 'She's not my type, and I thought I'd already made it clear that it's you I'm interested in. Unless I *didn't* make myself clear, in which case, let me rectify that.'

Shocked when Dale stepped forward and pulled her into his arms, Cheryl momentarily froze when he kissed her. It started off gentle but quickly became passionate, and all thoughts of Anna evaporated from her mind when he lifted her off her feet and carried her inside, kicking the door shut behind him.

Chapter 8

Bob was sitting up in bed when Cheryl arrived at the hospital that evening, and his face split into a beaming, toothless smile when he saw her.

'Hello, love. How's Cyril?'

'He's fine,' she assured him, pulling a chair up closer to the bed. 'I think he was a bit upset when I walked in instead of you last night, but he seemed to have forgiven me when I popped in this afternoon, 'cos he rubbed against my leg while I was feeding him.'

'He's a good boy,' Bob said fondly. 'Thanks so much for offering to look after him. Took a weight off my shoulders, that did.'

'It's my pleasure,' Cheryl replied. Then, looking around at the other patients, who all appeared to be sleeping, she whispered, 'Bit quiet in here, isn't it? You must be bored out of your mind.'

'It's God's waiting room,' he whispered back, pointing to the ceiling as he added, 'They've all got their tickets to meet the big man.'

'So why have they put *you* in here?' Cheryl asked, scared that it might have been discovered that he had a life-threatening illness since she'd left him the previous night. 'What have the doctors said?'

'Don't fret, I'm fine and dandy,' Bob said, reaching out to give her hand a reassuring pat. 'And my bonce is healing nicely, so me last few brain cells can't leak out.'

'It looks sore,' Cheryl remarked, eyeing the blood-encrusted scab that had formed over the cut.

'Can't feel a thing with all the painkillers they've pumped into me,' Bob chuckled. 'Might stay a bit longer if they keep topping me up like this.'

'No you bloody won't,' Cheryl shot back. 'Cyril will scratch my eyes out if you don't get your backside home soon.'

'He would that,' Bob agreed, settling back against his pillows. 'So, what's been happening there?'

'Nothing much,' Cheryl said, smiling to herself when her stomach fizzled at the memory of Dale making love to her on the hallway floor before moving on up to the bedroom for round two that afternoon. She had never in her life slept with a man so soon after meeting him, but she hadn't been with anyone since Chris, and Dale's passionate kiss had reignited a flame that she had thought was well and truly extinguished.

'Earth to Cheryl,' Bob teased, breaking into her thoughts.

'Sorry.' She snapped back to the present. 'What were you saying?'

'I was just asking if Chris brought you, or if you came on the bus?' said Bob.

'I'm not with him anymore,' Cheryl said, surprised to note that her stomach hadn't clenched at the mere mention of his name, as it usually did.

'Are you not?' Bob frowned. 'Oh, I am sorry, love. What happened?'

Used to his memory slips, but in no mood to get into a

discussion about her ex, Cheryl changed the subject, saying, 'Irene from down the road popped round when I was feeding Cyril this afternoon. She said to send you her regards.'

'Regards me arse.' Bob rolled his eyes. 'She can smell blood from a mile off, that one. Only woman I've ever known to take an empty shopping bag to the buffet at a funeral and leave with a full 'un.'

'You're terrible,' Cheryl laughed, amused by the image of their elderly neighbour rocking up to a wake with an Aldi bag in hand and shovelling sausage rolls into it.

'Only joking,' Bob said. Then, blowing a loud breath out through his gums, he flopped his head back on the pillow, saying, 'By 'eck, you've worn me out with all this gossip.'

'I'm sorry,' Cheryl apologised, concerned when she saw how exhausted and pale he suddenly looked. 'Do you want me to fetch the nurse?'

'No, I'll be reet in a minute,' he assured her, closing his eyes. 'Just a bit tired is all.'

Within seconds, his mouth fell open and his breathing slowed, and Cheryl quietly got up and made her way out when she realised he was sleeping.

Dale was waiting for her in the car park.

'Everything all right?' he asked as she climbed into the car.

'He's a lot better than yesterday,' she said. 'But I tired him out, poor thing.'

'Must be one of your superpowers,' Dale said, his eyes twinkling sexily in the car's dark interior. ''Cos you sure as hell wore *me* out earlier.'

'Don't be cheeky,' Cheryl said, smiling as she pulled her seat belt on.

Laughing, Dale reversed out of the tight space and set off for town, where he'd re-booked the table at the restaurant he'd intended to take her to the previous night.

Hours later, after a lovely meal and several bottles of wine – most of which Cheryl drank, because Dale wanted to keep a clear head for driving, they arrived back at Cheryl's house. Extremely tipsy and in no rush for the night to finish, she invited him in for a coffee, and was surprised when he politely declined.

'It's not that I don't want to,' he assured her, reaching across the divide to gently stroke her hair away from her face. 'But you're drunk and I don't want you waking up thinking I took advantage of you.'

'Why would I think that?' she asked, resting her cheek against the soft leather of her seat and giving him a seductive smile. 'It's not like we haven't already—'

'Yes, I know, and it was beautiful,' Dale interrupted. 'But you need to go to bed, and I need to go home. OK?'

'OK,' she conceded, sighing as she unclipped her seat belt.

'Hey, I hope you understand that I'm doing this for you not me,' Dale said, reaching for her hand when he saw her crestfallen expression. 'I know we've only just met, but you're different from every other girl I've ever dated, and I really like you, so I don't want to mess it up.'

'I really like you too,' Cheryl replied, tingling all over when she saw the sincerity in his eyes.

'Then let's take our time and do this properly,' Dale said, leaning over and kissing her before quickly pulling his head back. 'Now get out of here before I change my mind,' he ordered, pressing a button to release the door locks. 'I'll see you tomorrow – if I haven't been arrested for driving home with a raging hard-on.'

Laughing, Cheryl climbed out of the car and pushed the door shut. The warm glow inside her body repelled the cold night air like a physical shield, and she couldn't keep the grin off her face as she made her way inside after waving him goodbye. She had no idea how long this would last with Dale, or if he would even turn up tomorrow, as he'd promised. But the joy she'd felt since their first kiss had ramped up by a thousand tonight, and she truly felt, for the first time in a long time, that her life was about to get a whole lot better.

Chapter 9

Cheryl was both nervous and excited as she made her way home from work at the end of her first full week with Dale. He'd been coming round every night, and she still couldn't quite believe that a handsome, sexy man like him was interested in someone like her. She sometimes wondered if it – *he* – was too good to be true, but then he would sweep her up in his arms and kiss her, and the doubts would vanish as quickly as they had appeared – along with any residual feelings of guilt she had about Anna, who hadn't contacted her or answered any of her messages since their argument.

Dale's parents had flown home the previous day, and she would be meeting them for the first time that evening at their anniversary party. From the way Dale spoke about them, she knew they were a close family, but she hadn't forgotten the icy glare his mother had aimed at her and Anna that morning, so she was apprehensive about seeing her again.

Determined to make a good impression, Cheryl had closed the café half an hour early to make sure she had plenty of time to get ready. She had pretty much given up on making any effort with her appearance after Chris, choosing to slob around in jeans, with her face bare and her long red hair tied up in scruffy buns. But, tonight, she was determined to look her best, so she jumped straight into the shower as soon as she got home, then settled on the stool in front of her dressing-table mirror to curl her hair and apply her make-up before pulling on the lilac chiffon maxi-dress she'd bought in the half-price sale at the market-hall boutique.

Ready and waiting when Dale pulled up outside the house at 8 p.m., she checked her reflection in the hallway mirror before heading out.

'Wow,' Dale exclaimed, giving an appreciative whistle when she climbed into the car. 'You look amazing.'

'Thanks,' she said, smiling shyly as she pulled her seat belt on. 'I was worried the dress might be a bit too much.'

'It's perfect, like you,' he said, leaning over to kiss her before setting off. 'This is going to be such a great night. My mum's going to love you.'

Remembering how chic his mother had looked that morning, Cheryl had a sneaking suspicion that she would have preferred someone like Anna, who could afford designer clothes and salon-styled hair, for her son. But Dale had chosen her, and she liked him – a *lot*; so she swallowed her fear and made a silent vow not to allow her insecurities to overshadow her first meeting with his family.

Dale had told Cheryl that he had temporarily moved in with his parents after his landlord decided to sell his apartment in Manchester a few months earlier and issued him with a notice to vacate, but he hadn't told her where his parents lived, so she was intrigued when the lights of the city faded behind them as he drove into the countryside. Unable to see anything but the silhouettes of trees and hills in the faint light coming from the moon, she was shocked, when she glanced at the dashboard clock, to see that they had been on the road for forty minutes.

'I didn't realise you lived this far out,' she said. 'Do you live on a farm, or something?'

'Kind of,' Dale said. 'My folks both come from small villages in Poland, so they feel more at home out here in the sticks.'

Unable to visualise his glamorous mother swanning around the countryside in her fur coat and high heels, surrounded by sheep and cows, Cheryl sat up straighter in her seat when Dale turned off the road a few minutes later and drove along a narrow lane. He pulled up in front of a set of high, wrought-iron gates and pressed a button on his key fob to open them before driving onto a long, tree-lined driveway. Powerful security lights that were dotted along the grass verges came on as they passed, and her jaw dropped when she saw a huge white house sitting up ahead, with turrets on its roof, picture windows, and a bank of wide steps with columns on either side leading to a set of double front doors.

'Wow,' she murmured, craning her neck to take it all in as Dale drove around a circular fountain and parked beside a sporty Mercedes and a Bentley. 'This is incredible.'

'Not too shabby, eh?' Dale grinned, cutting the engine.

Amazed that he could be so blasé about living in an actual mansion, Cheryl climbed out and smoothed her dress down. Already in awe, her eyes widened when they reached the top of the steps and he ushered her into a spacious hallway that looked like it belonged in a Hollywood blockbuster, with a wide, curved staircase, marble flooring, glittering crystal chandeliers and ornately framed mirrors and oil paintings on the walls.

'Are you sure I'm dressed OK for this?' she whispered, sticking close to Dale's side as he took her coat and hung it and his own jacket on a stand behind the door. 'I feel like I should be wearing an evening gown and a tiara.'

'It's a family get-together, not a state ball,' he laughed, reaching for her hand. 'Now relax; this is going to be fun.'

Hoping that he couldn't feel the sweat on her palm, Cheryl clutched her handbag tightly as he led her to a door at the far end of the hall. It opened onto one of the largest, cleanest kitchens she had ever seen in her life, with state-of-the-art white goods and a marble-topped island in the centre that was laden with cling-wrapped platters of food.

A slightly built older woman with a silver bun was standing at the cooker, stirring the steaming contents of an enormous pan.

'Is that what I think it is?' Dale asked, walking up behind her and sniffing the air.

'*Tesh*,' she murmured, casting a hooded glance at Cheryl out of the corner of her eye.

'Oh, you're in for a treat, babe,' Dale said to Cheryl over his shoulder as he walked over to a ledge where numerous bottles of wine and spirits were standing. 'Rosa makes the best veal goulash in the world.'

'It smells lovely,' Cheryl said, smiling at the woman.

The woman dipped her gaze without returning the smile and turned the light down under the pan before scuttling away and disappearing through a door at the far end of the room.

'Did I say something wrong?' Cheryl asked when Dale handed her a glass of wine.

'Don't mind her, she doesn't speak much English,' he said, pulling a stool out from under the island. 'Now sit down and make yourself comfortable while I nip upstairs to get changed.'

'Don't be long,' Cheryl whispered, clutching his hand as she perched on the stool.

'I'll be two minutes, max,' he promised, leaning down to kiss her before sauntering out into the hall.

Cheryl sipped on her wine and listened as his footsteps ascended the stairs.

A few seconds later, Rosa reappeared carrying a large box.

'Can I help?' Cheryl offered, putting her glass down.

Rosa shook her head and flashed a glance at the door before laying the box down and lifting the lid to reveal a set of silver cutlery.

Unsure why the woman seemed to have taken an instant dislike to her, Cheryl took another sip of her wine and watched as Rosa laid out the knives, forks and spoons on another table before picking up the now empty box and leaving the room again.

At the sound of voices in the hallway a few minutes later, Cheryl stood up as Dale and his father walked in. She had only briefly glimpsed the man through the bedroom window in the early-morning light, and his back had been turned to her at that time so she hadn't been able to properly see his face. In the light now, wearing a black silk shirt, grey slacks and loafers, with his dark hair slicked back, he was a lot more handsome than she had imagined. He also had a distinctive aura of power about him that was reminiscent of the Mafia Dons in the old gangster movies her dad had been obsessed with when she was a girl.

'Dad, this is Cheryl,' Dale introduced them. 'Cheryl, my dad.'

'Hello, Mr Moran.' She nervously held out her hand. 'I'm really pleased to—'

'We don't stand on formalities round here, sweetheart,' he cut her off, pulling her into a hug that almost emptied her lungs of air. 'The name's Alfie.'

'Darling, have you seen my Cartier watch? I can't find it anywhere,' Dale's mother said, floating into the room on a cloud of perfume.

'Have you checked the junk box you keep on your dresser?'

Alfie asked, walking over to the drinks counter and pouring himself a glass of whisky.

'If you mean my grandmother's antique music box, yes I have,' she replied clippily. Then, pausing when she spotted Cheryl, she looked at her son and raised a questioning eyebrow. 'Is this her?'

'Sure is.' He grinned. 'Mum, Cheryl... Cheryl, my mum, Sonia.'

Cheryl swallowed nervously and forced a smile. The woman looked like a movie star in her figure-hugging, scarlet sequined dress and matching stiletto heels, with immaculate make-up and her golden hair coiled up and held in place with diamanté clips. Her skin was so smooth, Cheryl guessed that she'd probably had Botox – and possibly more invasive work done on her face. But the results were so good, it was impossible to estimate her true age.

'Oh, what a relief,' Sonia said, her diamond rings flashing like fire as she placed a hand on her breast. 'When you told me you were seeing one of those girls, I had a horrible feeling it was the other one.'

'Steady on, Mum,' Dale laughed. 'That's her best mate.'

'Every rose must have its thorn,' Sonia replied sagely. Then, turning to Cheryl, she held out her arms, saying, 'It's lovely to meet you, my dear. Welcome to our home.'

'Thank you,' Cheryl said, gaping at Dale in wonder over his mother's shoulder.

Sonia let go of her after a moment and slipped her arm through her son's, saying, 'Come and help me to...'

Unable to hear what the woman needed help with because they were already walking away, Cheryl sank onto the stool and reached for her wine. She'd been dreading meeting Dale's parents, but they had both greeted her so warmly, she was glad she had decided to come.

Across the room, Sonia opened a cupboard in which several barrels of beer were stacked and directed Dale and his father to carry them into the conservatory. As the men got on with that, Sonia went over to the cooker and lifted the lid off the pot on the stove top. She dipped a spoon in and tasted it, then took a jar out of a cupboard and sprinkled some of its contents into the pot before stirring it.

The front door suddenly opened and a cold breeze blew in and circled Cheryl's ankles, bringing with it the voices of a man, a woman, and what sounded like two young children squabbling.

'Hello...?' the man called out.

'In here,' Sonia called back, quickly replacing the lid on the pot.

A tall, dark-haired man wearing a smart suit walked in, and Cheryl immediately guessed that he must be Dale's brother, Stefan, when she saw how strikingly similar they looked; although this man had a seriousness about him that was at complete odds with Dale's levity.

'Darling, you made it.' Sonia approached him with outstretched arms.

'Of course,' he said, flashing a glance at Cheryl as he leaned down to give Sonia a quick hug before handing a bouquet of flowers to her.

'Oh, thank you,' she purred, sniffing them before calling: 'Rosa... come!'

The older woman scuttled out from behind the door at the far end of the room, and Sonia handed the bouquet to her, saying, 'Take these beautiful flowers my son bought me and put them in one of the crystal vases.'

Rosa nodded and carried the bouquet away just as two children entered the room: one, a chunky, dark-haired boy who looked to Cheryl to be around nine or ten, the other, a tiny slip of a fairer-haired girl who looked to be around four or five.

'*Babcia!*' the boy cried, launching himself at Sonia.

'There's my handsome Frankie boy,' she gushed, cupping his chubby cheeks in her hands before kissing him. 'Now step back and let me see how much you've grown.'

'It's only been a couple of weeks,' he laughed.

'A lot can change in a couple of weeks,' she said, straightening his tie.

As Sonia fussed over the boy, a pretty woman with an ash-blonde bob walked into the room. She pushed the girl forward, saying, 'Go and say hello to Grandma.'

'Hello, Gran'ma,' the girl said quietly.

'Hello, dear,' Sonia replied, patting her head before saying something to the woman.

She had spoken too quietly for Cheryl to hear what she'd said, but the woman didn't seem to have liked whatever it was, because her nostrils flared and a spark of anger flashed in her eyes.

Oblivious, Sonia placed her hand on Stefan's arm and guided him over to Cheryl, saying, 'Have you met your brother's friend, Cherry?'

'Um, no, not yet,' he said, flicking a hooded glance back at his wife, who was furiously scrubbing lipstick off the boy's cheeks with a tissue.

'Cherry, this is Stefan, my eldest,' Sonia said brightly, as if the terse exchange with his wife had never happened.

'Pleased to meet you.' Stefan extended his hand. 'But I thought Dale said your name was Cheryl?'

'Oh, did I get your name wrong?' Sonia asked. 'I'm so sorry, darling. Everything's been so hectic this week, I don't know if I'm coming or going.'

'It's fine, honestly,' Cheryl smiled. 'I was sorry to hear about your loss. It must have been a difficult time.'

'Thank you, you're very kind,' Sonia said, touching her arm. Then, turning her head at the sound of voices in the hall, she excused herself and rushed off to greet whoever had come in.

As soon as she'd gone, Dale strolled over and bumped fists with his brother.

'How's it going?'

'Good, thanks. You?'

'Couldn't be better,' Dale said, putting his arm around Cheryl. 'I take it you've met my girl?'

'Yeah, Mum introduced us,' Stefan said, glancing over Dale's shoulder when he spotted movement on the other side of the room. 'Sorry, need a quick word with Dad. Catch you in a bit.'

'He seems nice,' Cheryl said.

'He's all right,' Dale said, grinning as he added, 'If you're into nerds with no sense of humour.'

'Is that his wife?' Cheryl nodded towards the woman, who appeared to be having a stern word with her daughter as she settled her onto a leather armchair tucked away in an alcove behind the kitchen door.

'Yep, that's the lovely Estelle,' Dale drawled, a strange smile twitching his lips as he looked over at his sister-in-law. 'Life and soul of every party.'

Cheryl caught the sarcasm in his tone and guessed there wasn't much love lost between him and his brother's wife, but he picked up her empty glass before she had a chance to ask about it and walked away to get her a refill.

Sonia came back into the room with a group of guests, and the kitchen was soon alive with the sound of chatter, laughter and clinking glasses as they all helped themselves to drinks. Already intimidated by the grandeur of the house, and now

surrounded by older, expensively suited men and women drip-
ping in diamonds, Cheryl shrank into herself as she waited for
Dale to return with her drink. She had always known that his
family must be well off, but she had never dreamed they were
this wealthy, and she felt extremely self-conscious in her cheap
dress and charity-shop boots.

Unsure how long she'd been sitting there when Rosa came
over and started removing the cling film from the platters,
Cheryl slid off her stool to get out of the way when she heard
Sonia direct people to take a plate from a stack on the ledge
and help themselves to food. As the guests swarmed over to the
table, she went to the drinks counter and poured a glass of wine
before looking around for Dale. Picking up the scent of cigar
smoke drifting out through the conservatory doors, she glanced
inside and spotted him, his brother and nephew standing with a
group of men on a lighted patio outside. Alfie was in the centre
holding court, and she smiled when Dale threw his head back
and laughed along with the others at whatever his father was
saying. She was tempted to go and join him, but quickly decided
against it when she saw that no other women were there.

Her arm was jolted by a man carrying a tray laden with glasses
of whisky, and she murmured an apology and stepped aside to
let him pass before making her way to the quieter end of the
kitchen, where she took a seat on a straight-backed chair. A
short time later, the lights were dimmed and music drifted out
through a bank of wall-mounted speakers. A little bored by then,
and beginning to wonder why Dale had insisted on bringing her
if he'd had no intention of spending any time with her, Cheryl
watched as the guests broke away from their groups to dance.

Sensing after a while that she, too, was being watched, Cheryl
looked around and smiled when she saw Dale's niece staring at
her from the armchair, where she was now curled up under a

fur coat. When the girl gave a tentative smile in reply, she got up and went over to her.

'Hi,' she said, squatting down beside the chair. 'I'm Cheryl. What's your name?'

'Poppy,' the girl replied quietly, searching Cheryl's face with sleepy, cobalt-blue eyes.

'Oh, that's a lovely name,' Cheryl said. 'I had a doll called Poppy when I was a little girl. She was my favourite.'

'Mine's called Princess,' Poppy told her. 'I wanted to bring her, but Mummy made me leave her at home. Gran'ma says I'm too old for dolls.'

'How old are you?'

'Six.'

'Well, that's not too old for dolls,' Cheryl said, lowering her voice conspiratorially as she added, 'Don't tell your grandma, but I still sleep with my teddy, and I'm twenty-eight.'

'Are you Uncle Dale's girlfriend?' Poppy asked.

Taken aback by the directness of the question, and unsure how to respond since she and Dale hadn't put an official label on their relationship, Cheryl said, 'Well, we're friends, and I'm a girl, so I guess so.'

'You're prettier than Caroline,' Poppy said. 'Uncle Dale used to bring her for dinner, but they falled out so she can't come no more.'

'I see,' Cheryl murmured, wondering who Caroline was, since Dale had never mentioned her.

Before either of them could speak again, the girl's mother appeared, and Cheryl straightened up to introduce herself.

'Hi, I'm Cheryl. You must be Estelle?'

Ignoring her, Estelle leaned down and tucked the coat in around her daughter, saying, 'It's late. You're supposed to be asleep.'

'It's too noisy,' Poppy moaned.

'I don't mind sitting with her if she can't sleep,' Cheryl offered. 'I'm pretty tired myself, to be honest, so—'

'No thank you,' Estelle cut her off. 'We don't encourage our children to speak to strangers.'

'I'm actually here with Dale,' Cheryl said, guessing that the woman hadn't been told who she was.

'Lucky you,' Estelle said frostily. 'But you're still a stranger to my children, so leave them alone.'

'Of course,' Cheryl agreed, backing away.

She downed the rest of the wine in her glass and was heading over to pour another when she heard raised voices across the room and turned to see Sonia having what looked like a heated conversation with Rosa – although it was Sonia who appeared to be doing all the talking, while the older woman stared silently down at the floor.

Almost jumping out of her skin when Dale crept up behind her and wrapped his arms around her waist, she twisted round, and gave him a playful slap on the arm.

'Idiot! You scared the life out of me.'

'Couldn't resist,' he grinned. 'Where've you been? I was looking for you.'

'Oh really?' Cheryl raised an eyebrow. 'Funny that, 'cos you seemed pretty busy with your dad and his pals when *I* was looking for *you*.'

'Gotta get the business out of the way before the fun starts,' he explained. 'So what have you been up to while I was gone? Not talking to any men, I hope?'

Amused when he gave her a mock-accusing look, she said, 'Why? Would you be jealous if I had?'

'Why don't you try it and find out,' he said, his eyes twinkling even more brightly than usual as he pushed her back against the ledge and pressed himself up against her.

'How much have you had to drink?' she asked, getting a blast of his boozy breath.

'Not enough to stop me ravishing you,' he purred, kissing her neck. 'Come to my room and let me show you.'

'Stop it!' she whispered, putting her hands on his chest to hold him at bay. 'I'm not sleeping with you in your mum and dad's house.'

'They won't mind; they like you,' he persisted. 'Come on . . . you've got me in the mood now.'

'Well, get out of it, because it's getting late and you promised to have me home by midnight,' Cheryl reminded him.

'Seriously?' He gave her a pained look. 'The party's only just getting started.'

'I'm sorry,' she apologised. 'But you know I've got work in the morning.'

'Call in sick,' he urged, sliding his hand down her back and over her hip.

'I can't,' she said, grasping his wrist to prevent his hand from going any further. 'There's no one to cover for me.'

'So that's more important than me?' He pouted.

'No, of course not. But it's my job, and I can't afford to lose it.'

'Yeah you can. I'll look after you.'

'I don't need looking after,' Cheryl laughed, firmly pushing him away. 'Now tell me where the kettle is so I can make you a coffee and get you sobered up. Or do you want me to call an Uber?'

'No need, I'm not drunk,' Dale sighed. 'Just give me ten minutes to speak to a couple of guys, then we'll get moving.'

'Thanks.' Cheryl smiled. 'I'll get my coat.'

'OK, won't be long.'

When Dale had gone, Cheryl looked around for Sonia and spotted her with an elderly couple by the back door. She made her way over to them, but they were deep in conversation, so she hovered in the background, reluctant to disturb them. The lady of the couple noticed her after a while and murmured something to Sonia under her breath. Sonia snapped her head around, and Cheryl immediately thought she'd done the wrong thing when she saw how hostile her expression was. But it quickly morphed into a smile, and Sonia touched her arm, asking, 'Is everything OK, dear?'

'Yes, everything's fine,' Cheryl said, conscious that the old lady was scrutinising her. 'Dale's going to take me home, so I wanted to say goodnight.'

'You're leaving already?' Sonia looked disappointed.

'I have to be up early for work,' Cheryl said, feigning regret. 'But thank you so much for inviting me. I've had a lovely time.'

'It was my pleasure,' Sonia purred, air-kissing her cheeks. 'And you're more than welcome to visit us any time you like.'

'Thank you.' Cheryl smiled.

When Sonia patted her arm and turned back to the couple, Cheryl noticed Estelle standing alone a few yards away with a drink in her hand. About to smile when their eyes met, she decided against it when she noticed the sneer on the other woman's lips, and went off in search of Alfie instead.

The patio was empty when she reached it, and she gazed out across the vast lawn at the back of the house, at the rear of which she could see the silhouettes of several buildings. A couple of them had dim lights showing through their windows, and she guessed that they must belong to neighbours of the Morans when she saw the shadowy figures of people walking around outside.

She went back into the house and was on her way out of the

kitchen when she noticed that Poppy was still awake on the armchair. She had an urge to go and say goodbye to the child, but she didn't fancy putting herself in Estelle's firing line again, so she waggled her fingers instead and walked on through to the hallway to get her coat.

The security lights were off when she walked outside, and she gazed up at the sky as she descended the steps. Used to the city skyline, which was always suffused with artificial light, she couldn't believe how dark it was out there – or how brightly the stars were shining in their blanket of tar. It was quiet, too, with only the sound of the wind whistling through the leafless branches of the trees and the occasional screech of foxes in the distance to break the silence.

'Peaceful, isn't it?' a voice to her left said.

Jumping, Cheryl looked round and squinted at the dark figure of a man leaning against the bonnet of a car parked a few down from Dale's. His face was momentarily illuminated when he sucked on the cigarette he was holding and she smiled when she saw that it was Stefan.

'Oh, hi.' She walked over to him. 'I didn't see you there.'

'I'm taking a breather from the mad house,' he said. 'Are you off, or doing the same?'

'I'm off,' she replied, wrapping her coat tighter around herself. 'It's getting late and I've got to be up early for work, so Dale's taking me home.'

'You work?' Stefan raised an eyebrow.

'Yeah, I run a café,' she said, wondering why he sounded so surprised.

'Cool,' he murmured. 'So did you enjoy the party?'

'Yeah, it was good,' she lied. 'Dale's spoken about you all, so it was nice to put faces to the names.'

'Really?' Stefan gave a little grunt of bemusement. 'And did we live up to your expectations?'

Sensing sarcasm, Cheryl wasn't sure how to answer; but she was saved from having to try when the front door suddenly opened and light spilled down the steps. Seconds later, Estelle came outside and called Stefan's name.

'Shit,' he muttered, dropping the cigarette and grinding it out with his heel. 'You haven't seen me,' he hissed, ducking down behind the car.

'Stefan?' Estelle called again. 'Is that you down there?'

'Erm, no, it's me,' Cheryl said, stepping into the light.

'Oh.' Estelle folded her arms and scanned the darkness behind her. 'I thought I heard voices.'

'Must have been talking to myself,' Cheryl smiled. 'I do that sometimes.'

'Have you seen my husband?'

'No, sorry. Dale said he needed to speak to somebody before we leave, so maybe it was him?'

Estelle scanned the area behind her again and then turned to walk back into the house. Hesitating, she looked back and said, 'Friendly word of warning … don't get too cosy, 'cos the flavour of the month thing doesn't last long around here.'

At that, she disappeared through the door, slamming it behind her, and Cheryl stared at it in confusion, wondering what on earth she had meant.

'Has she gone?' Stefan whispered.

'Yeah,' Cheryl murmured, frowning as she turned back to him.

'Cheers for that,' he said, brushing the knees of his trousers as he straightened up. 'She doesn't like me smoking, but there's only so much I can take of these things before I need a nicotine hit. I'd best go back in before she comes looking for me again. If I don't see you again before you leave, take care.'

'You too,' Cheryl said.

Stefan trotted up the steps and disappeared inside the house. Seconds later, Dale came out.

'Ready?' he asked, pulling his car keys out of his pocket when he reached the bottom step.

Cheryl nodded and climbed into the passenger seat of his car when he opened the door for her. She pulled her seat belt on as he hopped into the driver's side, and took one last look up at the house before he reversed and spun the car around. It was the grandest place she had ever seen, and his mum and dad had been lovely to her; but she hadn't enjoyed the party at all – least of all her encounters with Estelle.

'Did you have fun?' Dale asked as he set off down the driveway.

'Yeah, it was nice to meet your family,' she replied.

'Well, my mum loves you, so you've made a good impression there,' he said, winking at her as he drove out through the gates.

Pleased to hear that his mother liked her, but curious to know why Estelle had been so offish, she said, 'I don't think your sister-in-law was too impressed. She came over when I was talking to your niece and basically told me to stay away from her.'

'Don't let it get to you; she's funny with everyone,' Dale said, looking each way before turning onto the road.

'Was she friends with Caroline?' Cheryl asked.

'Excuse me?' Dale snapped his head round and frowned at her.

'Watch the road,' she cautioned, gripping the side of her seat when he almost swerved into a hedge.

'Where did you hear that name?' he asked, his gaze back on the road.

'Poppy mentioned her,' Cheryl said, watching as his cheek

muscles twitched in the moonlight. 'She asked if I was your girlfriend, then told me that you used to take Caroline to their house for dinner. I take it she's an ex?'

'Something like that.'

'I'm only asking because you've never mentioned her. I wasn't quizzing Poppy, or anything.'

'I know.' Dale sighed. 'But she's part of my past that I'd rather forget.'

'It must have been serious if you get this uptight just hearing her name?' Cheryl probed.

'Not as serious as she wanted it to be,' Dale replied coolly. 'Truth is, she was a gold-digger, and when I found out, I finished it. That's why I've never mentioned her: because she meant nothing to me.'

'I see.'

'Hey, I hope you don't think I feel like that about you?' Dale asked. 'Because you are *nothing* like her.'

'It's OK, you don't have to reassure me.' Cheryl smiled. 'It's none of my business. I was just curious, that's all.'

'If it's any consolation, you've already made me happier than she ever did,' Dale said softly.

Cheryl shifted in her seat when she felt the familiar tingle in her stomach. Dale was almost thirty, so it was hardly a shock to learn that he'd had girlfriends before her – although it *had* crossed her mind to wonder why a good-looking man like him, with a great personality, wasn't married. But she was almost the same age, and she was still single, so it didn't really mean anything. And now that she'd seen where he came from, she figured it was understandable that he'd be cautious about who he dated.

Chapter 10

Cheryl had started to doze off by the time Dale turned onto her road, but she snapped awake when he said, 'Looks like the old man's home.'

Rubbing her eyes, she gazed at Bob's house in confusion as Dale pulled up outside her gate. Every light appeared to be on, and she could see someone moving around behind the thin living-room curtains.

'He's not supposed to be home until tomorrow afternoon,' she said, quickly unbuckling her seat belt. 'And he wasn't there when you picked me up earlier, 'cos I'd been in to feed Cyril just before you got here.'

'Well, you said he was looking a lot better after your last visit, so maybe they decided to discharge him early,' Dale reasoned.

'Yeah, maybe,' she murmured. 'But he can't move that fast, so someone must be with him.'

'Didn't you say they'd sorted out a care package for when he came out?'

'Yeah, but surely they wouldn't be here this late unless there's a problem,' Cheryl said, scooping her handbag up off the floor of the car and rooting her keys out of it. 'I'd best go take a look; make sure he's OK.'

'Want me to come with you?' Dale offered.

'No, I'll be all right,' she said. 'Go back to the party. I'll speak to you tomorrow.'

She leaned over and gave him a quick kiss, then hopped out of the car and rushed up Bob's path.

'Bob?' she called as she let herself into the house. 'It's Cheryl. Why didn't you ring to tell me you were—'

Tailing off as she walked into the living room and saw that it had been ransacked, she narrowed her eyes when she spotted Bob's daughter, Fiona, rooting down the side of his armchair.

'What the hell are you doing?' she demanded.

Fiona jumped as if she'd been electrocuted, and spun around to face Cheryl with a look of shock and guilt on her gaunt face.

'Fuckin' 'ell, man! What you creeping up on me like that for? You nearly give me a heart attack.'

'What are you doing?' Cheryl repeated.

'Nothing,' Fiona sniffed, scratching her arms with filthy nails. 'I was just...'

'Just what?' Cheryl demanded, taking in the dark hollows under the woman's eyes, and the fresh welts on her arms that only served to highlight the track marks beneath.

'Is everything all right?' Dale asked, coming into the doorway behind Cheryl and frowning when he saw the state of the room. 'Who's this?' he asked, stepping further in when his gaze landed on Fiona.

'Bob's daughter,' Cheryl told him. 'And it looks like she's robbing the place.'

'Fuck you, I ain't robbin' no one,' Fiona retorted angrily. 'He's me dad, so I've got every right to be here. More right than *you*.'

'Bob gave me a key,' Cheryl argued. 'And I know for a fact that *you* haven't got one, so how did you get in?'

'None of your business,' Fiona snarled, squaring up to her. 'Now wind your neck in and fuck off home before you get hurt.'

'By *you?*' Cheryl snorted, pushing her away. 'Christ, I knew you were scum, Fiona, but I didn't think even *you* would stoop so low as to burgle your own father when he's in hospital.'

'He ain't coming out, so what does he care?' Fiona shot back.

'Actually, he's coming home tomorrow,' Cheryl corrected her. 'But you'd know that if you'd bothered to visit him, like I've been doing for the last week.'

Fiona blinked rapidly at this news, as if she'd genuinely thought her father was on his deathbed – which, to Cheryl, made it even worse that she'd broken into his house to grab whatever she could.

'I don't have to answer to you,' Fiona muttered after a moment.

'OK, I'll call the police so you can tell *them* what you're doing,' Cheryl said, pulling her phone out of her pocket.

'Touch that an' you're dead,' a low male voice warned. 'And don't test me, sweetheart, 'cos it'll take less than two seconds to slit your throat.'

Cheryl snapped her head round and saw two men standing in the hallway: one bald, tall and stick thin, the other shorter and wider, with a mess of wild hair and even wilder eyes – and both holding knives.

'You've had it now,' Fiona crowed. 'Should've fucked off when you had the chance.'

Cheryl froze, her gaze riveted to the blades. Terrified that Dale was going to get stabbed when he stepped in front of her, her legs almost buckled with relief when the men clocked him and bolted for the door.

'What the fuck?' Fiona squawked, panic in her eyes. 'Davie? ... Lemmo? Get back here, ya bastards!'

'They won't be doing that,' Dale said. 'And if I was you, I'd go after them. Unless you'd rather wait for the police?'

Visibly rattled, Fiona bared her nicotine-stained teeth at

Cheryl, hissing, 'You've got no right to kick me out of me own dad's house.'

'She's not, *I* am,' Dale asserted.

Fiona opened her mouth as if to continue the argument, but something about the way Dale was looking at her changed her mind, and she pushed past Cheryl and stalked out, leaving the front door wide open behind her.

'Jeezus, she reeks,' Dale said, wrinkling his nose when she'd gone.

'Yeah, she does,' Cheryl agreed, her nostrils flaring in anger as she looked around. 'Look at the state of the place. How's Bob supposed to come home to this? And where the hell's Cyril?' she added, when it occurred to her that she hadn't seen or heard the cat. 'If they've hurt him, I swear to God...'

'Calm down,' Dale said, pulling her into his arms. 'He'll be around somewhere. I'll help you to look for him.'

'No, it's OK; he'll be scared if he sees you,' Cheryl said, making an effort to pull herself together. 'You get going, or the party will be finished before you get home.'

'Sod the party,' Dale argued.

'Dale, please, I'll deal with this,' Cheryl insisted. 'You did enough getting rid of that lot.' Then, frowning when she remembered the looks on the men's faces before they legged it, she said, 'Did you know them, by the way? It looked like they recognised you.'

'It's the suit.' Dale grinned. 'Junkies always think I'm police, for some reason. Now, if you're insisting on making me leave, at least let me check the house is secure before I go,' he went on, changing the subject as he walked out into the hallway. 'The front door lock's intact,' he said over his shoulder after looking at it. 'So they probably got in through a window.'

'I made sure they were all locked earlier,' Cheryl said, heading for the kitchen, where she immediately saw the back door standing open and splintered wood on the lino. 'They got in this way. Looks like they kicked it in.'

Dale followed her into the room and looked at the door. 'The lock's a goner, but I can board it up for now. The guys have left their gear over at the house, so give me a minute while I get some tools.'

'Thanks,' Cheryl said, grateful that he'd come in when he had. She wouldn't have had a problem getting rid of Fiona on her own, but she dreaded to think what might have happened if he hadn't been there to chase the knife-wielding men away.

When Dale left to get the tools, Cheryl headed upstairs and found Cyril hiding under Bob's bed. Aware that he would freak out if she took him downstairs while Dale was boarding up the door, she gave him a couple of soothing strokes and then left him there, closing the bedroom door behind her.

'I've just had a call from my dad and I need to get back home as soon as I'm finished here,' Dale told her when he came back a short time later carrying a toolbox and a sheet of wood. 'I'm not happy about leaving you alone, but I know you won't come back with me, so I've arranged for a couple of the guys to come over to keep an eye on this place.'

'You didn't need to do that,' Cheryl protested. 'I'll be next door, so I'll hear if anyone tries to break in again.'

'I'm not having you putting yourself at risk,' Dale said firmly. 'And the guys are already on their way, so it's too late.'

'OK,' Cheryl conceded, too tired to argue about it.

'Good girl,' Dale said, winking at her.

Bemused by his choice of words, Cheryl pottered about in the living room while he got to work on the door; righting the overturned furniture and closing the drawers that had been rifled through. She had no idea if Fiona and the men had managed to steal anything, but it could only have been small things if they had, because none of them had been carrying anything noticeable when they left. She just hoped Bob hadn't left any money lying around, because that would definitely be gone.

'All done,' Dale said, appearing in the living-room doorway a little while later with the toolbox in his hand. 'My guys will do a proper repair tomorrow, so give me the key and I'll leave it with them.'

'I'll need it to feed Cyril before I go to work.'

'OK, just drop it off over there when you're done.'

'Will do,' Cheryl agreed. 'And thank you.'

'My pleasure,' Dale said, kissing her before stepping outside. 'See you tomorrow.'

'Can't wait.' She smiled.

When he'd gone, Cheryl coaxed Cyril out from under the bed and fed him before heading home. As she slotted her key into her own front door, the workmen's van pulled up across the road, and she waved to the two men who hopped out. The younger of them grinned and waved back, but the other, a serious-faced man who she'd guessed might be in charge, merely nodded before following his colleague into the house. Glad that Dale had made the decision to call them over, because she doubted she'd have got much sleep for worrying about Fiona and those thugs coming back, she went inside, kicked off her boots and headed up to bed.

Across the road, Jakub Kowalski dragged a chair up to the window of the master bedroom. His crew had finished plastering the walls and ceiling in there a couple of days earlier, and it had been painted just that morning, so the smell was still heavy in the air. Cracking the window open an inch after taking a seat, he unscrewed his flask and tipped an inch of vodka into the lid. He could hear Aleksander moving around downstairs and guessed that the man was probably making up one of the single beds that had been delivered the previous morning in preparation for the soon-to-be-incoming tenants. He would be sound asleep within seconds of his head hitting the mattress, but that was fine by Jakub, because he knew his friend would be up and on his feet again in an instant if he needed him.

When the young woman's bedroom light went out across the road, Jakub settled back in the chair and scanned the area for signs of movement. It was all quiet, and he released a heavy breath as his gaze came to rest on her house again. Raising his cup into the light coming from the street lamp outside, he murmured, '*God be with you,*' before downing the fiery liquid in one.

Chapter 11

Cheryl had slept well, reassured by the knowledge that Dale's men were watching the house, and she woke feeling refreshed when her alarm went off at 6.30 a.m. After getting dressed and feeding Cyril, she went across the road to drop Bob's key off with the workmen. The front door was open but nobody answered when she rang the bell, so she stepped inside, calling, 'Hello?'

A radio was blasting music on the floor above and she could hear male voices, so she called out again, louder this time. As she waited for someone to come down, she took the opportunity to look around. Bob had told her that the house was huge, but this was the first time she had ever seen the inside, and the hallway alone seemed larger than the entire ground floor of her house. Freshly painted in white, it had a wide staircase to the left and several doors on the right, stretching to the back of the house.

The first door, which she presumed led into the living room, was open, and she stepped forward and poked her head inside. It was a big, square room with a high ceiling, dado rails and a ceiling rose. A large, open fireplace with an ornate iron grate occupied the centre of the wall facing the door, and the bay window looked out onto the recently tidied front garden. It had all the grandeur of the Victorian era, and she could almost visualise herself sitting in front of the fire at night, with oil lamps burning and a glass of wine in her hand.

Snapped out of her daydream by the sound of footsteps on the stairs, she quickly stepped back and smiled at the man who came down. He was the older one, and she wondered if he had slept when she saw the dark circles under his eyes.

The man hesitated when he saw her, then gave her a questioning look as he descended the last couple of steps. 'How you are come in?'

'The front door was open,' she said. 'I just came to drop this off.' She held out Bob's key. 'Dale told me to give it to you.'

'Ah, yes,' he said, taking the key and slipping it into his pocket. 'Is to repair door.'

'Thanks so much for doing it,' Cheryl said. 'And I really appreciate you watching the house last night.'

'It was not a problem,' he replied.

'Right, well, I'd best get going before I miss my bus,' Cheryl said, backing towards the door. 'Thanks again.'

The man nodded, and she gave him a hesitant smile before leaving the house. He had one of the most intense stares she'd ever seen, and his deep, heavily accented voice made him seem almost sinister.

She glanced back at the house when she turned to close the gate, and felt a shiver ripple down her spine when she saw him looking out at her through the bay window.

Pretending she hadn't noticed him, she turned and quickly walked away.

Excited about Bob coming home, Cheryl clock-watched the day away. Luckily, it was another slow day so she was able to close up early, and she made her way home with a bag of Bob's favourite sandwiches and a bottle of milk to make him the super-strong brew he'd been complaining he was missing while in hospital.

Showered and changed, ready for her date with Dale later that evening, she rushed out of her house when a taxi pulled up outside Bob's at 6 p.m.

'Hiya, love,' he beamed, clutching her hand when she opened his door to help him out. 'My, it's good to be back.'

'Good to have you back,' she said, taking his bag with her free hand. 'It hasn't been the same round here without you.'

'Missed my moaning, have you?'

'More than you know,' she laughed.

As if he'd sensed that his master was back, Cyril was waiting behind the door, and he moved faster than Cheryl had ever seen him move when he weaved around Bob's ankles, crying loudly.

'There's my boy,' Cyril grinned, reaching down to stroke him. 'Did you miss me?'

'Careful,' Cheryl cautioned, scared that he was going to fall over. 'Don't want you back in hospital before you've even had a chance to sit down.'

'No way them buggers are getting their paws on me again,' Bob grunted as he straightened up and headed into the living room. 'No offence to the nurses, 'cos they were lovely; but them young doctors don't know their arses from their elbows.'

'Well, you're home now,' Cheryl said, guiding him to his chair. 'And if you behave, you won't have to go back.'

'I won't be moving from here again, believe you me,' Bob said, releasing a sigh of relief as he sat down. 'Now that's what I'm talking about.'

'I'll make you a cuppa,' Cheryl said.

'You're an angel.' Bob smiled. 'Where's me remote?'

'On the table next to you.' Cheryl pointed it out. 'And don't go falling asleep, because your carers will be here soon.'

'Waste of bloody time if you ask me,' Bob grumbled. 'I've got you if I need help with anything.'

'I can't be here in the daytime, because I'll be at work,' Cheryl reminded him. 'And now I'm seeing Dale, I can't always guarantee I'll be around at night either.'

'Who's Dale when he's at home?'

'The son of the man who bought Edna's place. You met him last week when the alarm went off, remember?'

'What's up with this?' Bob said, seeming not to have listened to a word she'd just said as he pointed the remote at the TV and repeatedly pressed the 'ON' button.

'It hasn't been used for a while, so it might need to warm up,' Cheryl said.

'It's never taken this long before.'

'Well, quit jabbing it like that and give it a minute while I make your tea. And I've got some of your favourite butties, if you're hungry?'

'Stupid bloody thing,' Bob muttered, still jabbing the button.

Glad to have him back where he belonged, albeit a little more cantankerous than usual, Cheryl shook her head in bemusement and left him to it.

As she waited for the kettle to boil, the doorbell rang. Thinking that the carers had arrived early, she rushed to answer it, and was surprised to find Dale on the step.

'Hey, gorgeous.' He gave her a kiss. 'Thought you might be here when I got no answer at yours. Everything OK?'

'Yeah, just making Bob a cup of tea,' she said, waving him inside. 'Come in.'

'How's he doing?'

'He's really happy to be home, but there's something wrong with his telly, so I've left him messing with the remote. Go and see if you can help him while I finish up in the kitchen.'

'Maybe you'd best introduce us first?' Dale suggested. 'I doubt he'll remember me, and I don't want him getting freaked out, thinking some random guy's walked in off the street.'

'Good point,' Cheryl said, impressed by his thoughtfulness.

'Did you tell him about last night?' Dale asked as she reached out to open the living-room door.

'No, I don't want to upset him. Oh, and thanks for having your guys fix the door. They did a great job; even cleaned up after themselves.'

'My pleasure.' Dale winked. 'Now let's go sort old Bobby out, so I can get you to myself.'

Whispering, '*Stop it!*' when he slid his hand down her back, Cheryl jerked away from him and opened the door.

'Bob, this is Dale.'

'Eh?' Bob looked up and frowned when he saw Dale. 'Don't tell me you're my carer? I was expecting a woman.'

'No, he's my friend,' Cheryl said. 'And he's going to help you with the TV.'

'Good luck with that.' Bob slumped back in his chair. 'I think it's buggered.'

'Let me see what I can do,' Dale said, walking over to him.

Smiling when Bob said, 'Thanks, lad,' and handed the remote over, Cheryl went to the kitchen and finished making his tea before plating one of the sandwiches. The TV was on when she carried them into the living room, and she winced at the volume.

'Christ, I'd forgotten how loud you have it,' she yelled, placing the cup and plate on Bob's side table. 'What was wrong with it?'

'It was unplugged,' Dale said, giving her a meaningful look as he added, 'Looks like someone might have been planning to have away with it last night.'

Aware that he was talking about Fiona, Cheryl shook her head in disgust. Before she could think too much more about

it, the doorbell rang, and she said, 'Turn that down; that'll be
the carers,' before rushing out into the hall.

Smile in place as she opened the door, it quickly slipped when
she saw that it was Fiona.

'Talk of the devil,' she said, stepping outside and pulling the
door to behind her. 'What do you want?'

'I need to see my dad,' Fiona said, switching the bulging bin
bag she was carrying into her other hand.

'Why?' Cheryl folded her arms. 'Didn't you get enough last
night? Or did I catch you before you managed to steal anything
valuable enough to sell?'

'I wasn't stealing. I was trying to get the house ready for him
coming home.'

'Oh, now I've heard everything,' Cheryl spluttered, gaping at
her in disbelief. 'You didn't even know he was coming out until
I told you.'

'Look, I know what you think of me, and I get it,' Fiona said
quietly. 'But that weren't my fault last night. They made me do it.'

'You're the one who brought them here,' Cheryl reminded her.
'And what if your dad had been home and they'd threatened him
like they threatened me?'

'I wouldn't have let them do anything.'

'How would you have stopped them?'

'I just would have. Now is he home, or what?'

'Yes he is. But he needs rest, so I'm not letting you bother
him.'

'It's not up to you,' Fiona argued. Then, narrowing her eyes,
she said, 'You've told him, haven't you? That's why you're acting
like this – 'cos you've grassed me up and turned him against me.'

'Actually, I haven't. But only because it would break his heart
if he knew what you'd done.'

'But I haven't done anything. Please, Cheryl, I just want to see him.'

'I'm not being funny, Fiona, but he didn't get ill overnight. If you care that much about him, where have you been for the last few years while he's been going downhill?'

'I've visited,' Fiona said defensively.

'Once in a blue moon. But you never stay long when you do.'

'He's never asked me to.'

'He shouldn't *have* to ask,' Cheryl said pointedly. 'You've got no idea how much he's been struggling. If I didn't bring him food every day, he'd probably have starved to death by now.'

'It's all right for you; you can afford it,' Fiona griped. 'I've got nothing. And now Davie's kicked me out, thanks to you and your mate, I'm homeless an' all.'

'Don't try to blame us for that,' Cheryl shot back. 'I don't see why you'd want to be with him anyway, if you reckon he forced you to rob your own father. What kind of man does that?'

'Yours ain't no saint, so don't be lecturing me about mine,' Fiona said bitterly. 'Least Davie don't pretend to be something he isn't.'

Before Cheryl could ask what she meant by that, a car pulled up at the gate, and her heart sank when two women wearing blue tabards stepped out.

'Is this Robert Baker's house?' one of them asked as they strolled up the path.

'Yeah, he's in the living room,' Cheryl said, forcing a smile as she stepped in front of Fiona to open the door for them. 'But call him Bob; he hates anyone using his full name.'

'Noted,' the woman chuckled.

'I'm his daughter, I'll take you in,' Fiona said, skirting around Cheryl and pushing through the door.

Furious that the bitch had got one over on her, but aware that

80

there was nothing she could do without causing a scene, Cheryl waited until the women had gone inside before following.

Bob had muted the TV and was regaling Dale with tales of his antics as a young man. He paused when the living room door opened, and his face lit up when he saw Fiona.

'Hello, love. This is a nice surprise.'

'Hiya, Dad.' She rushed over and gave him a hug. 'Sorry I couldn't get to the hospital, but I haven't been too well.'

'I can see that,' Bob said, taking in her skinny frame and greasy hair. 'Sit yourself down.'

Fiona turned and made a move towards the couch, but froze when she saw Dale already sitting there.

'I'll, er, sit on the footy,' she said, turning back to her father and reaching down to pull an ancient footstool out from under his chair.

'Hello, Bob, I'm Sharon and this is Gill,' one of the carers said. 'We're going to be looking after you till you're back on your feet.'

'I'm not an invalid,' he grunted.

'They're here to help, so don't be rude,' Cheryl chided, giving Dale a hooded *not now* look when he glowered at Fiona, who was sitting as close to her father as she could get without actually sitting on his lap.

'Sorry,' Bob said contritely. 'I'll behave, I promise.'

'Good, or you'll have me to answer to,' she mock-warned. 'Anyway, you need to have a chat with these ladies, so we'll leave you to it. I'll pop round when I get home; make sure you're OK.'

'Thanks, love.' He grasped her hand. 'What would I do without you, eh?'

'Come on, Dad, she said she's got to go,' Fiona piped up.

'Yeah, sorry. You get off and have fun,' Bob said, letting go of Cheryl's hand. 'I'll see you later.'

'I'm staying, so there's no need for you to come back,' Fiona said, boldly looking Cheryl in the eye, as if daring her to argue about it.

'Well, aren't we the popular one?' Sharon teased Bob. 'Two lovely lasses fighting over who gets to take care of you. If only all our other clients were so lucky, eh, Gill?'

'I'm his daughter, so it's my duty,' Fiona said self-righteously. 'She's just a neighbour, so it wouldn't be right to put it on her.'

'We're friends as well as neighbours, so it's no problem,' Cheryl replied through a fake smile. 'I'll see you later, Bob.'

'That'll be nice,' he said. 'And it was good to see you, Chris,' he added when Dale stood up. 'I was starting to think you'd skipped the country.'

Sensing that Dale was about to correct him when he opened his mouth, Cheryl grabbed his arm and walked him to the door, saying goodbye to the carers as she went.

Outside, Dale slid his arm free and jumped into the car without opening Cheryl's door first, as he usually did.

'Are you OK?' she asked as she climbed into the passenger seat.

'Not really,' he replied coolly. 'I'm just wondering why you didn't say anything when the old man called me by your ex's name?'

'There was no point,' Cheryl said. 'I told you he gets confused sometimes.'

'And yet he didn't have any trouble remembering *your* name,' Dale said, giving her a side-glance as he threw the car into drive.

'He's known me for ten years and sees me every day, but that's only the second time he's ever met you,' Cheryl reminded him. 'And he's just come out of hospital, so he's probably not thinking straight.'

'And that makes it all right, does it?' Dale asked. 'So when you meet my folks for the second time, you'd be OK if they called you Caroline?'

'That's different,' Cheryl said quietly. 'They're not old and suffering from dementia.'

Dale stared out through the windscreen and drove on without replying, and Cheryl sat in awkward silence beside him. He was obviously deeply offended about Bob confusing him with Chris, but she'd told him about Bob's memory problems, so she wasn't sure why he was taking it so personally.

After several tense minutes, Dale released an audible sigh and reached across the centre console for Cheryl's hand.

'I'm sorry,' he apologised. 'That was out of order. It pissed me off, but I shouldn't have taken it out on you.'

'It's OK,' Cheryl said, relieved that it was over. 'I understand why it upset you, and I promise I'll correct him if he ever does it again. I just didn't want to get into it in front of Fiona and his carers.'

'You're a good woman,' Dale said, smiling at her as he turned into the car park of the restaurant where he'd booked a table. Twisting in his seat to face her after parking up, he added, 'I don't think you realise how much I like you.'

'I like you too,' Cheryl replied shyly.

'Please tell me I haven't blown it?' Dale peered into her eyes. 'I'd hate to lose you because I let my jealousy get the better of me.'

'Jealousy?' Cheryl drew her head back. 'You're jealous of *Bob*?'

'Not him, your ex,' Dale said sheepishly. 'I know it's stupid, but when you didn't set Bob straight, it kind of felt like you weren't bothered.'

'You're right, it *is* stupid,' Cheryl said. 'You know how much I hate Chris.'

'Do you, though?' Dale asked. 'Because if there's any feeling still there, I'd rather know before I get in too deep.'

'He put me through hell, and I feel sick whenever Bob talks about him as if he's still around,' Cheryl insisted. 'Or should I say I *used* to feel sick, until I started seeing you and realised it didn't affect me anymore.'

'Really?'

'*Really*,' said Cheryl. 'You say I don't realise how much you like me, but that goes both ways.'

'So I'm forgiven?' Dale grinned.

'I wouldn't go that far,' Cheryl teased. 'But on a more serious note, if Bob's going to upset you every time you see him, maybe it's best if you didn't come in with me next time.'

'Hopefully you won't have to keep going that often now his daughter's staying there,' Dale said. 'And that's not me telling you to stay away,' he quickly added. 'But I can't see you wanting to spend too much time with *her*.'

'I'd prefer not to see her at all,' Cheryl agreed. 'But I don't trust her, and Bob's been good to me, so I'm not going to stop going round there.'

'And I wouldn't dream of asking you to,' Dale said. 'But I would like you to spend less time worrying about everyone else and more time concentrating on us, because I really feel like we've got something special here.'

'So do I,' Cheryl said, realising that she actually meant it.

'That's all I needed to hear,' Dale said, leaning over to kiss her before opening his door. 'Now, let's go eat. Then I'm taking you home to ravish you.'

'Promises promises,' Cheryl quipped, relieved that he was back to his usual happy, laid-back self.

Back on the estate, Fiona was pacing her father's living-room floor. He'd started to drift off while the carers were still there, so the women had helped him upstairs and into bed before leaving.

He was fast asleep now, with his revolting cat, who had hissed like a viper when she'd popped her head round the door, curled up beside him, keeping guard.

It was a few hours since Fiona had last had a fix, and she didn't even have any cigarettes to calm her nerves as the withdrawal pains started kicking in. A search of her dad's coat pockets, the drawers, and down the back of the chair and sofa had yielded almost thirty quid, which was more than enough for a wrap of gear and twenty fags. But Davie, who always scored for her, wasn't answering his phone; and she couldn't approach any of the local dealers herself, because she owed them all money and knew she would get battered if she showed her face.

Unsure what to do, Fiona stopped pacing when she spotted a paper bag with the distinctive green logo of a pharmacy sticking out from the side of her dad's chair. Hoping the hospital might have sent him home with morphine, she ripped it open and tipped the small white boxes it contained onto the coffee table. Pleased to find two boxes of tramadol capsules among the antibiotics and various other medications, she popped four capsules out of a strip and made her way to the kitchen to get some water. It wouldn't be as strong as a morphine high, but it would certainly take the edge off the withdrawal pains until she could get her hands on some proper gear. In the meantime, she would use the money she'd found to buy a bottle of booze, which would triple the strength of the capsules.

After washing the capsules down, she spotted three keys sitting in the middle of the kitchen table. Guessing that they were for the back door, which she noticed had been repaired after Davie had kicked it in the previous night, she slid one off the little metal ring that was holding them together and slipped it into her jeans pocket. As that nosy bitch next door had smugly pointed out, her dad had never given her a key to the house;

but now she had this one, she'd be able to come and go as she pleased. And when the old bastard kicked her out, which he inevitably would at some point, because they had never been able to spend more than two days in each other's company without getting into a full-blown argument, she would be able to sneak in at night and kip on the sofa.

Still fuming with Davie for dumping her, just because she'd called him a coward for bottling it when he saw Cheryl's poncey man, she pulled her jacket on and headed out to the local off-licence. She would give him a couple of days, she decided; let him realise what he'd lost and come crawling back to her. Which he would, she was sure, because no other bird had ever been able to satisfy his freakish sexual appetite like she did.

The front door slammed shut when Fiona left the house, and Bob woke with a start. Groggy from the painkillers the carers had urged him to take before they left, he thought he was still in hospital and reached for the cord to summon the nurse to ask for a glass of water. The cord wasn't there, and he remembered he was home when Cyril stretched out beside him and gave a croaky little meow.

'Sorry, boy, did I wake you?' he said, smiling as he tickled Cyril under the chin and felt the vibration of his purrs.

Contented to be back where he belonged, with his best pal by his side, Bob lay there for several minutes, relishing the peace and quiet after a week of ghoulish groans and beeping machinery. After a while, realising that he wasn't going to get back to sleep any time soon, he decided to get up and make a cup of tea.

His head started spinning when he eased himself up into a sitting position, so he waited for it to stop before pushing the blanket off his legs and dropping his feet to the floor. His chest felt tight and he banged it with his fist to loosen the built-up phlegm when he started coughing. He hadn't smoked in years, but his lungs had been scarred by his sixty-a-day habit of old *and* the asbestos he'd breathed in at the school where he'd worked in his younger years. By rights, he ought to have kicked the bucket a long time ago, but God obviously had other plans for him, he reckoned.

Sighing at the thought of all the people who hadn't been so lucky to make it this far, not least his wife, who had passed away from breast cancer when Fiona was a teenager, he slowly got up. As he was making his way across the room to get his dressing gown off the hook on the back of the door, Cyril jumped down off the bed and weaved between his ankles, tripping him up. He landed with a thud and grimaced when pain flared in his hip. Too weak to get up, and afraid to try because he was sure he'd heard something snap, he banged his fist on the floor to attract Fiona's attention. But all that came back to him was silence.

Chapter 12

Cheryl woke with the scent of Dale's aftershave in her nostrils, and she smiled when she opened her eyes and saw him sleeping beside her. He'd never stayed the whole night before, so this was the first chance she'd ever had to study his face without being distracted by his sexy eyes. He'd told her that his mother had been a beauty queen when she'd met his father aged eighteen, and she was still a stunningly beautiful woman even now; but Dale's looks definitely came from his father, from his dark hair, to his chiselled jawline, straight nose and nicely shaped lips. His brother, Stefan, had also inherited those looks, but he didn't have the same twinkle in his eyes that Dale and his father both had; and he had a taller, thinner frame, which she thought gave him the appearance of a nerdy science teacher.

Smiling when Dale stirred after a few minutes, she said, 'Morning.'

'Hey,' he said, his sleepy voice softer and deeper than usual. 'Sleep well?'

'Like a baby. You?'

'Same,' he grinned, rolling over to face her. 'Must have been all that good loving.'

'The booze probably played a large part,' she teased,

remembering how drunk they had both been after drinking the two bottles of wine they had brought home from the restaurant.

'Nah, it was all this,' he said, sliding his hand up over her stomach to caress her breast.

Shivering at his touch, Cheryl glanced at the clock on the bedside table and wriggled away from him when she saw that it was almost time to get up.

'Oh, it's like that, is it?' Dale pouted, propping himself up on his elbow and resting his head on his hand when she climbed out of bed. 'You've had your fun and now you're done with me?'

'I need to take a shower and get ready for work,' she said, leaning down to kiss him as she pulled her dressing gown on.

'Not so fast, lady.' He leapt out of bed. 'If you're taking a shower, so am I.'

'You're not at home now,' she reminded him, giggling when he wrapped his arms around her and carried her out of the bedroom. 'I haven't got a fancy walk-in, so you'll have to stand in the bath with me.'

'I love me a bit of rough,' he growled, biting down on her shoulder.

Dressed, and tingling all over after their shower session, Cheryl felt giddy with excitement as she and Dale left the house a short time later. They had made love under the cascading water and Dale had held her in his arms and told her that he loved her, and she had said that she loved him too. And it was true. She *did* love him – as stupid as that would undoubtedly sound to anyone in their right mind, given that they had only been together for two weeks.

The Transit van was parked across the road, and Dale said he needed to nip over to have a word with the workmen before driving her to work. The house had been in a terrible state when his father had gone to view it for the first time, but the workmen had made short work of the repairs and decorating and were now almost finished. The beds had already been delivered, and the rest of the furniture and white goods were due to arrive that afternoon. And once that was all in place, the tenants would be moving in.

Dale had told Cheryl that the tenants were all women whom his father had employed to work in the various care homes he owned. That was why he'd gone to bid on the care home in Didsbury at the auction that day: to create another haven for the aging Polish community in that area. But when he realised he'd accidentally bought Edna's place instead, he decided to use it to house his workers instead of leaving them to find their own accommodation, which usually left them at the mercy of slum landlords, who charged the earth for tiny rooms in squalid, overcrowded properties.

Cheryl knew that Dale's parents were both from Poland, and she thought it was great that his dad wanted to provide facilities for the people from his homeland. He was also generous to his employees, and she almost envied the women who would be moving into the house. Hell, after seeing that grand hallway and huge front room, she would be happy to live there *herself*.

Smiling at the thought of having all that room to swan around in like Lady Muck, she took out the key Bob had given her. About to slot it into the lock, she remembered that Fiona was there and decided to knock instead. No answer came, so she moved to the window and peered through the gap between the curtains. The room was dark, but she could see Fiona curled up on the sofa; an overflowing ashtray, several crisp packets and chocolate wrappers and an empty bottle of vodka on the floor beside her.

Bob wasn't in there and she guessed that he must still be in bed. He'd always been an early riser, so she was sure he would be awake, and she decided to pop up and see if he needed anything before his carers arrived.

Hoping that she didn't wake Fiona, because she couldn't be bothered dealing with that bitch today, she quietly opened the front door and tiptoed inside. The stairs creaked as she made her way up them, and she froze and listened for sounds of movement from the living room before continuing on up to the top.

Bob's bedroom door was closed, so she tapped on it before easing the handle down, whispering, 'Bob? It's Cheryl. Are you awake?'

He didn't answer and, thinking that he must be asleep when she saw that his curtains were still closed, she was about to creep back out when Cyril brushed against her leg and gave a little cry. Sensing that something wasn't quite right, because Bob would have got up if the cat was awake and asking for food, she slid her hand across the wall, feeling for the light switch. She squinted in the sudden brightness when the unshaded bulb lit up, and her stomach dropped into her boots when she saw him lying motionless on the floor, a few feet away from the bed.

'Bob!' she cried, rushing to him. 'Bob, wake up!'

His bare shoulder felt icy when she touched it, and her mind whisked her back to the previous week, when she'd found him in a pool of blood on the kitchen floor.

A faint groan shocked her out of her thoughts, and a wave of sheer relief washed over her when Bob's eyes flickered open.

'Oh, thank God,' she gasped. 'Are you OK? What happened?'

'I got up to make a cuppa and tripped over Cyril,' he croaked, shivering in the cold air. 'Where is he?' He twisted his head. 'I didn't fall on him, did I?'

'No, he's fine,' Cheryl assured him, grabbing his dressing gown to cover him. 'How long have you been here, and why didn't you shout for help? Fiona's downstairs.'

'I banged on the floor, but she mustn't have heard me,' Bob said. 'I've no idea what time it was, but it was dark, so she was probably asleep.'

Remembering the empty vodka bottle, Cheryl thought it more likely that Fiona had been unconscious, and she cursed herself for not popping in to check on him when she and Dale had got home the previous night, as she'd promised.

'Do you think you'll be able to get up if I help you?' she asked.

'I don't know, love,' he croaked. 'My hip's throbbing like a bugger.'

'Hello...' a cheery voice called out from the hallway below. 'Anyone home?'

'Up here!' Cheryl yelled, recognising the voice of the carer. 'Quick!'

On solo calls that morning, since it had been decided that Bob didn't need two carers while his daughter was helping out, Sharon Oakes caught the panic in the woman's voice and rushed up the stairs.

'What happened?' she asked. 'How long's he been here?'

'Since last night,' Cheryl told her. 'He tripped over the cat.'

'Oh, you daft sod,' Sharon said, kneeling beside Bob. 'I told you to call your daughter if you needed anything, so why were you out of bed?'

'Something woke me and I needed a brew,' he said. 'I heard a snap and my hip's hurting. You don't think I've broke it, do you?'

'Only one way to find out,' Sharon sighed. 'Probably means another trip to hospital, though.'

'Oh God,' Bob groaned. 'I can't go back there, love. It was hell.'

'Should've stayed in bed like I told you, then you wouldn't

have to,' she chided, patting her pockets. 'Damn, I've left my phone in the car. Give me a sec to get it and I'll call an ambulance.'

'I'll call them,' Cheryl offered, pulling out her own phone.

"S'goin' on?' Fiona croaked, appearing in the doorway as Cheryl started speaking to the emergency services.

'Your dad's taken a bit of a tumble,' Sharon told her. 'But don't worry; she's calling for an ambulance.'

'He don't need an ambulance, he's just after attention,' Fiona sneered, prodding Bob's leg with her toe. 'Get up and quit messing about.'

'Stop that!' Sharon barked, slapping her leg away.

'Oi, that's assault,' Fiona protested.

'So, sue me,' Sharon glowered.

'Cheryl?'

Hearing Dale's voice as she finished the call, Cheryl pushed past Fiona and popped her head round the door.

'I'm upstairs. Bob's had a fall.'

'Is he OK?' Dale asked, running up to her.

'He's conscious, but he's hurt his hip. Help us get him onto the bed.'

'No!' Sharon held up her hand to stop Dale when he walked further into the room. 'We need to wait for the paramedics. If he's broken something, moving him could do serious damage.'

'Yeah, you're right,' he said, stepping back.

'Is it always this cold in here?' Sharon asked, turning her attention back to Bob.

'He doesn't like to put the heating on,' Cheryl told her.

'The prices them rip-off merchants charge, no I bloody don't,' Bob grunted. 'I spend most of me time in the front room, and I've got me fire in there, so that's enough.'

'Agh!' Fiona squawked. 'Get away from me, you little shit!'

Cheryl snapped her head round and saw Fiona drawing her foot back to kick Cyril, who had crawled out from under the bed, where he'd hidden when Sharon came in. 'Leave him alone!' she bellowed, scooping Cyril up off the floor. 'And don't you ever let me catch you doing that again, or I'll—'

'It's getting a bit crowded in here,' Sharon called out sharply. 'Somebody needs to go downstairs and keep an eye out for the ambulance.'

'*She* can go, seeing as she thinks she's his daughter,' Fiona sniped, jerking her chin up at Cheryl before flouncing out of the room.

'I'll go,' Dale said. 'And you calm down,' he added to Cheryl, kissing her on the forehead before heading downstairs.

'Well, he's a bit of all right, isn't he?' Sharon said approvingly. 'Good looks *and* a good heart. You don't find many of them these days.'

'Yeah, he's a good one,' Cheryl agreed, gazing down at Bob, who now had his eyes shut. 'Is he OK?'

'Looks like he's having a little nap,' Sharon said quietly as she pushed herself up to her feet. 'He can't have slept much if he's been on the floor all night. Good job he had his dressing gown to keep him warm.'

'He didn't. I put it over him when I came in.'

'Bloody hell; he's lucky he didn't freeze to death.'

'I know,' Cheryl replied, walking over to the window when she heard sirens in the near distance. She drew the curtain back and saw Dale standing by the gate below. 'They're here,' she said when an ambulance pulled up seconds later.

Two paramedics climbed out, and Dale directed them into the house.

'All right, lads,' Sharon said, smiling when the pair came into the room. 'Took your time, didn't you?'

'You got lucky; we'd just finished a job close by when the call came in,' one of them told her. 'So who've we got here, then?' he asked, looking down at Bob as he pulled on a pair of latex gloves.

'This is Bob,' Sharon said. 'He's seventy-seven and was discharged from hospital yesterday. He had a fall during the night, and his friend' – she nodded at Cheryl – 'found him and covered him up just before I got here.'

'OK, let's take a look at you, bud,' the man said, crouching next to Bob.

Sharon moved over to stand beside Cheryl to give the men room, and asked, 'Do you want to go with him if they take him in?'

'I can't,' Cheryl said guiltily. 'I've got to go to work.'

'What about madam?' Sharon gestured in the direction of the bathroom, where Fiona had gone after leaving the room.

'Doubt it, but you should probably ask,' Cheryl said, readjusting her grip on the cat when he started wriggling to get free. 'If they do take him, I'll keep Cyril at mine,' she added. 'No way I'm leaving him with *her*.'

Sharon didn't reply, but the look on her face told Cheryl that she approved of the decision.

'OK, nothing appears to be broken,' the paramedic said to Sharon when he and his colleague had finished their preliminary checks. 'And Bob here is insisting that he's not coming with us, so we're going to get him into bed and leave him in your capable hands.'

'Are you sure there's nothing else wrong?' Cheryl asked, putting Cyril down now there was no need to take him.

'Nothing obvious,' the man remarked. 'But once he's off the floor and comfortable, we'll hook him up to check his BP and heart, and what have you.'

'I couldn't half do with a cuppa,' Bob said.

'I'll make you one before I go,' Cheryl said, smiling down at him.

'No, you get off; I'll do it,' Sharon insisted. 'And don't be worrying about him, pet. I'll make sure he's got everything he needs.'

'Thanks,' Cheryl said. 'And thank you both, too,' she added to the paramedics.

They both smiled, then took hold of Bob's arms, ready to lift him.

'I'll call round after work,' Cheryl told him as he braced himself. 'And, this time, do as you're told and stay in bed,' she added mock-sternly.

'Yes, boss,' he grinned.

Glad that he was looking more like his old self again, Cheryl said goodbye and quickly made her way out to where Dale was waiting for her in the car.

Chapter 13

Three of Cheryl's regulars were already waiting outside The Bluebell Café when Dale dropped her off at the market hall after leaving Bob's. Apologising, she let them in and made them all a cup of tea before starting her morning routine. She was happy that Bob hadn't suffered any serious injuries, and very grateful that Sharon, the carer, was there to keep an eye on him. Once Sharon had gone, however, he would be left at the mercy of Fiona, and that worried her. But there was nothing she could do about it, so she tried to put it out of her mind and get on with her work.

It was a slow morning, and an even slower afternoon, but she used the time between customers to clean the fridge and do a stock-check.

Sure that no one else would come once Glenda – a wisp of a woman in her eighties, who was always the last to leave – had gone, Cheryl was loading the dishwasher when the little bell over the door jangled, and she was surprised to see Dale standing on the other side of the counter when she walked back into the café.

'Hey,' she smiled. 'What are you doing here? I thought you had to wait in for the furniture?'

'It was delivered this morning, so it's all done,' he told her. 'I had to nip into town for a meeting, so I thought I'd call in and see how you were getting on. Looks like I timed it perfectly,' he added, glancing at the empty tables. 'Are you ready to lock up?'

'No, I've got another hour yet,' she said. 'Sit down. I'll make you a brew.'

'No offence, but I'd rather get going,' he said, following as she made her way into the kitchen. 'I'm parked on double yellows.'

'You should be all right,' she assured him as she switched the kettle on. 'The wardens don't come round very often.'

'I'd rather not take the risk,' Dale said. 'And, to be honest, now I've seen how deserted it is round here, I'm a bit worried about you being here on your own. It's already getting dark out there, and there's no one around to help if someone tries to rob you.'

'There's a security guard, so I'm quite safe,' Cheryl assured him. 'Now stop worrying and let me get on with the cleaning.'

'I've got a better idea,' Dale said, taking her coat off the hook it was hanging on and lifting her handbag up off the ledge. 'Leave it till morning.'

'I can't,' Cheryl protested, resisting when he grabbed her hand and started pulling her towards the door. 'There's food out that needs putting away.'

'It'll keep,' Dale said, switching the light off and opening the door. 'Ladies first.'

Laughing when he did a mock-bow and waved for her to step out ahead of him, Cheryl said, 'OK. You win. But don't make a habit of turning up out of the blue like this, or you'll get me sacked.'

Dale laughed and watched as she locked the door, before taking her hand and leading her to the car.

*

Fiona was standing in Bob's doorway talking to two men when Dale pulled up outside Cheryl's house a short time later. She flashed a glance at them as they climbed out of the car, then said something to the men and gave a surreptitious nod in their direction before retreating into the house and closing the door.

The men looked shifty as they walked out through the gate, and Cheryl glared at them until they scuttled away. Annoyed that Fiona had brought her druggy friends to Bob's door, she was about to march to the house to confront her when Dale grabbed her arm and steered her up her own path, saying, 'Leave it, you haven't got time. My mum's expecting us at six, so you need to go get ready.'

'What?' Confused, Cheryl stopped walking and looked up at him. 'You never mentioned anything about going to see your mum.'

'I wanted to surprise you,' he said, plucking her keys out of her hand and unlocking the front door.

'But we were only there a couple of nights ago, why would she want to see me again so soon?' Cheryl asked. 'Oh God, she's not going to vet me, is she?'

'Why would she do that?'

'To see if I'm good enough for you.'

'Don't be daft,' Dale laughed. 'It's a family dinner, that's all.'

'But I'm not family,' Cheryl said, almost tripping over the doorstep when he ushered her inside.

'Looks like you are now,' Dale countered. 'You should be honoured,' he went on. 'My mum invited you, and she hasn't liked a single girl I've ever dated.'

'Not even Caroline?' Cheryl asked, mentally kicking herself as soon as the name left her mouth, because it made her sound like she was obsessed with the woman.

'Definitely *not* her,' Dale replied bluntly. 'She saw her for exactly what she was the first time she ever clapped eyes on her. Now stop talking about *her* and go make yourself gorgeous while I check that the tenants are settling in OK.'

'Oh, are they here already?' Cheryl asked. 'That was fast.'

'My dad doesn't let the grass grow,' Dale said. 'Now scoot.' He slapped her backside. 'I won't be long.'

Curious to see the new tenants, Cheryl waited until Dale had left before rushing up to her bedroom. It was already quite dark outside, so she wasn't surprised to see lights on in the house across the road. There were no curtains hanging at the windows, and she pressed her nose up against the net curtain covering her own window when she spotted a young, dark-haired woman moving around in the front bedroom.

An older woman came outside, and Cheryl ducked when Dale followed a few seconds later. The pair walked to the gate and had a short conversation, then the woman handed a parcel to Dale, and he, in turn, took something out of his pocket and handed it to her before strolling to his car. Afraid to stand up in case he saw her and thought she'd been spying, Cheryl reached up and slid the curtains shut before heading into the bathroom to take a quick shower.

Chapter 14

Dale's mother opened the front door when he and Cheryl arrived at the house that evening. She was dressed less formally than on the previous occasion, in navy culottes and a white silk blouse, but she still looked like a movie star with her immaculate hair and make-up.

'Sorry we're late,' Dale apologised, kissing her cheek. 'Traffic was a nightmare.'

'Well, you're here now,' she said, reaching up to straighten his tie before turning to greet Cheryl. 'It's lovely to see you again, dear. I'm so happy you were able to make it.'

Unsure why, because she hadn't thought she'd made much of an impact on her first visit, Cheryl said, 'Thanks for inviting me.'

'But of course,' Sonia purred, waving her inside. 'You're part of the family now.'

Cheryl slipped her coat off as she stepped into the hallway. Dale had hung it up for her the previous time she was there, but he and Sonia were already heading to the kitchen, so she held onto it and followed them.

Stefan, Estelle and their son, Frankie, were sitting at one end of the kitchen table, and two elderly women were sitting at the other end. They all looked up when Sonia strolled in and announced that the latecomers had arrived. Stefan nodded hello to Cheryl before rising to shake Dale's hand. Estelle, who looked like she'd dipped herself in a vat of foundation before coming out, ignored them both and quietly berated Frankie, who was noisily marching his knife and fork on the tabletop as if they were toy soldiers.

'Look who's here,' Sonia said, linking her arm through Dale's and walking him to the end of the table.

'Hey,' he beamed, looking as delighted to see the old women as they were to see him. 'Nobody told me you were coming.'

After fussing over him for a few moments, one of the women jerked her chin up and flashed a hooded look at Cheryl. '*Kto to jest?*'

'This is Cherry; Dale's lady friend,' Sonia said, waving Cheryl over. 'Cherry, these are Alfie's aunts, Alicja and Zuzanna.'

Cheryl noted that Sonia had misnamed her again, but felt too shy to correct her. Instead, she smiled politely at the old ladies, and said, 'It's lovely to meet you.'

They both scrutinised her through narrowed eyes, then Alicja muttered something to Zuzanna, whose gaze immediately slid to Cheryl's stomach. Cheryl had no idea what had been said, but she suspected it had something to do with her weight. She wasn't fat by any means, but she always put on a few extra pounds when she was due for her period, and she self-consciously clutched her coat tighter to hide her belly.

'Behave,' Sonia chided, giving the old ladies a mock-stern look before taking Cheryl's arm and leading her back to the other end of the table. 'Don't listen to them,' she whispered. 'They are both a little...' She circled her finger at her temple.

Cheryl smiled and quickly sat down when Sonia pulled a chair out for her directly opposite Estelle. As she looped it over the back of the chair, she noticed Estelle smirk before whispering something to her son, and her jaw clenched when they both laughed.

'Estelle, *please*.' Sonia gave her daughter-in-law a pained look. 'Do you always have to be so loud?'

Estelle instantly fell silent, and Cheryl's inner bitch hissed a jubilant *Ha*! when a heat rash broke out on the woman's chest and spread up her throat to her cheeks.

As Sonia took her seat next to the aunts, Alfie and two burly men in suits, who Cheryl later learned were his cousins, walked in from the conservatory. They all greeted Dale with handshakes and back slaps, then Alfie noticed Cheryl and walked up behind her chair and placed his large hand on her shoulder and gave it a squeeze.

'Welcome back, sweetheart. Glad you could join us.'

'Thanks,' she said, smiling shyly. She had been nervous the first time she met Alfie and his wife, but she was even more so tonight, given that this was a more intimate, family occasion. But they were both being so lovely, she didn't know why she'd been so worried.

As if a silent bell had been rung, Rosa appeared and served dinner. Cheryl thanked her, but the woman moved on without responding before silently disappearing through a door at the rear of the room.

The family seemed to have a lot of catching up to do, and they laughed and chatted their way through the meal. They were speaking in Polish, so Cheryl didn't understand a word of it; and Estelle seemed to be equally in the dark as she ate in stony-faced silence.

When everyone had finished eating and Rosa had cleared away the plates, the men rose to their feet, and Cheryl gave Dale a questioning look when he too got up.

'Whisky and cigar time,' he explained with a grin.

'You're not leaving me, are you?' she whispered, clutching his arm when he leaned down to kiss her.

'It's tradition,' he said. 'The men talk business, the women gossip. It'll give you a chance to bond with my mum,' he added, winking at her.

Dismayed by the thought of being forced to make small talk with the women, Cheryl watched as Dale, his nephew and the other men strolled into the conservatory. Sonia was nice enough, even if she did seem to have a problem remembering her name; but Estelle made her feel uncomfortable, and the aunts, like Rosa, didn't appear to speak English, so she knew she was in for an awkward time of it.

'At last,' Sonia said, smiling conspiratorially when the men had gone. 'Now who's ready for a *real* drink?'

In unison, both aunts held up their empty glasses, making Cheryl wonder if they did speak English, after all, since they had clearly understood the question.

Sonia took a bottle of vodka out of the fridge and poured large measures for the aunts before walking down to Cheryl.

'Drink up,' she ordered, gesturing to her glass, which still had an inch of wine in it.

Cheryl did as she'd been told and watched as Sonia half-filled the glass with neat vodka.

'Is there any Coke?' she asked.

'What she say?' Alicja called out.

'She wants Coke,' Sonia told her.

'No, no, no,' Alicja chuckled, wagging a gnarled finger at Cheryl. 'We take like man.'

'Put hair on chest,' Zuzanna chipped in with a mischievous glint in her eyes.

Sonia laughed and walked round to Estelle.

'Not for me, thanks; I'm driving,' Estelle said, covering her glass with her hand before pushing her chair back. 'Please excuse me, I need to ring the sitter to make sure Poppy's settled.'

Sonia pursed her lips when Estelle walked out into the hall-way and pulled the door shut behind her.

'Ridiculous woman,' she said, rolling her eyes at Cheryl. 'She treats that child like a baby, then wonders why she still behaves like one.'

Cheryl didn't agree. She thought Poppy was a perfectly normal little girl, and she'd felt quite sorry for her at the anniversary party; left alone in the corner, without the comfort of her favourite doll to keep her company. But it wasn't her business, so she gave an awkward smile and kept her mouth firmly shut.

'Come sit with us,' Sonia said, moving back to her seat and filling her own glass.

Cheryl got up and perched on the empty chair next to Zuzanna.

'*Na Zdrowie!*' Sonia said, raising her glass into the air.

Guessing that it was a toast when the aunts repeated what she'd said and raised their own glasses, Cheryl raised hers and then followed suit when they all downed their drinks in one. She instantly regretted it when the neat alcohol hit her throat and brought tears to her eyes, and she covered her mouth with her hand when she started coughing.

The old ladies cackled in delight, and Zuzanna whacked her on the back – with far more strength than a woman of her age ought to have, in Cheryl's opinion.

'Thanks,' she croaked, edging away before the woman could hit her again. 'I'm OK.'

'The first is always the worst,' Sonia assured her. 'The second will be smooth, like velvet.'

'I think I'd best stick to water,' Cheryl said, wiping her eyes on the back of her hand.

'Nonsense,' Sonia scoffed, leaning across the table to refill her glass. 'This is how we do it, and if you love my boy, you'll learn our ways.'

Alicja and Zuzanna raised their refilled glasses to Cheryl, urging her to join them in a second shot. Already a little tipsy, Cheryl picked up her glass.

'On three,' Sonia said. 'One ... two ...'

On three, they all threw their drinks back, and Cheryl was relieved to note that Sonia had been right when she drank hers and it felt much smoother on her throat than the first.

'We need music,' Sonia declared, slamming her glass down on the table and clapping her hands. 'Come help me, Cherry.'

As Sonia walked towards a door on the other side of the room, Estelle came back into the kitchen. Cheryl glanced at her as she rose to her feet, and almost laughed out loud when the woman gave her a sour look before sitting down and turning her back. Amused, she followed Sonia into a room that appeared to be used as storage for stacks of chairs and boxes.

'Wow, you've got a lot of fairy lights,' she said, noticing coils of multicoloured lights spilling out of one box. 'And is that Rudolph?' She pointed to a wicker reindeer standing in the corner.

'Christmas is a special time for our family,' Sonia said, tugging a karaoke machine out from under a chair. 'Alfie has his men decorate the garden and the front of the house, and it's so beautiful when it's all lit up at night. The children love it.'

'I bet they do,' Cheryl said, remembering how excited she herself had always been about Christmas as a child, although her parents had never gone as far as decorating the exterior of their house.

'You should come this year,' Sonia said. 'Unless you prefer to spend Christmas with your own family?'

'We don't really celebrate it anymore,' Cheryl said, pushing the memories out of her mind.

'Oh, that's so sad.' Sonia gave her a sympathetic look. 'Why would you not want to be together at Christmas?'

'My mum passed away a few years ago,' Cheryl told her. 'And my dad moved to Canada after he got remarried, so I don't see him very often.'

'No brothers or sisters, aunts or uncles who would allow you to join them?' Sonia raised an eyebrow.

'No, I'm an only child, and most of my relatives live quite far out, so it wouldn't be practical,' Cheryl said. 'But I'm used to it. So it doesn't really bother me.'

'No one should be alone at Christmas, so you will come to us,' Sonia said decisively as she handed two wireless microphones to Cheryl. 'Save me the agony of being left alone with Estelle when the men take their leave,' she added conspiratorially. 'I've tried so hard with her, I really have, but she sits there with that *face*...' She mimicked Estelle's expression of disapproval, then shook her head, saying, 'Why Stefan chose her to be his bride, I will never know. He would have been so much happier with a beautiful girl like you. But what can a mother do?' She raised her hands in a gesture of resignation. Then, smiling, she stroked Cheryl's hair and whispered, 'I'm so glad Dale found you, darling. I think you and I are going to have a lot of fun together.'

'Me too,' Cheryl said, grinning like a Cheshire cat as she followed Sonia back into the kitchen.

Chapter 15

Cheryl's mouth was bone dry when the alarm on her phone went off the next morning, and it took several moments before her vision cleared enough to see that she was in her own bedroom. Groping for her phone to shut it off, she lay still for a few minutes, breathing deeply in an attempt to settle her churning stomach. She had no recollection of coming home, and nor did she recall getting undressed and climbing into bed, so she guessed that Dale must have helped her.

At the thought of him, she turned her head to see if he'd stayed, but that side of the bed was empty and the pillows didn't look like they had been slept on. A wave of white-hot embarrassment washed over her when she had a sudden flash-back of herself singing karaoke at the top of her voice the previous night. The men had come back from their cigar and whisky session by then, and they had all been laughing – and she would bet her last penny it had been *at* her rather than with her, because she couldn't sing even when she was stone-cold sober.

Wondering if Dale had decided not to stay because he'd been annoyed with her for getting pissed off her head in front of his family, she checked her phone to see if he'd messaged her. He hadn't, so she messaged him instead, writing: *I'm so sorry*, along with the emoji of a girl with her hand over her face.

A second after she sent it, Dale rang, and she answered it nervously, fully expecting him to tell her off.

'Morning,' he greeted her jovially. 'Bet you've got one hell of a hangover?'

'A bit,' she admitted.

'I've never seen you so drunk,' he went on. 'It was hilarious.'

'I don't remember anything apart from singing my head off and everyone laughing,' she groaned. 'Your family must think I'm an absolute idiot.'

'Are you kidding me? They *loved* you,' Dale said. 'Anyway, I'm ringing to tell you my mum's booked a table for eleven thirty, so she says she'll pick you up at eleven?'

'What do you mean?' Cheryl was confused. 'I'll be in work at eleven.'

'Don't tell me you've forgotten?' Dale sighed. 'You arranged this with her last night. You're having lunch at The Ivy and going clothes shopping, then you're both booked in with her hairdresser.'

'*What?*' Cheryl had no recollection of talking to Sonia about any of that. 'I'm sorry, but even if I could go with her, there's no way I can afford any of that. Why didn't you check with me before you let her book it?'

'You really think anyone can stop my mum when she sets her mind on something?' Dale laughed. 'And if it's the money you're worried about, forget it. It's her treat.'

'Dale, I *can't.*'

'Babe, I know you'd had a few, but I heard the entire conversation,' Dale said. 'You planned the whole day together, and you said you couldn't wait, so what am I supposed to tell her now?'

'I don't know,' Cheryl moaned.

'You know what, it's fine; work's obviously more important,' Dale said coolly. 'She won't be happy, but I'm sure she'll understand.'

'Please tell her I'm sorry,' Cheryl said guiltily. 'I would never have agreed to it if I hadn't been so drunk. It was that vodka she gave me. It hit me like a—'

'Don't worry about it,' Dale interrupted. 'I'll see you later.'

'Are we OK?' Cheryl asked, but he had already cut the call.

When she left her house a short time later, Cheryl glimpsed Fiona looking out through the net curtains at Bob's living-room window, and she immediately felt guilty when she remembered that she had promised to call in on him when she got home last night. She contemplated popping in to see him now, but the thought of having to talk to Fiona when she already felt like shit instantly changed her mind. He would be all right, she was sure. And his carer would be there soon, so he would have everything he needed for the day.

As she walked out through the gate, a van pulled up on the opposite side of the road, and she glanced over when a group of young women came out of the house, followed by an older one who appeared to be hurrying them along. Cheryl smiled and raised her hand in greeting, but the girls immediately bowed their heads and climbed into the back of the vehicle.

The older woman, who had the blackest hair Cheryl had ever seen and the eyeliner to match, hurled a decidedly unfriendly look her way before climbing into the front passenger seat, and Cheryl muttered a sarcastic, 'Morning to you, too, neighbour,' before walking on.

*

In the back of the van, perched on the end of a narrow wooden bench that was bolted to the side wall, Agata Sikora watched through the wire meshed window as the woman who had smiled at them walked down the road.

Losing sight of her when the van set off in the opposite direction, she sighed as she gazed at the shabby buildings they were passing. The man who had interviewed her for the job she was starting this morning had painted a very pretty picture of Manchester, but the reality, so far, couldn't have been more different. She was twenty-two and had lived away from home the previous year, when she had been employed as a live-in nanny for six months. The other girls, however, who she had met for the first time at the airport yesterday morning, were mostly still in their teens and had never been away from their families, so there had been a lot of tears on the way over.

Dorothy, the woman who was sitting up front with the driver now, had met them at Manchester airport, and had collected their passports for safe-keeping before herding them all into this van. The drive from the airport to the Langley estate had been long, cold and uncomfortable, and Agata's heart had sunk when she saw how dark and depressing everything looked. Her spirits had momentarily lifted when they arrived at the beautiful house where they were now staying, but that tiny burst of joy had been short-lived and she had quickly realised that all was not as it seemed when they entered the house and Dorothy had informed them that they would be sharing rooms.

At their interviews, they had all been promised their own rooms, with en-suite bathrooms and locks on the doors to which only they would have the key. When some of the girls pointed that out, Dorothy warned them that she would have them taken straight back to the airport if they wanted to argue about it, where they would not only have to pay their own fare home, but would also have to repay their employer – in full – the money he'd spent to bring them over and secure their work permits. Agata didn't know if the others could afford to do that, but she certainly couldn't; and she needed the job far more than she needed her own room, so she had kept her mouth shut.

She was sharing with two girls called Janika and Lena, and the room they had been allocated was quite large, although the three single beds, three slim wardrobes and three chests of drawers that were crammed in there made it feel cramped. She had chosen the bed that was closest to the large bay window overlooking the front garden and the houses opposite, and had quickly unpacked her things and put them away before Dorothy called them down to the kitchen, where they were given parcels of chips and sausages to share among themselves.

As they ate, Dorothy – who it had turned out would be living in the house with them – had reeled off a long list of rules. There would be a rota for use of the bathroom, and no food or drinks were allowed in the bedrooms. Their rooms and all communal areas of the house were to be kept spotlessly clean at all times, and any girl caught slacking when Dorothy did her weekly inspections would be fined. They would be driven to and from work, and were strictly forbidden to leave the house for any other reason, or speak to anybody outside it or the care home.

Agata understood the need for a bathroom rota, and she thought the threat of fines for not keeping the house clean was a good idea, because it would deter any lazier girls from leaving their mess for the others to clean up. She wasn't so sure about the rule that forbade them from leaving the house or speaking to anybody outside it, however. It seemed a little excessive, but she reasoned that it was probably a temporary measure, designed to protect them until they properly settled in and were able to speak English more fluently. Manchester was a big, strange city, so it would be difficult for them to find their way home if they got lost and weren't able to communicate with the locals.

There had been more rules, but Agata had been too tired to take it all in. And she was even more tired now, after a restless night with little sleep. The smell of paint in the room had been so strong, they had been forced to leave the window open all night, which had not only let in the icy air, but also the sounds of people walking around and vehicles racing past late into the night – something which she and her roommates, who all came from small rural towns, were not used to at all.

Janika and Lena had fallen asleep at around 1 a.m., but Agata had still been awake when a car had pulled up outside an hour or so later, and she had watched the handsome man who had visited Dorothy earlier in the evening help a pretty, red-headed woman out of the car and into the house directly opposite. From the way the woman had been kissing him and clinging to him as they walked, Agata had presumed they must be a couple; but the man had come back out a few minutes later and had driven away, so she'd thought that maybe they were just friends.

That same woman was the one who had smiled at them as they had walked out to the van this morning, and Agata had wanted to smile back, but Dorothy had jabbed her in the back and hissed at her to keep her head down. But she *would* smile next time she saw the woman, she decided, because it was her *right* to do so.

Just as it was her right to move out of the house as soon as she had saved enough from her wages to be able to afford to rent a place of her own, because she refused to spend one minute longer that she absolutely had to under Dorothy's evil eye.

Chapter 16

Cheryl was still feeling down about the conversation she'd had with Dale as she stepped off the bus in town and walked the rest of the way to the market hall. Surprised, when she turned the corner, to see police vehicles parked at either end of the road, she spotted Saul, the market security guard, standing behind a strip of police tape, and quickly made her way over to him.

'What's going on?'

'Bomb scare,' he said, squinting at her through the smoke from his roll-up, which smelled suspiciously like weed. 'I was about to open up when the feds swooped in. They reckon they had an anonymous tip-off, so now we've got to wait for the squad to do their t'ing.'

'Bloody hell,' Cheryl murmured, gazing over at the old building. 'Why would anyone want to blow up this place?'

'Inside job, if you ask me,' Saul mused, taking another deep drag on his smoke.

'What do you mean?' Cheryl was confused. 'Why would any of us jeopardise our jobs by doing something stupid like that?'

'I'm talking about the owner,' Saul said, giving her a meaningful look. 'Think about it ... there's only seven units still occupied out of the original forty.'

'Seven?' Cheryl cut in. 'I'm sure I counted eight yesterday. Who's gone now?'

'Cake woman,' Saul told her. 'She handed her keys in last night. So, like I said, that leaves seven; which means the owner's probably paying out more in overheads to keep it open than he's taking in rent. And he ain't gonna keep the place running on fumes, is he?' He took another drag, then said, '*Insurance*. You get me?'

Before Cheryl had time to think about it, she heard her name being called and turned to see Dale waving to her from the end of the road, where he was standing next to his car.

Excusing herself, she rushed over to him.

'What's happened?' he asked.

'There's been a bomb scare,' she said.

'A *what*?' His eyes widened in alarm. 'In the market?'

'Yeah, but it's probably a hoax,' she said, not at all sure that she was right about that, but *hoping* she was. 'What are you doing here?'

'I came to bring you these.' Dale produced a slim bunch of roses from behind his back. 'Sorry they're wilted; I grabbed them at a garage on the way over. They're my way of apologising for being off with you on the phone earlier.'

'You didn't have to do that,' Cheryl said, smiling as she took the flowers from him. 'And you've got nothing to apologise for. I totally understood why you were pissed off with me for letting your mum down. Was she OK when you told her?'

'Yeah, she was cool,' Dale said, scanning the police line as he spoke. 'So what's happening now?'

'Saul said they're waiting for the bomb squad to check the place out,' Cheryl told him.

'Saul?' Dale repeated.

'The security guard.' She nodded to where the uniformed man

was now chatting to one of the coppers. 'He thinks it might be an inside job.'

'How so?'

'I'm not sure, to be honest. Something about insurance, and the owner not letting the place run on fumes.'

'He's got a point,' Dale said. 'If things are as bad as you've told me they are, I'd want out if I owned the place.'

'Yeah, well, I hope it doesn't come to that,' Cheryl said quietly, dreading the thought of being out of a job.

'Hey, Chez, you might as well go home,' Saul said, strolling over at that moment. 'The feds don't know how long they're going to be in there, so the owner told me to lock it down for the rest of the day.'

'Any chance I can get in there for a minute if they give it the all-clear?' Cheryl asked. 'I left some food out on the ledge last night, and I need to bin it before it goes off.'

'You can hang around if you want, babes, but there's no guarantee we'll get in,' Saul said. 'I'm giving it an hour, max, then I'm off.'

Watching through narrowed eyes as the man walked away, Dale said, 'That was a bit familiar. How well do you know that dude?'

'Who, Saul?' Cheryl said, frowning when she picked up an edge in his tone. 'Since I started working here after I left school.' Then, smiling, she said, 'Don't tell me you're jealous? He's the same age as my dad, *and* he's gay.'

'Know that for sure, do you?' Dale asked, no amusement in his eyes when he looked down at her.

'I do, actually. I've met his husband.'

'Yeah, well, you can't be taking chances,' Dale muttered. 'I know plenty of guys who've played the gay card to fool women into trusting them before hitting them with the *oh, actually, I think I must be bi, 'cos I'm starting to fall for you* shit.'

'I find it hard to believe any woman would fall for that,' Cheryl laughed. 'But even if Saul was straight, he's not you, so I wouldn't be interested.'

'Make sure it stays that way,' Dale said, smiling again as he walked round to the driver's side. 'Anyway, hop in. I've got a meeting in half an hour, but I can drop you off first; give you a chance to get changed before my mum picks you up. I just need to let her know you're free so she can rebook the appointments she cancelled.'

'No, don't do that,' Cheryl said. 'Like I just told Saul, I need to get in and get rid of that food I left out.'

'So you'd rather do that than spend the day with my mum?' Dale raised an eyebrow.

'No, of course not. But I don't need environmental health on my back because you dragged me out of there before I could clean up yesterday.'

'OK, have it your own way,' Dale sighed. 'But you're missing out, big time.'

'We can do it another day,' Cheryl said, relieved that he hadn't gone back into a mood with her for swerving his mum again. 'And thanks again for the roses. They're lovely.'

'Not as lovely as you,' he said, winking at her before climbing into the car.

Chapter 17

It was almost two hours before the police gave Saul the all-clear and Cheryl was able to get into the café and bin the food she'd left out. It felt eerie in there with all the shutters down on the units, and it was especially scary knowing that whoever had made that anonymous call to the police might have done so to test their response before coming back and planting a bomb for real. Saul was still adamant that the owner was behind it, but Cheryl didn't see what benefit the man would gain from pulling a stunt like that, because she was pretty sure that an insurance company would only pay out for actual damage, not just the threat of it.

After leaving the hall, Cheryl walked into Ancoats to pick up some shopping at Best Before Superstore: the budget supermarket that sold food that was close to or just past its sell-by date at massively discounted prices. It opened after she started work, and was usually closed by the time she finished, so it was a rare treat to be able to stock up on the groceries she needed for a fraction of what she would pay for the same items at the rip-off shops on the estate.

Eager to see how Bob was getting on, and to give him the strawberry flan she'd bought him, she called round at his place on her way home.

'What do you want?' Fiona demanded when she answered the door.

'To see Bob, obviously,' Cheryl said, her hackles instantly rising.

'Well, he don't wanna see *you*,' Fiona replied, stepping back.

'I don't believe you,' Cheryl said, putting her hand out to stop her from closing the door.

'I don't give a shit what you believe,' spat Fiona. '*I'm* his daughter, not you; and now I've moved in, it's my job to protect him from users like you, so piss off.'

Cheryl was furious when Fiona slammed the door in her face. She pulled Bob's key out from her bag and slotted it into the lock, but it didn't turn. At the sound of tapping, she snapped her head round and clenched her teeth when she saw Fiona waggling a bunch of shiny new keys at her through the living room window.

Aware that the bitch must have had the lock changed, no doubt at Bob's expense, Cheryl raised her chin and walked away. She couldn't force her way in, so she decided she would pull the same trick Fiona had pulled the other day, and slip inside when the carer turned up that evening.

Unused to having time on her hands during the week, Cheryl placed the wilted roses Dale had bought her into a vase and put her shopping away, then ate a sandwich and drank a cup of tea before rolling her sleeves up to give the house a long-overdue clean.

In the bedroom after finishing downstairs, she gazed over at Edna's house as she changed her bedding. She knew she ought to stop thinking of it that way now Dale's father owned it, but it would always be Edna's place in her heart – and probably everyone else's on the road, as well.

The thought of Edna brought Bob back to mind, and Cheryl found herself getting angry all over again when she recalled the confrontation with Fiona. She knew damn well that Bob would never say he didn't want to see her; they had been friends for too long and had helped each other out too many times for that to ever happen. This was Fiona's doing, for sure. She had taken advantage of her father's ill health to worm her way into his house, and now she had her feet under the table, she seemed hell-bent on keeping Cheryl away from him. It was jealousy, pure and simple. She hated that Cheryl and Bob were so close and obviously saw Cheryl as a threat to her inheritance – as laughable as that was, considering he didn't have two brass farthings to his name. But Bob loved his daughter and would be happy to think that she was there because she cared about him and wanted to look after him, so there was nothing Cheryl could do about it.

Ready and waiting when the carer's car pulled up outside Bob's gate at just gone six that evening, Cheryl grabbed the strawberry flan out of the fridge and rushed out to meet her.

'Hi,' she called out as the woman approached Bob's door. 'I'm Cheryl; we met last night. And this morning.'

'Yeah, I remember,' the woman said, smiling when Cheryl joined her on the step. 'How's he been this afternoon?'

'I don't know, I haven't seen him yet,' Cheryl said. 'Sorry, I forgot your name?'

'It's Sharon,' the woman said, eyeing the flan as she rapped on the door. 'That for me?'

'Sorry, no, it's for Bob,' Cheryl told her. 'They're his favourites.'

'Lucky Bob,' Sharon said, rolling her eyes in mock-envy.

The door opened, and Fiona peered out through the crack, saying, 'You can come in, but she can't.'

'Don't be so stupid,' Cheryl said irritably. 'I want to see Bob.'

'I've already told you he don't want to see you,' Fiona shot back.

'Am I missing something?' Sharon looked at each of them in turn.

'She's a thief and I don't want her in here,' Fiona said. 'And neither does my dad.'

'You liar,' Cheryl spluttered. '*You're* the one who tried to rob him, not me.'

'Prove it,' Fiona sneered. 'Oh, that's right... you can't, 'cos it never happened. Unlike *you*, filling your pockets every time you come round.'

'You'd better shut your mouth before I shut it for you,' Cheryl warned, infuriated that the bitch was twisting it around and making her look bad in front of the carer. 'I've never stolen off anyone in my life.'

'That's not what me dad says.'

'Ladies, I'm sorry, but I've got four more people to see after Bob,' Sharon interjected. 'So I really need to get cracking.'

'Like I said, *you* can come in, but she ain't stepping foot in here again,' Fiona asserted. 'This is my house and I know me rights.'

Cheryl wanted to argue that it was Bob's house not hers, but she didn't want to delay the carer any longer, so she took a deep breath to calm herself, then handed the flan to Sharon, saying, 'Can you give this to Bob, please?'

'He can't have that,' Fiona sneered. 'It'll play havoc with his diabetes.'

'Shows how well you know him, 'cos he hasn't got diabetes,' Cheryl replied tartly. Then, to the carer, she murmured, 'Please give him my love,' before flashing one last murderous glance at Fiona and heading back to her own house.

*

Half an hour later, Cheryl's doorbell rang, and her heart skipped a beat when she looked out through the window and saw the carer on the step.

'Has something happened?' she asked, yanking her door open. 'Is Bob OK?'

'He's fine,' Sharon assured her. 'Still quite weak, but a lot better than he was this morning. He asked me to thank you for the flan.'

'Bless him,' Cheryl murmured, sad that she hadn't been able to see his face, because she already missed his gummy little smile.

'Look, it's not my place to interfere, and I probably shouldn't be telling you this,' Sharon said, lowering her voice as she cast a surreptitious glance next door to make sure Fiona wasn't watching. 'But I know you're worried about Bob, so I thought you should know she's talking about putting herself down as his official carer.'

'Are you kidding me?' Cheryl gasped. 'She's hardly seen him in years. And she's an addict, for God's sake.'

'Unfortunately, she's also his next of kin,' said Sharon.

'She's doing this to spite me, because I caught her and her skanky mates breaking into his house while he was in hospital,' Cheryl spat. 'I didn't report her, because I knew it would upset Bob, but I wish I had now. There's no way they'd let her be his carer if they knew about that.'

'If she does apply, he'll probably get taken off my list,' Sharon said. 'But while I'm still able to see him, I'm happy to pop round and let you know how he is.'

'It'll probably be better if you text me,' Cheryl suggested. 'Knowing her, she'll take the funnies if she sees you coming round, and I don't want her making things difficult for you.'

'OK, give me your number,' Sharon said. 'And don't worry

about madam,' she added quietly. 'I'll be keeping a close eye on her, and I won't hesitate to put a report in if I see anything concerning.'

Cheryl thanked Sharon and swapped numbers with her, but it boiled her blood to think of Fiona masquerading as Bob's carer and claiming whatever extra benefits came with the title. Still, at least he was safe while Sharon was looking out for him – however long that lasted.

Chapter 18

Cheryl woke up feeling sick and she clamped her hand over her mouth, jumped out of bed and rushed to the bathroom, only just making it to the toilet in time before throwing up.

She'd been feeling queasy for a few days and had put it down to the stress of the ongoing situation next door, which had been dragging on for over two months by then, with no sign of Fiona backing down and allowing her to visit Bob. Fortunately, Sharon was still calling in on him twice a day and had kept her promise to message Cheryl and let her know how he was doing. But it was still upsetting that she couldn't see him for herself.

As she waited for the dry heaves to subside, Cheryl wondered if she had caught the winter vomiting bug she'd heard her customers talking about, or if the Indian takeaway she and Dale had shared last night hadn't agreed with her. Dale had said his was fine, but hers had tasted weird and she hadn't been able to finish it all. Either way, it wasn't pleasant, and when, at last, she felt safe to move away from the toilet, she contemplated calling her boss to tell him that she wouldn't be able to open the café today. That would be the responsible thing to do, but then she wouldn't get paid, so she immediately dismissed the idea.

*

The café wasn't busy that morning, which Cheryl was glad about since her stomach still felt off; but lunchtime was horrendous. A new construction site had opened up around the corner a few weeks earlier and the workmen had taken to coming to The Bluebell for lunch; which had been a godsend as far as the takings were concerned, but a nightmare for Cheryl, who had forgotten how exhausting it was to cater for a load of hungry men.

Her stomach was in turmoil as she cooked and served the greasy bacon and egg butties they had all ordered, and she was almost fit to collapse by the time they'd finished eating and gone back to work. The café was empty by then, and she decided she'd had enough and was going to lock up early as she gathered the dirty plates and cups off the tables. But no sooner had that thought entered her mind than the bell over the door jangled, and Cheryl silently groaned when one of her older customers walked in.

'Hi, Nell.' She forced a smile. 'Tea?'

'Yes, please,' Nell replied, perching her bird-like body on the chair she always favoured, at the corner table by the window. 'With a pinch of—'

'Salt,' Cheryl finished for her, easily remembering the old lady's peculiar little habit of taking salt in her tea instead of sugar, because she had never met anyone else in her entire life who drank their tea that way.

When she'd made the drink, Cheryl carried it over and placed it on the table. The old lady thanked her. Then, looking her in the eye, she asked, 'How far on are you?'

'Oh, I'm not pregnant,' Cheryl said, guessing that the woman had clocked her sickly complexion and jumped to conclusions. 'I'm just feeling a bit iffy today.'

'Are you sure about that?' Nell raised a wispy eyebrow. 'I'm rarely wrong about these things.'

'Well, I'm afraid you are this time,' Cheryl insisted, smiling before heading back to the kitchen.

As she loaded the builders' plates into the dishwasher a few seconds later, she frowned as she replayed Nell's words in her mind. It hadn't even crossed her mind that she might be pregnant, but now the seed had been planted, she had to admit that she might have missed the occasional pill while she'd been seeing Dale. She'd had a period shortly after the dinner party at his parents' house when she'd got drunk and made a fool of herself, but she genuinely couldn't remember if she'd had one after that.

Nell had gone by the time Cheryl came back out onto the shop floor. Surprised, because she usually stayed a lot longer, Cheryl took a twenty-pound note out of the till, mentally promising to put it back as soon as she got her next wages, then locked up and nipped to the pharmacy around the corner.

Back at the café a few minutes later, sitting on the toilet, she stared at the stick she'd just peed on, and felt her head spin when the words *Pregnant 4–5 weeks* appeared in the tiny window.

Still in shock on the bus ride home, with the pregnancy test wrapped in a sandwich bag inside her handbag, Cheryl stared out through the rain-lashed window and wondered how on earth she was going to tell Dale that she was pregnant. They had discussed just about everything else during the short time they had been together, but they had never once mentioned children, so she had no clue if he'd ever even thought about having his own.

Scared that he might react badly when she told him that, because she had possibly forgotten to take her pill, he was going to be a father, she was still agonising over how to broach the subject with him when the bus dropped her off at her stop. It was pitch dark by then, and the wind was blowing the rain every which way as she walked through the high-rise side of the estate. There were no kids out kicking footballs tonight, or women standing around gossiping over a fag, and she clutched her bag more tightly than usual when she spotted a hooded man sheltering in the shadows of the concrete bin cupboards.

The man followed Cheryl with his eyes as she passed, and she quickened her pace as she walked on to the narrow alleyway that led to her side of the estate. Six-feet-high walls stood on either side of the path, and it was unnerving to walk through there at the best of times, given that it wasn't overlooked by any of the houses beyond or flats behind. Tonight, with her instincts already screaming at her to hurry up and get into the light, she hesitated at the mouth of the alley and contemplated making a detour instead.

The sound of footsteps behind her made the hairs on the back of her neck stand on end, and she broke out in a cold sweat when she glanced back and saw the man from the bin cupboard running towards her wielding a stick. He was on her before her brain had a chance to tell her legs to move, and a blinding light exploded in front of her eyes when the stick connected with the side of her head.

Chapter 19

Light began to seep in at the edges of the dark cloud Cheryl had been floating on, and she groaned when she tried to open her eyes and felt a sharp pain slice through her head.

'Nurse!' a muffled male voice called out. 'She's coming round!'

Seconds later, Cheryl felt a warm hand cover hers, and a brighter, female voice, said, 'Can you hear me, love? If you can, give my hand a little squeeze.'

'Her fingers moved,' the man said.

'Yes, they did,' the woman affirmed. 'Stay with her while I find a doctor.'

Still drifting in and out of the fog, Cheryl heard receding footsteps, and then another, even warmer hand gripped hers. She felt her hair being gently stroked, and heard the man's voice urging her to open her eyes.

'Dale?' she croaked.

'Yeah, it's me,' he said, relief audible in his voice. 'Can you see me?'

Cheryl tried again to open her eyes, but the pain in her head made her feel sick and she swallowed dryly as a bitter taste flooded her mouth.

'Take your time,' he soothed. 'There's no rush.'

'Who do we have here, then?' a booming voice suddenly asked.

'Cheryl Taylor, aged twenty-eight,' the woman said. 'She was brought in earlier tonight with a fractured skull and a deep...'

The voice faded away, and Cheryl drifted back into the comforting darkness.

Dale was falling asleep on an armchair beside Cheryl's hospital bed when he heard her stir later that night, and he leaned forward and grasped her hand when he saw her eyelids flicker.

'Are you awake? Can you hear me?'

Cheryl opened her eyes and blinked in confusion when she saw the dimmed lights in the ceiling above her.

'Where am I?' she croaked.

'Hospital,' Dale told her, reaching behind her to press the button to summon the nurse. 'Don't try to move.'

'I need a drink.'

'Wait till the nurse gets here. I don't want to disturb any of the wires.'

'What wires?'

'They've got you hooked up to all sorts of machines,' he explained. 'It was touch-and-go for a while there.'

'Why? What happened?'

'You were attacked on your way home from work,' Dale said, anger in his voice now. 'Some bastard smacked you in the head with a metal pole and got off with your bag.'

'Ah, good, you're back with us,' a kindly voice said.

Cheryl swivelled her gaze and saw a nurse smiling down at her.

'I'm Janet, and I'll be looking after you tonight,' the woman said. 'How are you feeling?'

'Like I've swallowed broken glass.'

'Well, we'll get you sat up in a minute after I've checked your obs; see if you can take some water. OK?'

Cheryl nodded, but immediately wished she hadn't when a wave of nausea washed over her.

'I'm going to be sick,' she gasped.

'Take some nice deep breaths for me, there's a good girl,' Janet said, helping her to sit up before thrusting a kidney-shaped bowl into her hand. 'It's probably morning sickness, so it should pass in a minute.'

At those words, Cheryl inhaled sharply and cast a nervous glance at Dale.

'It's OK, I already knew,' he said.

'I'm sorry,' she murmured, guiltily dipped her gaze. 'I was going to tell you when I got home.'

'Sorry for what?' he asked. 'It's the best news *ever*.'

'Really?' She peered at him in disbelief.

'*Really*,' he laughed, leaning down to kiss her. 'I'm gonna be a dad!'

Chapter 20

Sharon Oakes checked her phone as she left Bob Baker's house, but there was still only one tick on each of the messages she had sent to Cheryl that week, which told her that Cheryl still hadn't seen them. That seemed strange, because Cheryl usually replied right away, so she decided to call round and check that everything was all right while Bob's daughter was out and there was no chance of her being caught visiting the enemy. In all honesty, she doubted Fiona would even notice even if she *had* gone there, because the woman always seemed to be on her phone. She rarely even looked at Sharon, and didn't seem particularly interested in her father, either. But Bob wasn't overly bothered, as far as Sharon could tell; quite content to be left to watch his horse racing in peace.

There was no answer when Sharon rang Cheryl's bell, and she couldn't see any lights on inside when she looked through the letter box. The air in the hallway smelled a little musty, and she wondered if Cheryl might have gone on holiday and couldn't get a Wi-Fi signal, hence not seeing the messages.

Sure that was all it was, and that Cheryl would reply when she was able, Sharon climbed into her car and set off to her next job on the other side of the estate.

*

Across the road, Agata Sikora watched as the blonde woman's car turned the corner at the end of the road and disappeared from view. She had guessed that the woman was a care worker, because her blue tabard was very much like the ones Agata and the other girls wore at the care home, and she wished she could speak to her and ask if her employers had any vacancies she could apply for. Unfortunately, Dorothy was always at home whenever the woman arrived, so she hadn't been able to risk sneaking out in case she got caught and sent packing back to Poland. As much she would love to go home, because she absolutely hated her life here, there was no way she could pay for the flight when she and the others still hadn't been paid for the almost three months' work they had done so far. Dorothy claimed that their money was being withheld by their employer as payment for living in this house, their food, their uniforms and the toiletries and sanitary products that were provided for them. Agata didn't believe her and suspected that Dorothy was keeping their money for herself, but there was no one to turn to for advice on the matter, so there was nothing she could do about it.

Agata despised Dorothy. She was a cruel woman with a foul temper, and she would lash out at the girls if they did something to annoy her, so they were all terrified of her. And there was no respite at the care home, because Mr Davies, the man who ran the place, was cut from exactly the same cloth as Dorothy and was always yelling at the girls and physically pushing them around. Agata stayed quiet and kept her head down both at home and at work, so she had managed to avoid their wrath so far. But she'd been brought up to speak out against injustice, so she wasn't sure how much longer she would be able to hold her tongue before she snapped.

Mr Davies had changed the rota today, so now, despite already

completing her usual day shift, Agata was being made to work
the night shift as well. She had managed to sleep for a couple of
hours after the van had dropped them off that afternoon – which
hadn't been easy since there were still no curtains to block out
the light coming through the window. It was now dark outside,
and she wished she could climb back into bed for a couple more
hours. But there was zero chance of that happening, because her
room-mate, Janika, had insisted on putting the overhead light
on so that she could do her make-up. Agata had no idea why
she was trying to make herself pretty when they still weren't
allowed to leave the house, but the girl had snapped at her
when she'd asked her to turn it off, so she'd given up trying to
reason with her.

Turning from the window when their other room-mate, Lena,
entered the room with her hair wrapped in a towel, signalling
that the bathroom was now free, Agata took her uniform off its
hanger and carried it down the corridor. Unlike the bedrooms,
which had no locks, the bathroom had a bolt on the door, and
she slid it into place and slipped out of her pyjamas, then quickly
washed and dressed before heading back to her room.

Lena and Janika were sitting together on Janika's bed, giggling
over a book Lena had in her hand. Heart leaping into her throat
when she glimpsed the cover and realised it was her journal,
Agata marched over and snatched it out of the girl's hand.

'Do not touch my belongings,' she snapped, shoving the book
into her bag.

'*I am so sad*,' Lena mocked, repeating things that she had read
in the journal. '*My heart cries for the sound of my mother's voice
and the smell of her bread*... You are so pathetic.'

Agata ignored her and looked around to make sure she hadn't
left anything else that was personal on display before grabbing
her coat and walking out. Tears were burning her eyes, but she

determinedly blinked them away before knocking on Dorothy's door to ask her to unlock the front door so she could go out and wait for the van.

As tired as she was, she was actually looking forward to spending the night at the care home. Dorothy often stayed there during the day and would sit with Mr Davies in his office, drinking. Tonight, neither of them would be there, and she intended to relish every moment she was away from them, and also from her roommates. The night manager would be there, and the doors would be locked so she wouldn't be able to go outside, but it still felt like freedom to Agata.

Chapter 21

Cheryl gazed out through the window of her third-floor hospital room, searching for Dale's face among the people who were milling about down below. She'd been in there for a week, and while it hadn't been too bad on the general ward where she'd had people to talk to, here, in the private room Dale's parents had insisted she be moved into after hearing about the baby, she had been bored out of her mind.

It was a very nice room, with a TV, a phone and its own bathroom, but she wasn't entirely comfortable with the fact that Dale's parents had been paying for her care. They, however, adamantly refused to entertain the idea of her going back onto an NHS ward, where she and the baby would be at risk of picking up a nasty bug.

Dale's visits had been the highlight of her stay, but they hadn't been anywhere near as regular as she would have liked, since his father had put him in charge of a new business he had recently purchased, which was taking up a lot of his time. Still, she was being discharged today, and she was hoping to see a lot more of him once she was home.

Looking round expectantly when she heard the door opening behind her, she was disappointed when Amy, the nurse who'd been looking after her, popped her head in.

'Still no sign?'

'No.' Cheryl shook her head. 'He must have got held up.'

'Well we're about to serve lunch, if you'd like some? I know you didn't fill in the menu because you thought you'd be gone by now, but—'

'No thanks, I'm fine,' Cheryl cut in. 'I'm not really hungry.'

'Still feeling sick?'

'A bit.'

'The joys of pregnancy, eh?' Amy rolled her eyes. 'Hopefully it won't last much longer.'

'It's already eased a lot,' Cheryl said, grateful that it hadn't lasted as long as some of the women on the ward had told her theirs had lasted.

A bell rang in one of the other rooms and Amy excused herself and rushed off to answer it.

Cheryl took another look out of the window and then sat on the bed and pulled her phone out of the plastic bag containing the clothes and toiletries Dale had brought in for her. Her old phone had been in her stolen handbag, along with her keys, her purse and her debit card. Dale had changed her locks, cancelled her card and bought her the new phone, but she'd been gutted to hear that all her contacts and messages were gone and there was no way to get them back because she had never backed her phone up. She wasn't too bothered about her contacts, because Anna was the only friend she had really stayed in contact with until their fall out, and if she heard from her dad once a year it was a miracle. But she really needed to speak to her boss, and she missed getting her daily updates about Bob.

About to call Dale now to ask how long he was going to be, she said, 'At last!' when the door opened and he strolled in.

'Sorry, I had to nip into town to pick something up,' he said, leaning down to kiss her.

'Better late than never,' she said, smiling as she stood up. 'Let's go. I'm dying to get home and have a cup of tea.'

'In a minute,' Dale said, pushing the door shut. 'I need to do something first.'

'I've already told you, I am *not* having sex in here,' Cheryl hissed. 'Private doctors might knock first, but they still...' Tailing off when he got down on one knee in front of her, she said, 'What are you doing?'

'I know this isn't the most romantic time or place to do this, but this has been burning a hole in my pocket all day,' Dale said, sliding a small black box out of his pocket and opening the lid to reveal a sparkling diamond ring nestled in the velvet interior.

'Are you being serious?' Cheryl gaped at him.

'Never been more serious in my life,' he replied softly. 'I knew you were the one the first time I saw you, and now you're carrying my baby, I think we should make it official.'

'This is too fast,' she murmured, sinking onto the bed. 'We've only known each other a few months.'

'I know you well enough to know this is right,' Dale insisted, getting up and sitting beside her. 'I love you, and I want our son to have my name.'

'He'll have it anyway,' said Cheryl. 'And it might be a girl.'

'I wouldn't care either way, but this is a boy,' Dale said with certainty as he slid his hand over her still-flat stomach.

Cheryl had no idea what sex the baby was, but right then she was more concerned about Dale wanting to marry her when they had only known each other for such a short time. Afraid that he was doing it out of some misplaced sense of duty, she said, 'If you're doing this because you think it's the right thing to do, there's really no need. I'm happy to carry on as we are, then talk about this again when we've had a chance to really get to know each other.'

'I already know everything I need to know, so why wait?' Dale asked.

'I just want us both to be sure we're doing it for the right reasons,' said Cheryl. 'Our relationship is great now, but we've both thought we loved other people and ended up realising they were totally wrong for us.'

'So you don't trust me?' Dale asked bluntly.

'Of course I do,' Cheryl replied without hesitation.

'Then why are you tarring me with the same brush as your ex?' Dale asked. 'It didn't work out with him, but that doesn't mean *we* can't make it work.'

'I'm not comparing you to him,' Cheryl insisted. 'I'm just saying we both need to be certain it's what we want before we take the next step.'

'I am certain,' Dale said. 'I love you, and I want my child to be legitimate. I'm sorry if you think that's weird, but it's important to me. And if you think I'm rushing it, it's only because you're going to get bigger the longer we wait, and I don't want you feeling uncomfortable on the day.'

Cheryl looked at him and saw the sincerity in his eyes, 'Is this really what you want?' she asked.

'More than anything.' He smiled.

'OK,' she murmured. 'Let's do it.'

'Are you sure?' Dale asked. 'I don't want you to feel like I'm pushing you into it.'

'I'm positive,' Cheryl said, smiling as she held out her hand. 'Ask me again.'

Grinning, Dale plucked the ring out of the box and dropped to his knee again.

'Cheryl Taylor...' he said softly. 'For the second and *last* time, will you marry me?'

'Yes,' she said, blinking back the tears that welled in her eyes as he slid the ring onto her finger.

Chapter 22

In Dale's car after leaving the hospital, Cheryl couldn't stop smiling as she twisted her engagement ring this way and that in the sunlight coming through the window. It was the most beautiful ring she had ever seen in her entire life, and the fact that Dale had personally chosen it for her made it all the more special.

Dale had insisted on taking her to his parents' house to celebrate their good news. She would have preferred to go home first to take a bath and get changed, but he was so excited, she hadn't had the heart to refuse. She had only been there twice before, and both of those times had been at night, so she had never seen how magnificent it looked in daylight. Unlike the dilapidated farmhouses they had passed along the way, which became more spaced out the further they travelled, the house, when it came into view as they drove through the gates, looked like an actual mansion.

'I didn't realise it was so big,' she said, taking in the fields on either side, which seemed to stretch for miles. 'How do you find your way around without getting lost?'

'You get used to it,' Dale said, leaping out to open her door after parking up. 'Watch your step,' he cautioned, guiding her up the steps with his hand on her back. 'Don't want you falling and hurting my boy now, do we?'

Loving how protective he was, Cheryl smiled as they walked into the hallway after reaching the top of the steps.

'Darling...' Sonia cooed, sailing out from the kitchen on her usual cloud of perfume and hugging Cheryl warmly. 'How are you feeling?'

'Tired, but OK,' Cheryl said. 'Thanks so much for everything you've done,' she went on. 'I'll pay you back as soon as I can, I promise.'

'Nonsense.' Sonia flapped her hand dismissively. 'You're family now, and we take care of our own. Now let me take a look at you.'

She pushed Cheryl back and looked her over, concern in her face as she scanned the bruising on her cheek and around her eyes, and the bald spot where her hair had been shaved off to allow the doctor to stich the four-inch gash she'd sustained along with her fractured skull.

'Oh, you poor thing,' she said. 'Your beautiful hair is ruined.'

'It's already starting to grow back,' Cheryl said, self-consciously touching the spot.

'Well, let's hope it gets a move on, or we'll have to get you fitted for a wig before the wedding,' Sonia said.

'Oh... you already know?' Cheryl said, casting a glance at Dale as Sonia grasped her hand to look at the engagement ring.

'Of course; my boy tells me everything,' Sonia said. 'This is divine,' she declared, giving Dale an approving smile. 'You have impeccable taste, son.'

'He must get that from you,' Cheryl said.

'Well, he certainly didn't get it from his father,' Sonia chuckled. 'Now let's get you sorted before Alfie and the others get here,' she went on, taking Cheryl's arm and walking her towards the stairs. 'I knew you wouldn't have anything suitable for a party with you, so I picked out a dress, shoes and some fresh underwear for you. There's also a make-up kit, so you can hide those nasty bruises before the party starts.'

'Party?' Cheryl glanced back at Dale in confusion, but he just shrugged, as if he had no clue what was going on.

'You've just agreed to marry my son, so of course there's going to be a party,' Sonia said, leading her up the stairs. 'We'll discuss you moving in later,' she went on. 'That way, I'll be able to make sure you're eating properly and getting all the rest you need while you're carrying our little one.'

'I think there's been a misunderstanding,' Cheryl said, almost tripping over the last step onto the landing, because the carpet was so thick. 'I've got my own house.'

'Here we are,' Sonia said, seeming not to have heard her as she waved her into a spacious bedroom. 'Your clothes are there,' she gestured to the king-size bed, on which a garment bag was laid next to a new bra, panties and tights. 'The bathroom's through here.' She opened a door to reveal an en suite containing a claw-footed bathtub, a sink and a toilet. 'And this is the dressing room.' Yet another door, revealing a room that was lined with floor-to-ceiling mirrors on one side; a built-in wardrobe and numerous shelves and drawers on the other; along with a dressing table with lights around it, upon which sat a range of make-up items. 'Right, I need to nip downstairs to check on the caterers,' she said, glancing at her watch. 'Alfie will be home soon, and the guests will start arriving around six, so don't take too long.'

A little overwhelmed by the speed with which everything was happening, Cheryl looked around the room when she was alone. It was more like a luxury hotel suite than a bedroom, and she could see Sonia's stylish touch in everything from the matching, ornately carved furniture, to the – again matching – bedding and drapes, and the expensive wallpaper with its delicate embossed swan design.

Sighing at the thought of having to endure a party when all she wanted to do was go home and relax, she gazed out of the window, which overlooked the garden at the rear of the house. It was far larger than she had realised when she'd seen it in the dark from the patio the first time Dale had brought her here. There was a fence around the lawn area, and another part was sectioned off for what appeared to be a vegetable patch and a chicken coop. But it seemed their land didn't stop there, because there were gates in the fencing leading to fields which seemed to stretch for miles with no other buildings in view, apart from the cottages she had glimpsed the outlines of that same night; alongside which, she could now see, a couple of static caravans were standing.

She heard a vehicle and switched her gaze to the right when a Transit van drove into view on a dirt path on the other side of the fence. Sure that it was the same one that the workmen who had renovated Edna's house had used, she guessed that the men must live in the cottages and caravans when it pulled up in front of them. Four men hopped out, and one of them walked round to the back of the vehicle and opened the doors, allowing seven more men out.

The door opened behind her, and Cheryl turned from the window as Sonia popped her head inside.

'Haven't you tried it on yet?' Sonia asked, looking pointedly at the still-zipped bag.

'No, sorry, I got distracted by the view,' Cheryl said. 'Your garden is incredible; must be great in the summer.'

'Yes, it's lovely,' Sonia said off-handedly. 'Now hurry up and get changed. Dale told me your size, so it should fit, but we haven't got much time to find you something else if it doesn't.'

'Sorry,' Cheryl apologised, walking over to the bed. 'I'll try it now.'

Sonia nodded and withdrew her head, and Cheryl quickly unzipped the garment bag and took out the evening dress. It was a beautiful shade of purple, with long sleeves, a sweetheart neckline and a full, flowing skirt. It still had its price tag attached, and her eyes widened in shock when she saw that it had cost almost seven hundred pounds. Reluctant to touch it, never mind wear it, she laid it carefully on the bed and went into the bathroom to wash her underarms; terrified that she would get sweat on the soft fabric and ruin it.

Relieved to find a tin of deodorant among the expensive toiletries in the bathroom cabinet, she sprayed it liberally under her arms and her breasts before carrying the clothes into the dressing room. The dress fit perfectly, and she loved how the soft material moulded itself to her body and made her look shapely and feminine in a way that none of her own clothes ever had. Guessing that was why Sonia always looked so fantastic – because she could *afford* to – Cheryl smiled to herself as she turned in front of the floor-length mirrors, viewing herself from every angle.

After preening for a while, she sat on the padded stool in front of the mirror and switched on the lights. She didn't wear make-up often, so she'd never been overly good at applying it; but her face was so pale and the bruising so vivid, she knew she had to at least try to make herself look better.

Fifteen minutes later, as she was applying a coat of cherry-hued lip gloss, Dale appeared behind her, and she almost jumped out of her skin, when he murmured, 'Holy fuck.'

'You idiot,' she gasped, spinning round on the stool. 'I didn't hear you come in.'

'I was hoping to catch you naked,' he said, grinning as he looked her over. 'You look amazing. Get up and let me see you properly.'

'Do I look all right?' she asked, self-consciously smoothing the skirt down as she stood up.

'Perfect,' he assured her. 'Oh, and here... my mum forgot to give you these.' He passed a shoebox to her.

Cheryl sat back down and opened the box. 'Oh, they're gorgeous,' she said, taking out the strappy, jewelled sandals. 'But I'll never be able to walk in those heels.'

'Course you will,' Dale said, pulling her into his arms when she stood up after slipping the sandals on. Spotting the label, which was hanging over the back of the collar of the dress, he whistled softly through his teeth and said, 'Looks like I'm going to have to give you a bigger allowance than I was planning to if you're going to keep up with my mother. No wonder my old man's always complaining that she's bankrupting him.'

'I earn my own money, so there'll be none of that,' Cheryl said, placing her hands on his chest to hold him at bay when he tried to kiss her neck.

'Ah... about that,' he said, giving her an awkward smile. 'I didn't want to tell you while you were laid up in hospital, but the café's been closed down.'

'What?' Cheryl felt like she'd been punched. 'Please tell me you're joking?'

''Fraid not.' He shook his head. 'I called into the market and got your boss's number off that security guard, so I could let him know you wouldn't be coming in for a while. He said to tell you he'd been about to let you go anyway. Apparently, he's been struggling to keep up with the rent for the last couple of years.'

'Oh God, I need to speak to him,' Cheryl said. 'Have you still got his number?'

'No, I jotted it down then threw it away after I spoke to him. But that's not all.'

'What now?' Cheryl groaned, wondering what could possibly be worse than losing her job.

'As of next week, the whole market's shutting down,' Dale said. 'The owner found a buyer and it's getting turned into apartments.'

'I don't believe this.' Cheryl slumped down on the stool when her legs started shaking.

'To be honest, I think it's the best thing that could have happened,' Dale said. 'You know I never liked you working there.'

'I loved it,' Cheryl replied tearfully. 'What am I supposed to do now? No one's going to take me on while I'm pregnant.'

'You don't have to do anything,' Dale said, squatting down in front of her and peering up into her downturned eyes. 'I know you're upset, but you'll never have to worry about money again now we're getting married.'

'I've paid my own way since the day I left school,' she sniffled. 'It's not your responsibility to look after me.'

'That's not how marriage works,' Dale argued. 'Not in my family, anyway. Like my mum said, we look after our own; and now you're mine, it's my job to provide for you. So snap out of whatever this is and let's enjoy our special day. OK?'

Cheryl felt as if the bottom had fallen out of her world, but Dale was right: this *was* a special day, and she didn't want to ruin it for him, so she sniffed back the tears and nodded.

'You sure?' Dale asked. 'If you can't face it, I'll go down and tell my mum to call the party off. She won't be happy after spending the whole day pulling it all together, but you and the baby are my priorities.'

'I'll be fine,' Cheryl insisted. 'I had a wobble, but I'm all right now, I promise.'

Dale peered at her for a few more seconds, as if to make sure that she meant it. Then, smiling, he stood up and helped her to her feet, saying, 'Come on, then. Let's go show the world what a lucky bastard I am.'

Chapter 23

The caterers had arrived by the time Dale led Cheryl down the stairs, and people were rushing in and out carrying trays of food and boxes of alcohol from the van that was parked at the foot of the steps outside. Feeling a little unsteady in the unfamiliar, too-high heels, Cheryl clutched Dale's hand as they made their way into the kitchen, where Sonia was bossily ordering the caterers around as they laid out the food on the long table.

'Wow,' she murmured, staring around in amazement when she saw that the entire room had been decorated with bunting, helium-filled balloons and a large banner that read *Congratulations on your engagement!* in fancy gold letters. 'How did she get this done this so fast?'

'They don't call her wonder woman for nothing,' Dale said proudly. Then, his expression darkened when a girl carrying a large stack of sandwich trays accidentally banged into Cheryl. 'Hey! Watch where you're going!' he yelled.

'It's OK,' Cheryl said, touching the girl's arm when she saw the shock and fear in her eyes. 'I'm fine. Don't worry about it.'

Scowling at Cheryl as the girl scuttled away, Dale said, 'Don't do that again.'

'Do what?' Cheryl frowned. 'It was an accident, so I was just letting her know I was OK.'

'Sorry.' Dale sighed, holding up his hands. 'I didn't mean to snap at you, but it pissed me off that she barged into you and didn't even apologise.'

'Actually, she did, but you obviously didn't hear her,' Cheryl said. 'So now you should apologise to *her* for jumping down her throat.'

'OK, boss,' Dale said, smiling again as he reached for her hand. 'I'll take her aside when things calm down and have a quiet word. But, for now, let's get you out of the way before somebody knocks you over.'

'I hope you're not going to try to wrap me in cotton wool for the rest of my pregnancy?' Cheryl asked, only half joking.

'I wouldn't dare,' Dale laughed, leading her into the conservatory and over to a small couch in the corner. 'Now, sit there while I get you a drink. What do you want?'

'Any chance I could have a cup of tea? I've been dying for one since we left the hospital.'

'Whatever my lady wants, my lady shall have.' Dale performed a mock bow.

Thanking him, Cheryl sat down and watched as he headed back into the kitchen. The patio doors at the far end of the room were standing open and she shivered when she felt the cold air creeping in. Through the window, she could see two tall heaters that looked like Victorian street lamps standing on either side of the doors. They were casting a rosy glow over the decking as the sky began to darken, and she was tempted to go and stand beneath them to warm herself up.

Before she could move, she heard soft footsteps padding towards her and looked round to see Rosa approaching carrying a steaming cup.

'Is that for me?' she asked.

Rosa nodded and leant forward to place the cup on the

table. As she straightened up, she looked Cheryl in the eye and murmured something under her breath.

'Sorry?' Cheryl tipped her head to one side. 'I didn't quite catch that.'

Rosa dipped her gaze and scuttled away, and Cheryl frowned as she watched her go. She was certain she'd heard the woman say *you should leave*, but that couldn't be right, because Rosa didn't speak English. Or maybe she spoke a little and her accent had made it sound like that, when she might actually have said *here's your tea*. The two phrases did sound similar.

But whatever Rosa had or hadn't said, it amazed Cheryl that Rosa had not only spoken to her, but had also looked her in the eye after purposefully not doing either of those things the previous times they had met. It was a small step, but it felt like a breakthrough of sorts, and Cheryl smiled as she reached for the cup and took a sip of the hot, sweet tea.

The guests started to arrive at 6 p.m., and Sonia insisted on personally introducing Cheryl to each of them. There were far too many names for her to remember, but she smiled politely and thanked those who congratulated her on her engagement. Happy, when Stefan and Estelle arrived, to see that they had brought Poppy along, as well as their son, Frankie, she went over and said hello to the adults before leaning down to speak to the little girl.

'Hi, there.' She smiled. 'You look so pretty.'

'Thank you,' Poppy replied shyly. 'I like your dress.'

'Yes, it's *very* nice,' Estelle drawled, looking Cheryl over with the hint of a smirk on her scarlet-painted lips. 'Looks rather familiar though.'

Cheryl knew Estelle was taking a dig at her because it was obvious that she would never be able to afford a dress of that quality; but she had already decided that she wasn't going to play her games anymore, so she smiled, and said, 'Thank you; Sonia lent it to me. And, can I say, you look beautiful tonight. That peach tone really suits you.'

Estelle's eyebrows inched up, and Cheryl could see that the compliment had thrown her when she saw a flash of uncertainty in her eyes. Dale denied that Estelle and his ex, Caroline, had been friends, but if he'd taken her to their house for dinner, as Poppy had said he had, then they had to have formed *some* kind of friendship; which would explain why Estelle had been such a bitch to her. But they were going to be sisters-in-law, so she was determined to break down the wall Estelle had erected – as hard as she suspected that might be.

The party got progressively louder as the night wore on, and Cheryl retreated to the armchair in the alcove, where Poppy had spent most of the night at the first party. Her feet were swollen, so she took off the sandals to give them a break. But she'd hardly had time to enjoy it when Dale came over to tell her that his dad was about to give a toast, and she had to force her feet back into the sandals.

In agony, she clung to Dale's hand as he walked her through the guests who had formed a semicircle around Alfie and Sonia at the far end of the room.

'Here she is,' Alfie said, putting his arm around Cheryl's shoulders. 'My beautiful daughter-in-law.'

'Soon to be,' Sonia corrected him, pushing a glass of champagne into Cheryl's hand before handing one to Dale.

'This young lady has stolen my boy's heart,' Alfie went on. 'And we all know how hard she must have worked to achieve *that* with his track record,' he added with a chuckle that was echoed by most of the men in the room. 'Joking aside,' he continued, squeezing Cheryl's shoulder to let her know he meant no offence. 'We're delighted to welcome her into the family, and everyone who's here tonight to celebrate their engagement is also invited to the wedding. So make sure you keep the date free when you receive the official invite or you'll have the missus on your case. And I'm sure you all know her well enough to know that nothing short of *death* will excuse you if you she invites you to one of her bashes.' He paused and winked at Sonia, who playfully slapped his arm. 'Anyway, this is the beginning of a beautiful relationship, so let's raise a glass to my son and his beautiful fiancée. *Gratulacje!*'

Touched when the entire room raised their glasses and repeated the toast, Cheryl was taken aback when Sonia tapped her arm and gestured for her to drink.

'I can't,' she whispered, pointedly dipping her eyes towards her stomach.

'Nonsense,' Sonia scoffed. 'I drank all the way through, and there's nothing wrong with my boys.'

Cheryl glanced at Dale to see how he felt about it, and was surprised when he nodded and raised his own glass to her. She had heard that it was bad for women to drink during pregnancy, and she'd thought Dale would have strong opinions on the matter, considering how protective he had been so far. But he and his mum didn't seem to think it would be a problem, and she couldn't deny that one little drink to ease the tension in her shoulders was tempting, so she raised the glass to her lips.

A flash went off as someone took a photograph close by, and Cheryl jumped and almost spilled champagne on the dress. Glad that Sonia had moved away to talk to somebody and hadn't witnessed the near disaster, she put the glass down and rubbed her wet hands together to dry them.

'Oops, sorry,' Stefan said, bumping into her.

Turning, Cheryl smiled when she saw that he was holding Poppy, who had her arms round his neck and her head resting on his shoulder.

'Someone looks tired,' she said.

'Someone's *always* tired,' he replied wearily, rolling his eyes. Then, more seriously, he said, 'Those bruises look nasty.'

'Oh, are they showing?' Cheryl touched her cheek self-consciously. 'I covered them with foundation, but I've been a bit hot, so it must be wearing off.'

'It's not that bad,' Stefan reassured her. 'And you can't see it at all at a distance. Sorry to hear what happened, by the way. Must have been scary.'

'Yeah, it was, but it could have been a lot worse,' she said. 'The cut's mostly healed now, and it was only a hairline fracture, so they didn't have to put any plates in.'

'You're very lucky,' he said. 'And congrats on the baby.'

'Thanks.' Cheryl smiled. 'It was a bit of a shock, and I wasn't sure how Dale was going to react, but he's really happy about it.'

Stefan's gaze intensified and Cheryl sensed that he wanted to say something, but Estelle came over at that exact moment and pulled him aside. Noting some tension between the pair when they had a hushed conversation, she left them to it and went off in search of Dale. He was nowhere to be seen, and she guessed he'd slipped off for whisky and cigars when she saw that his father and several of the other men had also disappeared. Tired, and in desperate need of a wee, she slipped out into the hallway and made her way up the stairs to use the en suite in the fancy bedroom and re-cover the bruises that were starting to show through.

Switching the bedroom light off when she'd finished, she was about to head back down when she heard shouting outside. Curious, she walked over to the window and peered out over the land. It was dark out there, but the moon was casting a ghostly light over the cottages and caravans, and she squinted to sharpen her vision when she spotted a shadowy figure running away from the buildings and jumping over a fence before disappearing into the field. A security light came on, illuminating several of the workmen milling about, and she wondered what was going on when she saw Dale and two other men run across the lawn to join them, followed by Alfie, who was holding what appeared to be a big stick. One of the workmen pointed towards the field, but the light went out so she couldn't see anything else. About to move away, she sucked in a sharp breath when a bright light flashed in the field and she heard a booming sound in the distance.

'What are you doing up here?'

Almost jumping out of her skin at the sound of Sonia's voice, Cheryl spun round to face her as the overhead light came on.

'I-I needed the toilet,' she stammered. 'Then I heard noises outside. I think someone might have been shot!'

'It's the foxes,' Sonia said unconcernedly as she walked over and drew the curtains. 'They prowl around at night and kill the livestock, so we have to shoot them.'

'Oh, I see,' Cheryl murmured, feeling foolish for immediately assuming that something more sinister was going on.

'Well, now we've cleared that up, we should go back to the party, because some of the guests are about to leave,' Sonia said, guiding her towards the door with a hand on her back. 'It's been a lovely night, hasn't it?'

'It really has,' Cheryl agreed. 'But I'm tired, so I think I'll probably go soon, too.'

'You're quite welcome to stay,' Sonia offered as they walked down the stairs.

'Thanks, but we came straight here from the hospital, so I really need to go home and make sure everything's OK,' Cheryl said.

'That's a shame,' Sonia sighed. 'We could have started planning the wedding over breakfast. I've already got a few ideas,
and I'm thinking Christmas, here in the garden.'

'Christmas is only six weeks away,' Cheryl reminded her.
'Don't you think that's a bit fast?'

'The sooner the better, I'd say.' Sonia raised an eyebrow. 'Unless
you *want* to waddle down the aisle with an enormous belly
poking out of your wedding dress?'

'No, definitely not,' Cheryl murmured.

'You do want this, don't you?' Sonia asked, peering at her
when they reached the hallway.

'To marry Dale? Yeah, of course,' Cheryl said, hoping she
hadn't given the impression that she had doubts about their
relationship. 'I'm just a bit overwhelmed with it all.'

'Then stop thinking about it and let me take the strain,' Sonia
said. 'Organising functions is my forte.'

'I can't leave it all to you, that wouldn't be fair,' Cheryl objected.
'I just need to sleep, then I'll be fine.'

'Excellent.' Sonia smiled. 'So go home tonight and pack what
you need, then come back tomorrow and stay for a few days so
we can start the ball rolling.'

Cheryl sighed as she followed Sonia back into the kitchen.
The woman was chomping at the bit to get started and Cheryl
had a feeling she would take over the entire thing if left to her
own devices. As lovely as this house undoubtedly was, it was
more like a show house than a home, and Cheryl was desperate
to get back to her own house and sleep in her own bed, the
mattress of which had moulded itself to her shape over the
years. But this wedding was her and Dale's day, and she didn't
want Sonia choosing her dress or deciding what flavour cake
they would have at the reception, so she'd had no choice but to
agree to stay.

Chapter 24

Dale had dropped Cheryl off at midnight, and she had been secretly relieved when he'd told her that he wasn't going to stay because he'd arranged to meet up with some of his friends who hadn't been at the party to celebrate his engagement. He'd still been full of life, but she'd been fit to drop, so all she'd wanted was to crawl into bed and fall asleep without worrying about him lying awake beside her.

Woken by the alarm at 7 a.m., she felt properly rested for the first time all week, and she was able to think more clearly about everything that was going on. Impending wedding aside, she had a lot of things she needed to sort out; the most pressing being the need to find another job while she was still able to work. Her wages hadn't landed in her account yet, but when they did, they would cover her rent and bills for the next month; and she was also going to speak to her boss about giving her some kind of severance pay. He had already told Dale he'd been struggling to pay the café's rent for a while, so she had no doubt he would cry poverty to get out of giving her any extra money. But the workmen who had been coming in for the last few weeks had definitely boosted his profits, so she figured he owed her *something* for managing the place single-handedly for so long.

If all else failed, she decided she would claim benefits until she was back on her feet. She had never claimed anything before, because she had walked straight into the job at The Bluebell after leaving school; but she had paid her taxes, so she was entitled to ask for help when she genuinely needed it. Fortunately, Sonia and Alfie were insisting on paying for the entire wedding and reception, because it would have been a registry office affair, followed by a bring-your-own-bottle party if she'd had to find the money to contribute towards it. But her own living expenses were nothing to do with them, and she wouldn't be asking Dale for help with them, either. It was all well and good him telling her that she would never need to worry about money again once they were married, but she had paid her own way her entire adult life, and she had no intention of becoming a kept woman.

The thought of Dale reminded her that they still hadn't discussed what was going to happen after the wedding – where they were going to live, for example. She loved her little house, but she honestly couldn't see Dale being willing to move out of his family's grand home to live on this estate. And even if he did agree to move in here, there was only one bedroom, so it might not even be big enough for them and a baby.

At the thought of the baby, she sat up and lifted her pyjama top to look at her belly. On the outside, there wasn't the slightest hint of the tiny human that was growing inside, but knowing that it was there was mind-blowing. She'd had a couple of scares when she was with Chris, and had been genuinely relieved on both occasions to find that it *was* only a scare. At the time, she had told herself that she was terrified of getting pregnant because she was too young for the responsibility, but she now believed it was probably her instincts warning her that Chris wasn't the right man for her.

But he was her past and Dale was her future, and she smiled as she switched her gaze to her ring. It truly was one of the most beautiful rings she had ever seen in her life, and it still didn't feel real that Dale had planned the proposal and collaborated with his mother to throw the impromptu party without her suspecting a thing. She just wished her own mum was still here to witness it all and help with the planning.

The usual sensation of sadness settled over her at the thought of her mother. She'd been so beautiful, with her flame-red hair, which Cheryl had inherited, and her lovely singing voice – which Cheryl definitely *hadn't* been blessed with. But she had also been a deeply conflicted woman, swinging from crazy highs to dangerous lows.

Cheryl was the one who had found her after she took her last overdose, and she had never forgotten the way her father reacted when he'd walked in on the scene a couple of minutes later. Any normal man would have tried to revive her, but Cheryl's dad had merely looked down at his wife, and murmured: 'Oh well, that's the end of that, then.' Cheryl had never completely forgiven him for those cold words, although he had vehemently denied ever saying them when she confronted him years later. As she got older, she had started to understand how difficult it must have been for him to live with her mum, but it still stung, and she'd been glad when he'd moved to Canada to start a new life, because it allowed her to put it all behind her.

Now she was on the verge of starting her own next chapter, she pushed the dark memories back into their box and climbed out of bed to pack for her stay at Dale's house.

Bob's front door was standing slightly ajar when Sharon Oakes arrived. Tapping on it, because his daughter had threatened to report her the last time she'd walked in 'uninvited', she pushed it further open and called, 'It's Sharon . . . Anyone home?'

When no answer came after a minute, she stepped inside and

popped her head around the living-room door. The smell of stale smoke and sweat hit her in the face, and she wrinkled her nose as she looked at the mess. Fiona's filthy quilt was in a heap on the sofa, and an overflowing ashtray was balanced on the arm of it, while the floor around it was littered with chocolate wrappers and beer cans the lazy cow hadn't bothered to put in the bin.

The woman herself was nowhere in sight, so Sharon walked to the foot of the stairs and called her name to make sure she wasn't in the bathroom before making her way up to Bob's bedroom.

Bob was awake and sitting up in bed in the darkness when she entered his room, and he gave her a gummy grin, saying, 'Morning, Cheryl, love. How's the weather out there?'

'It's Sharon, not Cheryl, and it's fine,' Sharon said, walking over to open his curtains. 'Ready to get up and have your breakfast?'

'Aye,' he said, pushing the quilt off his legs.

'What have you done now?' Sharon asked, frowning when she saw a fresh bruise among the faded tattoos on his scrawny arm.

'No idea,' Bob said, looking at it as if it was the first time he'd seen it. 'Must have banged it on the bedside table in the night.'

'How about we move it a bit, so it's not so close to the bed?' she suggested. 'Those corners are sharp, and we don't want you smacking your head on it.'

'Thanks, love,' Bob said, wincing as he dropped his feet to the floor.

'Are you in pain?' Sharon asked as she wiggled the heavy bedside table a couple of inches to the right.

'Just my hip giving me a bit of jip,' he said.

'Well, you need to take those painkillers regularly, like the doctor told you,' Sharon advised as she helped him to his feet. 'They have to build up in your body to keep the pain under control, so taking them sporadically won't be giving you the full benefit.'

'They don't give me enough, and they run out too fast if I take 'em regular,' Bob grumbled.

'I'm afraid I can't help you with that, 'cos I'm not allowed to interfere with your medication,' Sharon said, walking him out onto the landing. 'But have a word with your doctor when you get a chance. Maybe they've made a mistake with the script.'

'Aye, I'll try,' Bob said.

Leaving him to use the toilet and have his morning wash, Sharon went back to his bedroom and quickly made the bed before setting out his clothes for the day.

Downstairs a short time later, she settled Bob in his chair with the TV remote, then opened the window a little to air out the room while he flicked through the channels. It wasn't her job to clean up after his daughter, but she hated the thought of him having to sit in her mess all day, so she folded the foul-smelling quilt and then scooped up the rubbish and carried it into the kitchen.

That room wasn't as bad as the living room, because Sharon always did a little clean-up after she'd prepared Bob's food in the mornings and evenings; but there was a nasty smell in there today that turned her stomach. Guessing that something must have gone off inside the bin bag that was standing behind the back door, she held her breath as she untied the knot in it to put in the rubbish she was carrying.

It took a few seconds to comprehend what she was looking at when she opened the bag, but when it hit her, she recoiled in horror. There, among the rubbish, with an old teabag and a used sanitary towel on his head, was Cyril; his eyes glazed, his tongue sticking stiffly out of his unmoving mouth.

As she stared at the pitiful sight, Sharon felt a bubble of pure anger rise into her chest. Bob would *never* have put his beloved cat in the bin, so it had to have been Fiona; which made her wonder if Bob even knew about it. She very much doubted he did, because he would have been really upset, and he hadn't said a word to indicate that anything was wrong.

Cursing Fiona under her breath, Sharon peeled a new bin liner off the roll under the sink and stuffed her hands inside it. As she carefully lifted Cyril's body out of the old one, she reasoned that there was a possibility, albeit remote, that Fiona might have found him dead and had put him in the bag to prevent her dad from seeing him while she nipped out to find a box that was suitable to bury him in.

'Yeah, right,' she muttered, standing up to unlock the back door. 'And pigs might fly!'

Unsure what to do with Cyril after carrying him out into the yard, she was looking for a suitable place to leave him where the foxes wouldn't be able to get to him when Cheryl came out into her yard and walked over to the low fence.

'Morning,' Cheryl whispered, casting a furtive glance at Bob's door to make sure Fiona wasn't there. 'How's he doing?'

'Oh, you're back,' Sharon said, a frown creasing her brow as she walked over to her. 'He's OK, but I've, um, got a bit of a problem.'

'Why, what's up?' Cheryl asked, concerned by her expression. 'That bitch isn't giving you trouble, is she?'

'No, it's not her; it's *this*.' Sharon held up the bag.

'What is it?' Cheryl asked, pulling a face when she got a whiff of the smell coming from it. 'A dead rat, or something?'

'A dead *cat*,' Sharon corrected her, giving her a meaningful look.

'Not Cyril?' Cheryl gasped. 'Oh no, what happened?'

'I've got no idea,' Sharon sighed, placing the bag gently on the ground. 'I found him in the bin in the kitchen.'

'You're kidding?' Cheryl stared at her in disbelief. 'How the hell did he get in there? Do you think he climbed in looking for food and got trapped?'

'He might have got in by himself, but I'm pretty sure it wasn't him who knotted the bag,' Sharon replied ominously.

'Fiona,' Cheryl spat, reaching the exact same conclusion Sharon already had. 'If I find out she did something to him, I swear to God she'll regret it. Bob must be heartbroken.'

'To be honest, I don't think he knows,' Sharon replied. 'He hasn't mentioned him, anyway.'

'Poor Bob,' Cheryl said sadly.

'And poor *you*,' Sharon said, peering at Cheryl's face when she noticed the bruises for the first time. 'What happened?'

'I was mugged coming home from work last week.'

'Bloody hell, it's getting worse round here. I've got an old lady I see in the flats, and she was telling me some bloke got murdered over there a couple of days back. She reckons they caved his head in with a metal bar; left him in such a state they could only ID him from his fingerprints.'

'Seriously?' Cheryl asked. '*I* got whacked with a metal bar. And it happened by the flats.'

'Oh my God!' Sharon's eyes widened. 'Do you think it was the same person?'

'It'd be a bit of a coincidence if it wasn't. I was lucky, 'cos I only got a cut and a hairline fracture; but that could easily have been me.'

'Well, I'm glad it wasn't.'

'Me too,' Cheryl agreed, shuddering at the thought.

Turning her head when she heard a noise coming from Bob's house, Sharon saw Fiona taking her jacket off in the hallway, and said, 'Madam's back. Best get in and sort Bob's breakfast before she reports me for neglecting him.'

'Before you go, here's my new number,' Cheryl said, passing a piece of paper over the fence. 'The mugger stole my phone, so I had to get a new one and lost all my contacts.'

'Ah, that'll explain why you haven't been seeing my messages all week,' Sharon said, taking it and slipping in into her pocket. Then, narrowing her eyes when she spotted the ring on Cheryl's finger, she said, 'Is that what I think it is?'

'It sure is.' Cheryl smiled, holding out her hand. 'He proposed at the hospital when he came to pick me up yesterday. I'm going over to his place this afternoon to start planning the wedding with his mum.'

'I couldn't be happier for you, love,' Sharon said sincerely as she leant down and gingerly picked up the bag.

'Thanks,' Cheryl said. 'And can you give Bob my love? I miss the old bugger.'

'I think it's mutual,' said Sharon. 'He keeps calling me Cheryl.'

'Oh, bless him.'

'Hey, I didn't tell you that so you could start worrying again,' Sharon chided. 'If it makes him happy to think I'm you, that's fine by me. Now go start planning your wedding to that lovely man of yours. You've got a good one there.'

'I really have,' Cheryl agreed.

'And don't worry about Cyril,' Sharon whispered before moving away from the fence. 'I'll make sure he gets a proper burial, even if I have to take him home and put him in my garden.'

'Thanks,' Cheryl murmured, wishing she had grass instead of the concrete slabs that masqueraded as gardens on her block, because she would happily have buried poor old Cyril herself.

Chapter 25

Anna was woken by the sound of her phone vibrating on the wooden top of her bedside table. Blindly groping for it, she knocked it onto the floor, where it rattled around on the floorboards instead. Prising an eye open, she leant over the edge of the mattress to get it and groaned when she saw *Moneybags* on the screen. She immediately dismissed the call, only for the notifications to pop up, telling her that it was the fourth time he'd tried to get hold of her in the last hour. Wondering what the hell was so urgent that her father would hassle her at 10 a.m., when he knew she didn't like being disturbed before noon, she got her answer when a message appeared on the screen a few seconds later. He told her to ring him back ASAP to let him know if it was her who had withdrawn money on the credit card he'd given her strictly for emergencies; and if it was her, *why*, when she'd only received her monthly allowance a couple of weeks earlier.

Irritated, she dropped the phone back onto the floor, and rolled onto her back, muttering, 'Maybe if you gave me enough to fucking live on in the first place, I wouldn't have needed to use it to get cash!'

Awake now, with a mouth that tasted like stale alcohol and the contents of an ashtray, she was about to get up and go for a glass of water when she saw a lump under the quilt on the other side of the bed. Wary, because she had no recollection of inviting anyone back there the previous night, she stared at the lump, wondering who the hell it was. Greta had called her at around 1 a.m. to tell her she was throwing an impromptu party with some people she'd met at a club, and she remembered going up to her apartment on the floor above and doing a few lines of coke. But after that, it was a total blank.

Unnerved by the thought that she had brought a total stranger into her apartment when she was in that state – and, worse, had let them stay the night, when she had a strict rule *never* to let one-night-stands stay after fucking them – she eased the quilt off her legs and was tiptoeing to the door to get her dressing gown when the lump turned over. Able to see the face now, her eyes almost popped out of their sockets when she saw who it was, and she whispered, 'No fucking *way!*'

Grinning when the man stirred and she saw his eyelids fluttering, she leant over him, purring, 'Morning, handsome.'

'Morning,' he replied sleepily. 'Time is it?'

'Almost ten.'

'Ten?' Dale's eyes snapped open and he abruptly sat up. 'Fuck! I'm gonna be late. Why didn't you wake me?'

'I didn't even know you were here,' she told him truthfully. 'But now you are, how's about I get back in bed and—'

'What the fuck?' Dale cut in, staring at her as if he'd never seen her before in his life. 'Who are *you*, and what are you doing in my room?'

'I think you'll find it's you who's in *my* room,' Anna laughed. 'And you know exactly who I am, so let's not play games.'

Dale looked at the unfamiliar floral duvet, the pink velvet curtains and the mess of women's clothes strewn around the floor before snapping his gaze back to the woman. With her matted hair extensions, her puffy lips and the black streaks of eyeliner smeared around her eyes, she looked like a hooker, and he wondered if Tommy and the other lads had spiked his drink and set him up with her. It was exactly the kind of stunt those fuckers would pull for a laugh – and he would skin every single one of them alive when he got his hands on them.

'If you're expecting money, forget it,' he said as he snatched his boxers up off the floor and dragged them on. 'They hired you, so they can pay.'

'What are you talking about?' Anna gave him a bemused look.

'I'm talking about Tommy and the others, obviously,' Dale snapped as he looked for his trousers. 'They're the reason I'm here, aren't they? Fuckers must have carried me in, 'cos I sure as hell didn't walk in here by myself.'

'I don't know anyone called Tommy,' Anna said truthfully. 'And I've got no clue how you got here, 'cos I can't remember anything after getting to Greta's and doing some coke.'

'Who the fuck's Greta?'

'My mate. She lives on the next floor up, and she invited a load of blokes back for a party last night. You must have been with them.'

'I wasn't at a party; I was at a club with my mates.'

'Yeah, and Greta told me she met the guys at a club, so that must have been you lot,' Anna said. 'I'm not complaining,' she went on, perching on the side of the bed and stroking his bare arm. 'I just wish I could remember what we did when we came back here, 'cos this was so meant to be. I'd have had you ages ago if Cheryl hadn't pulled a fast one and thrown herself at you.'

'You what?' Dale pushed her hand off and glared at her. 'Where did you hear that name?'

'God, you've got a short memory.' Anna rolled her eyes. 'She was my best mate. *Was* being the operative word, the way she went behind my back to get her claws into you.'

'No...' Dale leapt to his feet and stared down at her in horror. 'This can't be happening.'

'Oh, but it is,' Anna said, lying back on her elbows and giving him a sexy smile. 'Fate, or what?'

'This ain't fate, it's a fuckin' set-up,' Dale spat, yanking his shirt on. 'It was *you* who spiked my drink, wasn't it? You were getting your own back on Cheryl.'

'What you on about?' Anna was confused.

'Don't fuck with me,' Dale hissed, pinning her to the mattress with his hand around her throat. 'I know your game, but you picked the wrong one, bitch. If Cheryl finds out about this, you're a dead woman walking.'

'You're hurting me,' Anna cried, digging her nails into his wrists in an effort to get him off her. 'I can't breathe!'

'Remember this feeling, 'cos this is your one and only warning,' Dale snarled, lowering his face and staring into her eyes. 'Keep that stinking mouth of yours shut. Understood?'

'*Yes!*' Anna cried, scared that he was going to strangle her. 'I won't say anything, I promise. Please just leave.'

'With pleasure,' Dale said, pushing himself away from her and snatching his jacket up off the chair in the corner. At the door, he turned and said, 'And don't even think about calling the police, 'cos I've got cops on the payroll and I can make you disappear like *that*...' He snapped his fingers and then walked out.

Terrified, Anna held her breath until she heard the front door open and close. Heart pounding, she crept to the bedroom door and peeped out into the hall to check he'd actually gone before running to the toilet to throw up.

*

Dale kept his head down after leaving the apartment. Wary of being caught on CCTV, because that would prove he'd been there if the bitch decided to push her luck and report him to the cops, he gave the elevator the swerve and jogged down the stairs to the ground floor. It was cold when he pushed out through the door at the bottom, but he was still sweating, so he looped his jacket over his shoulder and quickly walked away from the block.

He didn't remember a thing after meeting up with Tommy and the lads last night, and it disturbed him that he'd woken up naked in that skank's bed. The fact that she was Cheryl's ex-best mate and they had fallen out over him made it way too much of a coincidence for his liking. What were the chances of him getting his drink spiked – which he was convinced it had been – then ending up with *her* on the day he got engaged to Cheryl? It had to have been a deliberate attempt to sabotage the wedding. But was it all that bitch's doing, or had Tommy and the lads played a part? Either way, if Cheryl found out, he was fucked.

Anna was an unknown quantity to him, so he had no idea if she would heed his warning and keep her mouth shut, or go running straight to the police – or Cheryl herself. She couldn't reach Cheryl by phone, because she didn't know her new number, so she wouldn't be able to drop him in it that way. But she would be able to catch her at home if he didn't get there first, so he needed to find his car ASAP and get Cheryl over to his mum's.

Relieved, after walking through town, to find his car parked behind the club, he tossed his jacket into the back and hopped into the driver's seat. Pausing just long enough to call the client he was supposed to be having a meeting with in ten minutes, he apologised and made up some bullshit story about a family emergency before arranging to meet up later in the afternoon instead. Then, reversing out of his spot with a squeal of rubber, he drove over to Cheryl's place.

Chapter 26

Cheryl hadn't expected Dale to pick her up until later in the afternoon or early evening when he'd finished work, so she was surprised when his car pulled up outside her house shortly after her conversation with Sharon.

'Aren't you ready yet?' he asked when she opened the door.

'Not quite,' she said, waving him inside. 'You're early.'

'My first meeting was shorter than I expected, so I thought I might as well get you over there while I've got a couple of hours to spare,' he said, picking up the small case she'd packed, which was standing in the hallway. 'Grab whatever else you need while I put this in the car.'

'Haven't you been home yet?' Cheryl asked when she climbed into the passenger seat a few minutes later and noticed he was wearing the same clothes as the previous day.

'Er, no, not yet,' he said, throwing the car into drive as soon as she'd closed the door. 'I slept on my mate's couch.'

'Must have been a good night?' Cheryl said, guessing that he'd had too much to drink if he had decided not to drive home.

'I've got no idea,' Dale replied sheepishly. 'They already had the tequila shots lined up when I got there, and I don't remember a thing after the third round.'

'Are you safe to be driving now?' Cheryl asked.

'I'm absolutely fine,' he assured her, although he actually had no idea *what* was still in his system. Even if he hadn't been spiked, he had obviously drunk way more than he should have to not remember anything, and he would be in serious shit if he was pulled over, so he slowed down.

Cheryl noticed the reduction in speed and relaxed her grip a little on her handbag on her lap. She had been in the car with him many times and was always a little nervous when he put his foot down; especially on the unlit country roads at night, when it was impossible to see anything apart from silhouettes and shadows. He always laughed and reminded her that he knew those roads like the back of his hand whenever she asked him to slow down, so now she just held her breath when it got a little hairy. But if he'd been that drunk last night, his reactions might still be off, so she was glad that he'd decided to moderate his speed without her having to ask.

'So how was your night?' Dale asked, settling back in his seat as they left the city – and any chance of Anna grassing him up – behind. 'Did you sleep well?'

'Yeah, it was great.' Cheryl smiled. 'The hospital bed was OK, but it's impossible to get a proper rest with all the noises from the other rooms.'

'Well, you won't have to do that again once we get you off that estate and out of the danger zone,' Dale said. 'One of the lads told me that some bloke was done in a few nights back, at the same place where you were mugged.'

'I know, Sharon told me this morning.'

'Who's Sharon?'

'Bob's carer.'

'Oh yeah, I remember her. Nice woman.'

'She really is,' Cheryl said. 'Anyway, she said another of her old people who lives in the flats told her about it, and they made a right mess of him. But get this,' she added ominously. 'They did it with a metal bar, so it might have been the same one who attacked me.'

'Bloody hell, that's way too close for comfort,' Dale murmured. 'The sooner we get you out of there for good, the better, 'cos there's no way our boy's growing up in the middle of that shit.'

'Or *girl*,' Cheryl said, smiling at him.

'Whatever,' Dale grinned. 'Just saying, no kid of mine is growing up on the Langley. So I don't care how much you like it, we will *not* be living there when we're married.'

That answered the questions Cheryl had intended to ask regarding their future living arrangements, and she felt strangely OK about it. Strangely, because right up until that point she had thought she would argue about it if he said what he'd just said. She did love her little house, and she would definitely miss Bob; but in all honesty, there was really nothing else around there that she was connected to in any meaningful way. And Dale was right; the murder, so soon after her own attack, and the fact that the same weapon had been used, kind of sealed the deal for her. If it was too dangerous for grown men and women to live round there, there was no way she wanted to raise her child there.

'So where *will* we live?' she asked.

'My mum and dad's place to start off with,' Dale said. 'Then we can look for somewhere of our own once our boy's here.'

'Or *girl*,' Cheryl reiterated, determined to keep reminding him that the child might be female, because she'd sensed from the way she'd seen his parents treat Frankie and Poppy that his family placed more value on males. It was only a suspicion, and she hoped she was wrong, but she wanted to nip it in the bud before it even became an issue.

'Or girl,' Dale agreed, giving Cheryl a smile that instantly settled her fears.

*

Dale had rung ahead to let his mum know he was bringing Cheryl over earlier than planned, and Sonia was waiting on the top step when they drove up to the house.

'Morning, my darlings,' she greeted them both warmly. 'How did you sleep, Cherry?'

Amused that the woman was *still* misnaming her, Cheryl said, 'Yeah, really good, thanks. There's nothing quite like your own bed, is there?'

'Well, hopefully you'll grow to feel the same about your bed here,' Sonia said, smiling as she linked arms with her. 'Let's go and get a cup of tea while Dale takes your case upstairs. I had lots of lovely brochures delivered so we can get started right away.'

'Great,' Cheryl said, as eager as Sonia clearly was to get cracking, because the sooner they were done, the sooner she would be able to go home and start doing a clear-out of all the stuff she didn't want to take with her when she and Dale started their new lives together.

Settled at the kitchen table, enjoying the tea and delicious butter pastries Rosa had served, Cheryl smiled when Dale came back downstairs a short time later, showered, shaved and changed into a fresh suit. He looked so sexy with his wet hair slicked back, and she inhaled the scent of his aftershave when he leant down to kiss her, before then kissing his mother.

'OK, my two favourite ladies in the entire world, I'm off,' he said, lifting one of the pastries off the plate as he spoke. 'Have fun while I'm gone. And *you* make sure you get some rest,' he added, pointing a mock-stern finger at Cheryl.

'I'll be looking after her, so don't you worry,' Sonia said. 'Now go.' She dismissed him with a flap of her hand before turning her attention back to the bouquet brochure she and Cheryl had been looking at before he came into the room.

Catching his eye over Sonia's head, Cheryl smiled and mouthed, 'Bye.'

Dale winked at her in return and took a bite out of the pastry as he strolled out.

It was almost 7 p.m. before Dale and Alfie arrived home. Cheryl, under orders from Sonia, had taken a long soak in the claw-footed bathtub in her en suite an hour earlier. Rosa had drawn the bath for her and had added essential oils, the scents of which had relaxed her brain after a full-on day of wedding planning, while the oils had left her with glowing, velvet-soft skin.

Out on the patio, relaxing on a comfortable chair under the heaters, Cheryl was sipping on a vitamin-packed smoothie Sonia had insisted she drink and gazing up at the darkening sky. She had been dreading staying, but the peace of the countryside was already working its magic on her, and she smiled contentedly when Dale strolled out to join her and asked how her day had been.

'It's been really lovely,' she told him truthfully. 'Your mum's been so nice, and Rosa made the most amazing lunch for us.'

'Only the best for you and my boy,' he grinned, leaning down to kiss her. 'Or girl,' he added, holding up his hands as he straightened up again.

'Your mum wants to book me in for a 4D scan so we can find out the sex for sure,' Cheryl said quietly. 'But I think I'd rather wait and see. What do you think?'

'Hadn't really thought about it,' Dale said, taking a seat in the chair next to hers. 'I think it would be kind of cool to know,' he went on. 'That way, we'll know what colour clothes to buy.'

'I hope you're not going to be one of those dads who won't let his son wear anything except blue and white?' Cheryl teased.

'There's plenty of other colours, as well,' he replied. 'Just not pink. OK?'

'We'll see,' Cheryl laughed. 'So how's *your* day been?'

'Busy,' he said. 'But I thrive on busy, so it's all good. That reminds me, I'll be going to London in a couple of days for some meetings my dad's set up with some new investors. I should only be there a day or two, but I was thinking it might be nice if you came with me?'

'No!' Sonia said firmly, walking out onto the patio before Cheryl could answer and handing a glass of whisky to Dale. 'We've only just got started on our project, and we don't have much time, so this one stays with me.'

'Well, that's me told,' Dale laughed, raising the glass to his mother before taking a swig.

Me too, Cheryl thought, taking another sip of the smoothie. She had never been to London and would have loved to go with him, but she supposed Sonia had a point. They had been working on the wedding plans all day, but they had only made a concrete decision about the flowers for her bouquet, the wedding arch and the reception tables so far, so there was still a mountain of things to work through.

'Anyway, I came out to tell you both that dinner will be served in ten minutes,' Sonia said before heading back into the house.

'Does she actually live in the kitchen?' Cheryl asked Dale quietly when she'd gone. 'The house is huge, but I swear she hasn't moved away from the table all day.'

'It's her command centre,' Dale said. 'She only uses the best rooms for formal occasions, like when my dad's got important clients to schmooze, or when the mayor and his wife come over for dinner.'

'The *mayor?*' Cheryl's eyes widened.

'My old man's very well connected,' Dale said, giving her a mysterious smile as he stood up. 'Come on, let's get you inside before it starts getting any colder out here.'

Cheryl was perfectly warm under the heater and had been enjoying the solitude out there, with only the sound of the wind rustling through the trees, and the chattering of birds making their way home to their nests for the night. She was actually so relaxed she could easily have slept out there, but she'd already learned that Sonia ran her household like a well-oiled clock, and she wasn't about to disrupt everyone else's routine by dawdling outside when dinner was about to be served.

In bed later that night, as Dale slept in his own room down the corridor, and Alfie and Sonia were in their room in between, Cheryl gazed out at the moon through the window and considered how different her life was compared to a few short months earlier.

The loan shark's visit had been the catalyst for her meeting Dale, and that had set everything that followed into motion. It still amazed her that, in one short conversation, he had persuaded those men to leave her alone, when she herself had been trying for months to get them to stop pursuing her over Chris's debt. But he'd had the exact same effect on the men who had burgled Bob's house with Fiona that night, who had bolted at the mere sight of him. To Cheryl, it just proved that power didn't come from being the biggest thug in the village; it came from being a decent, hard-working man who refused to be cowed by people who thrived on taking advantage of weaker people. Like the boy who stands up to the bully everyone else is terrified of, and reveals him for the coward he truly is.

Alfie exuded that same aura of power, and both he and Dale

were the types of success stories that thugs like the loan shark and Fiona's mates could only dream of being. After living with a pure chancer like Chris, who gave it the Big I Am without actually doing anything that didn't benefit him personally, being with Dale was an absolute breath of fresh air. Not only did he work hard, he was also extremely kind and good-natured, and she loved how protective he was of her and their baby. She also adored how close he was to his family, and how much they seemed to genuinely enjoy each other's company. Tonight, at the dinner table, without the distraction of the guests who had been present every other time Cheryl had been there, they had talked and laughed as they ate, and she had felt truly grateful to them for making her feel like part of the family.

She wasn't sure how comfortable she would feel once Dale went off on his trip to London, but she had only been invited to stay for a few days while they got the majority of the wedding plans underway, so she would probably be home by the time he left. She hoped so, because there was a lot that needed to be sorted out there if she was going to give up the house. Alfie and Sonia had already said that she should move in with them, as Dale had suggested on the drive over; but she was sure that they wouldn't want her cheap furniture mucking up the place while she and Dale looked for a home of their own, so she would have to find a charity that was willing to come and pick it all up before she handed her keys back to the council.

She still needed her furniture for now, so she wasn't going to waste any time worrying about it. More pressing was the issue of contacting her boss about severance pay, while also looking for a new job so she'd be able to contribute once she and Dale found a new place. She was sure she had written her boss's number down in one of her old address books, but she hadn't been able to find it before Dale had picked her up that morning, so she would have to wait until she got home in a few days to search for it. And there was no point asking if she could use a computer to look for another job while she was here, because Dale had already told her that she didn't need one, so that would also have to wait until she got home.

Those things aside, everything else seemed to be heading in exactly the right direction, and Cheryl smiled as she closed her eyes and settled down to sleep. She'd had a moment of doubt about how fast things were progressing, but Dale and his parents had made her feel so secure, she was no longer terrified of what lay ahead. She had the perfect man, who loved her as much as she loved him and wasn't afraid to tell her so. And they were going to be married and have a child who would never know a day of loneliness or fear in his or her life. What more could she – or *any* woman – possibly want?

Chapter 27

Estelle had been summoned to her mother-in-law's house, and she wasn't looking forward to it since Stefan had told her that Cheryl was temporarily staying there while she and Sonia planned the wedding. The very thought of it set Estelle's teeth on edge, because she knew it would be the Sonia Moran show from start to finish. Cheryl had probably fooled herself into thinking that she had a say in the proceedings, but Estelle had pegged her for a people-pleaser from the off. And if *she'd* seen it, Sonia definitely had as well, and she would manipulate the silly cow in order to get her own way in every single aspect of the wedding.

After being kept waiting several minutes for the gate to open – deliberately, she suspected – Estelle parked up outside the house and hustled Frankie and Poppy up the steps, hissing at Frankie to behave or there would be no burgers and ice cream on the way home. It felt wrong to bribe him, and she knew that Stefan wouldn't be happy about her giving their son fast food when he was already overweight and too lazy to exercise. But Stefan wasn't here to help her out, and Frankie was starting to understand that men could do as they pleased in this family, so she had to do *something* to keep him in check while she still could.

'You're late,' Sonia chided when Estelle and the children entered the kitchen after Rosa had let them in.

'Sorry,' Estelle murmured, instantly feeling got at – an art that Sonia had perfected over the years. 'I've actually been waiting at the gate.'

'I opened them at five so you could drive straight in, because that was the time I told you to be here,' Sonia replied coolly. 'But you were late, so I had to close them again. You know we can't let just anybody walk in here at will; especially when the men aren't around to protect us.'

Feeling awkward, because she knew for a fact that Sonia had not opened the gates, much less closed them again, and had also pretended not to see Estelle's car on the monitor screens, Cheryl smiled at Estelle when Sonia turned her attention to the children. The smile wasn't returned, but Estelle didn't dole out any of her usual dirty looks, so Cheryl took it as an achievement of sorts.

Rosa came in after a few minutes and settled the children at a smaller table at the end of the kitchen with glasses of orange juice and a plate of biscuits to share, before filling the kettle to make tea for the women.

At the main table, Sonia informed Estelle that she had called her over so the children could be measured for their wedding outfits.

Estelle frowned as if this was the first she'd heard of it, and said, 'But we told you me and Stef were going to sort their clothes out.'

'As best man, *Stefan* will be far too busy being measured for his own suit,' Sonia said, placing heavy emphasis on her son's full name, Cheryl noticed. 'And you don't know the theme, so how on earth could you possibly choose what they're to wear?'

'Maybe if you told me the theme I could try?' Estelle ventured.

'Absolutely not,' Sonia said with finality. 'Cherry and I have already planned everything between us, and we can't have the ring bearer and the flower girl ruining the theme because their mother thinks she knows better.'

'Ring bearer and flower girl?' Estelle repeated, her frown deepening as a heat rash appeared on her neck. 'Nobody told me about this.'

'It's their uncle's wedding, at their grandparents' house, so of course they'll have starring roles,' Sonia replied smoothly. 'Stefan and I discussed it when he came over the other day, and he's fine with it.'

Cheryl squirmed in her seat when she saw the anger and frustration in Estelle's eyes. She'd witnessed Sonia speaking down to the woman before, but there had always been other people around on those occasions, so it hadn't felt quite so intense.

'Ah, they're here.' Sonia gestured to the CCTV monitor, on the screen of which two vehicles, one behind the other, could be seen approaching the main gates. 'And perfectly on time,' she added pointedly.

Estelle's shoulders sagged when Sonia strode out into the hallway to answer the door after pressing the button to release the gates. Feeling guilty, Cheryl said, 'Sorry about the confusion, Estelle. I honestly thought you knew.'

Estelle looked up and coolly met her gaze. 'We're not friends, so please don't patronise me,' she said spikily. 'And, just so you know, you're not his first and you won't be the last, so enjoy this while you can.'

Later, after Estelle had taken the children home, Cheryl tried to make sense of what the woman had said to her. It had sounded like some kind of warning, she thought; as if Estelle was implying that Dale had been engaged or married before and it hadn't worked out. But if that *was* what she'd meant, Cheryl didn't believe her, because she was sure that Dale would have told her.

Unless it was Caroline.

Dale always reacted angrily to that name, and Cheryl had often wondered if their relationship had been more meaningful than Dale cared to admit. But he and Cheryl weren't teenagers trying to prove their love for each other by pretending there had never been anyone else; they were both adults who had lived with and loved other people before they met, so why would he lie about it?

Still mulling everything over when Dale came home later that evening, Cheryl waited until dinner was over and he and his father had shared their nightly whisky and cigar hour before joining him on the patio to speak to him in private.

'I need to ask you something,' she said, taking a seat across from him under the heaters. 'Estelle brought the kids over earlier to get fitted for their wedding outfits, and she said something weird when your mum was out of the room.'

'Everything 'Stelle says is weird,' Dale grunted, squinting as he relit the butt of his cigar. 'I thought you'd have cottoned on to that by now?'

'She's usually just a bitch,' Cheryl said, wafting the noxious-smelling smoke away from her face. 'But this was different; like a warning, almost.'

'About what?'

'I'm not sure,' Cheryl said, conscious that she needed to choose her words carefully to avoid upsetting Dale or dropping Estelle in it. 'She said I'm not the first and I won't be the last, so I should enjoy this while I can.'

'Meaning?'

'I've no idea, that's why I'm asking you.'

'Beats me?' Dale said, shrugging as he took another drag on the cigar.

'OK, I need you to be totally honest with me,' Cheryl said, figuring there was no point beating around the bush. 'If there's anything you haven't told me because you think it might upset me, I want you to know that I honestly don't care what happened in your past.'

Dale drew his head back and gave her a bemused smile. 'Now you're starting to sound weird.'

'I'm only letting you know that I won't hold it against you if there's something you haven't told me.'

'Like what? If you've got something specific in mind, babe, spit it out or we'll be here all night.'

'Have you been engaged or married before?' Cheryl blurted out.

'*What?*' Dale spluttered. 'Are you actually being serious right now?'

'Yes, I am, because I need to know,' Cheryl said, watching his face closely. 'I already told you I don't care, because the past is the past. But if everyone else knows something and I don't, that's not fair.'

'OK...' Dale sighed and leaned forward in his seat to peer into her eyes. 'I'll tell you the truth, but are you sure you're ready for it?'

Already dreading the worst, but prepared to stand by what she'd said and not hold it against him, Cheryl took a deep breath and nodded.

'I have...' Dale said slowly, leaving a long pause before continuing: '...*never* been engaged or married. Not to anyone, *ever*, because I've never been with a girl I wanted to make that kind of commitment to. You're the first, and you *will* be the last, so whatever weird shit Estelle's planted in your head, forget it.'

Cheryl saw the sincerity in his eyes and breathed a sigh of relief. 'OK, I believe you. And I'm really sorry I had to ask.'

'You can ask me anything you want, any *time* you want,' Dale said. 'But do yourself a favour and stop trying to play nice with Estelle, because she's not worth the headache you'll get trying to figure out why she's got such a huge chip on her shoulder.'

'I've kind of figured that out already,' Cheryl agreed. 'And I know your mum's really tried with her as well.'

'Which should tell you that it's not just you she's got a problem with,' said Dale. 'So leave her to her weird little fantasy life and concentrate on us.'

Cheryl smiled and nodded her agreement. He was right. Estelle seemed to have a problem with everyone and everything, and she wasn't going to waste any more time trying to figure the woman out when there didn't seem to be any reason for her hostility.

Chapter 28

The children were in bed, and Estelle was pacing the living room swigging a glass of wine when Stefan arrived home later that night. Still furious about being made to drive all the way over to her in-laws' house for a stupid measuring session that could have been done anywhere, she launched into him when he stepped into the room after hanging his jacket in the hall.

'Why have you and your mother decided that Frankie and Poppy are going to be the ring bearer and flower girl without discussing it with me first?'

'Do we have to do this now?' Stefan sighed, flopping onto the sofa. 'I've had a long day.'

'Join the club,' Estelle snapped, standing over him with her hands on her hips. 'But mine didn't only involve getting the kids to school, doing the laundry, the shopping and the cleaning; I got summoned to your mother's house, as well. So I had to drive over there and sit outside the gate for ten minutes, as punishment for being five minutes late, only to find out that you and her have been conspiring about *my* children behind my back; getting them fitted for clothes we said *we* were going to buy.'

Stefan listened to her tirade. Then, raising an eyebrow he said, 'Have you finished?'

'I've only just started,' she replied angrily. 'I've had enough of your family, and I'm sick of your mother treating me like shit.'

'First off, I only heard about the ring bearer and flower girl stuff last week,' Stefan began. 'But my mother said she'd already discussed it with you, so that's why *I* didn't mention it: because I assumed it was all in hand.'

'Well she *lied*,' Estelle spat. 'Because she never said a word to me about it until I got there this afternoon. And boy, didn't she enjoy sticking it to me in front of your brother's latest tart!'

'They're getting married and having a baby,' Stefan reminded her.

'So?'

'So I don't think it's fair to call her that when he's obviously serious about her.'

'Oh, I see,' Estelle said quietly, her eyes flashing fire. 'I knew it.'

'Knew what?' Stefan asked wearily, although he already knew exactly where this was headed.

'You're defending her because you fancy her,' Estelle snarled. 'And don't deny it, because I heard the way you were talking to her at that farce of an engagement party.'

'I was asking her if she was all right – like any normal person would if they knew someone had just come out of hospital after being attacked,' Stefan said coolly. 'She's my brother's fiancée, so what am I supposed to do? Ignore her and pretend this wedding isn't happening and we're not involved? I know you'd probably like that, but that's not how this family works.'

'It's your family, not mine,' Estelle shot back. 'And what do you mean by *"normal person"*? Are you implying that I'm *not* normal because I've got no time for that whore?'

'Why do you always have to blow everything out of proportion?' Stefan groaned, raking his fingers through his hair when he felt his scalp tighten. 'You're sending my blood pressure through the fucking roof with this shit.'

'Oh, that's *my* fault, is it?' Estelle sneered. 'So it's not your interfering fucking *mother* or your *father*, who treats you like an absolute joke, who are responsible?'

Stefan had heard as much as he could stomach, and he rose to his feet.

'Oh no you don't,' Estelle barked, shoving him back down with both hands on his chest. 'You're not running away from this one. You're gonna sit there and tell me why you let your mother make decisions about my children without asking my permission.'

'I'm going to get a drink,' Stefan said through gritted teeth as he stood up again. 'And I suggest you go for a walk or something, to calm yourself down.'

'Don't tell me what to do,' Estelle hissed, getting up in his face. 'I've had your mother treating me like an idiot all afternoon, and I'm sure as hell not letting you do the same in my own home.'

Peering down into her eyes, Stefan said, 'You need help.'

'Yes, I fucking do,' Estelle shot back angrily. 'Help to get away from you and your toxic family.'

'You know where the door is,' he replied. 'And no one's stopping you from using it. But don't think you're taking my children with you.'

'They're *my* children, not yours,' Estelle screeched, slamming her fists into his chest. 'I'm the one who's stuck with them all the time while you run round after your brother and your father, licking up their scraps while they swan off with all the real money. Why can't you be more like them? Huh? Why can't you grow some balls and tell them to give us our fair share?'

'So now the truth comes out,' Stefan said, scowling when her word-arrows hit their mark. 'You don't hate Cheryl because of who she is, you hate her because she's got the man you wish *you* could have. Well, guess what, Estelle... Dale wouldn't look *twice* at you!'

'I could have him if I wanted him,' Estelle retorted angrily.

'Don't make me laugh,' Stefan sneered. 'My brother might be a lot of things, but he would never betray his own blood. And as for saying my mother treats you like shit, I've seen her try to include you in stuff and you throw it back in her face. You know what your problem is? You're so fucking jealous of what they've got, you can't stand it. But that's theirs, and *this* is ours...' He swept his arm around the room. 'This is what *I've* worked for; what *I've* earned. But if it's not good enough for you, go find someone who can give you the life you think you deserve.'

'Maybe I'll do that,' she spat. 'And I'll make sure this one's mother is *dead* so I don't end up with another weak little mummy's boy!'

'Good luck finding someone who'll put up with your psycho shit,' Stefan scoffed. 'Leave, don't leave, I honestly don't give a shit anymore,' he went on. 'But if you try to take my kids, you will regret it. They're part of my family, whether you like it or not; and they *will* be taking part in this wedding – with or without your permission.'

He pushed past her at that and walked out of the room, and Estelle let out a roar of frustration and launched an ashtray at the wall when she heard the front door open and then slam shut.

Chapter 29

Cheryl slept in late on the morning Dale left for his London trip, and she was gutted when she woke to find a note on the bedside table telling her that he hadn't wanted to wake her because she'd looked so peaceful, but that he would ring as soon as he got there.

Cursing herself for forgetting to set her alarm, because she'd told Dale she wanted to go home while he was away and had asked if she could hop in the taxi with him, she got up and took a shower before heading downstairs.

Alfie always left the house early, so she'd known he wouldn't be home when she walked into the kitchen, but she was surprised to find that Sonia was also out. It felt strange being in the house by herself, and she made a cup of tea and carried it out onto the patio. It was one of her favourite places and she loved to sit in silence and feel the beauty of nature all around her; although she rarely got the chance to do it in daylight, because Sonia was always up before her and would have the brochures and notepads laid out on the kitchen table so they could get straight to work, and it was often dark by the time they finished.

It was a cold day, and the wind sounded fierce as it ripped through the bare branches of the trees and propelled the dark clouds across the sky. As she sat down, movement by the cottages caught her eye, and she frowned when she saw two men loading something large into the back of a jeep she hadn't seen before. Wary, because she didn't know if it was someone who was meant to be there, she eyed the vehicle as it drove slowly along the dirt track. As it passed by the fence to her right, she raised her hand in greeting when she spotted the older man, whom she'd given Bob's keys to after the break-in, at the wheel. He gave the slightest of nods in return, and she sighed as she settled back in her seat, wondering if she ought to have stopped him and asked for a lift home. But he and his team had finished working on Edna's house, so she doubted he'd be going that way.

The thought of home brought Bob to mind. He would have been her natural choice to walk her down the aisle since she had no way to get in touch with her dad after losing his number along with her old phone. She knew she had written it down somewhere, along with her boss's number, but she didn't really see the point of looking for it, because she doubted he'd come. It was a long, expensive flight, so she couldn't really blame him; plus, he knew she didn't like his wife, so that would make things doubly awkward. In all honesty, she would have preferred Bob to do it; but it was going to be a long day, and Sharon had told her that Bob was getting weaker and less active, so she had decided not to put him on the spot by asking him.

Fortunately, Alfie had volunteered to do the honours, so she would have *someone* to walk her up the aisle; but she was conscious that the lack of people on her side was going to look very strange. After losing her phone and all the numbers she'd had stored in it, she didn't have any way to contact any of her distant relatives or old friends; but she couldn't remember the last time she'd spoken to any of them, anyway. The only one she'd really kept in any sort of regular contact with was Anna, but the girl hadn't responded to any of her calls or messages in the wake of their fight over Dale, so she didn't really want to invite her to their wedding and risk her making a scene.

The realisation that her world had shrunk so small while she'd been on the *work, eat, sleep, repeat* treadmill weighed heavily on Cheryl's mind. Working long hours for little pay had pretty much wiped out her social life, but she hadn't really minded not being able to go out clubbing, because she liked being at home. But her inability to think of even one person to invite to the wedding slammed home just how isolated she had become over the last few years.

'Friends come and go, but family are forever,' Sonia had said when Cheryl had explained why she didn't have any names for the guest list. 'You're part of *our* family now, and we take care of our own.'

That last phrase seemed to be a Moran motto, but Cheryl hadn't really understood what it meant until now, because her own family had never been that close. Now she'd seen how tight and loyal Dale's family were, she was grateful that they had allowed her to be a part of it – and even more grateful that her child would get all the love that was coming his or her way.

A noise behind her told her that somebody was in the conservatory, and she turned her head and smiled when Rosa appeared in the doorway holding a small fleece blanket.

'Morning.'

'Is cold, so I bring this,' Rosa replied quietly, handing the blanket to her.

'Oh, thank you,' Cheryl said, touched that the woman had done that for her.

'You need more thing?' Rosa asked, surprising Cheryl because it was the most she had ever spoken in her presence, and her English was better than expected.

'No, I'm fine, thanks,' Cheryl said. 'I made myself a tea.' She held up the cup. 'Would you like to sit with me?' she asked then, thinking it would be nice to get to know the woman a little better since Rosa had made this approach of her own accord.

'No, I need work,' Rosa said, instantly dipping her gaze.

She murmured something else that sounded like thank you before rushing back into the conservatory, and Cheryl watched her through the window until she disappeared into the kitchen.

Dale had told her that Rosa had worked for his parents since before he was born, and had acted as a nanny for him and Stefan, as well as doing all the cooking and laundry for the family. Cheryl thought she looked a little old to still be responsible for the day-to-day care of a huge house like this one, but nobody else seemed to think there was a problem, and she'd never heard Rosa herself complain about it. Then again, why would she when, according to Dale, she had her own lovely suite of rooms on the far side of the house, and was regarded as part of the family?

It was almost lunchtime when Sonia arrived home and sailed into the kitchen on her usual cloud of perfume.

'Ah, good, you're dressed,' she said when she saw Cheryl sitting at the table looking through the brochures. 'Get your coat, we've got an appointment.'

'Who with?' Cheryl asked, hoping that Sonia hadn't gone ahead and set up the fancy scan, because she'd already decided that she didn't want to know the sex of the baby until it was born.

'A wedding dress designer,' Sonia said, glancing at her watch. 'Now hurry; we need to be there in the next hour or we'll miss it.'

'I thought we'd already decided on the dress?' Cheryl said, following her into the hall.

'I changed my mind about that one,' Sonia replied, heading for the door.

Frowning, because it was news to her that Sonia had decided against the dress, Cheryl pulled her coat on and went upstairs to grab her handbag before joining Sonia in the car.

'Is this really necessary?' she asked, pulling on her seat belt. 'I thought the one we chose was perfect.'

'It was nowhere near special enough,' Sonia said. 'And you're very lucky this designer agreed to see you,' she went on as they set off down the driveway and drove out through the gates. 'I had to pull in a huge favour, because she's so exclusive she has a three-year waiting list.'

'Wow,' Cheryl murmured, dreading to think how much the woman must charge if she was that highly sought after.

'She's also extremely picky about who she takes on as a client,' Sonia went on, not even pausing to check for vehicles on the road as she turned onto it from the lane. 'So let me do the talking, and make sure you don't do anything to upset her.'

'I'll try not to,' Cheryl promised, gripping the sides of her seat and digging her heels into the mat when Sonia put her foot down.

She had never been in a car with Sonia before, but it was easy to see who Dale had inherited his love of speed from, and she spent the entire journey into Manchester with her heart in her mouth.

The designer was a woman called Kat Silver, and her look was every bit as exotic as her name; from her short, metallic purple hair, matching lipstick and tights, to her studded leather mini-dress, biker boots and two full sleeves of tattoos. Cheryl was surprised, because she'd expected someone older and as groomed as Sonia, given the gushing way Dale's mother had spoken about her. And Sonia looked equally surprised; so much so that Cheryl wondered if she might have thought twice about making the appointment if she'd know, what the must-have designer actually looked like.

The gowns that were on display when Kat showed them into her spacious workroom were spectacular, and the walls were lined with photographs of Kat and various women, some of whom Cheryl recognised as famous singers and actresses. A glance at Sonia's face told her that she too was impressed as they took their seats on a well-upholstered purple sofa, which was separated from a matching chair by a long, low steel table that looked to Cheryl like something she had seen an autopsy being performed on in a true crime programme.

'I'm guessing you like purple?' she commented as Kat walked over carrying an armful of sketch books and catalogues and took a seat on the chair.

'It's the colour of female empowerment,' Kat smiled. 'And I like to empower my sisters to be the most beautiful brides in the fucking world.'

Cheryl saw Sonia's eyebrow shoot up and had to bite her lip to keep from laughing out loud. She loved Kat already, and prayed that Sonia wouldn't change her mind about her as quickly as she had changed her mind about the dress Cheryl had previously chosen.

The next hour was spent looking through design templates and discussing lengths, necklines, sleeves, embellishments – and numerous other details that began to blur into one for Cheryl after a while. Kat then made a few quick sketches of what she thought they wanted, all of which looked absolutely amazing to Cheryl.

After discussing the finer details for a little longer, Kat told them to leave it with her and she would get back to them in a couple of days with two designs based on their preferences.

Impressed by the woman's talent and vision, Cheryl made her way outside to wait while Sonia discussed payment. The reception area and workroom were situated on the first floor of the building, while the ground floor housed a shop with a *KS* logo etched into the glass door. Gazing at the various dresses on display inside, Cheryl spotted a woman sitting on a chair towards the rear of the shop holding a glass of champagne, and she smiled to herself when a younger woman came into view wearing a beautiful, pure white gown embedded with crystals.

Tears welled in Cheryl's eyes when the older woman covered her mouth with her hand, as if the vision had made her emotional, and she quickly turned away from the window when she realised they were probably mother and daughter. Blinking them away, along with the thought that she didn't have her own mother to share this experience with, she hugged herself as she waited for Sonia to come out.

Minutes passed with no sign of Sonia, and Cheryl stamped her feet on the pavement and blew on her fingers as the icy air started to bite. A woman rushed around the corner, and Cheryl murmured, 'Sorry,' and stepped back when they almost collided. The woman kept going, and Cheryl's heart skipped a beat when she caught a glimpse of her face.

'Anna?' she called out.

The woman abruptly stopped walking and turned her head.

Cheryl smiled, but it quickly slid off her lips when she saw Anna's face visibly pale at the sight of her.

'Sorry,' she apologised. 'I know you probably still don't want to talk to me, but I opened my mouth before I had the chance to think about it.'

'Is *he* with you?' Anna asked, looking around.

'Who, Dale?' Cheryl said. 'No, he's in London. Are you OK?'

'I'm fine,' Anna muttered, hunching her shoulders against the wind. Then, narrowing her eyes when she noticed which shop Cheryl was standing outside, she gave her a questioning look.

Cheryl caught it and immediately understood what she was asking. 'Yes,' she said, giving a sheepish smile as she held up her hand to show Anna the ring.

Anna looked at the ring, then slid her gaze down to Cheryl's stomach, where a tiny bump was beginning to show.

'You're pregnant?' She frowned.

'Yeah, but it's OK,' Cheryl said, aware that Anna probably remembered how worried she'd been when she had thought she was pregnant with Chris's child in the past. 'We're both really happy about it.'

Anna stared at her for several moments without speaking, but Cheryl knew her well enough to know she had something on her mind. Guessing it was the unresolved issue of who had spotted Dale first, she decided to tackle it head on.

'Look, I know you weren't happy about me and Dale getting together, and I'm really sorry if I hurt you. But it's been months now, and I've missed you. Can't we put it behind us?'

'I need to tell you something,' Anna said quietly. 'But you've got to promise you won't tell him it was me who told you.'

Confused, Cheryl said, 'Dale?'

Anna nodded, and looked around again, before saying, 'You remember my mate Greta? Well, she had a party a few nights back.'

'Right?' Cheryl murmured, wondering what that had to do with her and Dale.

'It was really late, and there was loads of booze and coke, so I was off my head,' Anna went on. 'She'd brought some blokes back from a club,' she continued, peering pointedly into Cheryl's eyes as she spoke. 'I didn't know any of them. Least I didn't *think* I did. But when I woke up the next morning, I—'

'Ah, there you are,' Sonia said, pushing out through the door behind Cheryl before Anna could go on. 'I was waiting for you upstairs. We thought you'd gone to the bathroom.'

'No, I've been out here talking to my friend,' Cheryl said. 'Anna, this is Dale's mum, Sonia.'

'Yeah, I remember,' Anna said, flashing a glance at Sonia. 'Sorry, I've got to go. Good luck, Chez.'

'How rude,' Sonia sniffed, linking her arm through Cheryl's when Anna turned and walked away. 'If she's supposed to be your friend, it's no wonder you didn't want to put her on the guest list.'

Cheryl nodded, but she had an unsettled feeling in the pit of her stomach as they made their way back to the car. Whatever Anna had been about to tell her, her instincts told her it wasn't good, and she wondered if Anna might have been assaulted by one of the men at Greta's party and had wanted to tell her because she hadn't had anyone else to confide in. But if that was the case, why had she asked her to promise not to tell Dale that she was the one who had told her? It didn't make sense.

Another thought began to edge its way in, but Sonia said her name before it could take root, and Cheryl snapped out of her thoughts when she saw that they were back at the car. As she climbed into the passenger seat, she wished she'd thought to ask Anna for her number so she could call her when she got back to the house and find out what was troubling her.

'Well, *that* went well,' Sonia said, breaking into Cheryl's thoughts again as they set off. 'It'll add an extra ten thousand or so onto the bill, but it will be worth every penny to have Kat Silver on the label.'

'Bloody hell, that's a lot,' Cheryl spluttered. 'Maybe we should stick with the original dress.'

'No, I didn't like it,' Sonia said. 'And Alfie and I are paying, so you don't need to worry about that. You just make sure you stick to the diet I've put you on now Kat's measured you, because we don't need you bursting the seams on the day.'

A little offended by the implication that she would gain excessive weight because she ate too much, and not because she was carrying a baby that was growing by the day, Cheryl forced a smile and gazed out through the window. They were only a few days into the planning, and it had been pretty relaxed and fun so far. But the mention of money had reminded her just how much it was all going to cost, and she felt guilty that Dale's parents had effectively been forced into paying for everything because she – a stranger to them, in all honesty – had slept with him and fallen pregnant.

Dale had told her that he'd ended things with Caroline because she was a gold digger, and she wondered now if that was what Sonia and Alfie thought of *her*. Or, worse, did they think she had deliberately got pregnant to trap Dale, assuming that his Catholic family would compel him to marry her?

'Are you all right, darling?' Sonia glanced at her. 'You're very quiet.'

'I didn't realise everything was going to cost so much,' Cheryl said. 'I told Dale we should wait until I've had a chance to look for another job so I could save up to help pay for the wedding, but he wanted the baby to be born with his name, so—'

'How many times do we have to tell you that we *want* to do this?' Sonia cut in. 'This isn't only about you, don't forget. Dale is our son, and you're providing us with another grandchild, so of course we want to celebrate in style.'

'I'm sorry,' Cheryl sighed. 'I just didn't want you to think I was after his money.'

'You'd be lucky,' Sonia laughed. 'Now, stop thinking silly things and remember that we're all very fond of you.'

'Thanks,' Cheryl said, smiling as her short burst of doubt fizzled out.

Chapter 30

Dale was away for four days, which had felt like an eternity to Cheryl, and he arrived home like the conquering hero, bearing flowers and perfume for Cheryl and for his mother, and a ridiculously expensive bottle of whisky and a box of cigars for his father.

After secreting themselves away for an hour to sample the whisky and cigars while they discussed business, Dale and Alfie came back to the kitchen, where Cheryl and Sonia were putting the finishing touches to the order of the wedding service. Between them, the women had pretty much covered everything during Cheryl's stay, and there were only a few minor things left to sort out. So when Dale told Cheryl to pack her bag because he was taking her home, she didn't need telling twice.

Alfie and Sonia were waiting in the hallway with Dale when she carried her small case down from the bedroom, and she thanked them both for a lovely stay.

'Be good, and stick to that diet while you're away,' Sonia said as she hugged her goodbye. 'I'll see you in a few weeks.'

'Can't wait,' Cheryl said, looking forward to the small hen party Sonia had planned to hold at the house for her, with just a few of Sonia and Alfie's female relatives who would be joining them for the pamper sessions Sonia had lined up. If Estelle had also been coming, she wouldn't have been so happy about it; but the woman had already cried off, using the excuse that Stefan would be at the stag do and there was no one to look after the children, so it was all good, in Cheryl's opinion.

In the passenger seat of Dale's car a couple of minutes later, Cheryl smiled when he climbed behind the wheel after putting her case in the boot.

'I've missed you so much,' she said, reaching out to stroke his hand as he threw the car into drive and set off towards the gates.

'I've missed you too,' he said, grinning at her. 'Why do you think I'm taking you home?'

Cheryl felt a flutter in the pit of her stomach and smiled as she settled back in her seat. Sonia had forbidden them to share a room at the family home before they were married, which had been fine by Cheryl, because she would have been far too embarrassed to share a bed with their son knowing that it went against their traditional values. But she couldn't deny that she had missed the intimacy of lying naked in his arms after making love. And he'd obviously missed it, too.

As they drove into Manchester, Dale told her about his trip and the investors he'd brought on board for another of his father's building projects. It appeared that Alfie had managed to get his hands on a substantial piece of land only a five-minute walk from Manchester city centre, and they were planning to construct an American-style mall that would smash the Arndale Centre out of existence. It all sounded very important and exciting, and Cheryl could tell that Dale was proud of himself for single-handedly securing the investments his father needed. But she was more interested in where he'd stayed, and what he'd done in his downtime between meetings.

'You're turning into my mum,' Dale laughed when she asked

about his hotel. 'Ignore the nitty-gritty and jump straight to the good stuff.'

'I hope that's not some kind of dig?' Cheryl asked.

'Not at all,' he assured her. 'That's exactly how it should be. The men make money; the women take care of the home – and us.'

'You're such a chauvinist,' Cheryl teased.

'No, I'm a realist.' Dale grinned. 'I'm liking the new look, by the way.'

'Thanks.' Cheryl reached up to stroke her hair, which had been coloured and styled by Sonia's hairdresser a couple of days earlier. 'I wasn't sure about it at first, but I think your mum was right about going shorter.'

'She's got excellent taste,' Dale agreed. 'The new style's good, as well,' he added, glancing approvingly at her navy culottes and cream blouse.

'They're your mum's,' Cheryl told him. 'I didn't take much, because I was only supposed to be staying a couple of days. I think she got sick of seeing me in the same two outfits, so she gave me a few of her old things.'

'It suits you. Makes you look more like a Moran woman.'

'I'm not a Moran yet.'

'Soon will be,' Dale said, sending a little shiver down her spine with one of his sexy winks. 'That reminds me, I've got something for you. It's in the glovebox.'

Curious, Cheryl opened the glove compartment and took out the small gift-wrapped package that was sitting inside.

'What is it?'

'Open it and see.'

Carefully peeling the paper apart to reveal a small black velvet box, Cheryl opened it and saw a wishbone-shaped ring inside, studded with glittering diamonds.

'Oh, wow, it's beautiful.'

'You can't wear it yet,' Dale said, placing his hand over hers when she went to take the ring out of its cushion. 'It's for after we're married; to show the world that you belong to me for eternity.'

'I don't need a ring to prove that,' Cheryl smiled, gazing at it for a few more seconds before closing the lid. 'But thank you. It's lovely.'

'You're welcome,' Dale said. 'I've got something else to tell you,' he went on. 'We're going to buy your house.'

'You can't; it's a council house,' Cheryl reminded him.

'We can't, but *you* can,' Dale countered. 'With our money, obviously,' he added before she could tell him that she couldn't afford it. 'We've been looking into it, and as a long-term tenant they'll sell it to you at way below market value.'

'But I thought we'd decided it was going to be too small for us and the baby?'

'Yes, and it would be. But we can use it to house some of our employees.'

'Oh, right... like those girls in Edna's place?'

'Exactly. But you're the tenant, so it'll have to be in your name. What d'you think?'

'Sounds OK in theory,' Cheryl said. 'But I'm sure there's some sort of clause that says I'd have to live it in for a certain length of time after buying it.'

'Don't worry about the small stuff,' Dale replied. 'All you need to do is set it in motion with the council, then go to the bank to arrange a mortgage.'

'Won't they want to know how I'm proposing to pay for it without a job?'

'Ah, but you *do* have a job,' Dale grinned. 'As of this morning, you're the official PA of a Black Swan director. *Me*,' he elaborated when she gave him a questioning look. 'You're on the payroll already, and my dad's having the paperwork drawn up so you can show the council and the bank proof of your salary.'

'Wow, you've really thought about this, haven't you?' Cheryl said. 'But don't you think you should have talked it over with me before you started making plans with your dad?'

'It was his idea,' Dale said. 'He mentioned it on the phone when I was in London, so I didn't have a chance to tell you. I didn't think you'd mind, because it seems like a waste to hand it back to the council when we've got people who need it. And it's an investment, so it benefits everyone.'

'I suppose it does,' Cheryl agreed, warming to the idea of a young woman, or maybe even two, being able to enjoy her lovely little house after a hard day caring for the elderly patients in Alfie's care homes. 'So when do I get my first pay cheque?' she asked.

'You're marrying your boss; what more do you want?' Dale laughed.

Later that night, a few hours after Dale had gone home – under orders from his mother, who had, apparently, extended the no-sharing-a-bed-until-they-were-married rule to Cheryl's house as well as her own; Cheryl woke from the sleep she had fallen into after their passionate lovemaking session. Her skin was still tingling from his touch, and her thighs were aching as she climbed out of bed to use the toilet.

Her sleep-fogged mind guided her in the direction of the en suite at Dale's house, and she was amused when she almost walked straight into the wall after pulling her dressing gown on. She had lived in this house for ten years and could walk around blindfolded without stubbing her toe or banging into anything, yet one short week in Sonia and Alfie's grand house had made it feel tiny, almost like a doll's house. She would genuinely miss it when she moved out, because she had spent her entire adult life there, and she would love to know that the next tenant appreciated it as much as she had; which was why the idea of Dale and his dad buying it to house one of their employees appealed to her. She'd been a bit worried that it might not actually be legal to use somebody else's money to buy it, but as Dale had pointed out, she could have taken out a loan for all the council knew; and he'd assured her that they would run everything past their solicitors before they moved ahead with it, so she was determined not to worry about it.

In the bathroom, washing her hands after using the toilet, she noticed the security light come on in her backyard. Concerned when a vision of Sharon holding the bag containing Cyril's body flashed into her mind, she jogged down the stairs to look out through the kitchen window in case it was a fox. She knew it was natural for animals to forage for food, but she couldn't bear the idea of Bob's boy being ripped to pieces if Sharon had buried him out there.

With the kitchen light off, she peered out through the glass and scanned both her own and Bob's yards. There didn't seem to be anyone out there and she was about to go back to bed when the security light went out, but hesitated when she caught a shadowy figure flitting past in the corner of her eye. Scared that it might be someone looking for a house to burgle, she shoved her hand into the pocket of her dressing gown to grab her phone, but realised that she had left it on the bedside table.

She noticed a faint glow in the alleyway and, seconds later, she heard her gate creaking open and a narrow torch beam illuminated the concrete slabs.

'Agata, get out here!' a voice hissed. 'I know you're round here somewhere, and I *will* find you. And when I do...'

The security light came on again as the torch-holder neared the house, and Cheryl saw that it was the older woman she had seen going in and out of Edna's house with the younger ones. Much closer now, her face clearly visible in the bright light, she looked even older than Cheryl had initially thought; and her eyes, encircled by thick black eyeliner, looked positively evil.

Curious to know what she was doing, Cheryl quickly unlocked the back door and stepped outside.

'Can I help you?'

'Oh, hello…' The woman looked like a deer caught in headlights. 'Sorry, I didn't realise anyone was in.'

'Well, I am, so what do you want?'

'I'm looking for one of my girls. I don't suppose you've seen anyone creeping around out here?'

'Only you,' Cheryl replied bluntly, folding her arms.

'I've seen you with Dale,' the woman said, giving her a sinister smile. 'So you probably know I'm looking after his dad's new girls?'

Cheryl nodded but didn't say anything. Dale had told her that his dad had specifically recruited girls from his own country to work in his care homes, both to give them the opportunity to earn good money to send home to their poor families, and also because they spoke the language of the elderly Polish people he catered to. He had housed them in Edna's place to keep them out of the clutches of rogue landlords, and she had assumed that this woman was there to look after them in some kind of housekeeper capacity, like Rosa. But the nasty way she'd been talking to whomever she was looking for when she came into the yard hadn't sounded very nurturing to Cheryl.

'I'm Dorothy.' The woman held out her hand but quickly dropped it again when Cheryl didn't move. 'My girls don't speak much English and some of them are quite immature,' she went

on. 'I'm doing my best to keep them safe, but the one I'm looking for is a little unstable. She's quite gullible, and she tends to
make up stories to get sympathy, so I'm concerned she'll get
herself into a dangerous situation if she gets picked up by the
wrong kind of person. D'you know what I mean?'

Cheryl didn't have the faintest idea what she meant, and she
had no wish to stand there talking to this woman any longer,
so she said, 'If I see her, I'll send her your way. But right now,
I need to sleep, so if you don't mind...' She gestured towards
the gate.

Dorothy narrowed her eyes and quickly scanned the yard.
Then, nodding, she said, 'Sorry for disturbing you,' before
retreating into the alleyway.

Cheryl closed the gate behind her and pushed the bolts into
place. She listened until the footsteps in the alley had faded,
then turned and headed back to the house. Almost at the door,
she heard a muffled cough and spun round. It sounded like
it had come from the tiny shed at the rear of her yard, and
she approached it cautiously and slowly opened the door; more
scared of the spiders that were probably living in the unused
space than of the girl she suspected was hiding in there.

'Hello?' Cheryl whispered. 'Can you hear me?'

No answer came, but she could hear someone breathing heavily, and as her eyes slowly adjusted to the darkness she picked
out a pale face in the corner. It was definitely the girl the woman
had been looking for, but her figure was so slight, she could
easily have been a child.

Conscious of what Dorothy had said about the girl's mental
state, Cheryl squatted down so she was on the same level, and
said, 'Don't be scared, I'm not going to hurt you. I just want to
make sure you're all right?'

The girl didn't answer, but Cheryl could see the fear in her eyes.

'Are you hurt?' she asked. 'Do you need me to get help for you?'

The girl's eyes widened, and she shook her head and seemed to draw even further back into the shadows.

'It's OK,' Cheryl said, holding out her hand to show that she wasn't a threat.

It was icy cold in there and Cheryl was already shivering, despite her dressing gown, so she could only imagine how cold the girl must be, since she appeared to only be wearing a nightdress.

'Look, you can't stay out here,' she said, speaking slowly, because she wasn't sure if the girl could understand her. 'Come inside and get a hot drink?' She gestured towards the house and mimed lifting a cup to her lips.

'She... she will find,' the girl whimpered. 'Please no tell her I am here, miss.'

'She's gone,' Cheryl said. 'Come...' She held out her hand. 'You'll be safe, I promise.'

The girl's eyes searched her face for a moment, and then she slowly rose to her feet. She was shaking from head to toe, so Cheryl quickly took off her dressing gown and placed it around her shoulders before leading her out of the shed and into the house, closing and locking the door behind them. She led her into the living room, switched on the table lamp and gestured for her to sit down.

'I'm Cheryl,' she said when the girl perched, as stiff as a rod, on the sofa. 'What's your name?'

'Agata,' the girl murmured, looking around nervously.

'Wait there,' Cheryl said. 'I'll get you that drink, and then we'll talk. OK?'

Glad when Agata nodded, because she'd been afraid the girl might bolt as soon as her back was turned, Cheryl went to the kitchen and switched the kettle on before nipping upstairs to get a cardigan and her phone.

When she carried the drinks back to the living room a couple of minutes later, Agata was sitting exactly where she'd left her.

'It's hot chocolate,' she said, handing a cup to her before taking as seat at the other end of the sofa.

'Thank you,' Agata said quietly, her hands still shaking as she gripped the cup.

'Do you want to tell me what happened?' Cheryl asked. 'That woman, Dorothy, who was looking for you, did she do something to scare you?'

Agata dipped her gaze, and Cheryl saw her knuckles whiten as she tightened her grip on the cup.

'Did she hurt you?' she probed.

Agata's chin wobbled. Then, so quietly that Cheryl almost couldn't hear her, she said, 'She bring man.'

'A man?' Cheryl repeated, wondering if she was referring to one of Alfie's workmen. 'A Polish man?'

'No, he is English,' Agata murmured, a tear trickling slowly down her cheek as she spoke. 'She... she make me go wait for him in room under house, but I climb from window and run. I hear Dorothy come look for me, so I hide.'

'What would she have done if she'd found you?' Cheryl asked, already guessing what the answer would be.

'She will beat me,' Agata said, swiping at the tears that were flowing freely now. 'I am sorry, I should not be tell you.'

'Yes you *should*,' Cheryl said gently. 'I can help you.'

'I have seen you and I think you are kind woman,' Agata said. 'But Dorothy is not like you. She is not good in here.' She placed her hand on her chest.

'Tell me what's been happening,' Cheryl urged.

Agata shook her head and clammed up, and Cheryl guessed that whatever was going on, the girl was seriously scared of the repercussions of talking about it. Unwilling to give up, Cheryl gently probed, asking specific questions to see what Agata's response would be. Gradually, she began to form a picture – and it wasn't a pretty one.

It seemed that, far from being the house-mother she'd made herself out to be, Dorothy ruled the house like a tyrant; forcing the girls to stay in their rooms when they weren't working, and punishing them if they didn't obey her every command. Also, it appeared that none of the girls had received any money yet, despite the fact that they had all worked every single day since arriving in the country, because Dorothy claimed their money was being used to house and feed them, and also to pay Alfie back for the cost of bringing them over. Agata also mentioned that Dorothy had recently started to bring men in, and she had sent Agata to wait for him in a 'room under the house' in which there was only a bed, which Cheryl presumed must be the cellar.

Agata had clammed up again after letting that last bit slip, and Cheryl could only imagine what would have taken place if the girl hadn't escaped. It sounded like a pretty desperate situation, and she was convinced that Dale and Alfie didn't know about any of it, because she had lived with them and knew they would *never* allow their staff to be treated so badly. She was so angry, she wanted to call the police, but she had only managed to elicit little bits of Agata's story, so she doubted the police would fare any better – if Agata even agreed to speak to them in the first place. So, instead, she decided to call Dale and get him to deal with it.

Sensing that Agata might get scared again if she told her that she was calling Dale in, Cheryl offered her another drink. In the kitchen, with the door closed, she rang Dale as she waited for the kettle to boil. His phone went straight to voicemail, so she left him a whispered message after the beep; asking him to come over as soon as he could, because she had one of his dad's girls there; and to please not speak to Dorothy until he got here and heard what she had to say.

Chapter 31

Dale was on the verge of falling asleep when Cheryl's message came through, and he muttered, 'Shit!' and jumped out of bed after listening to it. He tried to call her back, but his calls went unanswered, so he went to his parents' room and tapped on their door.

'Dad? Are you awake? We've got a problem at the new house.'

'What's going on?' Alfie yanked the door open and blinked at him.

'Cheryl just sent me this,' Dale said, pressing play so his father could hear the voice-note.

Sonia came onto the landing in time to hear most of it. Frowning, she told Dale to call Cheryl back and find out exactly what was going on.

'I've tried, but she's not answering,' he said.

'Then go over there,' she ordered. 'This could be serious. And *you* need to speak to Dorothy,' she added to Alfie. 'I told you that bitch couldn't be trusted.'

'She's Marcin's widow; I had to give her a chance,' Alfie muttered.

'Well, this is where your bleeding heart got you,' Sonia berated him. Then, turning to Dale, she pushed him towards his room, saying, 'Hurry up and go. We need to know what's going on.'

'I'll call you as soon as I've spoken to her,' Dale said, rushing back to his room to get dressed.

Dorothy was standing by the gate sucking on a cigarette when Dale's car pulled up. She had searched the area to no avail for Agata, and had finally called Alfie when it became obvious that she wasn't going to find her. He had been mad at her for losing one of his girls, and she'd heard his wife in the background, screeching at him to sack her. Fortunately, he was more level-headed than his fiery wife, and he'd told her that he would speak to her in the morning, which would give her the time she needed to formulate her story.

Alfie had also told her that Dale was on his way over, but she hadn't expected him to get here so fast. Nervous, because she didn't know if his girlfriend might have spoken to him to complain about her trespassing in her backyard, she opened her mouth to tell him her side of the story as he climbed out of the car, but he stopped her before she could speak and ordered her to go inside, telling her that he would come over to talk to her in a minute.

Frowning when he strode over the road, Dorothy guessed that his girlfriend *had* reported her, and she muttered a curse under her breath as she went back into the house.

Agata almost jumped out of her skin when the doorbell rang.

'Is her,' she whispered. 'She find me.'

'It's not her,' Cheryl reassured her. 'It's my fiancé,' she said, pointing to the ring on her finger in case the girl didn't understand the word. 'He's here to help, so stay here while I talk to him. OK?'

Agata looked like she wanted to throw up, and Cheryl gently touched her shoulder and told her that everything was going to be all right before heading out into the hall, pulling the door shut behind her.

After checking the spyhole to make sure it was Dale, and that he was alone, she opened the door to let him in.

'Thanks for coming so fast,' she said quietly, leading him to the kitchen.

'What's going on?' he asked. 'You didn't say much in your message.'

'After you left earlier, I fell asleep, but I woke up needing the loo,' she told him. 'The back security light came on while I was in there, and I was worried that Sharon might have forgotten to take Cyril's body home and that a fox was trying to get at him, so I came downstairs to chase it off.'

'*What?*' Dale looked like he had no clue what she was talking about.

Remembering that she hadn't told him the story of Sharon finding Cyril in the bin, because he'd taken her by surprise when he'd turned up much earlier than expected to take her to his parents' house that morning, she said, 'I'll tell you another time. Anyway, while I was looking out through the kitchen window, I caught that Dorothy woman sneaking into my yard, and I heard her threatening the girl.'

'Threatening her how?' Dale's frown deepened.

'She was basically telling her that she'd better come out of wherever she was hiding, or else,' Cheryl said, unable to recall the woman's actual words. 'I went out to ask what she was doing, and she said one of her girls had gone missing and she was worried about her because she's immature and could be in danger if the wrong person got hold of her.'

'Sounds about right,' Dale said. 'They are very young. That's why my dad moved Dorothy in with them: to keep them safe while they get used to living in England.'

'Well, it doesn't sound like she's keeping them very safe to me,' Cheryl huffed. 'I found the girl hiding in my shed after I sent Dorothy packing, and she's absolutely terrified of her.'

'Why, what's she told you?'

'I've only managed to get little bits out of her, but it sounds like Dorothy is quite cruel to them,' Cheryl said. 'And did you know that none of them have been paid yet, because *she* keeps it all to cover their living expenses? And that's not even the worst of it,' she went on indignantly. 'Dorothy has been bringing men to the house and forcing the girls to sleep with them in the cellar.'

'She said that?'

'I wasn't easy to understand her, because she lapses into Polish quite a lot, but that's what I took from it, yeah. She said there's a bed in the room under the house, and Dorothy chooses a girl to go down there with the man. Agata was chosen tonight, but she climbed out of a window and ran away.'

'Where is she now?'

'In the front room. But be gentle; she's really scared.'

'Don't worry, I just want to talk to her,' Dale said.

Cheryl led him to the living room and went in ahead of him. 'Agata, this is Dale. He's your boss's son and he's going to help you, so just tell him everything you told me.'

Agata shrank back at the sight of him, but Dale gave her a reassuring smile and took a seat on the chair facing the sofa. He asked Cheryl to give them a minute, so she went out into the hall and pulled the door to behind her. Listening for a moment and hearing Dale speak softly to the girl in Polish, she decided she had done the right thing by calling him instead of the police, and she made her way to the kitchen to wait for him to finish.

It was a good fifteen minutes before Dale came out of the living room, and Cheryl asked if everything was all right when she saw that he was frowning.

'I'm not sure,' he said. 'Talking to her is like trying to get blood out of a stone, but something isn't quite adding up to me about the cellar thing. You said she told you there was nothing but a bed in there?'

'Yeah, that's right. And Dorothy chooses one of them to go down there with the man.'

'Well, last time I looked, the cellar was crammed with boxes from the furniture that was delivered the day they moved in. And the decorating stuff was down there as well.'

'Dorothy must have cleared it out.'

'To be honest, I don't think she'd be physically capable of moving it at her age. There's some pretty heavy shit down there.'

'So what are you saying?' Cheryl frowned. 'You think Agata's lying?'

'No, I'm not saying that. But I can't blindly believe her without talking to Dorothy as well. She's worked for my dad for a long time, and she was married to one of his closest friends from back home, so I need to be sure of the facts before I accuse her of something this serious.'

'She's obviously not going to admit it,' Cheryl said. 'And don't forget I heard her threatening the girl.'

'I'll take a look in the cellar and see for myself,' Dale said. 'And, believe me, if there *is* a bed in there, Dorothy's going to get what's coming to her. In fact, why don't you come with me? That way, you can back me up if I find something and Dorothy tries to deny it.'

'What about Agata?'

'She'll be safe here till we get back,' Dale said. 'Lock the doors so no one can get in.'

Nodding, Cheryl pocketed the back door key and followed him out into the hall. She popped her head around the living-room door and told Agata she would be back in a minute, then followed Dale outside, double locking the front door behind her.

When Dale and Cheryl entered the house across the road, Dorothy was sitting on the small sofa in the former living room, which was now her room; sucking on a cigarette.

'Fuck's sake, Dot,' Dale complained, wafting the cloud of smoke that was hanging in front of his face with his hand. 'I thought my dad told you not to do that in here. It's only just been decorated.'

'Sorry, but I'm really stressed out,' Dorothy apologised, stubbing the cigarette out in an ashtray on the coffee table.

'This is Cheryl,' Dale said, gesturing to where Cheryl was standing in the hallway.

'We've met,' Dorothy said, standing up and giving Cheryl a weary smile. 'Sorry if I spooked you earlier, love. It's been an absolute nightmare over here tonight, and I realise I might have come across a bit harsh, like. But I was worried about the girl.'

Cheryl didn't reply, but Dale filled the gap, saying, 'We need to see the cellar.'

'Of course,' Dorothy replied, taking a bunch of keys out of a drawer and walking out into the hallway.

She stopped at a door that was concealed behind the staircase and fiddled with the keys until she found the right one. Pulling the door open after unlocking it, she switched the light on, then stepped back to let Dale and Cheryl get past.

Cheryl followed Dale down a narrow set of wooden steps. There was another doorway at the bottom, but this one had no door so they were able to see straight into the cellar.

'Ah…' Dale said. 'I thought so.'

'I don't understand,' Cheryl murmured, taking in the mess of ladders and decorating equipment stacked in one corner of the small space, and the boxes haphazardly packed, floor to almost ceiling, in the rest. 'She said there was nothing but a bed down here.'

'I did say something didn't feel right about it,' Dale sighed. 'That's why I needed to see it for myself, because I knew there was no way Dorothy could have cleared it out, then moved it all back in here in the time it took you to call me tonight. Plus, if it had been moved tonight, where did *they* come from?'

Cheryl followed his finger when he pointed something out, and saw several large cobwebs strung between the walls and the boxes. Realising that they couldn't possibly have been spun in the last hour, she glanced guiltily back up the stairs to where Dorothy was waiting for them by the top. The woman had looked sinister in the backyard, and she'd sounded pretty nasty, too; but she now looked old and frail, and there was no way she could have lugged all this stuff inside in the forty minutes or so it had taken Dale to drive here.

'Thanks for that, Dot,' Dale said when he and Cheryl climbed back up the steps.

'No problem,' she said, re-locking the door. 'But can I ask what you were looking for? If you've lost something, I can keep an eye out for it.'

'It's OK, I just needed to check everything was still in there,' Dale said.

'I wish it wasn't,' Dorothy said, rolling her eyes. 'Your lads told me they were going to clear it out, and I'm worried it might start attracting rats if it's left much longer. There's a funny smell, and I'm sure some of them might have dropped food in there.'

'Don't worry, I'll sort it,' Dale promised.

'Thank you,' Dorothy said. Then, concern in her eyes, she asked, 'What are we going to do about Agata?'

'She's safe for now,' Dale assured her. 'But she said some stuff that needed looking into; that's why I'm here.'

'What kind of stuff?' Dorothy asked. 'Only I was telling your friend here that she's got a habit of making up stories, and it's been causing a lot of trouble between the girls. I was going to talk to your dad about her, because I actually think she might have something wrong with her. She's hard work, and I'll admit I get angry and end up shouting at her sometimes, but it's not easy to keep your cool when you're faced with this nonsense day in, day out. And she's causing problems at the home, as well. Ray told me some of the residents have reported money going missing when she's been there on her own.'

Cheryl's head was spinning as she listened to the old woman reel off the problems she'd been having with Agata. It was the complete opposite of what the girl had said, and she was struggling to accept that she had so easily swallowed what might have been a complete pack of lies. One thing was indisputable: there was no bed in that cellar. And those well-established cobwebs proved that the boxes had not been put there to cover up what Agata claimed had been happening down there.

'She's a nice enough girl, but she's been acting strange since day one,' Dorothy continued, following as Dale ushered Cheryl towards the front door. 'I know they're all young and missing their parents, and God knows I've done my best to try to be a substitute mother to them all; but there's only so much I can do.'

'I'll talk to my dad,' Dale promised, stepping outside. 'And I'll let you know what we decide before I leave.'

'Thanks,' Dorothy murmured, giving them a sad smile as she closed the front door.

'What happens now?' Cheryl asked as they walked back to her house.

'If Dorothy's right, it sounds like the girl's got mental issues, so I'm going to get my dad to send his GP over,' Dale said. 'I'll take her over there and stay with her till he gets here.'

'You can bring him here, if it's easier,' Cheryl offered, sad to think that Agata was struggling so badly that she needed the intervention of a doctor, when all she'd wanted to do was come to England and work to help out her family.

Cheryl sat with Agata while Dale called his father. They had decided it would be best not to forewarn the girl in case she tried to run again, so Agata was visibly shaken when the doctor arrived twenty minutes later and told her who he was. Fortunately, he was Polish, which meant he could properly communicate with her; and Cheryl, who had retired to the kitchen again, was surprised to hear Agata speaking more freely to him than she had to Dale.

When Dale and the doctor came out into the hallway after a while and had a hushed conversation, Cheryl joined them and asked what was going on.

'He reckons she's displaying symptoms of extreme paranoid delusions,' Dale said, as the doctor walked outside with his phone to his ear.

'What does that mean?'

'That she's imagining stuff and thinks we're all trying to hurt her,' Dale sighed. 'She's getting agitated and he said she's at high risk of self-harming, so he's arranging to get her admitted to a psych ward where she can be properly assessed, then he's going to sedate her.'

Unable to watch when the doctor came back carrying a briefcase that she guessed contained his medical gear, Cheryl went back to the kitchen. But even with the door closed, she could hear the terror in Agata's voice. When the girl suddenly started screaming, it was one of the most harrowing sounds Cheryl had ever heard, and she was sobbing when Dale came in after everything went quiet a few minutes later.

'I'm sorry you had to hear that,' he said, putting his arms around her and stroking her hair. 'But she'll be OK now, I promise.'

'It's so sad,' Cheryl cried. 'I know it was all lies, but I honestly think she believed it was true.'

'The doc says that's typical of this kind of psychotic episode. But I've spoken to my dad and he's going to pay for her treatment, so she'll be fine soon, I'm sure.'

'What'll happen to her when she's better?' Cheryl asked, blowing her nose on a piece of kitchen roll.

'We're going to send her home,' Dale said. 'This didn't come out of nowhere, and her family have probably been dealing with it for years, so they'll be better equipped to look after her than us. We'll send money over so they can afford whatever medication she needs in the future.'

'That's so kind,' Cheryl murmured.

'We look after our own,' said Dale. 'Anyway, she's quietened down now, so I'm going to carry her out to the doc's car, then I'm going to follow them over to the unit to sign the paperwork.'

Cheryl nodded, but her heart was breaking for Agata, and she had to blink away a fresh set of tears when she walked into the living room behind Dale and saw the unconscious girl curled into the foetal position on her sofa. She'd met many liars in her life, Chris being the absolute king of them all; but she had never witnessed anybody have an actual mental breakdown before, during which their sense of reality was so warped they became convinced that their delusions were true and people really wanted to harm them. It was so sad, and Cheryl could only imagine how terrifying it must have been for Agata.

Watching from her doorstep as Dale and the doctor drove

away a short time later, Cheryl felt guilty when she spotted
Dorothy watching through her window across the road. It was
scary to think how much trouble the woman could have got
into tonight, based purely on the ramblings of a girl who was
suffering severe delusions. Now Dorothy had explained what
had been going on in that house, Cheryl totally got why she'd
sounded so pissed off when she came into the yard. But at least
Agata was going to get the help she needed now, thanks to Dale
and Alfie, so it had all worked out for the best.

Chapter 32

Cheryl didn't get much sleep after Dale and the others had left, because she kept hearing Agata's pitiful screams and seeing the terror in her eyes. Determined not to dwell on it when daylight began to seep through the curtains, she took a shower and got dressed, then walked around the house opening all the curtains and windows to let the fresh air in – and the traumatic memories out.

About to make herself a cup of tea, she remembered she had no milk and pulled her coat on to nip to the shop around the corner. As she stepped outside, she saw Sharon climbing out of her car, and called, 'Morning.'

'Hey, you're back.' Sharon smiled. 'How are the wedding plans coming on?'

'Great. We've pretty much got everything sorted now. Only a few minor things left, but we'll probably tackle them nearer the day.'

'Exciting times. But you'd better make the most of it, 'cos it's all downhill after the actual wedding,' Sharon teased.

'Thanks,' Cheryl laughed. 'Way to cheer a girl up after a hard night.'

'Why, what happened?' Sharon asked.

'I honestly wouldn't know where to begin,' Cheryl sighed. 'But never mind me, how's Bob?'

'He's doing OK. Why don't you come and see for yourself?'

'What about Fiona?'

'She hasn't been here for the past two days, so I'd say you're safe.'

'Have you got a key?' Cheryl asked. 'I used to, but she changed the locks.'

Sharon rolled her eyes, and said, 'She tried to stop me getting one, but the agency told her they'd stop me coming if she didn't co-operate, so she had no choice. Anyway, give me a sec to check she didn't come back last night, then come in. I'm sure it'll cheer Bob up no end.'

Excited by the thought of seeing her old friend again, even if only briefly, Cheryl watched as Sharon let herself into the house. A few seconds later, she popped her head out again, and said, 'All clear.'

Bob was still in bed when Sharon tapped on his bedroom door, but he was wide awake and sitting up, and he beamed at her when she walked in.

'Hello, love.'

'Morning,' she trilled. 'You've got a visitor.'

'Who's that then?' he grunted. 'Undertaker come to measure me up, has he?

'You're a morbid old bugger, you,' Cheryl mock-chided from the doorway.

Bob snapped his head round at the sound of her voice, and she felt the sting of tears in her eyes when she saw the shock and delight in his.

'Cheryl,' he said, his hands shaking on the end of his skin-and-bone arms as he reached out to her.

'How are you, love?' she asked, smiling as she walked over to the bed. 'I haven't half missed you.'

'I've missed you, too,' he said, clutching her hands tightly. 'Why did you stop coming? I didn't upset you, did I?'

Still fighting the tears, Cheryl forced herself to maintain the smile and shook her head as she perched on the edge of the bed. 'Course you didn't, you daft sod. How could you ever upset me? You've been like a dad to me.'

'Don't let the other one hear you saying that, or she'll get jealous,' Bob whispered. 'Thinks I'm pretty special, she does,' he went on, his eyes twinkling as he winked at Sharon over her shoulder. 'Wishes I were twenty years younger.'

'Try forty,' Sharon snorted, busying herself with getting his clothes ready for the day.

'Eeee, it's good to see you,' Bob said, his attention back on Cheryl. 'Hasn't been the same round here without you and Cyril.'

Cheryl flashed a glance at Sharon and guessed that she hadn't told Bob what had happened when she pressed a finger to her lips.

'Someone left the back door open and he slipped out,' Bob went on. 'Haven't seen him since, but Sharon reckons he'll have got lost and been taken in by a nice family, don't you, love?'

'Absolutely,' said Sharon. 'Who wouldn't want a lovely boy like him?'

'I'll keep an eye out for him,' Cheryl said.

'Thanks, love.' Bob squeezed her hands. 'Now, how's your Chris?'

'He's fine,' Cheryl said, surreptitiously shaking her head at Sharon when the woman opened her mouth to tell him it was Dale not Chris.

'I see they've renovated Edna's place,' Bob said, abruptly changing the subject. 'Them girls are a funny lot, though, aren't they? Always scuttling in and out with their heads down. What's that all about?'

'No idea,' Cheryl said, reluctant to even think about that house right then.

'Her who's in charge is a rum old bag, though, isn't she?' Bob continued. 'Poor Edna would turn in her grave if she saw the blokes she entertains in there of a night.'

'How would you know something like that?' Sharon asked, tutting at him.

'How d'you think?' he grinned, letting go of Cheryl's hand to take an ancient pair of opera glasses out of the drawer of his bedside table.

'Dear Lord, I'm taking care of a peeping Tom,' Sharon muttered, shaking her head in despair.

'Behave!' Bob protested. 'There's nowt mucky about wanting to see what's going on in the outside world. And I don't even get to do that half the time, 'cos you keep shutting me curtains.'

'Well, pardon me, I'm sure,' Sharon huffed, flashing Cheryl an amused look.

Cheryl didn't return it; she was too busy thinking about what Bob had said about men going into the house at night.

'I just hope the new owners found the trapdoor before she moved in,' Bob went on. ''Cos she looks like the type who'd have away with it all, that one.'

'Trapdoor?' Cheryl repeated. 'I thought there was a proper door to the cellar?'

'There is, to the main one,' said Bob. 'But Edna and her hubby needed somewhere to stash their valuables, so they bricked half of it off and hid the trapdoor to the smaller one under the carpet in the back room. I only know about it 'cos Edna called me over there to help her get it open after her old man died. She needed some paperwork he'd left in there; made me swear on me life I'd never tell a soul.'

'And now you've told *us*,' Sharon pointed out. 'Remind me never to tell you any of my secrets.'

'Edna's long gone, love,' Bob sighed. 'And I reckon I'll be joining her soon enough, so I'll make me peace with her when I see her.'

'Rubbish, you're going nowhere,' Sharon said, smiling as she walked over to the bed. 'Ready to get up?'

'Aye,' he said, patting Cheryl's hand. 'And you'll be heading off to work, I suppose?'

'Not today,' Cheryl said, standing up. 'But I've got a few things I need to take care of, so I'll get out of your way.'

'You'll come and see me again, won't you?'

'Of course,' she promised, leaning down to kiss his stubbly cheek.

'Bye, love. And say hello to Chris for me.'

'Will do,' Cheryl said, nodding goodbye to Sharon before walking out and down the stairs.

Her head was reeling again, and she struggled to put her thoughts in order as she walked to the shop to get the milk she needed. When she had brought Agata in from the shed last night, she had genuinely believed her story, and had been shocked to find out that the girl had made it all up after having some kind of breakdown. But now Bob had confirmed that Dorothy *did* have men going in there at night, and – more importantly – had told her there were *two* cellars, she wondered if Agata had been telling the truth after all. If so, and Dorothy had found the trapdoor to get into the second cellar and had been using it as Agata had described, then she was the liar, and poor Agata had been sedated and sectioned for absolutely nothing.

Cheryl doubted that Dale and his parents knew about the other cellar, or he would have asked to see it when they went over there to check Agata's story about there being nothing but a bed in there. She knew they trusted the woman and would be disappointed to hear that she had been lying to them, but they didn't only have Agata's word to go on now, they also had Bob's; so even if they didn't want to believe it, they could at least talk to the other girls to see if they corroborated Agata's story.

Chapter 33

Sharon was climbing into her car when Cheryl got home from the shops, but she jumped back out when she spotted her, and rushed over with a slip of paper in her hand.

'I meant to give you this earlier,' she said. 'But you left before I had the chance.'

'What is it?' Cheryl asked.

'Someone called Anna called round at yours while you were away,' Sharon told her. 'She said she's been trying to ring you but couldn't get through. I told her you'd lost your phone, but I didn't want to give out your number without asking you first, so she gave me hers instead. I actually meant to text it to you, but I've got a memory like a sieve.'

'Thanks,' Cheryl said, pocketing the paper.

'She seemed a bit edgy,' Sharon went on. 'Asked me to make sure you were alone when I gave it to you.'

'We haven't been talking for a while,' Cheryl said, her mind still on Dale and what he might do when she told him what she'd learned.

'Probably wants to make friends, eh?' Sharon smiled. 'Anyway, best get off before my next lady thinks I've forgotten about her.'

'Thanks again for sneaking me in to see Bob,' Cheryl said.

'Any time,' Sharon replied, walking back to her car.

In the house, Cheryl made a cup of tea and then rang Dale. He answered quickly, and she smiled when he purred, 'Hello, beautiful. You've caught me between meetings.'

'I won't keep you long,' she said. 'I just needed to tell you something I've heard about that Dorothy woman.'

'Oh, yeah?'

Cheryl relayed what Bob had told her about seeing men going into the house at night and about the second cellar.

'Interesting,' Dale murmured when she'd finished.

'*Interesting?*' she repeated. 'It's more than interesting; it proves Agata was telling the truth.'

'Not necessarily,' Dale said. 'She's got mental issues, don't forget.'

'Yeah, probably caused by being forced to sleep with men and being treated like a slave and having her wages stolen,' Cheryl blurted out. 'You need to look into this and find out what's going on, 'cos you see stuff like this on the news all the time: young girls being forced into prostitution right under their neighbours' noses. I've a mind to go over there myself and ask her what the hell she thinks she's playing at.'

'Do *not* go over there,' Dale barked.

'*Excuse* me?' Cheryl spluttered, taken aback by the sharpness of his tone.

'Sorry, didn't mean to snap,' he apologised. 'I just don't want you getting involved if there is something going on. What else did the old man tell you?'

'Nothing. Only what I told you.'

'And did you say anything to him about what happened last night?'

'No, I was only in there a few minutes.'

'OK, let's keep this to ourselves,' Dale said. 'My dad will

deal with it, and we don't need the hassle of people round there gossiping.'

'Of course,' Cheryl agreed, all too aware that her neighbours would do exactly that if they got the slightest whiff of any scandals at Edna's place.

'Right, I need to get off, so I'll see you later,' Dale said. 'And put something sexy on,' he added quietly. 'I might have been banned from staying over, but I'm sure as hell not going without sex till the wedding.'

'I don't own anything sexy,' Cheryl laughed. 'But even if I did, it probably wouldn't fit me anymore.'

'Well, we'll have to go shopping and fix that then, won't we?' Dale chuckled. 'Catch you later.'

'Bye,' Cheryl said, smiling as she cut the call.

Glad that he'd taken her seriously and had promised to get his dad to look into the Dorothy issue, Cheryl pulled Anna's number out of her pocket and typed it into her phone.

'Hi, it's me,' she said when Anna answered after several rings.

'Who's me?' Anna asked warily.

'Cheryl,' she said, remembering that her name wouldn't have come up on Anna's screen since she was calling from a new number. 'Bob's carer gave me your note.'

'Took her long enough,' Anna grumbled. 'I thought you were ignoring me.'

'I've been away, so this is the first time I've seen her in a while,' Cheryl explained. 'And you're the one who fell out with me, don't forget.'

'I know, but I'm over all that now.'

'Is that why you came round?' Cheryl asked hopefully. 'To make friends?'

'No, I came to warn you,' Anna said. Then, wary again, she asked, 'Are you on your own?'

'Yeah, Dale's working,' Cheryl said, frowning when she re-membered that Anna had acted weird about him when she'd seen her outside the wedding dress boutique. 'When I saw you last week, you started telling me something, but then stopped when Sonia came out.'

'I didn't want to discuss it in front of her, 'cos I knew it'd get straight back to him,' Anna replied. 'And like I said then, if I tell you, you've got to promise you won't tell him it came from me.'

'What's going on?' Cheryl asked, not liking the sound of this. 'You know I'm pregnant and we're getting married in a few weeks, so if this is about Dale, just tell me.'

'Promise first.'

'Fine, I promise.'

'And he's definitely not there?'

'*Anna!*'

'Sorry, but I need to be sure,' Anna said. 'And when you hear what I've got to say, I hope you don't blame me, because I had no idea till I woke up.'

Cheryl's mouth had started to go dry and her stomach was churning. 'No idea about what?' she asked, already dreading the answer.

Anna didn't speak for a few seconds. Then, quietly, she said, 'I think I slept with him.'

Cheryl had been standing by the window as they talked, but her legs started shaking so violently at hearing those words, she slumped down on the sofa.

'What do you mean, you *think* you slept with him?' she demanded. 'You either did or you didn't.'

'I'm pretty sure we did, 'cos I found a used condom in my bin and I hadn't had anyone round in a while before that,' Anna replied guiltily. 'But, like I said, I didn't even know he was there until I woke up. And I don't think he realised who I was until I mentioned you, then he went off on one.'

Cheryl's head was spinning, and she couldn't make sense of what she was hearing.

'Start at the beginning,' she ordered. 'And don't leave anything out. I want to know *everything*.'

By the time Anna had finished her story, all thoughts of Agata and the goings-on across the road were erased from Cheryl's mind, and her heart was pounding so hard, she thought it might explode right out of her chest. The party at Greta's place had, it transpired, been on the same night that she and Dale had got engaged. Greta had met some men in a club and had invited them back to her place because they had a load of coke and booze. One of them had fancied Greta and given her his number, hoping to hook up with her in the future. His name was Tommy – the same name as the mate whose sofa Dale had told Cheryl he'd slept on that night.

Anna claimed she had been off her head and couldn't re-member a thing after the first few lines and shots. She didn't recall seeing Dale before she zonked out, but she vividly remem-bered waking up next to him the following morning. She'd admitted she had been happy about it at first; considering it payback for Cheryl stealing him from her. But that had quickly changed when Dale realised who she was and pinned her to the bed with his hand around her throat, threatening to make her disappear if she told Cheryl or reported him to the police.

Cheryl didn't want to believe it, but Anna had described the tattoo of a black swan on Dale's thigh. The only way she could have known about that was if she'd seen it; and she could only have seen it if she had seen Dale without his trousers.

Her heart was broken, but she was also angry when she

remembered how Dale had turned up at hers earlier than arranged that morning, still wearing the same clothes, and had rushed her over to his parents' house. Now she knew where he'd really spent the night, she suspected he'd been in a hurry to get her out of there because he was scared that Anna, unable to reach her by phone because she didn't have her new number, might come over to tell her about it in person.

Cheryl's head was in bits as she went over and over everything Anna had told her. There was a chance, albeit small, that her friend had made the whole thing up to spite her, and that she had found out about his tattoo from one of his friends that night. With that in mind, she decided that she would speak to Dale and give him the chance to tell his side of the story before she made any firm decisions. Anna claimed she'd been so high she didn't remember actually having sex with him, and if he'd been in the same state and admitted as much, they might have something to work with. But even if he did admit it, she couldn't ignore that he had outright lied to her about sleeping at his friend's house; and if it was true that he'd threatened Anna to make her keep her mouth shut, that was another red flag. She had seen glimpses of his temper, but his outbursts never lasted long, so she hadn't been overly worried about it. But if he was hiding a darker side, his mask would eventually slip, as it had with Chris, and she didn't want to spend the rest of her life walking on eggshells waiting for him to erupt, because that wouldn't be good for her *or* the baby.

Chapter 34

It was almost 6 p.m. before Dale's car pulled up outside, and Cheryl's stomach flipped when she heard him slot his key into the front door. But it wasn't the usual flip of pleasure at the thought of seeing his handsome face and being held in his arms; it was a horrible, sickly feeling of apprehension.

'Hey.' He gave her a weary smile as he walked into the living room and slipped his jacket off. 'What a day. I must have done more miles in the last few hours than I've done all week. But I've hooked us two new investors, so it's all good.'

He paused when he realised she wasn't smiling and hadn't spoken, and tipped his head to one side.

'You OK?'

'I'm fine,' Cheryl said, breathing deeply and evenly in an effort to keep her emotions under control. 'Sit down. We need to talk.'

'Sounds ominous,' Dale murmured, still looking at her questioningly as he went to sit beside her.

'Not there,' she said. 'On the chair.'

'What's going on?' He frowned. 'You're acting weird. If this is because I'm late, I did try to get away earlier, but the investor made the meeting run over, so—'

'I'm not interested in your meetings,' Cheryl interrupted brusquely.

'So what is it then? It's not the baby, is it?'

'No, it's not the baby. Now will you please sit down?'

'For God's sake, Cheryl, what's going on?'

'Do you remember the night we got engaged?'

'Yeah, of course I do.' Dale gave a cautious smile as he perched on the chair. 'It was one of the best nights of my life.'

'Really?' Cheryl raised an eyebrow. 'And why's that?'

'Because you said yes to my proposal, obviously.'

'And your mates were happy about the engagement, were they? The ones you met up with for drinks after you dropped me off that night.'

'Yeah, they were made up for us.'

'And you went back to Tommy's place after you left the club and slept on his sofa?'

'I've already told you I did,' Dale said, giving her a questioning look. 'Why are you asking about it now?'

'Because I don't believe you,' Cheryl said bluntly.

Dale narrowed his eyes and stared at her. 'Has someone been talking shit about me? 'Cos I'm telling you now, whatever they've said, it's a lie. I was with Tommy all night, and I'll ring him so you can ask him yourself, if you want?'

'No thanks,' Cheryl said coolly as she slid the ring off her finger and placed it on the table in front of him. 'You've already told me everything I needed to know, so you can take that and leave.'

'Babe, what the fuck's going on?' Dale asked. 'At least tell me what I'm supposed to have done so I've got a chance to defend myself.'

'That *was* your chance, but you lied, so there's nothing else to say,' Cheryl said, standing up. 'Oh, and don't think Tommy's going to back you up, because he's already confirmed you were at the party.'

'What?' Dale looked confused. 'How have you spoken to Tommy? You don't even know him.'

'Dale, stop it,' Cheryl sighed. 'I know what you did and I gave you the chance to be honest about it, but you're obviously not going to be, so please just go.'

'No.' Dale shook his head and rose to his feet. 'I love you, and I'm not losing you because some stupid bitch is spreading lies about me.'

'I never mentioned a woman, but thanks for admitting that you *were* with one that night,' Cheryl said, folding her arms.

'I was not with a woman,' Dale replied adamantly. 'Not in the way you mean, anyway.'

'In what way *were* you with one, then?' Cheryl probed.

'OK, I did go to a party,' Dale sighed. 'But I was already pissed before we left the club, so I had no clue where the guys were taking me. I didn't tell you because I knew how bad it would look, but I swear nothing happened.'

'If you were that far gone, how would you know if anything happened?'

'I just do,' Dale insisted. Then, gazing at her, he said, 'Look I know where this has come from, and I totally get why you're mad at me, but don't you think she might be doing this to hurt you? You said it yourself, she was jealous when I chose you, so this would be the perfect payback.'

'I want to hear it from you,' Cheryl said. 'Did you or did you not spend the night with her?'

'That's not how I'd describe it,' Dale replied. 'Yes, I did wake up at her place, but I swear on my life nothing happened.'

'Swear on the baby's life,' Cheryl said, holding his gaze.

'What?' Dale drew his head back.

'You heard me. If you're telling the truth and nothing happened, swear on the baby's life.'

'OK, I swear.'

'On the *baby's* life,' Cheryl repeated slowly.

'This is fucked up,' Dale said, raking his fingers through his hair. 'I've admitted everything, so why can't you believe me about this?'

'You didn't admit it, I had to drag it out of you,' Cheryl said flatly. 'And the fact that you won't swear on the baby tells me you're still lying, so I'd like you to leave.'

'OK, I'll go and give you time to calm down,' Dale agreed. 'But this isn't over. We're getting married and having a baby, and that's more important than this bullshit.'

'We are *not* getting married,' Cheryl shot back. 'And I haven't decided what I'm doing about the baby yet.'

'What?' Dale's eyes darkened. 'You'd better not be saying what I think you're saying.'

The switch in his mood was chilling, and Cheryl quickly backtracked when she realised she'd gone too far.

'I'm not saying anything,' she murmured. 'I'm tired and upset, and I need time to think.'

'Well, think about *this*,' Dale said, his voice low and menacing as he walked towards her and stared down into her eyes. 'If anything happens to my baby, I'll make sure that you and that bitch regret it for the rest of your lives.'

'Dale, you're scaring me,' she croaked, unable to move when she felt her back hit the wall.

'I've been good to you,' he went on. 'And when you get your head straight and quit with this bullshit, I'll give you a better life than you could ever imagine. But if you *ever* threaten to hurt my kid again, it's game over.'

Too scared to respond, Cheryl could barely breathe as she waited to see what he was going to do next. Flinching when he stepped back and straightened his tie, she thought her legs were going to collapse beneath her when he turned and snatched his jacket off the back of the sofa and the ring off the table before walking out.

As she heard the front door close behind him, followed by the slam of his car door and the screech of rubber as he took off, she stumbled to the sofa, slumped down and placed her head between her knees to keep from throwing up. She had genuinely thought he was going to hit her, and she understood why Anna had been reluctant to tell her about him sleeping at her place if he'd threatened her in the same way.

But it wasn't only fear that was making Cheryl feel sick, she also felt guilty for intimating that she might be considering an abortion. For one split second, it *had* crossed her mind, but she should never have spoken the words out loud, and the tears streamed down her cheeks as she cradled her belly, and whispered, 'I'm so sorry.'

As he drove away from Cheryl's house, Dale's burst of anger died down and regret crept in. He wanted to turn the car around and go back to apologise, but he'd seen the fear in her eyes and doubted she'd let him in, so he rang his mother instead.

'Mum, I've fucked up,' he said when she answered.

'What have you done?' Sonia asked.

Dale told her what had happened, and she listened in silence until he reached the part about threatening Cheryl.

'You idiot!' she snapped. 'The wedding's only three weeks away. Do you know how much money we've spent, and how many people have already RSVP'd?'

'I'm sorry.'

'Never mind sorry. Get it sorted!'

'I can't, Mum. I really scared her, and I don't think she'll ever forgive me.'

Sonia was quiet for a moment. Then, taking control, as she always did when Alfie or one of the boys fucked up, she said, 'OK, I'll deal with it.'

'How?' Dale asked. 'She's not going to change her mind; I could see it in her eyes.'

'We'll see about that,' Sonia replied.

'That's not all,' Dale went on. 'She rang me earlier to tell me that someone told her there's two cellars at the new place and they've seen men going in there at night, so now she thinks Dorothy's running some kind of sex slave operation.'

'Shit!' Sonia muttered. 'I told your father that bloody house was going to bring nothing but trouble.'

'Well, he needs to sort it,' Dale said. 'The last thing we want is people thinking we're involved in dodgy shit.'

'Leave it with me,' Sonia said.

'Which bit?' Dale asked.

'All of it,' snapped Sonia. 'You've done enough damage for one night, so don't be going round to Cheryl's again until I've had a chance to talk to her.'

'OK,' Dale agreed, glad that she'd taken charge, because Cheryl was more likely to listen to her right now. 'Thanks, Mum.'

Sonia cut the call without responding to her son's thanks and walked out onto the patio, where Alfie was sitting in his favourite spot under the heaters, enjoying his first whisky and cigar of the night.

'I've got to go out,' she told him. 'Your son's done something stupid and I need to fix it.'

'Which one?' Alfie squinted at her through the smoke.

'Take a guess,' she muttered.

'What's he done now?' Alfie asked. 'He'd better not have fucked it up with that new investor.'

'It's Cheryl,' Sonia told him. 'She found out he slept with her mate on the night they got engaged, and now she's called things off and is threatening to get an abortion.'

'She's what?' Alfie scowled.

'Don't worry, I'll set her straight,' Sonia assured him. 'But we've got another mess that *you* need to deal with...'

Cheryl was still huddled on the sofa when the doorbell rang an hour after Dale had left. In no fit state to speak to anybody with her eyes swollen from crying, she ignored it and willed whoever it was to go away.

The bell rang again, followed by the sound of a key being inserted into the lock. Dale was the only person who had a key, and she leapt up and faced the door, unsure what kind of mood he would be in when he entered.

Almost fainting with relief when Sonia walked in, she said, 'How did you get my key?'

'Dale gave me a copy when he had your locks changed while you were in hospital,' Sonia said, dropping her handbag onto the table and looking round. 'Well, this is ... *cosy*.'

'I like it,' Cheryl replied defensively, folding her arms. 'And I'm not really in the mood to speak to anyone right now.'

'I'm not just anyone,' Sonia said, taking a seat on the sofa and patting the cushion beside her. 'Sit down and let's talk, woman to woman.'

'I don't mean you any disrespect, but I'm really tired,' Cheryl said, standing her ground. 'I'm going to make a cup of tea and go to bed, so—'

'Tea's not good for you at this time of night,' Sonia interrupted, giving her a disapproving look. 'I know you're upset, but pumping caffeine and tannins into your body isn't good for the baby.'

Irritated, because she'd had a gutful of being told what she should eat and drink while she was staying with Dale's family, Cheryl bit her tongue and reminded herself that Sonia had been good to her and none of this was her fault.

'Dale told me what happened,' Sonia went on. 'So how are we going to put this right?'

'We're not,' Cheryl muttered, perching on the other end of the sofa.

'He knows he messed up and he deeply regrets it,' Sonia said. 'But you gave him a scare, too, so you can't lay all the blame at his feet. You know how much family means to us, and the thought of you denying him access to his son – or *worse* – was bound to push him over the edge.'

'I know.' Cheryl guiltily dipped her gaze. 'I told him I didn't mean it, but he was really mad. I've never seen him like that before.'

'He's a man, and they react differently to threats than we do,' Sonia reasoned. 'They get fired up and fly off the handle, and that can be frightening for a woman. But, as I said, you have a part to play in this, so it's not all on him.'

'It's not just about the baby,' Cheryl said quietly. 'I don't know if he told you all of it, but he cheated on me.'

'That meant nothing.' Sonia flapped her hand dismissively. 'He doesn't even remember it.'

'Maybe not, but it still happened,' Cheryl said, astounded that Sonia was trying to brush his betrayal under the carpet as if it was something trivial.

'He's a man,' Sonia sighed. 'It's what they do.'

'So you'd be OK if Alfie cheated on you?' Cheryl asked.

'We're married, so that's never going to happen,' said Sonia. 'And Dale will be faithful once you and he are married. But until those vows are exchanged, you're both still single in the eyes of the Church, so it isn't considered a sin.'

'It is to *me*,' Cheryl shot back indignantly. 'And there's no going back from this, so if you're trying to make me change my mind, forget it.'

'My concern is my grandchild, so I need to know your intentions,' Sonia replied evenly. 'You claim that you didn't mean what you said to my son, but the thought must have crossed your mind for it to make its way out of your mouth, so how are we to know that you won't go ahead and do it?'

'To be honest, this really isn't your business,' Cheryl said, growing tired of being lectured. 'I like you, and I appreciate everything you and Alfie have done for me, but this is my life and my body, and I'm the only one who gets to decide what to do with it.'

Sonia peered at her through narrowed eyes for several long moments. Then, smiling tightly, she said, 'Whatever you decide, Alfie and I will support you.'

'Thanks,' Cheryl said, glad that she'd regained control of the situation.

'Right, I can see you're getting tired, so I'm going to make us both a drink, then get on my way,' Sonia said, taking a box of herbal teabags out of her handbag. 'It's a chamomile and violet infusion; perfect for helping you to relax and taking some of the stress out of my long drive home.'

'Not for me, thanks.' Cheryl stood up. 'I'm going to bed.'

'Are you sure?' Sonia raised an eyebrow. 'They're highly recommended.'

'Positive,' Cheryl said, opening the door.

'As you wish,' Sonia conceded, dropping the box back into her bag. 'I hope we see you soon, dear.'

Cheryl forced a smile and showed her out, then quickly closed the front door and slid the bolts into place. She didn't like that Dale had given his mother a key, or that he still had one himself; but she couldn't afford to change the locks, so she would keep the front door bolted and go in and out via the back door until things cooled down, she decided.

After watching Sonia drive away, Cheryl went upstairs to her bedroom and looked over at the house across the road. Lights were on in some of the rooms, but curtains had recently been fitted, so she couldn't see anybody in there.

Sighing, she drew her own curtains and then changed into her pyjamas before climbing into bed. She was tired and upset, and all she wanted to do was fall asleep and wake up to find that everything had been a horrible dream.

Chapter 35

There were seven missed call notifications and ten text messages on Cheryl's phone when she woke the next morning; all from Dale, apologising for scaring her and begging her to give him another chance. Still too upset to talk to him, she put her phone on silent so she wouldn't hear if he called again.

It was a bitterly cold day, but she needed to do a bit of shopping before she settled down to do a serious job search, so she pulled on her coat and let herself out through the back door. Sharon was in Bob's yard, emptying the bin, and she nodded hello when the woman spotted her and waved.

'How's it going?' Sharon asked, smiling as she walked over to the fence.

'Good,' Cheryl lied, not wanting to tell her what had happened, because she didn't know the woman well enough to bore her with her personal dramas. 'Bob OK?'

'He seems a bit tired today. But madam's back, so I think that's part of it. He's never as talkative when she's around.'

'Probably sick of her being there. He's lived alone for years and likes his own company.'

'Baffles me how a nice man like him can have a moody so-and-so like her for a daughter,' Sharon remarked. Then, grimacing, she said, 'Sorry, that was out of order. I'm not supposed to talk about my clients' personal stuff.'

'You're only saying what I think every time I see her, so don't worry about it,' Cheryl said. 'He deserves so much better.'

'He really does,' Sharon agreed. 'But hey ho … Like they say, you can choose your friends, but you're stuck with family forever – whether you like it or not.'

'Very true.'

'Did you see anything going on across the road last night?' Sharon asked, abruptly changing the subject. 'Only Bob reckons three men went in there in the early hours, and one of them had a scuffle with some bloke before chasing him off. Between you and me, I think he might have been dreaming, bless him. The nosy bugger spends so much time looking over there, it must play on his mind while he's sleeping.'

'I didn't see or hear anything,' Cheryl said, hoping that Alfie had decided to check the place out because of what she'd told Dale.

'Are the girls who live in there foreign?' Sharon asked.

'They're Polish,' Cheryl told her. 'Dale's dad owns a few care homes, and he flew them over to work for him.'

'Ah, I thought so. My mate works opposite a residential home, and I popped over to see her the other day and noticed the sign had the same logo as the one I've seen on the girls' uniforms.'

'Probably one of his, then.'

'I hope you don't think I'm being cheeky,' Sharon said sheepishly. 'But you couldn't ask if he's got any jobs going, could you?'

'You're not leaving Bob, are you?' Cheryl asked.

'No, I'll be keeping this job,' Sharon assured her. 'But the pay's not great, so I'm looking for something part-time to top it up. Preferably nights.'

'OK, I'll ask when I get a chance. But I'm not sure when it'll be.'

'No problem. I know you're busy organising the wedding, so there's no rush.'

Thinking that she might have a very long wait, Cheryl smiled, and said, 'I need to get going. Give Bob my love.'

'Will do,' Sharon said. 'And thanks again.'

Cheryl waved goodbye and walked out of the yard, pulling the gate shut behind her. She'd almost reached the end of the alleyway when she spotted Dale's car driving past, and she quickly stepped through the open gate of the last house on the block, so she could hide if he came back. Confident that he mustn't have seen her when he didn't, she slipped out and walked quickly down the road in the opposite direction.

Dale parked outside Cheryl's house and hopped out of the car. He'd tried calling her numerous times, but she hadn't answered or replied to his messages, so he'd decided to call round in person. His mum had said it was obvious she'd been crying last night, and he was hoping that meant she still cared and would agree to talk to him now she'd had a chance to calm down and think things over.

He knew she was up because the curtains were open upstairs and down, so he rang the bell. She didn't answer, so he tried again after a few seconds, then squatted down and pushed the letterbox open.

'Cheryl, it's me,' he called, his voice echoing off the hallway walls. 'I know you've read my messages, and I get that this might be too soon, but I just want to see you and make sure you're OK.'

Again no answer came, and he couldn't hear any sounds of movement coming from inside, so he pulled out his key and slotted it into the lock. Frowning when it didn't turn, he waggled it a few times and then pulled it out.

'She's just nipped out,' a voice said behind him.

Turning, he saw that it was the old man's carer, and asked, 'Any idea where she's gone?'

'I think she said she was going to the shops,' she told him. 'Congratulations on your engagement, by the way.'

'Cheers,' he said, pleased to hear that Cheryl hadn't told the woman that she'd called the wedding off, which gave him hope that he might still have a chance to win her round.

'You're a lucky man,' she said.

'I know,' he agreed, nodding goodbye when she gave a little wave before walking to her car.

Dorothy had been watching Dale through the window, and her heart sank when he walked away from the redhead's house and started heading her way. The late-night visit from Alfie and a couple of his men had left her feeling jittery, and she'd barely slept a wink after they'd gone. That little bitch escaping and running her mouth off to Dale's lady friend had fucked everything up, and she'd felt sure that Alfie was going to sack her after roasting her for attracting unwanted attention to the house. He hadn't done it last night, but he might well have changed his mind and sent Dale to do it instead.

'Fuck me, you look rough,' Dale said, walking into the hallway when she opened the door.

'I had a bad night,' she muttered, crossing her arms. 'So what's this? Alfie want me out, does he?'

'If he wanted you gone, he'd have told you himself,' Dale said, giving her an ominous look as he added, 'Just think yourself lucky it was him who came round last night and not my mum, or you really would be history.'

'None of this is my fault,' Dorothy protested. 'It's that fucking Agata's doing. If she hadn't blabbed to her across the road—'

'That's my fiancée you're talking about, so watch your tone,' Dale interrupted sharply. 'And it *is* your fault, because it was your job to keep an eye on her.'

'I did my best,' Dorothy whined. 'But I warned you from the start that she was a slippery one, so it's not all on me.'

'Whatever,' Dale said dismissively, glancing at his watch. 'Right, I need to get going, so hand the money over and I'll be off.'

Dorothy reached inside her bra and pulled out a folded envelope.

'*Seriously?*' He pulled a face when she handed it to him.

'It's all there,' Dorothy said, thinking that he was questioning how slim it was. 'So is that it? Are we all square?'

'For now,' Dale said, dropping the envelope into his pocket and wiping his hand on his thigh before heading for the door. 'But you won't be so lucky if you fuck up like that again.'

'Trust me, I won't,' Dorothy said, breathing a sigh of relief as she closed the door behind him.

Chapter 36

Cheryl's day got progressively worse as it wore on. The only three jobs she'd found that she had any chance of being considered for had already gone by the time she filled out the online application forms; and her old boss, whose number she had managed to find after searching the house, hadn't answered any of her calls, so she'd pretty much resigned herself to the fact that she wouldn't be receiving any sort of severance pay from him.

But the worst part came at 6 p.m., when Dale usually came round after finishing work. She knew he'd called round after she saw him that morning, because Sharon had told her, so when he didn't turn up at his usual time, the loneliness crept up on her like a snake and wrapped itself around her wounded heart. She knew she shouldn't care after everything he'd done, but it upset her that he seemed to have given up without a fight, and she found herself jumping up to look out of the window every time she heard a car outside or footsteps on the pavement.

Sick of tormenting herself, she made her way up to bed at eight and flipped through the TV channels, hoping to find something that would take her mind off the mess her life had become. Nothing held her interest, and she was about to turn off and try to get some sleep when her phone vibrated on the bedside table. She snatched it up, hoping it would be Dale, and sighed when she saw Anna's name on the screen.

'Babe, I need to tell you something,' Anna blurted out when she answered the call. 'But I haven't got long, so please don't interrupt.'

'What's wrong?' Cheryl asked, instantly picking up on the tension in her old friend's voice. 'Are you OK?'

'I'm fine,' Anna replied, sounding far from it. 'Look, I know you're already mad at me, and this is probably going to make it ten times worse, but I've been feeling really guilty since I spoke to you yesterday, and I need to tell you the truth about me and Dale.'

'Go on,' Cheryl said, a sickly feeling stirring in her stomach.

'You know I was pissed off at you for getting off with him after I told you I liked him,' Anna went on. 'So when I saw you that day and you told me you were getting married and having his baby, I wanted to hurt you. That's why I told you I'd slept with him.'

Confused, Cheryl said, 'Why are you changing your story? Dale's already admitted he stayed at yours.'

'Yeah, but he doesn't know what really happened,' said Anna. 'He *was* here, but I lied about us having sex. Truth is, he was unconscious when they brought him here.'

'Who's *they*? You're not making any sense.'

'His mates. It was Greta's idea. She knew we'd fallen out over him, so when she brought those blokes back and I pointed Dale out to her, she thought it would be funny to get back at you by setting him up. He was totally out of it, so we got his mates to carry him to mine and put him in my bed.'

'Why would his friends do something like that? They'd gone out to celebrate him getting engaged.'

'Because they're idiots and they wanted to fuck with his head, sort of like the stuff they do at stag parties,' Anna said. 'But Greta's been talking to Tommy and he told her he feels shit about it and is going to tell Dale what they did, so I thought I'd best tell you before it goes any further.'

'Are you being serious right now?' Cheryl asked, unable to believe what she was hearing. 'Have you any idea what you've done? I split up with him because of what you told me, and I could have lost the baby!'

'I'm really sorry,' Anna said. 'I just wanted to show you how it feels to have someone take your man off you.'

'He was never yours to start with,' Cheryl reminded her angrily. 'Christ, I knew you could be vindictive, but I can't believe you've done this. We've been best mates since we were kids. I *trusted* you.'

'I said I'm sorry,' Anna said tearfully. 'What more do you want me to do?'

'Go fuck yourself,' Cheryl hissed. 'And don't ever call me again!'

Furious, she cut the call and screamed in frustration as she hurled her phone across the room. Anna had pulled some stunts over the years, but this was by far the most malicious, and she cursed herself for ignoring her instincts when they'd tried to warn her that the bitch was doing it to spite her. Dale had told her he didn't remember a thing, and now she knew why: because he'd been unconscious when his friends planted him in Anna's bed. But what was she supposed to do now? She had taken Anna's word over his and said the worst thing imaginable about their baby, and she wasn't sure that she could forgive herself, so how the hell was *he* supposed to?

As the anger subsided, remorse crept in, and she retrieved her phone and brought up Dale's number. She stared at it for a long time, trying to muster the courage to actually ring it.

The doorbell rang before she had the chance, and her stomach flipped when she peeped out through the window and saw him standing on the path below. Praying that he hadn't come to have another go at her, she pulled her dressing gown on and went downstairs.

'Hi...' Dale gave a tentative smile when she opened the door. 'Sorry if I woke you, but I wanted to check in on you before I head home. Don't worry, I'm not expecting you to speak to me,' he went on. 'I just wanted to tell you I'm really sorry for what happened yesterday. That wasn't me, and I won't blame you if you never—'

'Come in,' Cheryl interrupted, opening the door a little wider. 'We need to talk and it's too cold out there.'

'Are you sure?' He hesitated.

'Yes,' she insisted, waving him inside. 'Go and sit down. I'll put the kettle on.'

Cheryl made two cups of tea and carried them into the living room, where Dale was perched on the armchair with his elbows resting on his thighs and his hands clasped together between his knees.

'Thanks for letting me in,' he said when she put his cup on the table before taking a seat on the sofa. 'I know I don't deserve it after what I did.'

'It wasn't all your fault,' Cheryl said guiltily. 'I should never have said what I did about the baby, and I'm really sorry.'

'Nah, it's on me,' Dale insisted. 'I got frustrated because I knew I'd fucked up by not telling you what happened that night, but I honestly didn't remember. I still don't, but I *do* know I would never knowingly cheat on you.'

'You didn't,' Cheryl said, clutching her cup tightly to stop her hands from shaking. 'It was a set-up.'

'What d'you mean?' Dale frowned.

'Anna made it up to get back at me for stealing you off her,' Cheryl sighed. 'She told me about you going to that party and said you'd slept together, and I knew you were lying when I asked you about it, so I thought it must be true. But she rang again just before you got here and told me nothing happened. She says you were already out of it when she got there, so her and Greta got your mates to carry you to her place and put you in her bed for a laugh. That's why you didn't know where you were when you woke up. She reckons Tommy feels guilty about it and is planning to tell you, and that's why she told me: because she knew I was about to find out.'

'Why would she do this?' Dale shook his head in disbelief. 'It's sick.'

'Because she wanted to hurt me. But at least we know the truth now.'

'That's one good thing, I guess,' Dale said. 'I should never have lied to you, but I was scared you'd finish with me if I told you the truth. Then you did anyway, so more fool me.'

'I'm sorry,' Cheryl apologised. 'I didn't want to believe her, but when she told me about your tattoo, I thought the worst. But she obviously saw it when your mates took your pants off and put you in her bed.'

'I don't blame you,' Dale said. 'You only had her word to go on, and she's your best mate, so what were you supposed to think?'

'Yeah, but I know what a bitch she can be, so I shouldn't have automatically believed her.'

'I knew exactly what she was the first time I saw her,' Dale sneered. 'But she's irrelevant. All I'm interested in is where we go from here.'

'I don't know,' Cheryl murmured. 'I feel guilty for making you think I was going to get rid of the baby, and I don't blame you for kicking off. But you really scared me.'

'I know, and I'm disgusted with myself,' Dale replied quietly. 'I love you more than I've ever loved anyone in my entire life, and I would never do anything to hurt you.'

'I love you, too,' Cheryl sighed. 'But if we can be that horrible to each other so soon into our relationship, how can we be sure it won't happen again?'

'It won't,' Dale insisted. '*She* caused this, because she's jealous that you got what she couldn't have. But we shouldn't let her ruin it for us. We've got a baby on the way, and I want to be a hands-on father, not some stranger who visits every other weekend.'

'I want that too.'

'Then let's put this behind us and start over,' Dale said, moving to sit beside her. 'I know I scared you, but I swear that will never happen again. You and the baby are my life, and I never want to go through another day like today.'

'Neither do I,' Cheryl murmured, resting her head on his chest when he pulled her into his arms.

'God, I've missed this,' Dale said huskily as he held her. 'You've got no idea how terrible my day's been, thinking I'd lost you.'

'Mine hasn't been so great, either,' she admitted. Then, drawing her head back when he pulled his phone out of his pocket, she said, 'What are you doing?'

'Calling my mum to tell her the good news,' he grinned. 'She's been on my case since she saw you last night, telling me how stupid I am for fucking up the best thing that ever happened to me.'

'That's so sweet,' Cheryl said. 'I was worried I might have offended her last night.'

'No chance,' Dale assured her. 'She classes you as the daughter she never had, so she'll be made up to hear we're back together. Subject of...' He reached into his pocket again and pulled out the ring he'd snatched off the table before leaving the previous night. 'Will you take this back?'

'Yes, I will,' Cheryl said, smiling as he slipped the ring onto her finger.

Chapter 37

Anna's face was wet with tears, and she cradled her bruised ribs as she hobbled into the bathroom. The vision looking back at her in the mirror was like something out of a horror film, and she clutched the edge of the sink to keep from collapsing when her legs almost gave way. Her left eye was already purpling and almost closed, her nose looked crooked, her lips were swollen and bleeding, and there was a bald patch on the side of her head where some of her extensions had been ripped out, taking her natural hair with them.

Jumping at the sound of a fist hammering on her front door, she turned away from the horrifying sight and made her way into the hallway. She knew it was Greta, because she'd called her a minute earlier and asked her to come down, but she checked the spyhole anyway, just in case.

'Oh my fucking God,' Greta gasped, covering her mouth with her hand when Anna opened the door and let her in. 'I'm calling an ambulance.'

'No!' Anna croaked, closing and double-locking the door. 'They'll tell the police.'

'Good,' Greta said, still staring at her. 'That bastard needs locking up.'

'He'll come back if I report him,' Anna said, grimacing in pain as she made her way to the sofa and gingerly sat down.

'You can't let him get away with this,' Greta argued, taking in the blood on the cream rug as she sat beside her. 'Christ, Anna, you sounded bad on the phone, but this is next level. Why the fuck did you let him in?'

'I didn't know it was him,' Anna told her. 'He had a baseball cap on and one of those yellow jackets, so I thought he was delivering something.'

'What did he do to you?' Greta probed. 'He didn't...?'

Anna knew that her friend was asking if she'd been raped and shook her head. 'No, he didn't touch me like that.'

'So what did he want?'

'He forced me to ring Cheryl and tell her I'd lied about sleeping with him.'

'Twat,' Greta said angrily. 'And you wonder why I've got no time for men.'

'I feel sick,' Anna groaned, still cradling her ribs as she rested her head back against the cushion.

Greta jumped up and ran into the kitchen to get her a glass of water.

'Babe, you really need to get checked over,' she said as she watched Anna try to take sips. 'Your nose looks broken, and he could have caused internal damage.'

'I'll be OK,' Anna insisted, shivering when some of the water spilled straight back out of her battered mouth and trickled down her chest. 'I'll tell my dad I had an accident and get him to pay for a nose job.'

'It'd have to be one hell of a fucking accident to do this much damage,' Greta replied, frowning as she took in the terrible bruising and the missing patch of hair. 'I wish to God I'd been here, 'cos that'd be *his* blood on the rug if I had been.'

'He'd only have done the same to you,' Anna said, fresh tears burning her eyes as she recalled the attack. 'I just don't get why he had to do this when I'd already made the call.'

''Cos he's a fucking animal,' Greta spat. 'No wonder Tommy told us to steer clear of him. He must be a right cunt if his own mates can't even stand him.'

'I'm worried about Cheryl,' Anna sniffled, carefully dabbing her cheeks with the back of her hand.

'Bollocks to that,' Greta replied indignantly. 'She's the one who caused this.'

'No, she's not,' Anna countered. 'She was really upset when I told her about him staying here, and I could hear how much I'd hurt her when I said I'd made it all up.'

'Well, maybe she'll think twice before she steals anyone else's man in the future,' said Greta. 'I've always thought she was a snooty bitch, but now I know how sly she is, she'd better hope I never get my hands on her.'

'She thinks it was all your idea,' Anna said. 'He told me to tell her you'd suggested it to get back at her.'

'I don't give a fuck what Sonia thinks,' Greta replied. 'I'm more concerned about you, and how we're going to make him pay for this.'

'We're not doing anything,' Anna insisted. 'He's already proved he can get to me any time he likes, and he'll probably kill me next time, so I'm not risking it.'

'I think you're making a mistake, but it's your call,' Greta conceded. 'Now please let me take you to hospital; I'm really worried that you might be more hurt than you think. If you're concerned about them calling the police, we can tell them you got mugged.'

Anna didn't want to face the inevitable questions, but the pain was pretty bad already, and she had a feeling it was only going to get worse, so she reluctantly agreed.

'OK, but promise you won't say anything about what really happened. I don't want to spend the rest of my life looking over my shoulder.'

'If that's what you want, I won't say anything,' Greta promised. 'But I swear to God, if I ever see him anywhere near you again, I'll—'

'Babe, leave it,' Anna implored. 'It's over now and I've got to let it go.'

'Fine,' Greta agreed. 'Let's get you to hospital, 'cos those lips are getting fatter by the second and I don't want to be in the firing line if they burst.'

Shuddering at the thought, Anna slowly got up and hobbled towards the door as Greta gathered together her phone, keys and coat. She wished she could call Cheryl and tell her what had happened, but she'd already changed her story, so she doubted her old friend would believe her. She just hoped Cheryl had the sense not to get back with the bastard, because if he was capable of doing this to Anna, God only knew what he might do to Cheryl or their child if they pissed him off in the future.

Chapter 38

It had been snowing all morning and everything was cloaked in a blanket of glistening whiteness as far as the eye could see. It was the perfect day for the Christmas Eve wedding Sonia had set her heart on, and Cheryl had to admit that it did look magical as she gazed down at the scene from the window of the bedroom where she'd been sleeping since Dale had brought her home after the Anna debacle.

It was Sonia who had suggested that she should stay until the wedding in order to avoid any further stress, and Cheryl, still shocked by Anna's betrayal, had gratefully accepted the invitation. Three weeks had passed since then, and in one short hour she would officially become Dale's wife. She was excited and nervous, but also a little sad that there was nobody from her side among the guests. It would have been nice to have her dad there to walk her down the aisle, but it was her mum's presence she was missing the most. She had long ago learned to live without her, but seeing how close Dale and Sonia were had made her feel the loss more acutely than usual. But as Dale and Sonia kept telling her, *they* were her family now, and she truly felt like she had been accepted into their fold – even if Estelle *was* still giving her the cold shoulder.

Cheryl hoped that relationship might thaw once she became

a fellow Mrs Moran, but she only ever saw Estelle at family functions, so she didn't really care if the woman wanted to keep things as they were. Sonia, on the other hand, had been amazing, and Cheryl appreciated the effort she had made to include her in the family. She had been a beauty queen when she'd met Alfie, but she had sacrificed her future in the fashion and modelling industry in order to support him when he moved to England to start up his own company. They had started out in rented accommodation, but his hard work, while she almost single-handedly raised their sons, had elevated them to the point that they had been able to buy this beautiful house and completely renovate it from top to bottom. Sonia was the glue that held the family together, and she was still supporting Alfie as he prepared to embark on the next stage of his life: running for mayor while his sons took more control of his other businesses. And Cheryl aimed to follow her example and support Dale and their child in the same way going forward.

A breeze circled Cheryl's bare ankles when the bedroom door suddenly opened, and she turned and smiled when Sonia came in, looking absolutely stunning in the royal-blue mother-of-the-groom outfit she had chosen for the day.

'The hair and make-up girls will be with you in a moment,' she said, offering one of two champagne flutes to Cheryl.

'Thanks, but I'd best not,' Cheryl said, touching her stomach, which had recently started to swell, necessitating an emergency visit from Kat, the designer, the previous day, to make last-minute adjustments to the dress.

'It's only apple juice,' Sonia assured her. 'I've asked the photographer to take some pre-wedding shots while they're getting you ready, and these glasses make for better optics.'

A tap came on the door as Cheryl reached for the glass, and the make-up artist and her assistant entered, along with the hair-stylist and photographer. As the first three laid out their equipment, the photographer snapped pictures of Cheryl and Sonia in various poses, culminating in one of them smiling lovingly at each other as they clinked glasses.

Alfie was standing in the hallway, looking suave in the silver-grey morning suit and royal blue cravat that all the men from Dale's side were wearing. Frankie was also there, in his pageboy outfit, alongside Poppy, who looked like a little princess in her peach flower-girl dress, holding a basket of rose petals.

'Wow,' Alfie said, gazing up at Cheryl as she slowly descended the stairs in her Swarovski-crystal studded dress and veil, with the vintage ermine stole Sonia had gifted her around her shoulders.

'Doesn't she look beautiful?' Sonia said, walking down to join him.

'Almost as beautiful as you,' he grinned, kissing her cheek.

'OK, let's get this show on the road,' Sonia said, issuing instructions to the children as she ushered them into the kitchen.

'Ready?' Alfie asked, offering his arm to Cheryl.

'I think so,' she replied nervously.

'It'll be over before you know it,' he said, placing his hand over hers and giving it a reassuring squeeze as they walked out through the conservatory and stepped onto the snow-covered carpet that had been rolled out across the lawn to the entrance of the marquee that had been erected at the rear of the garden that morning.

The wedding service was a traditional Polish one, followed by a five-course sit-down meal, speeches and the first dance. Cheryl was already tired, and her feet were throbbing after standing for hours in the strappy heels, but she didn't think she had ever felt happier than she did right then in Dale's arms, swaying to the music they had chosen in the twinkling light coming from the candles on the tables and the fairy lights strung across the ceiling of the marquee.

When the first dance came to an end, Sonia cut in, and Cheryl was happy to hand Dale over to her and take a seat. She took the opportunity to slip off her shoes, and looked around the room as she rubbed her aching feet. She hardly knew any of the guests, many of whom were Dale's relatives, while others were business and political acquaintances of Alfie's. Those who had flown over from Poland for the occasion were in high spirits, enjoying the family reunion, and Cheryl noticed that they seemed to have separated into male and female groups.

Catching three women from the latter group casting hooded glances in her direction as they whispered among themselves, Cheryl sighed and averted her gaze. They had all attended the hen party Sonia had thrown for her, but none of them had made the slightest effort to speak to her, and she sensed that they would have preferred Dale to take a Polish bride. But he had chosen her, and they would be gone as soon as this was all over, so she didn't care what they thought.

Poppy was sitting alone in a corner, and Cheryl got up and went over to her.

'Hi,' she said, smiling as she took a seat next to her. 'You don't look very happy. Where's your mum and dad?'

'Daddy's there,' Poppy said, pointing through the bodies on the dance floor to where Stefan was talking to a couple of elderly ladies. 'But I dunno where Mummy is.'

'How come you're not playing with your cousins?' Cheryl probed, nodding towards a group of boys and girls who were noisily chasing each other around the tables.

'Frankie told them not to play with me, 'cos I look stupid in my dress,' Poppy murmured.

'Well, that's not very nice,' Cheryl said. 'And it's also not true, because you look very pretty.'

'He says I look fat and ugly,' Poppy said. 'Like you,' she added, so quietly Cheryl almost missed it.

Unsure how to respond, Cheryl shifted in her seat. She'd never really spoken to Frankie, because he always stuck close to the men when they came over, but she hadn't known he felt that way about her.

'He only said it 'cos he heard Mummy say it on the phone,' Poppy went on. 'But he's just stupid.'

Cheryl was annoyed to hear that Estelle had been badmouthing her in earshot of the children, but she didn't want to upset Poppy, so she swallowed her anger and smiled, saying, 'Oh well, at least you and me get on OK.'

Poppy nodded her agreement and returned the smile.

'Hey, there you are,' Stefan said, appearing in front of them. 'Everything OK?'

'I was just checking Poppy was all right, but I'll leave you to it now you're here,' Cheryl said, wondering if he also shared his wife's opinion of her. She didn't think so, because he always made the effort to at least say hello when he saw her; but he probably thought it would cause friction with Dale if he ignored her, so it could be an act.

'It was a beautiful service,' Stefan said, peering into her eyes when she rose to her feet. 'I hope...' He tailed off without finishing the sentence, then smiled, and said, 'I'd best take this one inside and see if she needs the loo.'

Cheryl gave a tight smile and watched as he took Poppy's hand and led her away. His gaze was always intense, but it had been even more so just then, and she wondered what he'd been about to say.

Before she could dwell on it too deeply, she spotted Dale walking across the dance floor, and raised an eyebrow when one of his female cousins grabbed him, pressing herself up against him as she stood on her tiptoes and whispered into his ear. Her name was Katriona, and she was an eighteen-year-old beauty with a mane of glossy black hair and large breasts. The girl had been flirting with Dale ever since she had arrived two days earlier, but he hadn't shown any interest in her in that way, and Cheryl smiled when he extricated himself from her clutches now and walked away. She was about to follow him to tell him she was going back to the house to get changed, but lost sight of him when a group of men blocked her view.

Sidestepping the group, she made her way outside. It was pitch dark by then and the air was icy, but it had stopped snowing, and she pulled the stole tighter around her shoulders as she gazed up at the stars twinkling in the sky above the ghostly-white treetops. That view still mesmerised her, and she always slept with her curtains open so she could enjoy it from her bed.

Music was blasting out behind her, but in a lull between tunes, she picked up the sound of low voices coming from the side of the marquee and peeped around the corner to see who it was. The men from the cottages and caravans were sharing drinks around a table, and she felt awkward when the boss of the crew, whose name she now knew to be Jakub, suddenly turned his head and looked right at her. About to withdraw, she hesitated when he raised his glass into the air, as if toasting her. Smiling, she gave him a little wave before turning and making her way to the house.

The caterers were gathered in the kitchen grabbing a bite to eat out of sight of the guests, and she was embarrassed when they all looked her way. Thanking them when they offered their congratulations, she walked on through to the hallway. Stefan was coming down the stairs with Poppy in his arms, so she waited until he reached the bottom before heading up.

As Cheryl reached the landing, Rosa came out of her room pulling a suitcase.

'Is that my stuff?' she asked.

'*Tek.*' Rosa nodded. 'Miss Sonia tell me take to Dale room.'

'Ah, right,' Cheryl said, remembering that she would be moving into his room now they were married. 'Thank you.'

Rosa nodded, dipped her gaze and started to walk away. Then, hesitating, she glanced around furtively, as if to make sure they were alone, before turning back to Cheryl and raising her hand. For a split second, Cheryl wondered if the woman was going to stroke her face, but Rosa made the sign of the cross in the air between them and murmured something under her breath in Polish before scuttling away.

Bemused, Cheryl watched Rosa put the case into Dale's room before heading towards the second staircase at the far end of the corridor. Guessing that she'd just been blessed, she smiled to herself as she went into her bedroom.

The room was in darkness and the curtains were open, so she left the light off and struggled out of the heavy wedding dress. The emerald-green velvet dress she'd chosen for her evening outfit was still hanging in its bag on the back of the door, and she quickly slipped it on and smoothed it down before heading over to the window to take in the view one last time.

As she gazed out over the landscape, a cigarette glowed in the darkness by the fence to the left of the marquees, and she squinted when she spotted two shadowy figures, one of whom appeared to be waving their arms around as if having an argument. A bright light suddenly flared, illuminating the figures' faces, and Cheryl quickly stepped to the side of the window when she realised it was Stefan and Estelle. Obviously aware that they were now in plain view, Stefan flicked the cigarette away and marched back to the marquee, and Estelle scurried towards the house, swiping at her face as she went.

Cheryl was curious to know what had happened to make ice-queen Estelle cry. The pair never seemed happy, but the tension between them had become more noticeable in recent weeks. Stefan didn't seem to possess any of the levity Dale and his father had, rarely joining in with their jokes or offering any of his own at family dinners, and Cheryl imagined he would be incredibly boring to live with. If his wife had been any woman other than Estelle, she might have felt sorry for her; but now Poppy had told her that Estelle spoke badly about her behind closed doors, she had no sympathy for her whatsoever.

More at ease now that she was dressed like the other women and didn't stand out like a sore thumb, Cheryl re-joined the party. The booze was flowing freely, and the younger women were strutting their stuff on the dance floor, while the older ones sat and chatted and the men filled the tent with cigar smoke and raucous laughter.

She found Dale sitting at a corner table with a group of his male cousins and was happy when he told the guys to make room for her and patted the now-empty chair beside his. She couldn't understand a word they were saying, but she liked that the men seemed to approve of her and weren't giving her the side-eye or tossing dirty looks her way, like the women had been doing.

On her umpteenth apple juice of the day, all served in champagne flutes on Sonia's orders so nobody would suspect that she was pregnant, Cheryl's bladder felt like it was going to burst when Dale leaned towards her after a few hours and asked if she was ready to leave. Nodding, she clutched his hand as he made his way around the marquee saying goodnight to the guests before heading back to the house.

Giggling when they reached Dale's room and he insisted on carrying her over the threshold, she wrapped her arms around his neck as he picked her up and carried her inside.

'I've been waiting for this all day,' he growled, kicking the door shut and tossing her onto the bed before leaping on top of her.

'Get off,' she laughed. 'I need the loo.'

'It can wait,' he said huskily, kissing her as he reached down and unzipped his suit trousers.

'You're going to ruin my dress,' she protested, placing her hands on his chest to hold him at bay. 'And I really do need the loo.'

'*Now?*' he groaned.

'Blame your child for sitting on my bladder,' she teased, rolling away and dropping her feet to the floor. It was the first time she had ever been in his room, and she was surprised to see that it had a completely different layout to hers. It was furnished very differently, as well, with dark woods, muted wall-lights, and dark red wallpaper. 'Wow, this is a proper man's room,' she said.

'Just how I like it,' Dale grinned, pointing out a door in an alcove in the corner. 'Bathroom's that way. And don't be long.'

The masculine theme spilled over into the bathroom, with its floor-to-ceiling granite tiling and black and chrome accessories. It was stylish, but also very dark, and Cheryl hoped that Dale wouldn't expect her to decorate their own home in a similar fashion when they eventually found one.

Dale was waiting in bed for her when she came out of the bathroom a few minutes later minus her dress, and she shivered when he pulled her under the quilt and kissed her. They hadn't

slept together in three long weeks, so the sex was passionate –
and fast. Relieved about that, because she knew that some of
the house guests were already in their rooms across the corridor
and was paranoid that they might be able to hear them, Cheryl
rolled onto her side when Dale flopped onto his back.

'Night,' he said, his eyes already closed.

'Night,' she echoed, gazing at his handsome face as his
breathing slowed. It had been a long day and he'd had a lot to
drink, so she wasn't surprised when he started snoring after a
few seconds. Smiling, she snuggled closer and slid her arm across
his stomach, whispering, 'I love you,' as she closed her own eyes.

Chapter 39

Cheryl slept deeply and felt thoroughly rested when she woke the following morning. Relieved that the wedding was done, and excited to be waking next to her new husband for the first time, she rolled over to wish him happy Christmas. This would be the first morning since she'd got there that he wasn't heading out to work first thing, so she was surprised to see that his side of the bed was empty. Eager to see him, she took a quick shower and got dressed, then made her way down to the kitchen.

Sonia and the female family members who had stayed over were sitting at the table, in the middle of which were plates of the various pastries and delicacies Rosa had baked.

'Ah, you're up,' Sonia said, waving for her to take a seat. 'Sleep well?'

Katriona, who was sitting next to another of the younger cousins, smirked and whispered something to the girl, and they both giggled behind their hands.

Determined not to let the bitches think their rude exchange had bothered her, Cheryl smiled, and said, 'I slept really well, thanks. Dale did, too.'

'He could sleep through a hurricane,' Sonia chuckled. 'Did you enjoy your day?'

'It was lovely,' Cheryl replied. 'And Dale was so sweet, he

insisted on carrying me over the threshold when we got to our room after the party.'

One of the older women asked Sonia what she'd said, and Cheryl was gratified to see the flash of envy in Katriona's eyes when Sonia repeated her words in their language.

'Where is he?' she asked, glancing through the window into the conservatory as she sat down, to see if he was out on the patio.

'He and Alfie took the men hunting,' Sonia told her. 'It's a Christmas Day tradition, but they'll be back in time for dinner and the gift exchange.'

'Oh, right,' Cheryl murmured, acutely conscious of the fact that she hadn't bought a single thing. She hadn't had an opportunity to leave the house since coming back, because she and Sonia had spent the entire time tweaking their arrangements. But even if she had been able to go shopping, she didn't have the money to buy gifts.

As if sensing what she was thinking, Sonia said, 'I've had Rosa put yours under the tree with ours, darling. Can't wait to see what you bought me.' She gave a warm smile and winked at Cheryl, letting her know that she'd got her back.

Grateful, Cheryl returned the smile and reached for one of the pastries as the women resumed their chats around her. It was frustrating not being able to contribute to or understand the conversation, and she made a mental note to ask Dale to teach her their language as she bit into the pastry. As she ate, her gaze drifted over to Rosa, who was standing by the sink peeling a mountain of potatoes, behind which various other vegetables were heaped. Feeling sorry for the woman, she wiped the crumbs from her fingers and started to get up, but hesitated when Sonia asked where she was going.

'I thought I'd help Rosa,' she said.

'I don't think so, dear,' Sonia replied smoothly. 'She's a servant, and we don't demean ourselves by doing the work that we pay them to do.'

Again, one of the women asked what they were talking about, and Cheryl frowned when Sonia explained and they all turned and looked at her as if she was crazy. As much as she loved her now mother-in-law, she'd never been particularly comfortable with the way Sonia spoke to Rosa, and she especially didn't like hearing her being referred to as a servant. Housekeeper would have been a more fitting title, in her opinion, since Rosa seemed to do all the cooking, laundry and day-to-day cleaning. She had also been a nanny to Dale and Stefan when they were younger, which showed how long she had lived with the family. They had given her a suite of rooms, but she never seemed to leave the house or even take a day off as far as Cheryl had seen, so to call her a servant when she was so dedicated seemed harsh.

The morning dragged on and Cheryl was bored out of her mind as the women gossiped and cackled around the table while she sat in isolated silence. When Dale, his father and the menfolk came home from the hunt later that afternoon, she followed him up to their bedroom and threw herself down on the bed while he took a shower and got changed. It was the most relaxed she'd felt all day, and she wished they could have stayed up there all night. But that wasn't an option with dinner about to be served, so she plastered a fake smile on her lips and held his hand when he was ready to go back down to his family.

Stefan, Estelle and the children had arrived while they were upstairs, and Cheryl was surprised when the woman wished her a happy Christmas and flashed a quick smile at her. As relieved as she was to no longer be the only English woman in the room, and as preferable as this new-found civility was to the

usual hostility, she was under no illusions about Estelle's true
feelings towards her, so she wasn't expecting this to be the start
of a wonderful sister-in-law relationship.

As it was a special occasion, they were eating in the dining
room instead of the kitchen that night. It was a spectacular
room, with a long, polished-wood table in the centre, over which
a genuine crystal chandelier was hanging. Expensive artworks
lined the walls, and a bank of folding glass doors overlooked
the back garden, in front of which a baby grand piano that
matched the one in the hallway was standing. The table was
already laid, with silver candelabras at either end which lent a
homely atmosphere to the occasion; and the scent coming from
the beautifully decorated, real pine Christmas tree in the corner
only added to the ambience.

Rosa was a great cook, but she'd excelled herself tonight, and
the family tucked into the banquet with gusto; praising Sonia
with every bite, as if she herself had cooked it. Sonia smiled
benevolently, but didn't bother to point out that it was Rosa's
doing, not hers, which Cheryl thought a little odd. But they all
knew who had really done the work, so she figured they were
probably just complimenting her on her hosting skills and choice
of menu.

After dinner, they all moved to the seating area at the other
end of the room to exchange gifts. Cheryl still felt awkward
about the fact that she hadn't bought any, but that feeling
lessened when she saw that Dale's relatives had brought simple
handmade presents, including a lovely lace shawl for Sonia, and
knitted gloves for Alfie, Dale and Stefan. Sonia's gifts were every
bit as extravagant as Cheryl had expected, although she had no
idea when the woman had found the time to go shopping since
they had been so busy with the wedding in the last few weeks.
But Sonia had not only bought the gifts from herself and Alfie,

she had also bought gifts that were supposedly from Dale and Cheryl; hers being a bottle of her favourite perfume, over which she gushed as if it was a huge surprise.

Cheryl and Estelle each received a gold wristwatch from Sonia and Alfie, which blew Cheryl's mind, because nobody had ever bought her anything so expensive in her life. But her favourite gift by far was the gold locket Dale had bought for her, which had 'For my darling wife xx' engraved into the back of it.

Tears glistening in her eyes when he fastened the chain around her neck, she said, 'Thank you so much. I love it.'

'Not as much as I love you,' he whispered, kissing her softly on the lips.

As soon as Dale drew his head back following the kiss, Katriona appeared at his side. Her lips were smiling, but her eyes were narrowed to slits as she reached out and lifted the locket off Cheryl's throat to look at it. Dropping it after a second, she looked up at Dale and batted her lashes at him, and her voice was like syrup when she spoke quietly to him. Dale laughed and said something in return, and Cheryl smirked when the girl pursed her lips angrily and stomped back to her seat.

'What did she say?' she asked.

'She wanted to know why I hadn't bought her anything,' Dale said, reaching for a mince pie off the plate Rosa had placed on the coffee table.

'And what did you say?'

'I told her to wait till she's got a boyfriend and let *him* buy her something.'

Thrilled that he'd knocked the girl back and put an end to her games, Cheryl settled back in her seat to enjoy the rest of the night, reminding herself that Katriona would be leaving with the others in a couple of days, hopefully never to be seen again.

Chapter 40

'I need a job,' Cheryl said as she lay in bed watching Dale get dressed one morning.

It was six weeks since their wedding, and she'd quickly learned what her future was going to look like if she followed Sonia's example as life in the Moran household returned to normal. Now she no longer had the wedding to focus on, Sonia had slipped back into her routine of shopping, getting her hair and nails done, lunching with her lady friends, and having Botox top-ups. Cheryl had gone with her a few times, but she'd soon realised that lifestyle wasn't for her and had used her growing belly and swollen ankles as an excuse to get out of going again. That left her alone for hours on end with no one to talk to, and she hardly saw Dale since he was now working even longer hours than before the wedding and often only came home to shower in the evening before heading straight back out to have dinner with some client or other.

'You've already got a job,' Dale reminded her as he buttoned his shirt. 'We put you on the payroll months ago, remember?'

'Yeah, but it's not a *real* job,' she argued. 'And I'm bored off my head doing nothing all day.'

'I'm sure you could find something to do if you put your mind to it. My mum finds plenty to keep her occupied.'

'She enjoys that kind of thing, but I don't. I want to do something useful with my life – and earn some money while I'm doing it.'

'You're my wife, so it's *my* job to bring the money in,' Dale said, giving her a mock-stern look. 'You just concentrate on growing my son, 'cos he's the future of this family.'

'Or *she*,' Cheryl corrected him, for what felt like the millionth time. Then, sighing, she said, 'It's all right for you; you're over in Manchester seeing people every day while I'm stuck out here on my own.'

'So now you resent me for working to give you a good life?' Dale raised an eyebrow. 'Most women would give their left arm to have what you've got.'

'I'm not saying I don't appreciate it, but you're hardly ever home,' Cheryl moaned. 'Maybe I should take driving lessons, then at least I could go out.'

'Out where?' Dale frowned.

'To see my friends.'

'What friends? Last I heard, the only one you still saw was Anna. And that's not happening again after what she did.'

'I never said I wanted to see *her*,' Cheryl muttered. 'But I only lost touch with the others because I was working all the time, so it might be nice to catch up with some of them.'

'That's your past,' Dale said. 'This is your life now, and I don't understand why you're bitching about being stuck here when we've given you everything you could possibly want.'

Cheryl bit back the urge to tell him that *things* weren't enough; that rattling round in this big house day after day, with nothing to do and no one to talk to, was killing her. It wouldn't have been so bad if it was their own house, but this was Sonia's castle, and she wasn't even allowed to clean up, which she had always found relaxing. Mopping the floor, vacuuming the carpet, sleeping in sheets that she herself had washed and hung out on the line to dry... all simple pleasures that she missed more than she had ever thought possible.

'When are we going to start looking for our own place?' she asked, changing the subject.

'Babe, you know I haven't got time right now,' Dale said, pulling his suit jacket on. 'I'm already up to my eyes in it, and it's going to get even more intensive once my dad starts campaigning.'

'Can't we start looking before it gets to that?' Cheryl asked. 'I'd prefer to be in there before the baby's born.'

Dale had been combing his hair in front of the mirror, but he slammed the comb down at that and snapped his head around. 'For God's sake, Cheryl, can't you get off my back for two fucking minutes!'

'I was only asking; no need to bite my head off,' she said quietly, giving him a wounded look. 'You're the one who said we could start looking for somewhere after Christmas, and I really don't want to still be here when the baby comes.'

'Why not?' he asked. 'This is the best place you could possibly be, with my mum here to help you through the difficult bits.'

'I want to do it myself,' Cheryl insisted. 'It's our baby.'

'Yes, I know that,' Dale replied, sighing as he gazed down at her. 'And it will happen, but not right now, so can we talk about this another time? I really need to get going.' Smiling when Cheryl nodded, he said, 'See you later,' and leaned down to kiss her before leaving the room.

Frustrated, Cheryl flopped back against the pillows. She'd tried to talk to him about these things several times since the wedding, but he always shut her down before she could get him to commit to anything. It was almost, she thought, as if he didn't want to leave the family home and would be happy to raise the baby there. She couldn't deny that it would be a safer, more peaceful environment than the estate, but there were no neighbours within miles, so the child would have no friends to play with. And God only knew where the nearest nursery and schools were, so if they did stay here, she would have to get a car at some point. But Dale had yet to follow through on his promise to teach her to drive, and she hadn't received a single pay cheque from the job they'd supposedly given her as his PA, so she couldn't even look for an instructor herself.

Resigned to the fact that there was absolutely nothing she could do about the situation until she somehow managed to pin Dale down to start making plans, Cheryl took a shower and got dressed before heading downstairs.

Sonia had already gone out, but Rosa was in the kitchen preparing the meat for that night's dinner. Cheryl smiled and said good morning, and Rosa acknowledged the greeting with a nod and continued what she was doing.

'What are you making?' Cheryl asked as she filled the kettle.

'Is steak,' Rosa murmured.

'Nice,' Cheryl said. 'I'm making a cup of tea. Would you like one?'

Rosa shook her head.

'It's OK, we're alone,' Cheryl said, all too aware that Sonia disapproved of anyone speaking to Rosa outside of asking – or, rather, *telling* – her to do things for them.

Rosa pointedly swivelled her gaze to the bank of CCTV monitors on the shelf behind them, which were always on, day and night, showing views of both the exterior and interior of the house. Understanding that the woman was warning her that they could be being watched or listened to, because Sonia had an app on her phone that enabled her to view them remotely,

Cheryl felt her usual sadness at the thought that Rosa had been trained to remember her place as a mere servant.

'Sorry,' she murmured, leaving the woman to her work as she made herself a cup of tea and carried it into the conservatory.

Her conversation with Dale had got her thinking about her old life, and she pulled her phone out of her pocket and logged into her Instagram account as she took a seat on the sofa near the window. She'd set it up a few years earlier but hadn't really posted much, mainly because she hadn't thought that any of the old friends who had followed her would be remotely interested in hearing about her work at the café. She had enjoyed seeing their posts, though, and had often liked or commented on their photos. That had stopped when she'd started seeing Dale, so it was interesting to take a peek now and see what they were all up to.

She had intended to avoid Anna's page, but after scrolling through the other girls' updates, the temptation was too strong to resist. Anna, the selfie queen, had always posted a lot, but most of her recent posts were old photos of herself and her ex, Sean. At least Cheryl had *thought* they were old, but she realised they were actually new ones when she came across one of Anna grinning and flashing an engagement ring, with the caption: *I said yes!!!* Anna hadn't been engaged to Sean when he'd broken up with her, so they had obviously got back together, and Cheryl wasn't sure how she felt about it. On the one hand, she was happy for her old friend, because Sean was a nice man; but on the other, she resented that Anna had moved on so easily after almost destroying her life by lying about sleeping with Dale.

Annoyed with herself for allowing Anna back into her mind, Cheryl logged out of her account and looked out across the garden. Spring was on the horizon, but it was still cold out there, and the grass and patio were covered in a layer of frost. Thinking that she might take a walk and explore the land beyond the fence, she switched her gaze to the dirt track when she heard a vehicle and changed her mind when she saw the Transit van driving towards the cottages.

Aware that the older man, Jakub, often came back to pick up equipment after dropping the other men off at wherever they worked, she quickly made her way upstairs to grab her coat and pull on her boots. Then, checking that her house keys were in her bag, she left the house and made her way across the garden.

Jakub had parked up at the side of the caravans and the back doors were standing open. She could see him and someone else moving around inside the caravan, and she called out: 'Hello?' as she approached.

Jakub jumped out of the caravan, quickly closing the door behind him, and she smiled, and said, 'Hi. Sorry to disturb you, but I don't suppose you're going into Manchester, are you? Only I could do with a lift, if you are.'

Unsure if he'd understood her when he frowned and peered at her with his intense dark eyes, she pointed to the Transit van, then to her own chest, saying slowly, 'Can you take me to Manchester please? I need to see my doctor,' she added, touching her stomach. It was a lie, but she sensed that he'd be more prone to agreeing to take her if he thought it was for something official.

Jakub's gaze slid to her stomach before coming back to her face. Then, nodding, he said, 'Get in. I will be ready in minute.'

'Thanks.' She smiled. 'I really appreciate it.'

In the passenger seat a few seconds later, she glanced over her shoulder when Jakub came out of the caravan carrying a large bag and placed it in the back. As he closed the doors, the sun reflected off the metal flooring, highlighting a pool of something dark and wet.

'Is that blood?' she asked when he climbed into the driver's seat and started the engine.

'Oil,' he replied, turning the van around and setting off up the track. 'We had leak in bottle.'

'Thank God for that,' she half-laughed. 'I was thinking all sorts for a minute there.'

Jakub flashed a hooded side-glance at her as he drove out through the electric gates and pressed a fob on his keys to close them behind him. As he drove on through the countryside, Cheryl tried to make small talk with him, but made herself stop when he didn't respond and spent the rest of the journey huddled up against the door, staring out at the landscape.

When they reached Manchester, Cheryl asked Jakub to drop her off on the Langley estate. He pulled up at the bus stop where she had used to get off in the evening after finishing work, and she thanked him as she climbed out. He nodded and gave her one of his intense looks before driving on. Shivering, as much because of the look as the fact that she now had to walk past the high-rises and through the alleyway where she'd been attacked a few months earlier, she clutched her handbag tightly to her side and walked quickly on.

Her heart lifted when she reached her road, and she found herself smiling as she looked at the familiar houses and maisonettes. After living in Dale's huge house for so long, everything looked smaller and shabbier than she remembered, but it felt like home in a way that Dale's house never had, and she realised just how much she'd missed it when her own house came into view.

Eager to get inside, even though she knew it would probably stink in there and everything would be covered in dust, she yanked her keys out of her bag after pushing through the gate and quickly opened the front door.

'Honey, I'm home,' she called, grinning to herself as she stepped into the hallway.

The sight of a pair of dirty trainers at the foot of the stairs stopped her in her tracks, and she frowned as she stared at them, wondering where they had come from, because they certainly weren't hers.

Scared that squatters might have thought the house was abandoned and broken in, she warily opened the living-room door and looked inside, and her frown deepened when she saw more things that didn't belong to her littered around on the floor and the coffee table.

She was fumbling her phone out of her pocket to call the police when she heard a creak on the landing, and her heart leapt into her throat when she looked up and saw a young, wild-haired woman wearing a nightgown gazing down at her.

'Who the hell are you?' Cheryl demanded, nervously backing towards the front door in case there was someone else up there.

The woman didn't answer, and Cheryl saw that she looked even more scared that she herself was. She also noticed that the woman's stomach was swollen beneath the thin gown, and her bare legs were covered in bruises.

'Are you alone?' she asked, taking a step forward. 'Is somebody up there with you?'

The woman backed up a couple of steps and Cheryl held up her hand to show that she meant no harm as she started climbing the stairs.

'It's all right,' she said, softening her tone. 'I'm not going to hurt you. My name's Cheryl and this is my house.'

'J-Janika, she is hurt,' the woman stammered, pointing towards the bedroom. 'Baby.'

Recognising the accent and realising that the girl was Polish, Cheryl remembered Agata and wondered if this girl and the one she'd called Janika had also escaped from the house across the road. If so, Alfie obviously hadn't dealt with Dorothy as effectively as he'd thought, and the bitch was still up to no good behind his back.

The girl darted into the bedroom when Cheryl reached the landing. Following her, Cheryl saw another girl lying semi-naked and motionless on the bed; her face chalky white, her stomach and thighs smeared with blood.

'Oh my God,' she gasped, rushing over to the bed. 'What happened?'

The first girl pointed to a bloody towel on the other side of the mattress, and Cheryl's stomach flipped when she saw the tiny foetus inside it.

'I'm calling an ambulance,' she said, her hands shaking wildly as she pulled out her phone.

'Please, no!' the first girl cried. 'Dorothy has see, and she say she is take care of it.'

'Dorothy knows about this?' Cheryl asked, disgusted that the woman had left the girl here in this state. 'Where is she?'

'*You* help,' the girl begged, putting her hands together in a pleading motion.

'I'm not sure I can,' Cheryl replied honestly, looking down at the other girl again. 'I'll call Dale,' she said after a moment. 'It's OK,' she said when the girl's eyes widened with fear. 'He's my husband, and he's Dorothy's boss, so he'll help.'

'No,' the girl whispered, shaking her head as she backed towards the door. 'Dale is not good.'

'Yes he is,' Cheryl assured her. 'He helped Agata, and he'll help your friend, too.'

'Agata is dead,' the girl whimpered. 'Dorothy say they kill her.'

'No, they took her to hospital,' Cheryl explained, guessing that Dorothy had told the girls that she had been killed in order to scare them and keep them in line. 'They made her better and sent her home to her family.'

'I do not believe,' the girl said tearfully. 'Dorothy say she is dead, and we will all be kill if we do not obey.'

'Don't you worry about Dorothy,' Cheryl muttered, pulling up Dale's number. 'I'll make sure she never hurts any of you again.'

Chapter 41

Dale's phone vibrated on the tabletop. Glancing at it and seeing Cheryl's name on the screen, he turned it face-down and reached for the bottle of wine that was standing beside it.

'Another?'

'Do you need to ask?' Carmel Drake purred, holding his gaze as she slid her empty glass towards him.

Dale smiled and filled her glass before emptying the rest of the bottle into his own. Carmel was his mother's age, if not older, and it was clear that she had the same penchant for cosmetic procedures, because he knew all the tell-tale signs. She looked good for it, so he wasn't knocking her for that; and she'd kept her body in pretty good shape for an old bird, too. But her most attractive feature, by far, was her billionaire, political heavyweight husband, Benjamin Drake.

Black Swan didn't need the Drakes' money, because Alfie had amassed more than enough to keep the family in luxury for generations to come; and Stefan had done a great job of balancing the books to absorb the cash from the illicit businesses into the legit ones. But now their father had decided to throw his hat into the political arena, they needed everything to be squeaky clean. And that was where Carmel and the other investors, with their good names and impeccable reputations, came into the picture; with the added benefit, in Carmel's case, that Alfie would have access to Benjamin and his connections.

It had been clear to Dale from the moment they took their seats in the restaurant that Carmel was more interested in getting laid than in any business proposition he had for her, and he suspected that was why his dad had sent him along to seal the deal instead of coming himself: because his mum would have strung the old man up by his balls before she would let him entertain a thirsty vamp like Carmel. He had no intention of fucking her, but he was giving her the full charm offensive to make her *think* he would. And it seemed to be working, so he wasn't happy when his phone started vibrating again.

'If you need to get that, do it now while I powder my nose,' Carmel said, reaching for her handbag.

Dale smiled and nodded his agreement, then waited until she'd left the table before snatching his phone up.

'I'm in a meeting,' he said before his wife could speak. 'And it's a really important one, so—'

'This is important too,' Cheryl interrupted. 'I'm at my house and there are two girls here.'

'What?' Dale frowned. 'What are you doing there?'

'Never mind that, you need to get over here,' Cheryl said. 'I think one of them has had a miscarriage, and she's lost a lot of blood. I was about to call an ambulance, but the other girl's so scared, I thought I'd best talk to you first.'

'Don't call anyone!' Dale barked. Then, holding up his hand in an apologetic gesture to the diners at the surrounding tables, he lowered his voice, and said, 'I'll be there as soon as I can. Just sit tight and don't do anything.'

'OK, but you need to hurry,' Cheryl urged. 'I'm serious, Dale. This doesn't look good.'

'I said I'm coming,' he hissed, cutting the call as Carmel came back to the table.

'Trouble?' she asked.

'I, er, need to go and take care of something,' Dale said, sliding his wallet out of his pocket and gesturing for the waiter to bring the bill.

'Now?' Carmel pouted. 'I was hoping we could continue our chat somewhere more private. Surely you have people who can go in your place?'

'I'm afraid not,' he said apologetically, handing his card to the waiter.

'Really?' Her expression hardened. 'Then I guess we're done here.'

'Look, why don't I meet up with you when I've dealt with it,' Dale suggested. 'It shouldn't take too long. An hour at most.'

'Give your father my best wishes for his campaign,' Carmel replied, waggling her fingers goodbye before sashaying towards the door.

Hissing, 'Shit!' Dale raked his fingers through his hair as he watched her walk away. Then, making a snap decision, he went after her, saying, 'Give me two minutes to make a call and I'll be right with you.'

'I'll be outside,' she said, smiling like a cougar that was about to get the cream.

Cheryl was standing at the bedroom window, alternating between looking out for Dale's car and checking on the girl, who was, she'd discovered, still breathing. Aware that every second that passed could be putting the girl in more danger, she almost cried with relief when Sonia's car pulled up outside twenty minutes after she'd spoken to Dale. Guessing that he must have sent her on ahead, she told the other girl, who was huddled in the corner, sobbing quietly, to wait there before jogging down the stairs to let her mother-in-law in.

'Why are you here?' Sonia demanded as soon as she stepped inside. 'And how did you even get here?'

'I needed to come home and pick up some things, so Jakub gave me a lift,' Cheryl told her.

'Did he now?' Sonia murmured, a flash of anger flaring in her eyes.

'Didn't Dale tell you what's happening?' Cheryl asked, wondering why the woman seemed more interested in her being here than she was about the girls. 'I found two of Alfie's girls hiding in my bedroom. Dorothy must have broken in when she realised I was staying at your place and hidden them here so Alfie wouldn't find out they're pregnant. One of them looks like she's had a miscarriage,' she went on when Sonia didn't reply. 'I wanted to call an ambulance, but Dale said he'd deal with it when he got here. I hope he's on his way, because it really doesn't look good.'

'Doctor Nowak's coming, so he'll take care of everything,' Sonia assured her.

'Has anyone told Alfie?' Cheryl asked, confused as to why Sonia wasn't reacting more strongly to the awful news. 'Dale said he spoke to Dorothy and she convinced him she wasn't doing anything wrong, but she obviously lied.'

'Trust me, Alfie's employees do not lie to him,' Sonia replied coolly. 'Whatever's happening here, it has nothing to do with Dorothy.'

'But one of the girls told me that Dorothy was going to deal with it, so she knows they're here,' Cheryl argued. 'They're *pregnant*,' she repeated, wondering if Sonia had missed that bit. 'So Agata must have been telling the truth about them being forced to sleep with men. If you won't do something about this, I'm going to call the police myself. I told you about this months ago, but you obviously didn't take it seriously, and now look what's happened. It's disgusting she was allowed to get away with it for so long.'

'You need to calm down and concentrate on your own baby,' Sonia said sharply. 'Getting hysterical over something you know nothing about isn't good for you *or* him. Now go and sit down while I arrange for you to be taken home.'

'I *am* home,' Cheryl said, staring at her in disbelief. 'And I'm not being hysterical. I'm worried about that girl who might be dying on my bed, and the baby that's wrapped in one of my towels!'

A knock came at the door before Sonia could answer, and she said, 'That'll be the doctor. We'll discuss your concerns later. Until then, stay out of the way, because I don't want you getting any more upset than you already are.'

Cheryl was confused by Sonia's lack of reaction to the horrific news, but the woman had already turned to open the door. The doctor who had attended to Agata walked in, followed by two men who were wearing what looked like black scrubs, and Cheryl went into the living room and closed the door when she heard Sonia speak to them in Polish. Alone, she rang Dale again, and left a message when it went to voicemail, asking, 'Where the hell are you? Your mum and the doctor are here, but I need *you*.'

Unable to settle after sending the message, Cheryl gazed out of the window. The doctor's car and a black van with dark-tinted windows were parked behind Sonia's car, and some of the neighbours had come out onto their doorsteps, no doubt to have a nosy. She caught a movement in the corner of her eye and switched her gaze to Edna's house in time to see Dorothy coming out through the gate carrying a suitcase. The woman scuttled down the road with her head bowed, clearly hoping not to be noticed, and Cheryl rushed to the door, determined to go after her and stop her from getting away.

Her path was blocked by Sonia and one of the men in scrubs, who were standing in the hallway.

'Dorothy's getting away,' she said, pointing to the front door. 'She needs to be stopped! Call the police!' Forced to take a step back when the man walked forward, she looked at Sonia, asking, 'What's going on?'

'Sit down, dear,' Sonia said, taking a seat on the sofa.

Sure they were about to tell her that the girl on her bed was dead, Cheryl's heart sank as she sat next to her mother-in-law. She felt a sharp scratch and stared down in confusion when she saw that the man was injecting something into the back of her hand. Shocked, she snapped her gaze up to Sonia, but the woman's face immediately began to blur, and the room started to spin before everything turned black.

Chapter 42

Cheryl's head felt heavy and her mouth was so dry, her tongue was sticking to the roof of it. The room was dark when she prised her eyes open, and it took several moments before she was able to see the outlines of the furniture. Confused, because she had absolutely no recollection of coming to bed, she sat up and dropped her feet to the floor. Instantly snatching them up again when she felt rough floorboards beneath her bare soles instead of carpet, she rubbed her eyes and frowned when the unfamiliar shapes came into focus and she saw that this wasn't her and Dale's room.

'Dale?' she croaked.

No answer came and she realised she was alone when she saw that the other side of the bed was empty. She had no idea where she was, or how she'd got there, and she shook her head in an effort to clear her clouded thoughts, but it only made her feel dizzy.

A sliver of light under the door to her left caught her eye, and she slowly stood up and felt her way towards it. She twisted the handle, but it didn't open.

'Hello?' she called, pressing her ear to the wood as the fear began to rise. 'Can anybody hear me?'

She heard footsteps and quickly backed away from the door

at the sound of a key being slotted into a lock. The door creaked open, and she shielded her eyes with her hand when bright light flooded into the room.

'Why are you out of bed?' Sonia asked, taking her arm and guiding her back across the room.

'Where am I?' Cheryl asked, squinting at her. 'This isn't our room.'

'No, it's not,' Sonia affirmed. 'But it's where you'll be staying until you're better.'

'What do you mean?' Cheryl asked, sitting down hard when the backs of her knees hit the mattress. 'I'm not ill.'

'Yes you are,' Sonia said, helping her to lift her legs onto the bed before pulling the quilt over her. 'You had a breakdown and you've been in and out of consciousness for the last four days. Now relax and try not to get agitated. Rosa's going to bring some water so you can take your medication.'

'What medication?' Cheryl stared at her. 'I'm not on anything.'

'It's an antipsychotic Doctor Nowak prescribed after you threatened to kill yourself,' Sonia explained. 'Nothing to worry about.'

'No . . .' Cheryl shook her head, convinced that this had to be a nightmare, because it was too crazy to be real. 'There's no way I'd threaten to do that.'

'But you did, dear,' Sonia said, gently stroking her hair. 'We were in the kitchen talking and you said you needed the toilet, then I heard you shouting and found you at the top of the stairs threatening to throw yourself down. Luckily, Doctor Nowak was visiting one of our friends close by and was able to get here within a few minutes, or I dread to think what might have happened. He says you're suffering pregnancy psychosis.'

Cheryl's head was spinning and she couldn't make any sense of what she was hearing. She didn't remember any of that. In fact, the last thing she *did* remember was being driven somewhere and gazing out at the landscape, but she had no idea where she'd been going, or who had been driving.

'Don't think about it too hard,' Sonia advised. 'The brain blocks out the details of psychotic episodes to protect you from the trauma, so you just need to relax and let us take care of you.'

Cheryl swallowed the sickly taste that was flooding her mouth. Something about what Sonia was saying didn't feel right. If it was true that she'd threatened to kill herself, why had they locked her in here instead of taking her to hospital?

Before she could ask, a tap came at the door and Rosa entered carrying a jug of water and a glass.

Sonia slipped a small brown bottle out of her pocket and tipped two capsules into her hand as Rosa poured a glass of water.

'Take these,' she said, smiling as she handed the capsules to Cheryl. 'You'll feel a lot better in a few minutes, I promise.'

'No.' Cheryl shuffled further back against the pillow. 'I don't want them.'

'You *need* them,' Sonia insisted. Then, sighing, she said, 'If you refuse, I'll have no choice but to call Doctor Nowak and have him inject you instead.'

'*No!*' Cheryl gasped, trying to stand up. 'I need to get out of here.'

'If you try to leave, you'll be sectioned,' Sonia warned, placing a firm hand on her shoulder and pushing her back down onto the bed. 'You don't understand how serious this condition is. You threatened to *kill* yourself, and if you refuse help, they'll take the baby away as soon as it's born. Is that what you want?'

'I don't believe you,' Cheryl cried, starting to panic.

Sonia turned her head and spoke to Rosa in Polish, and

Cheryl's heart started pounding when the woman quickly left the room.

'If you've sent her to get the doctor, make her stop,' she begged. '*Please*, Sonia. There's nothing wrong with me.'

'You're ill, but you still need to eat, so I've told her to bring you some soup,' Sonia explained. 'I know you're confused, but I'm trying to help you, and that's going to be difficult if you keep fighting me.'

'Everything all right?' Dale asked, strolling into the room.

'She's resisting her medication,' Sonia told him. 'She thinks I'm lying about the psychosis.'

'Babe, it's OK,' Dale said, sitting on the edge of the bed. 'My mum's only trying to help. We *all* are.'

'But there's nothing wrong with me,' Cheryl whimpered, shrinking away from him.

'You've been unconscious for four days,' he said, stroking her tear-streaked face. 'You really scared us, sweetheart. It came out of nowhere and you could have seriously hurt yourself and the baby, so we had no choice but to call the doctor in to sedate you.'

'If that's true, why aren't I in hospital?'

'You're getting private treatment here that's better than any hospital,' Dale said, raising her chin with his finger to look into her eyes. 'Trust me; we only want the best for you and the baby. And the doctor says this psychosis thing will probably disappear as fast as it started once he's born.'

'I don't understand what's happening,' Cheryl said, frustrated that she couldn't remember anything.

'You need to relax and let the medication do its work,' Dale said softly. 'We all love you and want you to get better, and we're doing everything we can to keep you and the baby safe. Now take these and get some sleep,' he urged, holding out the capsules his mother had passed to him.

'You won't let them take the baby, will you?' Cheryl asked fearfully.

'*Never,*' he assured her. 'He's my boy, and I'll protect him with my life.'

Cheryl reluctantly took the capsules and put them into her mouth. She had never felt more confused in her life, and she couldn't think straight, much less remember anything. But Dale and Sonia were both insisting that she had threatened to kill herself, so she genuinely didn't know if she could trust her own judgement right then.

'There you go,' Dale said, smiling when she'd washed them down with water. 'Now I've got to go out for a bit, but I'll pop in later to see how you're doing. OK?'

Cheryl nodded and watched as he left the room, sidestepping Rosa, who had just come back carrying a tray containing a bowl of soup and a slice of buttered bread. The woman peered into her eyes as she placed the tray on the bed, and Cheryl felt like crying when she saw the concern etched on her lined face before she turned and walked out again.

Sonia had switched a lamp on, and she leaned over and fluffed the pillows behind Cheryl's head, saying, 'You'll be nice and comfortable now, so eat and then try to get some sleep. If you need the toilet, use the commode.' She pointed to a chair in the corner. 'I'll come back later and see how you're getting on.'

'Thank you,' Cheryl murmured.

'My pleasure,' Sonia smiled, following Rosa out and locking the door behind her.

Alone, Cheryl looked around. The room was small and cluttered compared to the other rooms in the Moran house; the furniture looked ancient, the wallpaper was old-fashioned and faded, and the roof was sloped on one side, which made her wonder if it was an attic room.

A tiny window beneath the slope caught her eye, and she lifted the tray off her legs and placed it to one side before getting up. The window was too high to see out of from the floor, so she carried the commode chair over and stood on that. The window had a rusted bar latch, and it took her several attempts to shift it. When, at last, it popped open, she sucked in the fresh, cold air and gazed out into the darkness, trying to locate where in the house she was.

Quickly pulling her head back when she heard voices down below, she spotted the faint glow of lights in the windows of the cottages and caravans in the distance, and realised she was at the rear of the house; probably directly above the patio, since that was where Dale and his father seemed to have most of their business chats. She picked up a female voice among the lower male ones, and guessed that Sonia must be out there, too; but they were speaking in Polish, so she couldn't understand what they were talking about.

Cheryl snapped her head round when she heard what sounded like a little girl crying and nervously scanned the darker areas of the room behind her. Visions of horror films she'd seen about people who were locked in attics full of ghosts leapt into her mind, and she quickly climbed down off the chair and got back into bed.

Heart rate slowly returning to normal when she didn't hear any more noises or see any ghostly figures, her stomach rumbled as she picked up the aroma of the soup, and she ate a little before laying the tray aside. She was starting to feel sleepy, but she fiercely resisted it, terrified that she might never wake up again if she allowed herself to drift off.

Chapter 43

Stefan had only been home from work for a couple of minutes when he received a call from his father ordering him to come over for a family meeting. It was a cold night, but the patio was the only place in the house that wasn't wired for sound, so that's where he, his parents and brother were now sitting beneath the heaters. He was tired and hungry and knew it probably wasn't a good idea to drink whisky on an empty stomach when he had to drive home again shortly, but what he'd heard so far had disturbed him so much, he needed it.

As Stefan poured a second shot, he glimpsed Estelle giving him the death stare through the kitchen window, where she'd been ordered to stay with the children. He had no clue why she had insisted on coming since she claimed to hate the place and never had a nice word to say about his mother. But she was so paranoid they would talk about her if she wasn't there, she refused to be 'left out', so she only had herself to blame if she was bored.

'So what's the plan?' Alfie asked Sonia, whom he was annoyed with for creating this latest shitstorm, since she was the one who had made the decision, without consulting him, to have their daughter-in-law drugged. 'You can't just keep her locked in the attic till the baby's born.'

'If she behaves, I won't have to,' Sonia said, leaning forward to refill her glass. 'But if she doesn't, that's exactly what's going to happen.'

'Someone's bound to come looking for her,' Alfie argued. 'She's not like those other girls. She's *English*, and English people don't just disappear off the face of the earth without someone reporting them missing.'

'Who's going to notice she's not around anymore?' Sonia asked. 'She has no family or friends; only that senile old man who lives next door and his common little carer.'

'The carer who texts her every day to give her updates about the old man?' Alfie replied sarcastically. 'Yeah, I'm sure *she* won't think it's odd if Cheryl suddenly stops responding.'

'But she won't stop, because I'll be doing it for her,' Sonia said, smiling slyly as she held up Cheryl's phone. 'I know you think this is a step too far,' she went on when Alfie shook his head in despair. 'But I will not allow her to put this family in jeopardy.'

'This is your fault.' Alfie turned on Dale. 'You could have had any girl you wanted, but you had to go and pick the one who lives across the fucking road from the new house. Now she knows about Dorothy and the girls, if she goes to the police when she gets out of here and they start digging, we're fucked.'

'That's not going to happen,' Sonia interjected before Dale could respond. 'Trust me, by the time I've finished with her, she'll think she imagined the entire thing.'

'You'd better be right, because the child's going to need its mother,' Alfie said. 'And don't kid yourself that no one'll wonder where she's gone, because someone *will* come looking for her eventually, I guarantee it.'

'This is exactly why I told you to get rid of that bloody house,' Sonia berated him. 'People on those scummy estates are too nosy for their own good. We've never had any of this trouble in the other houses, because rich people don't care what's happening in their neighbours' lives as long as it doesn't interfere with theirs.'

Pursing his lips thoughtfully, Alfie looked at Stefan, who had so far remained silent. 'What would you do, Son?'

'Why are you asking *me*?' Stefan replied coolly. 'You didn't trust me enough to let me know you were still dabbling in that shit while I've been working my arse off to legitimise the businesses, so why involve me now?'

'You're part of this family, and what's bad for one is bad for all,' said Sonia. 'So stop being so bloody self-righteous and answer your father.'

'OK, I'll tell you what I'd do,' Stefan replied bluntly. 'First, I'd sack Dorothy and shut down that whole operation. The woman's an absolute liability.'

'She's already gone,' Sonia told him. 'She did a runner when I went over there, so we moved the girls into one of the other houses and sent some of the men out to track her down.'

'I hope they find her, because she knows far too much.'

'Already found and dealt with.'

'Well, that's something,' Stefan said. 'As for the Cheryl problem,' he went on. 'You need to let her go home and raise her baby in peace, without *his* interference.' He jerked his thumb at Dale.

'It's my fucking baby as well,' Dale retorted angrily.

'You don't even like kids, so what do you care?' Stefan snapped. 'And you haven't got time to be playing at parenting now Dad's put you in charge of all those projects.'

'Ah, so that's what's really eating you,' Dale smirked. 'Your nose is out of joint because you're jealous Dad's put me in charge.'

'I'm in charge, not you,' Alfie cut in sharply. 'I might have given you more responsibility, but what's given can just as easily be taken away, and don't you forget it.'

'*I'll* look after the baby,' Sonia said, bringing them back to the subject at hand. 'He's a Moran, and he'll be raised as such.'

'And what if it's a girl?' Stefan raised an eyebrow. 'Still be as keen then, will you?'

'How *dare* you,' Sonia glowered. 'I am your mother, and you will speak to me with respect.'

'All right, enough of the dramatics,' Alfie said, slapping his hand down hard on the arm of his chair. 'We still need to decide what to do about Cheryl.'

'She stays where she is until the baby's born,' Sonia said with finality. 'She doesn't remember anything yet, but if her memory comes back and she decides to turn on us ...'

She left the rest of the sentence hanging, but they all knew what she meant, and Stefan wasn't having any of it.

'No,' he said firmly, looking his mother in the eye. 'She's done nothing wrong, and I won't let you deprive the child of its mother because of *your* bad decisions.'

'So what would you suggest?' Sonia asked. 'Set her free and wait for her to blow the entire family apart when she remembers what she saw?'

'Your mother's right,' Alfie sighed. 'I'm fond of the girl, but family comes first.'

'She *is* family,' Stefan reminded him. 'But even if she wasn't, there are better ways to handle this.'

'How?' Sonia challenged.

'Clean up the mess so there's no evidence for the police to find if she *does* end up talking to them,' said Stefan. 'And I don't only mean cleaning that house out, I mean quit the entire operation and concentrate on the legit businesses. If Dad's serious about running for mayor, the last thing he needs is someone to start digging and link him to the illegal stuff.'

'And what are we supposed to do with the girls?' Sonia asked. 'We can't just set them all free and hope they don't talk.'

'You still need care workers for the homes, so let them carry on doing that,' said Stefan. 'And you can still use the guys as labour, but start paying them properly so they can send money home. Trust me, they'll soon forget all the other shit if you give them what they came for in the first place.'

'I've got a better idea,' Dale said, grinning evilly. 'Round the lot of 'em up, fetch them over here and organise a hunt. I'm sure some of Dad's new pals would pay through the nose for the chance to test their shooting skills, and it'd give us great blackmail material for the future.'

'Don't be so disgusting.' Stefan glared at him. 'They're human beings, not fucking vermin.'

'Stef's right,' Alfie said. 'We need to make big changes, and *you* need to get Cheryl on side.'

'No worries.' Dale grinned. 'She loves me, so it'll be a piece of cake.'

'If we're done here, I'm off,' Stefan said, sinking the rest of his drink and slamming his glass down on the table. 'I need to get the kids home.'

'Before you go, I want a word,' Alfie said. 'In private,' he added, looking pointedly at Dale and Sonia.

Sonia got up without argument and walked into the house. Dale flashed his brother a look of pure contempt before following.

In the kitchen, Estelle watched out of the corner of her eye as Sonia walked through to the hallway and on into the living room, slamming the door behind her. Sliding off her seat when

Dale went over to the sink and downed the rest of his drink, she walked up beside him, and said, 'What's going on?'

'Family stuff,' he said dismissively, turning the tap on to rinse his glass.

'Where's Cheryl?'

'Sleeping.'

'We need to talk,' Estelle whispered, touching his arm.

'Leave it out,' he hissed, flashing a glance at Frankie and Poppy, who were watching them from the sofa at the other end of the room.

Nostrils flaring when he pushed past her and walked out of the room, Estelle told the children to tell their father she'd gone to the toilet if he came inside before she got back, and then rushed out into the hall.

Dale had already climbed the main stairs and was almost at the top of the narrow staircase that led to the attic rooms when he heard a creak. Turning to see Estelle coming up behind him, he hissed, 'What the fuck are you doing?'

'Why do you always have to be so cold?' she asked. 'I only want to talk.'

'About what?'

'Us, obviously.'

'Not this again.' He rolled his eyes. 'How many times do I have to tell you, there is no *us*. Never was, never will be.'

'That's not what you said when you were fucking me and telling me you loved me,' she reminded him. 'You said we'd be together when the kids were old enough for me to leave Stef.'

'And you believed me?'

'Yes I did, and I still do, because I know you meant it,' Estelle said, stepping closer and peering up into his eyes. 'You can pretend you don't care as much as you like, but we both know I'm the one you really want.'

'Behave,' Dale sneered. 'I only fucked you because I was bored and you used to look half decent before you piled the weight on. State of you now, I wouldn't touch you with *Stef's* dick, never mind mine.'

'You bastard,' Estelle gasped, tears springing into her eyes. 'I've been faithful to you.'

'Oh, so you haven't fucked Stef since we did it?' Dale raised a bemused eyebrow.

'Only when I absolutely had to, or he'd have got suspicious,' she replied defensively. 'I was waiting to be with you.'

'You've got patience, I'll give you that,' Dale laughed.

'You think this is funny?' she squawked. 'Well, let's see how funny everyone *else* thinks it is.'

She turned to march back down the stairs, but Dale seized her by the arm before she could take a step and slammed her up against the wall with his hand around her throat.

'Say one word to my family and it'll be the last time you ever open your mouth,' he warned. 'And it won't only be me you'll have to worry about, 'cos my mum'll rip your heart out and eat it before she lets you break up this family. Want to risk that, do you?'

'I *hate* you,' Estelle cried.

'Ditto,' spat Dale. 'Now get back to your own family and keep my fuckin' name out of your mouth.'

Smirking, he let her go, and she clutched her throat and almost fell down the narrow steps in her haste to get away.

Dale waited until she'd gone before continuing on up to the top and unlocking the first door. In the dim glow of the bedside lamp, he could see Cheryl lying motionless in the bed. Satisfied that she was out of it and wouldn't be able to cause any trouble, he quietly closed and relocked the door.

*

Eyes tightly closed, Cheryl listened until Dale's footsteps had receded before daring to release the breath she'd been holding. Her head felt like it was stuffed with cotton wool and she knew it wouldn't be long before the capsules knocked her out, but she had managed to get out of bed and creep over to the door when she'd heard Dale arguing with someone outside the room. She had been shocked to realise that it was Estelle – and even more shocked to hear what they were saying.

Making it back to the bed just before Dale opened the door, she had prayed that he wouldn't come too close; afraid that he would see her heart thumping like a jackhammer beneath the quilt and realise she was awake. Relieved that he hadn't come into the room, she opened her eyes and stared up at the ceiling. She had never in her wildest dreams suspected that Dale was interested in his sister-in-law, but now she knew they'd had an affair, she understood why Estelle had been an absolute bitch since they'd met. If the woman had been banking on dumping Stefan and running away with Dale when the kids were older, it must have killed her when he brought Cheryl home. She had no idea if the affair had happened before or after she'd started seeing him, but the fact that he had betrayed his own brother was not only disgusting, it also made a complete mockery of the so-called family loyalty the Morans were always banging on about.

Unable to fight the effects of the medication any longer, Cheryl closed her eyes when a wave of exhaustion washed over her. As the darkness pressed down on her, she prayed that she would quickly recover from the psychosis so she could go home and put some distance between her and Dale while she processed what she had learned tonight. If it turned out that the affair had happened before they met, she would consider trying to work things out; but if it had happened while they were together, there was absolutely no way back from that.

Chapter 44

Cheryl was woken by the sound of distant voices outside. Daylight was filtering in through the grubby little window, and the air in the room was icy as she climbed out of bed and stumbled over to the commode chair. The voices were coming from the cottages, where the workmen were getting into the Transit van and the Jeep, and she felt a twinge of resentment as she watched them set off down the dirt track, knowing that they were free to go about their days as usual while she was locked in this room. If she'd found herself in this same situation at her own house, she would have shouted for help, and people from all over the estate would have been there in seconds to kick the door in and rescue her. But out here, in the middle of nowhere, the only people who would hear her calls were Dale's family and the people who worked for them, so it was futile to even consider it.

She climbed down off the chair when the vehicles had gone and hurried back to the warmth of the bed. Resting her head on the pillows, she closed her eyes and breathed deeply and evenly in an effort to slow down the jumbled thoughts in her mind. Something in Sonia's story about her supposed breakdown was niggling at her. She'd been through some terrible times in her life, finding her mother dead being the absolute worst.

The fallout with her father, culminating in him remarrying and emigrating without her had been traumatic, and the breakdown of her relationship with Chris had broken her heart. But never once, throughout all of that, had she ever thought about killing herself, so why would she suddenly go crazy and threaten to do it at a time when she had everything to live for?

A vision of Doctor Nowak and two men in black entering her house flashed across her mind's eye, immediately followed by another of Sonia sitting on her sofa. She knew they couldn't be connected, because the only time the doctor had ever been to her house was after she'd found Agata hiding in her shed. And Sonia had only ever been there once, when she had turned up after Cheryl had kicked Dale out when he'd lied about staying at Anna's place. Those visits had been on different occasions, and both had taken place at night, and yet it had looked like there was daylight behind them in the visions. But the images had come and gone so fast, she honestly couldn't be sure *what* she'd seen.

Snapping her eyes open when she heard footsteps outside the room and a key being turned in the lock, Cheryl sat up as Sonia walked in looking as perfectly coiffed as usual.

'Morning.' Sonia smiled. 'Did you manage to sleep OK?'

'Yes, thanks,' Cheryl replied quietly, her gaze flitting to the open door behind the woman. The key was still dangling in the lock and she had a sudden urge to jump up, rush past Sonia and lock her in. Aware that she would probably get caught within seconds and be forcibly injected or sectioned, she dismissed the idea as quickly as it had come.

'Rosa will be up shortly with your breakfast, so you can put something in your stomach before you take your medication,' Sonia said, perching on the edge of the bed. 'I'm going to be out for most of the day, but I want to make sure you're comfortable before I go.'

'I'll be fine,' Cheryl said. 'And I don't need any medication. I'm not suicidal, and I'd never do anything to hurt the baby.'

'That's how you feel *now*, but who's to say you won't have another breakdown if you stop taking it?' Sonia asked. 'Doctor Nowak said this type of psychosis is tricky, because the episodes can strike at any moment. Do you really want to risk that?'

When Cheryl didn't reply, Sonia sighed and patted her hand, saying, 'I know you can't remember what you did, and you probably think we're being cruel keeping you locked up in here; but this is the only room in the house with a lock, apart from mine and Alfie's, so it's safer for you to stay in here for now. As soon as you're stable, you'll be able to move back in with Dale.'

Remembering the conversation she'd overheard the previous night, Cheryl's jaw clenched at the mention of Dale's name. She needed to speak to him to find out if the affair had happened before they got together, but Rosa appeared with her breakfast before she could ask Sonia where he was.

'About time,' Sonia said, irritably waving Rosa into the room.

As the older woman laid the tray on Cheryl's lap, Sonia took the small brown bottle out of her pocket and shook out two capsules. Handing them to Rosa when her phone started ringing, she gestured to the glass of water on the tray and said something in Polish before walking out onto the landing to take the call.

Rosa's lips tightened as she looked at the capsules in her hand, and she flicked a hooded glance at Sonia before turning back to Cheryl and peering deeply into her eyes as she held out her hand.

Cheryl sensed that the woman was trying to convey some-thing to her, but she wasn't sure what. Confused when Rosa's hovered her hand over hers, then withdrew it without dropping the capsules, she gave the woman a questioning look. Still peer-ing at her intently, Rosa gave the slightest of head-shakes before handing her the glass of water.

Aware that Sonia, who was still talking on her phone but had stopped pacing, was watching the interaction, Cheryl realised what Rosa was doing and raised her hand to her mouth as if putting the capsules into it before drinking some of the water, earning herself a smile and a nod of approval from Sonia.

Quietly thanking Rosa when she saw that the woman's hands were shaking as she slid the capsules into her cardigan pocket, Cheryl picked up a piece of the buttered toast off the plate on the tray and bit into it.

Sonia finished her call and gestured for Rosa to leave the room before pulling the door shut and locking it.

Sonia and Rosa had already been in to give Cheryl the capsules and something to eat when Dale got home from work that evening. Sonia had handed them to her this time and had stood over her and watched her put them into her mouth, so she had been forced to swallow them. Wary after seeing Rosa's reaction to them that morning, Cheryl had waited until she was alone and had then stuck her fingers down her throat and thrown them back up. Afraid that Sonia might spot them if she left them in the commode, she had fished the capsules out of the vomit and stuffed them into a small hole she'd found in the material on the side of the mattress.

When Dale came into the room, Cheryl kept her eyes closed and forced herself to breathe slowly so he would think she was sleeping when he sat down on the edge of the bed. He reeked of perfume and booze, and she could feel his breath on the flesh of her arm as he stared down at her. For a horrible few moments, she feared he might actually try to have sex with her, so when he got up and left the room, she almost cried with relief.

Chapter 45

Cheryl quickly got used to her new routine as the days passed. Dale had pretty much stopped visiting since she always pretended to be asleep when he was there, but Sonia and Rosa came twice each day – morning and afternoon – to bring her food, drinks and medication. If Sonia handed the capsules to her, she would hold them in the side of her cheek until she was alone, then spit them out and stash them in the mattress; whereas Rosa would pocket them if she was tasked with giving them to her.

As the drugs left her system and her memory started to improve, Cheryl was able to form a true picture of what had happened on the day before she'd woken to find herself locked in that room. She remembered that she had been bored and homesick and had asked Jakub for a lift into Manchester. He had dropped her off at the Langley estate, and she had gone home to find two of Alfie's girls in her house; one of whom was pregnant, while the other had suffered a miscarriage.

The memory of that tiny foetus loosely wrapped in one of her towels while its mother lay dying in a pool of her own blood on the bed had broken Cheryl's heart, and she'd cried for hours after recalling that awful moment. Her biggest regret was that she'd called Dale instead of the emergency services that day, but she had trusted that he would arrange to get the girl treated privately, as he had told her had been done for Agata.

Dale had promised to come and take care of everything, but he'd sent his mother instead; and Sonia had called in Doctor Nowak, who had arrived a short time later with two men in black scrubs – one of whom, Cheryl now remembered, had injected something into her hand that had knocked her clean out.

There had been no psychotic episode and she hadn't threatened to throw herself down the stairs. It was all a lie, concocted by Sonia to fool her into taking those capsules voluntarily, so they could keep her sedated while she was locked in there. She now knew *what* had happened, but she still had no idea *why*, and could only assume that Sonia had thought she'd stumbled onto something that could get the family into trouble. Whatever it was, she was locked in this room because of it, and was – so the Morans thought – still drugged up to the eyeballs. But how long were they planning to keep her there? And what were they intending to do with her and the baby when she gave birth?

Terrified to even think that far ahead, Cheryl played their game to the best of her abilities; acting groggy when they came to give her food and medication, and pretending she was sleeping if they bothered to look in on her outside the scheduled times.

But everything came to a head at the end of her third week of captivity, when Dale appeared during Sonia and Rosa's morning visit.

Sonia had a busy day planned and was eager to get the morning visit out of the way as quickly as possible. She had started working on the plans for Alfie's mayoral campaign, and the Cheryl situation was fast becoming a burden. But Alfie and Dale couldn't deal with it, because they were working long hours, so she had no choice but to keep going up there.

This morning, she stayed out on the landing, because Rosa hadn't yet emptied the commode and she didn't want the stench from it to attach itself to her clothes. She gave Rosa the capsules and ordered her to hurry up and give them to Cheryl, but as Rosa held out her hand to pass them to Cheryl, Sonia heard somebody coming up the stairs behind her and raised an eyebrow when she turned and saw that it was Dale.

'What are you doing here?' she asked. 'I thought you'd already left for work.'

'I was about to, but Dad asked me to give you this,' Dale said, handing a piece of paper to her, on which a phone number was written.

'What is it?' Sonia asked.

Dale didn't answer. Instead, eyes narrowed, he walked past her into the room and grabbed Rosa's shoulder, roughly turning her around.

'Is something wrong?' Sonia asked, walking in behind him.

In the bed, unable to understand Dale's reply to Sonia's question, because he spoke in Polish, Cheryl's stomach clenched with dread when she saw him reach into Rosa's pocket and pull out the capsules the woman had slipped in there seconds earlier. Wincing when he showed them to his mother and she saw the fury in Sonia's eyes, she cried, 'Stop it!' when Sonia seized Rosa by the front of her dress and started slapping her hard across the face.

'Dale, make her stop,' she implored when Sonia dragged Rosa out onto the landing, still hitting her and screeching at her.

'How long?' Dale asked, looking down at her.

'How long what?' she asked, tears welling in her eyes as she listened to the slaps and Rosa's cries of pain.

'*This.*' Dale shoved the capsules under her nose. 'How long have you not been taking them?'

'Long enough to know I'm not ill and never was,' she replied accusingly, locking eyes with him when the awful noises faded. 'I just can't figure out why you would do this to me when everything was so good between us. But, then again, you've been lying to me from the start, so it obviously wasn't as good as I thought.'

'You still going on about that bullshit Anna told you?' Dale sneered. 'She's already admitted she was lying, so why are you—'

'I'm not talking about that,' Cheryl cut in.

'What then?' Dale demanded.

About to tell him that she knew about him and Estelle, Cheryl changed her mind when she remembered how mad he'd been on the night she had finished with him. Already in a precarious situation, she didn't want to risk making it worse by revealing that she knew about his affair and had no intention of staying with him when she got out of there.

'Well?' Dale was still waiting.

'I just don't get how you could do this when you're supposed to love me,' she muttered. 'All I did was tell you about that poor girl losing her baby, and you said you'd deal with it, so why am *I* being punished? Dorothy's the one who caused all this, not me.'

'Trust me, she's been dealt with,' said Dale. 'And my mum's doing this to protect you, not punish you.'

'How is force-feeding me drugs protecting me?' Cheryl stared at him in disbelief. 'Don't you care that they're going into the baby through me? Or is that what this is about? Are you trying to make me lose it because you never really wanted it?'

'Don't be ridiculous,' Dale sighed. 'I was happy when you told me you were pregnant.'

'*Was?*' Cheryl repeated.

'Am,' he corrected himself. 'I know it probably feels like shit right now,' he went on, sitting down and reaching for her hand. 'But it's going to be OK, I promise.'

'I don't believe you,' she said, snatching her hand free.

'Get away from her,' Sonia barked, marching back into the room at that exact moment, her eyes still blazing.

Dale obediently stood up and Cheryl defiantly raised her chin when Sonia loomed over her.

'Going to hit *me* now?' she challenged. 'Same way you just laid into that old woman for absolutely nothing.'

'You are a stupid girl,' Sonia spat. 'All you had to do was take the damn capsules and everything would have been fine. But now I know Rosa's been lying about giving them to you, I'll have to arrange for the doctor to inject you instead.'

'Dale, help me,' Cheryl cried. 'If you care about me and the baby, you can't let her do this.'

'Don't try to manipulate my son, because his loyalty lies with us, not you,' Sonia hissed. 'We've given you the best care possible, and you've thrown it back in our faces, so this is your own fault.'

'No, it's not,' Cheryl argued. 'I did nothing wrong, and you've got no right to keep me prisoner. As soon as I get out of here, I'm going to tell the police everything!'

'And there we have it,' Sonia said, smiling nastily as she turned to Dale. 'Still think we can trust her, do you?'

Dale looked down at Cheryl and shook his head. 'You shouldn't have said that.'

'I'm sorry, I didn't mean it,' Cheryl spluttered, quickly back-tracking. 'I don't know what I'm supposed to have done, but whatever it is, I'll never do it again, I swear. I just want things to go back to the way they were.'

'Too late,' Sonia said. 'I gave you a chance and you blew it, so now we do things my way.'

Cheryl looked at Dale for support, but he shrugged and

handed the capsules he'd taken off Rosa to his mother before walking out.

'Sonia, please stop this,' Cheryl begged when he'd gone. 'I'll do anything you want.'

'Yes, you will,' Sonia agreed. 'But don't worry; it's only for a few more months. As soon as you've given birth, Dale will take custody and it'll all be over.'

'You can't take my baby,' Cheryl gasped, protectively covering her stomach with her hands.

'It's for the best, dear,' Sonia said. 'You've already threatened to kill yourself in front of witnesses, and we have photographs of you drinking alcohol at your engagement party and wedding when you were already pregnant, so no one will be surprised when it all becomes too much for you after the birth. Alcoholism and postnatal depression are a lethal combination,' she went on in a fake-sad voice. 'We did everything we could to help you, but you hid it from us so well we didn't realise how deeply damaged you were until it was too late.'

Heart pounding, Cheryl shook her head. 'No ... You can't make me kill myself. I won't do it.'

'We'll see,' Sonia replied coolly, glancing at her watch. 'Right, that's enough chatting. You've already made me late for my first appointment, so hurry up and take the capsules or I'll call Doctor Nowak.'

Terrified by the thought of being injected again, because the grogginess and confusion she had suffered the last time had been far worse than the effects of the capsules, Cheryl reluctantly did as she'd been told.

'See how easy it is when you accept that you can't fight me,' Sonia said, smiling as she smoothed the duvet over Cheryl's legs after checking her mouth to make sure she had swallowed them. 'Now eat your breakfast and get some sleep. If you're good,

I'll have someone empty the commode later,' she added as she walked to the door.

Cheryl lay still for a few minutes to make sure that Sonia had really gone, and then rushed over to the commode and made herself sick. Sure that whoever Sonia tasked with emptying it wouldn't bother to check the stinking contents, she quickly replaced the lid without fishing out the capsules and then looked around the room. She pretty much knew every nook and cranny in there by then, but she quietly opened the drawers of the old dresser in the corner and rooted through the oddments inside, searching for something she could use to try to pick the lock.

The dresser yielded nothing useful, so she turned her attention to a small wooden chest that was sitting beneath piles of books and newspapers. Coughing when she lifted them up and disturbed the dust that was covering them, she stacked them to one side and raised the chest's lid. It was filled with an assortment of creepy-looking dolls and various other toys, but right at the bottom she found a rusted tobacco tin, and her heart leapt with hope when she opened it and saw that it contained a load of old keys.

She pressed her ear to the door and held her breath as she listened out for sounds of movement. Nothing but silence came back to her, and she prayed that Sonia and Dale had both left the house as she slotted the first key into the lock.

It didn't fit and nor did any of the others, and the true horror of the situation weighed down on her like a ton of bricks when she realised she was never getting out of there. The thought of Dale having custody of the baby was terrifying, because he and Sonia had made no secret of the fact that they were hoping for a boy. If it was a girl, they could kill it and make it look like she had committed a murder-suicide; and everyone would believe them, because Doctor Nowak had already diagnosed her as suffering from a psychosis.

Like Agata.

As that last thought crossed her mind, a light bulb flickered to life inside Cheryl's head. She had felt foolish for blindly believing the girl's story after the doctor had delivered his diagnosis that night, and she had also felt guilty for condemning Dorothy before finding out the facts. It hadn't occurred to her at that time that Dale might be lying about his father investigating the woman and finding nothing untoward going on; *or* when he'd told her that Alfie had paid for Agata to be treated privately in England before sending her home with money for her future care. Even when she had found those other girls in her house, she *still* hadn't thought that he or his family were involved. But they had not only been involved, they were in control of the whole thing. And once she realised that, she understood why Sonia had turned on her when she'd threatened to report Dorothy to the police: because it would have dropped *them* in the shit, as well.

The Morans had drugged her and locked her up to prevent her from exposing them, and the doctor had diagnosed her with pregnancy psychosis in order to discredit her if she ever spoke out against them in the future; because nobody would believe her when there was already an official record that she had gone crazy and threatened to kill herself and her baby.

Whatever was in those capsules, it had made her so confused and groggy she would probably have ended up believing that she had imagined the entire thing if she'd carried on taking them, and Sonia might, eventually, have let her go. But now she had revealed herself to be a serious threat, Sonia had decided to get rid of her altogether to protect her precious empire.

What shocked Cheryl the most was the knowledge that Dale

had been going along with his mother's plan from the start, and had even tried to sweet-talk her into believing that she was genuinely trying to help her. If he could conspire against her so easily after proclaiming to love her more than he'd ever loved any other woman, she dreaded to think how he would treat the baby when it was born. Especially if it turned out to be a girl.

Sinking down onto the bed, Cheryl cradled her stomach as tears of utter helplessness flowed down her cheeks.

Chapter 46

Jakub Kowalski couldn't sleep. It was 3 a.m. and he'd spent the entire day and most of the evening digging holes in the field behind the cottages. His muscles were aching and his limbs felt like dead weights, but his mind was refusing to switch off, so he poured a large glass of neat vodka and rolled a cigarette, then went outside to sit at the table, hoping that the cold early-morning air would help to clarify his thoughts.

The moon was casting an eerie blue light over the landscape, and he squinted as he sucked on his smoke and scanned the windows of the boss's house on the other side of the vast garden. No lights were on, which told him that the family were sleeping. But why would a little thing like conscience keep *them* up at night when they had Jakub and the other guys to do their dirty work while they concentrated on rebranding themselves as upstanding members of the community.

Jakub had worked for Alfie Moran – or *Alfons Maron* as the man was known back home – for many years. In the early days, he had respected him for his commitment to create safe, loving homes for the ageing Polish community in Manchester, while also providing much-needed employment for the youth from their homeland. He had never understood why Alfie had decided to stray from the straight line and start dabbling in drugs, guns and prostitution when he had already amassed more money by then than he would ever need. But his grandmother had once told him that men who valued wealth over the lives of their fellow man had sold their souls to the devil, and Alfie was proving that to be an absolute truth.

Now Moran had decided he wanted to get into politics – no doubt spurred on by his bitch wife, who had always considered herself a lady and probably scented the chance to bag the title for real if Alfie managed to get in with the right people – he had embarked on a massive clean-up campaign, determined to eradicate anything that could link him to his past crimes. Dorothy had already been disposed of, which was nothing less than the bitch deserved, because she was every bit as evil as Sonia, in Jakub's opinion. And the women who ran the other whorehouses had been ordered to cease their operations and revert to keeping house for the girls who were employed at Alfie's care homes.

Those girls, and the young men who had been brought over to work as labourers in Alfie's other businesses, had been offered the choice of going home or continuing in their jobs, with the promise that their wages would actually be paid to them. They had all been warned, however, that, whichever choice they made, they would be hunted down and killed if they ever spoke out about the abuse they had endured – and their families would be made to suffer, too.

As Alfie's longest-serving employee, Jakub had been forced to turn a blind eye to many things he hadn't agreed with over the years. Unlike the kids who had been lured to England by the promise of good wages only to be enslaved and abused, he had always been well paid. That was why he had stayed, despite the constant battle with his conscience: because he was the sole provider for his family back home, and his elderly parents would have starved or died in agony if he hadn't been able to feed them and buy the medications they needed.

But everyone had a breaking point, and Jakub had finally reached his.

Shifting his gaze to the tiny window at the far right of the ground floor of the house, Jakub swallowed another mouthful of vodka and took a deep drag on his smoke. That room was Rosa's and she always slept with the light on, but the window had remained dark for several weeks. He also hadn't seen Rosa moving around inside the house, which was unusual since she did all the cooking, the laundry and most of the cleaning, and could often be seen moving around the kitchen. At first, he had wondered if she might have flown home for family reasons, but he recalled her once telling him that her parents were deceased and she had lost touch with her more distant relatives, so that seemed unlikely. He had then wondered if she was sick; but if that were the case, it had lasted a long time and she would surely have recovered by now. Unless she had died, and the family had arranged for her body to be removed and buried while he and the others had been working.

Acid burned in Jakub's gut at that last thought, and he downed the rest of his drink to douse it. Rosa was a kind, decent woman, and he despised the Morans for the way they had treated her over the years – Sonia, in particular. Time was fast running out, but he would not leave this place without checking to see if Rosa was still inside that house. The apocalypse was coming, and he didn't want her to get burned when the rest of them went up in flames.

In the attic, unnoticed by Jakub, Cheryl was also having a sleepless night, and she had been watching him through the tiny attic window as he sat at that table, smoking and drinking.

She'd always found him physically intimidating, but what really unnerved her about him was the fact that he was in charge of all the other men and, therefore, the closest to Alfie and Dale. Before she had known about the abuse Agata and the other girls had been suffering, she had often seen Jakub going in and out of their house, and she now believed that he must have known exactly what was going on, even if he wasn't directly responsible for any of it.

When Jakub stubbed out his cigarette and went back into the cottage, the security light above the door went out. Unable to see anything else, Cheryl climbed down off the chair and went back to bed. She was seven months pregnant, and her belly was growing bigger by the day, despite only being given sandwiches and the occasional Pot Noodle to eat, instead of the wholesome food Rosa had used to cook.

It was several weeks since Dale had caught Rosa with the capsules, and Cheryl was convinced that Sonia had done something terrible to her after dragging her out of the room that day, because she hadn't seen her since. That made her feel both guilty and sad, not only because Rosa hadn't deserved it, but because the woman was the only one who had shown her any genuine compassion since she'd been locked in there, and her presence, if only for a few minutes at a time, had been comforting.

Sonia now came alone to dole out the medication, and any pretence of friendliness or caring was long gone. Her tone was curt, if she bothered to speak at all during her increasingly short visits; and she refused to touch the commode, so it was often left for several days before Dale reluctantly emptied it. That was good for Cheryl, because none of them ever checked the contents and found the capsules she routinely vomited back up as soon as she was alone. The stench had permeated everything, and she imagined that the room would need fumigating after she was gone. But if it kept Dale and Sonia's visits down to a bare minimum, she was happy to live with it.

As the weeks had passed with nothing to do except sleep, eat, pace the floor, look out through the window and talk to the baby when it kicked and squirmed inside her, Cheryl felt as if she was losing her mind. The closer she got to the dreaded nine-month mark, the more scared she became; terrified that her child was going to be snatched from her arms as soon as it was born. She was also petrified by the thought of Doctor Nowak being brought in to deliver it, because she wouldn't put it past Sonia to have him inject her with something lethal as soon as it came out of her body – and possibly kill the child, as well, if it was a girl.

That last thought had been playing on her mind a lot, but a glimmer of hope had pierced the gloom a few days earlier, when a beam of morning sunlight coming through the window had glanced off something metal in the corner of the room. She hadn't noticed anything over there before in the many times she had searched the area, so she had taken a look to see what it could be and had discovered a metal ring sticking out from between two floorboards. When she had managed to wriggle it all the way out, she'd been astonished to see that it was attached to a rusty old instrument that looked like a cross between a pair of scissors and a pair of tweezers.

She had immediately thought that she could use the tool as a weapon to threaten Sonia into letting her go, but as the tips of the blades were flat and blunt, she doubted they would scare the bitch. With that option a no-go, Cheryl had turned her attention to the door. Since Rosa had stopped coming, she had noticed that Sonia had taken to leaving the key in the lock on the other side so Dale could let himself in to empty the commode if she was out, so she had tested the scissor-tweezers by inserting the flat tips into the keyhole. Delighted when they easily went in, but scared that she might accidentally knock the key out because her hands were shaking so badly, she had quickly withdrawn them and had stashed the tool inside the mattress. If she was really careful, she believed she would be able to grip the end of the key and turn it. But she knew she would only get one chance, so she had forced herself to wait until she was absolutely sure that she was alone in the house before attempting it.

This morning, after a torturous three-day wait, Sonia had answered her prayers when she'd taken a phone call, in English, before entering the room, and Cheryl had clearly heard her talking about an event at the town hall at 7 p.m. the following evening, to which she, Alfie and Dale had been invited as guests of honour.

It sounded like a prestigious event, and Cheryl knew that the social-climbing bitch would walk barefoot over broken glass to be there. That was why she couldn't sleep tonight: because her head was spinning at the thought that she might actually be on the verge of getting out of there, mixed with the fear that it could be a trap; that Sonia had somehow found out about the tool and had faked that call to fool her into thinking she was going to be alone in the house tomorrow. Knowing Sonia as well as she now did, Cheryl knew that was a very real possibility; but she'd already been warned that she was going to die as soon as the baby was born, so she had nothing to lose.

Chapter 47

The sun had begun to rise by the time Cheryl finally managed to fall asleep, so she was still tired when Sonia made her morning visit a few hours later. Thankfully, the woman only stayed long enough to watch her swallow the capsules before chucking a bottle of water and a limp, shop-bought cheese and tomato sandwich onto the bed and marching out again.

The afternoon visit was equally as short, and Cheryl had been relieved that Sonia hadn't questioned why her hands were shaking so badly that she dropped the capsules on her first attempt to put them into her mouth.

Cheryl's nerves had been sparking like live wires ever since, and the closer it got to evening, the more terrified she became. She guessed that the family would probably set off at least half an hour before the event was due to start, but Sonia had her phone and there was no clock in the room, so she had no way of knowing what time it was. She knew from her time in the main house that the workmen always came home between six and seven, so she decided that she would watch out for them and then count off a full hour in seconds before making her move.

The thought of her plan failing made Cheryl feel physically sick, so she pushed it out of her mind and concentrated on planning her escape if she managed to get the door open. She couldn't leave the house by the front, because there was no way she would be able to climb over the high gates or walls in her condition. But leaving by the back would be equally hazardous, because she would have to be really careful not to set off the security lights and alert Jakub and the other men, who would undoubtedly raise the alarm if they saw her – or, worse, mistake her for a fox and shoot her.

After mulling her options over, she decided that she would go sideways. There was an annexe at the far left of the house, accessed through the utility room. Rosa's suite was in there, but if, as she suspected, Rosa had been got rid of, those rooms would now be empty, because there was no other member of staff living in the house. If she could get in there, she might be able to climb out through a window and disappear into the fields at the side of the house before anyone saw her.

Praying with all her heart that she would be able to pull this off and save herself and the baby, Cheryl stood on the chair and looked out through the window to watch for the arrival of Alfie's men.

The sky had already darkened when the men got home twenty minutes later, and Jakub went upstairs to his room while the other men headed into the kitchen to share out the food they had bought on the way back. The sound of their chatter and laughter floated up through the floorboards as they ate and drank, and it disgusted him that they already seemed to have forgotten what they had all participated in the previous night. He knew he shouldn't blame them, because they had only been following orders, but the fact that they were showing no signs of remorse disturbed him deeply.

As he stuffed the few possessions he needed into his rucksack in preparation for disappearing after he'd done what he needed to do tonight, Jakub was conflicted about whether or not to warn Aleksander. As Jakub had been Alfie's right-hand man, so Aleksander had been his, and he liked him. But liking and trusting were two very different things, and Jakub couldn't afford to take the risk of having his plan blown apart if Aleksander betrayed him.

It was fully dark outside by the time Cheryl counted out the hour in seconds after seeing the Transit van and the Jeep pull up outside the cottages. There were lights glowing behind the windows, but no sign of anyone moving around outside, so she decided it was time to put her plan into motion.

Her heart was beating so fast and hard she could barely breathe as she retrieved the tool from the mattress, and her hands were shaking so violently it took several attempts to insert the tips into the keyhole and grip the end of the key. The shock when the key started to turn almost made her drop the tool, but she took a deep breath to steady herself before continuing.

Hardly daring to believe that the door was actually unlocked when the key stopped turning, Cheryl tentatively twisted the knob, and cried out in surprise when the door started to open. She clapped her hand over her mouth and held her breath as she listened for sounds of movement on the landing outside. When nothing came back to her after several moments, she slowly eased the door open and took a tentative step out of the room.

Merely standing on the other side of the door after being locked in that room for so long was both thrilling and terrifying, and she imagined it was how a wrongly convicted prisoner must feel when they were released. Still half-expecting it to be an ambush, however, she forced herself not to rush and crept towards the narrow staircase; slowly walking down, one step at a time. Scared that the Morans might be hiding around the corner waiting to pounce when she reached the bottom, she paused on the last step and listened; but the house was silent, so she moved on.

Several lights had been left on around the house, so she was able to see exactly where she was. The room she had shared with Dale was a few doors down the landing on the right, and she tiptoed towards it and peeked in through the open door to make sure that it was empty before nervously stepping inside. Clothes were strewn across the unmade bed, dirty cups and plates were littered around the ledges, and a glass was standing alongside a half-empty bottle of whisky on the bedside table. Rosa usually tidied the room on a daily basis, so it was unusual to see it in such a state; but it confirmed her suspicion that Rosa was no longer there.

Remembering that Dale always emptied his loose change into the top drawer of the dressing table before taking his trousers off at night, Cheryl looked around to make sure that no one was hiding in the shadows before darting around the bed. Hesitating when she spotted another glass standing on the table on what had been her side of the bed, her nostrils flared in disgust when she saw red lipstick smeared around the rim. She had never in her life worn that shade, so even if the room hadn't been cleaned since she last slept in there, it definitely wasn't hers.

The realisation that Dale had screwed another woman in their bed while she was locked in the attic, pregnant with his child and being forced to take drugs, made her want to throw up. And Sonia had to have known about it, because that bitch didn't miss a thing that happened under her roof. Furious, but all the more determined to keep her baby out of their evil clutches, Cheryl opened the dresser drawer and scooped all the money out, praying there would be enough for a cab ride back to Manchester.

Angered all over again when she opened the wardrobe and

saw that all her clothes had been removed, almost as if Dale had wiped every trace of her from his mind as well as his life, she grabbed one of his jumpers, a pair of jogging pants and a jacket out of his wardrobe. The nightdress and knickers she'd been wearing for weeks were filthy, and she couldn't remember the last time she'd taken a shower or a bath. But she couldn't afford to waste time worrying about how she looked or smelled, so she pulled the clothes on over the nightdress and looked around, hoping that her boots might still be there. They weren't, but Dale had plenty of pairs of trainers, some still in their boxes, so she chose a pair of them instead. After pulling on several pairs of his socks to pad them out, she slipped the jacket on and dropped the coins into the pocket before creeping back out onto the landing.

Cheryl looked out over the banister to check that nobody was on the ground floor and then carefully made her way down the stairs; one hand firmly gripping the rail, the other protectively covering her stomach.

Chapter 48

Stefan was sitting in the corner of the pub enjoying a quiet pint and a sandwich after another long day at the shop. He'd balanced the accounts of his father's various businesses to the point that it would take a forensic accountant to find any discrepancies; and his dad, in the meantime, had taken his advice and started closing down all the illicit arms.

He was happy about that, because Frankie looked up to his grandpa and uncle far too much for his liking, and he'd dreaded the thought of them sucking him into that world. The boy was already displaying a cruel streak, and Stefan was constantly telling him to leave his sister alone; that it was wrong for boys to hit girls, and if he caught him touching her or beheading any more of her dolls, there were going to be serious repercussions. So, yeah, he was happy to know that his dad was shutting down that side of things and his son would never be a part of it.

Finished with his sandwich, Stefan sank the rest of his beer and glanced at his watch before unhooking his jacket off the back of his chair. The pub was already filling up, and the chatter at the surrounding tables was starting to give him a headache.

Weaving past the groups that were coming in as he headed for the door after taking his empty plate and glass to the bar, he bumped shoulders with someone and immediately apologised.

'No, it's my fault,' the woman said. 'I wasn't looking where I was going.'

Recognising the voice, Stefan peered at her, at the exact same time she looked at him.

'Caroline.' He gave an awkward smile. 'Long time no see.'

'Yeah, it's been a while,' she said, glancing over his shoulder as she spoke.

'It's OK, I'm alone,' he said, guessing from her worried expression that she was checking if Dale was with him. 'How've you been?'

'Good, thanks.' She stuffed her hands into her jacket pockets. 'You?'

'Same as always.' He shrugged. 'Still mucking about with old shit.'

Caroline gave a knowing smile at that, and Stefan guessed that she knew he was alluding to the time Dale had brought her over to the shop when they'd first started dating. '*This is Stef; he's the boring one,*' he'd said by way of introduction. '*He mucks about with old shit while the men in the family get on with the* real *work.*' That had pissed Stefan off, but the slap-down had rebounded when Caroline had shown a genuine interest in his antiques, much to Dale's disgust, because he hated anyone stealing his thunder.

'I'll have to pop in some time if I'm passing,' Caroline said now.

'Great,' Stefan replied, doubting that she would.

An awkward couple of moments of silence passed, and Stefan was about to say that he should get going, when Caroline said, 'I heard your brother got married?'

'Er, yeah, a few months back,' he said, hoping that the news hadn't upset her too much. Dale hadn't told him much about their break-up, only that he'd dumped her because she had been pressuring him to get married and start a family, so it couldn't have been nice for her to hear that he had moved on and done exactly that with his next girlfriend.

'That's good,' she remarked, looking more relieved than upset, he thought.

One of the girls from the group she'd come in with called her name and she turned and held up her hand to gesture that she was coming. Then, smiling at Stefan, she said, 'It was nice to see you. Take care.'

'You too,' he said, watching as she pushed her way through to where her friends were standing at the bar.

Stefan patted his pockets for his car keys as he walked on towards the door. They weren't there, so he went back to his table to check if he'd left them there. The people who were now sitting there told him that they'd already handed them in, so he went over to the bar to get them.

Thanking the barmaid when she handed them over, Stefan turned to leave, but stopped in his tracks at the sound of Caroline's voice. She was standing with her friends a few feet ahead, and her back was turned to him; but he could hear every word she was saying, and it chilled him to the bone.

One of the other girls in the group spotted him staring and whispered something that caused Caroline to spin round.

'Oh God,' she said, approaching him with a guilty look on her face. 'You didn't hear that, did you?'

'Which bit?' Stefan asked. 'The bit about you catching my brother in bed with my wife? Or the bit about you pitying me 'cos I'm a nice bloke who didn't deserve that shit?'

'I'm so sorry, Stef.' Caroline squeezed her eyes shut and shook her head. 'If I'd known you were still here, I'd have kept my mouth shut.'

'What, and deprive your friends of a good laugh at my expense?' Stefan spat. 'Thanks for nothing, Caroline.'

He pushed past her and stalked out, but she followed him and ran in front to stop him.

'I know you're angry, but I wasn't gossiping about you or taking the piss,' she insisted. 'I was telling them who you were, because they're the ones who held me together after it happened, and they thought you were him.'

'Oh, so it's all right to tell your mates, but not me?' Stefan shot back accusingly. 'I'm the only idiot who doesn't deserve to know my brother's been fucking my wife – if it's even true?' He narrowed his eyes when it occurred to him that she might have known full well that he was standing behind her and could hear her every word. 'Please tell me you didn't just make it up to cause trouble because you're jealous he got married to someone else?'

'*What?*' Caroline screwed up her face. 'God, no! I was relieved when I heard about it. He was an absolute nightmare after I finished with him; kept turning up at my gym and work, begging me to get back with him. I thought I was going to have to get a restraining order, but he suddenly stopped coming. Then I heard he'd got a new girlfriend, and I prayed she'd stay with him for long enough to make him forget about me.'

'Come off it,' Stefan scoffed. 'Dale obviously didn't care that much about you if he was screwing around behind your back, so why would he bother harassing you? If anything, he'd have been glad to get rid of you so he didn't have to put up with you nagging him to get married and have kids.'

'Is that what he told you?' Caroline gave a bitter laugh. 'Wow! That's absolute bullshit. He proposed to me a few weeks after we got together, and I turned him down, because I didn't know him well enough to make that kind of commitment. And I said no every time he asked after that, as well, because I'd already started to see things I didn't like about him. And I certainly didn't want kids with him.'

'Whether or not that's true, it still doesn't explain why he'd be so desperate to get back with you if you'd caught him with Estelle,' Stefan argued. 'Surely he'd have been worried about you telling me the first time you had an argument.'

'If he'd known I'd seen them, yeah, he probably would have been worried,' Caroline replied. 'But I never told him.'

'Why not?' Stefan asked, struggling to make sense of her story.

'Have you *seen* your brother when he gets mad?' Caroline raised an eyebrow. 'If he'd thought I was going to grass him up, he would have threatened me into keeping my mouth shut. I probably shouldn't even be telling you now, because he'll make my life hell if he finds out,' she went on. 'But I meant what I said … you *are* a nice guy, and you didn't deserve it. I just hope that, whatever happens next, you don't end up getting hurt, because I know what a nasty piece of work he can be.'

'I won't argue with you about that,' Stefan muttered.

'I know he probably initiated it, but Estelle's not completely blameless,' Caroline said. 'The dirty looks she used to give me when Dale brought me to yours, I used to wonder if she thought I was after you and was warning me to back off. I never dreamed it was because she was jealous that I was with Dale.'

Stefan's teeth were tightly clenched as he digested what he had heard. He didn't want to believe that Estelle had cheated, and with Dale of all people; but he remembered how tense and snarky she used to get whenever Dale brought Caroline to the house. He'd always thought it was because she thought his brother brash and arrogant, but she had treated Cheryl in exactly the same way she had treated Caroline, so it was obvious she saw them as the problem, not Dale. And there could only be one reason for that: she had been jealous, because Dale was the one she had wanted all along.

'Are you OK?' Caroline's soft voice broke into Stefan's thoughts.

'Yeah,' he said, a glint of steel in his eyes when he met her gaze. 'A lot of things have just slotted in place, so thanks for that. And don't worry,' he went on. 'He'll never hear where it came from when it all comes out. You have my word.'

Caroline thanked him and then hugged herself as she watched him walk to his car. That sour-faced bitch he was married to didn't deserve him, and she wished she could have told him that he was a far better man that his brother could ever hope to be; and far more handsome and intelligent, as well. But he wouldn't have believed her, because he wasn't a walking ego like Dale.

Sighing when he drove away, she turned and walked back into the pub.

Chapter 49

The Mayor's ball hadn't properly started yet, but Sonia was already having the time of her life. As soon as she'd received the invite, she had commissioned the designer, Kat Silver, to make her an evening gown; determined to outshine every other woman in attendance and grab the attention of any photographers and reporters who were present.

Kat hadn't disappointed, and Sonia felt like the queen of England, never mind Greater Manchester, as she floated around the hall in the stunning gold gown embellished with Swarovski crystals, champagne glass in hand, charming the dignitaries and their dreary little wives, and flirting with the celebrities who had also been invited.

Alfie and Dale were networking on the other side of the room, and Sonia felt a rush of pride when she saw women melting at the hint of a smile from her handsome son; while Alfie, exuding the powerful aura of a true alpha male, already had the politicians and bigwigs eating out of the palm of his hand. This was an important night for making connections, and she couldn't have been happier with their progress so far.

Excusing herself when she heard the ping of a text message coming from her handbag, Sonia left the gentleman she had been talking to and moved to a quiet space to read it. It was

Cheryl's phone that had pinged, not hers, and she tutted when she saw that it was another boring message from the old man's carer; this one letting Cheryl know that he was back in hospital after suffering a heart attack. Eager to get back to the important people, and tired of having to play nice with this faceless Sharon creature, Sonia blocked the number, safe in the knowledge that the entire charade would soon be over and the woman would pose no threat if she decided to ask questions about Cheryl's whereabouts.

The thought of Cheryl reminded Sonia that she hadn't checked the security cameras at home since arriving at the town hall, and she pulled out her own phone and quickly logged into the app. Scrolling through the various views, she didn't immediately register the shadowy figure darting across the hallway. But when she flicked forward to the view of the kitchen, her stomach flipped over.

Panicked, she looked around for Alfie and then gathered up the skirts of her gown and rushed over to him.

Cheryl felt sick with fear as she crept through the kitchen. The light was on, and she desperately hoped that none of Alfie's men were outside and spotted her through the windows. If she'd been able to crouch, she would have crawled to the utility room on her hands and knees to stay low, but her stomach was so huge, it was physically impossible.

The door to the utility room was closed when she reached it, and she pressed her ear to the wood. She knew that Rosa was probably long gone, but Sonia hated doing chores, so there was always a chance she had found a replacement to take over the old woman's duties. Aware that this might be her only chance to get out of there alive, she forced herself to risk it and twisted the handle. There were no windows in that room so it was pitch

337

dark; but she'd been in there on a couple of occasions and knew that the door to Rosa's suite was directly opposite.

Still clutching her stomach, Cheryl held her other hand out in front of her to feel for potential obstacles as she made her way across the room. Almost there, she hesitated when she heard what sounded like faint groans and mumbled words coming from behind another door to the right of Rosa's suite. Frowning when she inched towards it and noticed a key in the lock on this side of the door, she wondered if maybe Rosa was still here, after all, and Sonia had locked her away to punish her after catching her with the capsules she'd been meant to give to Cheryl.

Frown deepening at another groan from behind the door, Cheryl quickly twisted the key. She knew that she was on borrowed time and needed to concentrate on making her escape, but Rosa had been good to her, and her conscience wouldn't allow her to leave without at least checking that the woman was OK.

Stepping inside the dark space after cautiously easing the door open, she just about managed to pull her leg back when her foot hit empty space. Shaken to realise she was standing at the top of a narrow flight of wooden steps and could easily have fallen, Cheryl placed her hand on the wall to steady herself before slowly making her way down.

The further down she went, the lower the temperature dropped, and the air began to smell musty and damp. Another odour hit her when she reached the bottom, and her stomach turned when she recognised it as the same stench that came from the commode when it hadn't been emptied for a while.

The groans sounded much closer now, and Cheryl could also hear the faint trickle of water. Covering her nose with her hand, she pushed open another door at the bottom of the stairs and squinted into the darkness. Able to make out the shape of what looked like a mattress on the floor ahead, with somebody lying on it, she took a tentative step forward, whispering, 'Rosa? Is that you?'

The groans stopped, and she heard the figure inhale sharply before raising their hand into the air. Positive that it was Rosa when she heard her murmur something in Polish, Cheryl rushed over to her.

'It's Cheryl,' she whispered, holding the old woman's outstretched hand and squinting down at her. 'I'm going to get you out of here. Can you walk?'

Jakub looked down at the men who were seated around the kitchen table. Some had their heads resting on the wood, while the others had their faces buried in the food still on their plates, and he prodded the legs of a couple of them with the toe of his boot to make sure that the vodka he had laced had done its work. Satisfied that it had and they would be unable to stop him if they woke up and tried to follow him, he looped the straps of his rucksack over his shoulders and let himself out of the cottage, then hopped the fence and trudged across the grass towards the big house.

The conservatory door was locked when he tried it, but he had the tools he needed to easily break in, before doing the same to the internal door leading into the kitchen. Aware that a silent alarm would have gone off as soon as he'd broken the seal on the first door, and that the Morans would be able to see him if they checked the CCTV, he strode into the utility room and was making his way towards Rosa's suite when he noticed that the cellar door beside it was standing open.

Frowning when he heard Rosa crying out as if in pain, he shrugged the rucksack off his back and took out the sawn-off shotgun he'd packed into it before quietly making his way down the stairs.

Rosa was clutching Cheryl's hand and kept repeating the same phrase over and over in Polish. Unable to understand what she was saying, and struggling to lean down far enough to help the woman up, Cheryl was pulling on Rosa's hand when the overhead light suddenly came on. Almost wetting herself with terror when she snapped her head around and saw Jakub standing in the doorway holding a shotgun, she shifted her position to shield Rosa and covered her stomach with her arms, crying, 'Please don't shoot. I'm pregnant.'

'I will not hurt you,' Jakub replied, his deep voice sending a shudder down her spine as he approached the bed. 'I came to look for Rosa. I have not seen her for long time and needed to know she is safe.'

'I t-think she might be ill,' Cheryl stammered. 'I heard her making noises and found her locked in here.'

Jakub squatted down at the side of the mattress and placed the back of his hand on Rosa's forehead. 'She has fever,' he said, slipping his arm under the old woman and gently lifting her off the mattress. 'Come,' he ordered, jerking his head at Cheryl before striding towards the door. 'Silent alarm has been activate and they will be here soon.'

Rosa was still mumbling in Polish, and Cheryl asked what she was saying as she followed Jakub up the stairs.

'She say she hoped you were death come to take her, because she is ready to die,' Jakub said. 'But I will take her for help to make sure she live.'

'Not to Doctor Nowak?' Cheryl blurted out fearfully as she followed him into the utility room. 'He lied and said I was ill, and Sonia's been giving me medication to keep me quiet,' she continued in a rush, although she wasn't sure why she was telling him any of this when he probably already knew. 'Please don't tell them you saw me out of the room,' she begged. 'They're going to kill me and take my baby.'

'They are *devils*,' Jakub spat, his jaw muscles twitching with anger as he walked on into the kitchen. 'I have done bad thing for them, but I have made my peace with God and this is over. I will take you and Rosa to safe place, then I will tell police everything.'

Chapter 50

Stefan had murder on his mind when he screeched to a halt outside the house and jumped out of the car. After speaking to Caroline, he'd gone home to have it out with Estelle; and, finally, after denying it and trying to twist it around and accuse *him* of being the cheat, the bitch had admitted that she was in love with Dale and had been planning to run off and set up home with him and the children.

It was hearing her plans for the children that had pushed Stefan over the edge. Estelle had made his life hell for years with her incessant nagging and spiteful putdowns, and he had done everything in his power to try to make her happy; but nothing he did was ever good enough for her, and now he knew why. From here on out, she could fuck whoever she wanted to, because he was totally and utterly done with her. But it would be a cold day in hell before he allowed his brother to play daddy to Frankie and Poppy while the cunt was torturing his own wife and planning to steal her baby.

Using his key to let himself into the house, Stefan threw the door open and marched across the hallway, yelling, 'Where are you, you bastard?'

*

In Jakub's arms, Rosa cried out at the sound of Stefan's voice. Tears streaming down her cheeks, she extended her hand towards him when he strode into the kitchen.

'What the fuck...?' Stefan stopped in his tracks and stared at Jakub in shock. 'What's going on?'

'I am taking her to doctor,' Jakub said calmly as he aimed the shotgun at him. 'I know you are not bad like the others, but I *will* shoot if you try to stop me.'

Rosa cried out again, and Cheryl was as confused as Stefan looked when she said, '*Mój syn... mój syn...*'

'What's she going on about?' Stefan asked, frowning at Jakub. 'Is she delirious?'

'No, she say because is true,' Jakub replied quietly. 'You are her son.'

'*What?*' Stefan's expression morphed from confusion to utter disbelief, and he gave a humourless laugh, saying, 'Don't be ridiculous, man. I'm the double of my dad.'

'Yes, you are,' Jakub agreed. 'But you do not look like your *mother*.' He spat out the word. 'Because she is *thief*.'

Unsure what that meant, and unable to understand any more of what they were saying when they both started speaking Polish, Cheryl edged towards the conservatory door. Jakub was protecting Rosa, but she knew that there were more guns in the house, and she was terrified that if she didn't get out of there before the family came back, they would get to the cabinet and force her back into the attic.

Chapter 51

In the back seat of Dale's car, Sonia had been watching the live footage from the CCTV cameras as he drove them back to the house at breakneck speed. The signal had started cutting out as soon as they hit open countryside, and she had screamed in frustration when she'd lost sight of Cheryl.

The signal came back at last as they drove through the gates and headed towards the house, and her eyes widened in alarm when she saw what was happening.

'Stef and Jakub are in there,' she squawked. 'Jakub's got Rosa and he's pointing a fucking sawn-off shotgun at Stefan! The bastard must have let them both out.'

'Traitorous cunt,' Alfie spat, already unclipping his seatbelt as Dale screeched to a stop.

'Stay there,' Dale ordered, looking back at Sonia as he hopped out of the car.

'No chance,' she snarled, tossing her own seatbelt aside. 'If that little bitch thinks she's getting the better of me, she's got another thing coming!'

Stefan had left the front door open and he was closest to the hallway now, so he'd heard the approaching car before the others did. Aware that it was probably his parents and his brother, he made a snap decision and barked, 'Run, Cheryl!'

Cheryl froze for a second, but then forced her legs to move when she heard car doors slamming, followed by running footsteps. She launched out through the open conservatory door and, holding onto her stomach with both hands, stumbled across the grass. Gasping for breath, she glanced back at the house and shuddered when she saw Sonia waving her arms around in the kitchen. Dale was standing behind her, while Alfie, who appeared to be talking, walked slowly towards Jakub with his hands held out in front of him in what appeared to be a calming gesture. Afraid for Jakub and Rosa, Cheryl heard sirens in the distance and snapped her gaze off the scene before stumbling on, desperately trying to stay close to the fence to avoid setting off the security lights.

As she reached the fence separating the garden from the fields, a boom echoed out across the land and she screamed when a shadowy figure suddenly appeared in front of her. She felt the heat of urine trickling down her legs when a firm hand covered her mouth and an arm snaked around her from behind and lifted her off her feet, and she squeezed her eyes shut and prayed to God to save her baby as she felt herself being half-dragged, half-carried towards the barn behind the cottages.

Epilogue

'Awwww, she's such a cutie,' Anna gushed, stroking the downy cheek of the tiny baby who was sleeping in the Moses basket next to Cheryl's sofa. 'And I love that she's got your hair. You must be so proud, babe.'

'I'm just thankful she made it,' Cheryl said, gazing at her beautiful daughter, with her perfect little turned-up nose and her wispy red hair.

She had only come home from hospital two days ago, after going into premature labour brought on by the events of that awful last night at the Morans' house a month earlier, when Jakub's young friend, Aleksander, who hadn't drunk as much of the laced vodka as the other men, had stumbled outside the cottage and dragged her to safety when he saw her fleeing from the house and heard the booms of the shotgun being fired. He had saved her life; because the doctors had told her that she'd gone into shock and would have died of hypothermia if she had made it into the field.

The same field where Jakub and the other men had, on the night before that incident, been ordered to bury the bodies of all the girls and young men who had chosen the 'go home' option Alfie offered them when he decided to clean up his businesses.

Cheryl had been heartbroken when she'd learned what had

happened to those young people, all of whom had been told to pack their bags for the flight home, only to find themselves being driven to the barn, where they had been shot through the head by Alfie and Dale before being chucked into the deep hole Jakub and the others had dug, with their partially burnt belongings tossed in on top of them.

And that mass grave wasn't the only one the police had discovered. Agata's body had also been found out there, along with that of the girl who had miscarried on Cheryl's bed, and the other pregnant girl, who had been killed because she had seen too much. There had been several others slaughtered for trying to escape, as well; the 'foxes', as Sonia had called them when Cheryl questioned her about the gunshots she'd heard when she had stayed with them after being mugged. And, lastly, the body of Dorothy, who, unlike the others, had been strangled to death instead of being shot – by Sonia, it had later transpired.

The Morans' land had been dubbed 'The Killing Fields' in the press, and the news stations had dedicated hours of airtime to reports of the arrest of 'crazed gunman' Jakub Kowalski, who had murdered his employers: upstanding businessman and mayoral candidate, Alfie Moran, and his former beauty queen wife, Sonia, and the attempted murders of their sons, Dale and Stefan. Drone video footage of the house of horrors had been played on a loop, along with footage of the police exhuming the bodies in the field, and Cheryl hadn't been able to switch her TV on for fear of accidentally seeing it and being dragged back into the nightmare.

Once it was revealed that Jakub had actually broken into the house that night in order to rescue Rosa and then hand himself in to the police to tell them everything before Alfie managed to wipe out every last trace of his crimes, the news reports shifted in tone to highlight the fact that the modern-day slavery trade was still very much alive in Britain, and Jakub was hailed as a hero by the public. And Dale, who had initially been portrayed as a victim, was subsequently arrested for the hands-on part he had played in his father's brutal empire.

'Are you OK, babe?' Anna asked, looking at Cheryl with concern when she saw that her friend was deep in thought.

'Yeah, I'm good,' Cheryl said, smiling sadly. 'Just thinking how lucky I am.'

'Understatement, or *what*,' Anna exclaimed. 'If you hadn't got out of there that night, this little one wouldn't be here right now. And nor would you,' she added, sitting next to Cheryl and hugging her. 'I can't believe I nearly lost you, and I'm so sorry for falling out with you over that creep. If he hadn't made me lie to you that night, you'd have dumped him and none of this would have happened.'

'Stop it,' Cheryl sighed, resting her head on Anna's shoulder. 'None of this was your fault, and I don't ever want to talk about *him* again.'

'I get that,' Anna said, stroking her hair. 'But have you thought what might happen if he tries to see the baby in the future? I've heard about men doing that: suing the mothers of their kids for access, even after they've been sent down for abusing them. It's totally fucked up, but it happens, so you need to be prepared.'

'It's not going to happen with me,' Cheryl stated fiercely. 'I'll kill him with my bare hands before he ever gets near my daughter.'

'And I'll be there to help you,' Anna assured her, popping her head up to look out of the window when she heard the gate squeaking open. 'You've got visitors,' she said, jumping up to go and answer the door.

'Who is it?' Cheryl asked. 'I'm not really in the mood to see anyone.'

'I think you'll want to see this one,' Anna grinned.

Cheryl sighed as Anna bounded out of the room. She'd forgotten how talkative the girl was, and she was already exhausted, but she was grateful that her friend had decided to come and stay to look after her while she recovered, because she wasn't sure she could have faced sleeping in the house alone with those horrible visions of that poor girl and her baby still so fresh in her mind. But she was *home*, and she and her precious daughter were both alive and doing well, so she refused to let herself slide back into the gloom she'd been buried under for the last few months.

The door opened and Cheryl looked up when Anna walked in, followed by Sharon, Bob and another woman, who she presumed must be a second carer. Tears flooded her eyes when Bob gave her a huge gummy grin, and said, 'Eh up, stranger.'

'You look amazing,' she said, reaching for his hand when he sat beside her. 'You've put on so much weight.'

'Give over flirting with me,' he chuckled. 'I'm already spoken for – ain't that right, Shazza?'

'In your dreams,' Sharon said, rolling her eyes in mock-despair as she walked over to take a peek in the Moses basket. 'Ahhhh, look at her,' she cooed. 'She's the absolute image of you, Cheryl.'

'Can I look?' the other woman asked, still standing nervously back.

Looking up at her and seeing her properly for the first time, Cheryl's eyes widened in surprise.

'*Fiona?* Wow, you look so different. I didn't recognise you.'

'I've been in rehab,' Fiona said, blushing as she flicked a glance at Sharon. '*She* made me go.'

'I told you about it in my texts,' Sharon said. 'Should have twigged it wasn't you answering, because it didn't sound like you; when I got blocked after sending you the one about Bob's heart attack, I figured you'd probably got sick of me bothering you with it all while you were trying to start your new life.'

'I would never have done that,' Cheryl murmured. 'I'm just glad he had you there to look after him while I was away.'

'She's been a bloody angel,' Bob said, squeezing Cheryl's hand as he gazed fondly up at Sharon. 'Got me to hospital in the nick of time, *and* sorted my girl out.'

'Only doing my job,' Sharon said, winking at Cheryl as she added, 'Don't be thinking you're special, or anything.'

'She loves me really,' Bob whispered, nudging Cheryl playfully. 'Now let me have a look at the little one, then we'll get off and leave you in peace,' he said, standing up and walking over to the Moses basket.

Watching as he leaned down and gently stroked her daughter's cheek, Cheryl felt her heart swell. He was such a lovely man, and she was so glad to see him back to his old self.

'Thanks for coming,' she said, standing up to give him a hug when he'd finished looking at the baby. 'I'll pop over and see you soon.'

'You'll be lucky to catch him in,' Sharon said. 'Now he's back on his feet, he's always out and about doing odd jobs for your neighbours.'

'Someone's got to look after the old buggers,' Bob said, grinning as he headed for the door.

As they left, a car pulled up outside. Already back on the sofa, Cheryl gave Anna a questioning look when she saw her frown as she gazed out through the window.

'Who is it?'

'Stefan. Do you want me to get rid?'

'No, it's OK. You can let him in.'

'Are you sure?' Anna asked.

Cheryl nodded, so Anna went out to answer the door. Seconds later, Stefan walked in carrying a bunch of flowers.

'I hope I'm not imposing?' he asked, standing awkwardly by the door. 'I rang the hospital to ask how you were doing and they told me you'd been discharged.'

'It's fine,' Cheryl said, smiling when she saw the concern in his dark eyes.

Stefan gave a guilty little smile in return and placed the flowers on the table, saying, 'I won't stay, because I'm probably the last person you want to see. I just wanted to make sure you were OK, and to tell you that if you need anything, call me.' He handed a small business card to her. 'Oh, and I've set up an account for the baby,' he added.

'Her name's Rosa,' Cheryl said when she caught him flicking a glance at the Moses basket.

'Really?' Stefan's eyebrows shot up. 'That's, um ... *surprising.*'

'Rosa saved our lives,' Cheryl explained. 'If she hadn't taken those capsules off me, we probably wouldn't be here now; and I'll never forget how kind she was, considering what she was going through herself. I had no idea what she'd suffered.'

'Neither did I,' Stefan admitted. 'I still can't quite believe it. Obviously, she was always there when I was a child, but I thought she was the nanny and my parents kept her on as housekeeper out of loyalty. I can't even begin to imagine how heartbreaking it must have been for her to be forced to watch me grow up thinking that *woman* was my mother, all because my father slept with her and got her pregnant when Sonia had been told she couldn't have children. The bitch didn't even want me; she just wanted to punish Rosa for having the gall to produce the heir she couldn't provide. The evil of the woman is incomprehensible.'

'I won't argue with you on that,' Cheryl said, shuddering at the memory of Sonia's wickedness. 'I hated the way she spoke to Rosa.'

'You and me both,' Stefan sighed. 'But at least she'll never have the chance to destroy any more lives, so it worked out well in the end.'

'Yeah, it did,' Cheryl agreed. Then, frowning, she said, 'Is Rosa *his* real mother, as well?'

'Dale's?' Stefan asked, guessing that was who she was talking about. 'No.' He shook his head. 'Apparently, another young maid caught my dad's eye, but Rosa reckoned she ran away after giving birth, so she got lucky.'

'Christ, what a disgusting mess they made of your lives,' Cheryl murmured. 'It can't be easy for you finding out that everything you've ever known was a lie.'

'I'm OK,' Stefan said. 'Being the "boring one" had its advantages,' he went on, making quote marks with his fingers. 'I genuinely had no idea about half the stuff my father and Dale were involved in; and what I *did* know, I refused to have anything to do with. I just wish I'd had the strength to report them and make them stop, but it took a real man like Jakub to do that.'

'Don't put yourself down,' Cheryl said kindly. 'You were up against three of the most manipulative people I've ever met. And you were *family*, so you couldn't have gone against them when you'd had the loyalty thing drummed into you your whole life.'

'I know. But I could have done *something*.'

'You did,' Cheryl reminded him. 'You're the one who persuaded them to stop the prostitution and slave racket.'

'And look how that turned out,' Stefan muttered. 'All those kids dead because they chose freedom over continuing to work for the man who had abused them. It's sickening.'

'And that's not your fault any more than Rosa getting locked up was my fault, because the capsules she withheld were meant for me,' said Cheryl.

'You're right,' Stefan conceded. 'Logically, I know all this, but I guess it's going to take time to forgive myself.'

'You'll get there.'

'Hopefully.' Stefan smiled. 'Once the divorce is out of the way and I know exactly where I stand financially, I've told Rosa that I'll take her home to see if we can find her family.'

'*Her* family?' Cheryl raised an eyebrow.

'Yes, I know it's mine as well,' Stefan said. 'But that's another thing that's going to take time. Finding out that someone is related to you when you've spent your entire life thinking of them as staff is a bit much to handle.'

'I can imagine,' Cheryl said. 'Take your time and be kind to yourself.'

'I will,' Stefan agreed. 'Anyway, before I go, I wanted to give you this.' He pulled an envelope out of his pocket.

'What is it?' she asked.

'The deeds to your house.'

'Sorry?'

'Ah ... you didn't know,' Stefan said. 'My father bought it while you were staying with them.'

'How?' Cheryl was confused. 'They talked about it and I started the process, but it never got completed.'

'It did,' said Stefan. 'They must have forged the rest of the paperwork. But that was pretty typical of them, because it appears that *my* name was on several of their properties without my knowledge. I can only assume they did it so they could leave me holding the can if something happened at one of the homes and they were sued. But it's all good if it keeps Dale from ever getting his hands on anything when he gets out.'

'Yeah, that *is* good,' Cheryl agreed.

'Right, well, I'll leave you in peace,' Stefan said. 'But please keep my number, and if you and baby Rosa ever need anything, don't hesitate to call.'

'I won't,' Cheryl agreed. 'And thanks for everything, Stefan. I always knew you weren't like them. You were extremely serious compared to them, which I admit I found intimidating; but the love I saw in your eyes whenever you spoke to your children showed me what a decent man you are.'

'Thank you, that means a lot,' Stefan said modestly. Then, stuffing his hands into his pockets, he said, 'Before I go, I, um, have someone with me who would quite like to meet you. But please don't feel obliged if it's too much.'

'Who?' Cheryl asked, giving him a questioning look.

'One second,' he said. 'She's in the car.'

'Wow,' Anna mouthed, gaping at Cheryl when he rushed out of the room. 'He is *hot!*'

'Behave, or I'll tell Sean,' Cheryl teased.

'Spoilsport,' Anna grinned. Then, turning her head when she heard footsteps in the hall, she smiled at Stefan when he came back into the room. But it was the woman who walked in behind him who caused her eyebrows to shoot up, and she murmured, 'What the hell...'

'Cheryl, this is Caroline,' Stefan said.

'Oh my God.' Cheryl stared at the woman. '*Dale's* Caroline?'

'Stefan's now,' Caroline said, smiling shyly as she slipped her hand into his.

'Really?' Cheryl said, unable to stop staring at the woman, because it was like looking at a prettier, slimmer version of herself, with the same red hair, the same shaped face and even the same smattering of freckles on her nose. 'Well, you've certainly upgraded with this one, because he's a far better man than his brother.'

'I know,' Caroline agreed, flashing another smile at Stefan before turning back to Cheryl. 'About the *other* one, thanks for agreeing to meet me, because I wanted to apologise for not warning you about him.'

'How could you have warned me?' Cheryl asked. 'You didn't even know me.'

'No, but I should have found out who you were when I heard he had a new girlfriend,' Caroline countered. 'It's been bothering me for a while, but I was so glad to be rid of him, I took the coward's way out and left you to it.'

'You were right to,' said Cheryl. 'Now I know what an evil bastard he is, you'd have been stupid to put yourself on his radar again. I just wish I'd had the sense to dump him before anyone else got hurt,' she added, glancing guiltily at Anna.

'We both know how charming he can be when he's hunting his prey, so you weren't to know how bad it would get,' Caroline said. 'I'm just happy that you and the baby are free of him now.'

'Me too,' Cheryl agreed.

'Well, he's certainly got a type, I'll give him that,' Anna remarked, looking from Cheryl to Caroline and back again. 'No wonder he wasn't interested in me.'

'Think yourself lucky,' Stefan remarked. Then, to Cheryl, he said, 'We'll get going and leave you in peace. Put my card somewhere safe, and please don't hesitate to call me if you ever need anything.'

'Thanks,' Cheryl said, staring after Caroline in disbelief as Anna showed them out.

As Stefan and Caroline climbed into his car, Anna scowled when she spotted a familiar face walking along the pavement.

'What do *you* want?' she demanded, folding her arms when he pushed through the gate.

'To see Cheryl, obviously,' Chris said. 'I couldn't believe it when I saw all that stuff about her on the news; being held prisoner in that massive house by her own husband and his family. That's sick, man.'

'Ah … I get it.' Anna gave a knowing smirk. 'You think she's got money because her husband's family was rich, and you've come to try to sweet-talk your way back into her life. Well, fuck you, dickhead. My girl's dealt with enough crap this past year, and you ain't getting anywhere near her.' She closed the door in his face at that, and walked back into the living room where Cheryl was feeding Rosa, who had woken up while she was outside.

'Were you just arguing with someone?' Cheryl asked.

'Nah, just wiping some shit off my shoe,' Anna said, sitting down beside her and stroking the baby's downy red hair. 'Now hurry up so Auntie Anna can have a hold.'

Acknowledgements

All my love, as ever, to Win, Michael, Andrew, Azzura, Marissa, Lariah, Antonio, Marlowe, Ava, Amber, Martin, Jade, Reece, Diaz, Azariah, Auntie Doreen, Pete, Lorna, Cliff, Chris, Glen, Toni, Natalie, Dan, Rayne, Amari, Zi, River, Silvia, Paul, Lee, Elle, Val, Norman, Liz, Richie, Julie and co, and the rest of my clan – past, present and future.

Huge thanks to my agent, Sheila Crowley; my editor, Leodora Darlington, and all at Orion; Wayne Brookes; Jeanna Polley and Ian Martin.

Much love to Betty and Ronnie Schwartz, KC, Katy and John, Jayne and Nev, Tracy, Laney, Tasha, Rik, Chris and Allan, Jo and Dom, Brian and Jac, Louis Emerick, Jodie Prenger, Steve Evets, Joe Gill, Gary Shail, and Sean Ward.

Big shout out to my old friends in Warrington and Hulme, and to my readers and friends on FB, X and Insta. And a very special mention to Tode, Carolyn Caughey, and Sharon Oakes – in whose honour one of my characters in here is named; all sadly gone, but fondly remembered.

Heavenly love to my dad, and all the loved ones who are no longer here; RIP x

Exclusive Q&A with Mandasue Heller

What inspired you to write *The Family*?

When I start a book, I rarely have a solid idea of what it will be about. There's usually a vague image of a character or an event in my mind, and I type it out and run with it to see where it takes me. With *The Family*, the vision I saw was of a once-grand, now derelict old house sitting in the middle of a council estate. I've always been fascinated by rundown and abandoned old properties, and if I lived opposite one, as Cheryl does in this book, I'd be itching to get inside and explore. Cheryl doesn't get to do that, but her involvement with the new owners and occupiers of the house change her life in ways she could never have imagined. I guess my message here is that old saying: all that glistens is not gold.

This is your twentieth book, which is quite the achievement! How did the writing process for this differ to books you've written before? Do you find it gets easier to finish a manuscript the more books you write?

I'd been a professional singer for many years before I wrote my first book, and never imagined that I would be capable of finishing one, never mind twenty! My first was a pure passion project. I had spent ten years in the notorious Hulme Crescents, and it was like no place I'd ever lived before – or since. I had experienced the best and the worst of humanity there, and I wanted to write about it because of the life-changing effect it'd had on me. I decided very early in the process that I didn't want to write about real people, so I created my own characters and dropped them into the environment. I wrote quite a few in that setting, but the Crescents no longer existed, so I eventually branched out into different areas, which inevitably changed the tone of my writing over time.

As many as I've now written, it definitely doesn't get easier. But I actually think that's a good thing, because I don't ever want to get to the point of thinking that I've cracked this writing lark and can just churn them out. Each book is its own complete story, and my characters become living, breathing entities in my mind long before I submit the finished version. That's quite a pressure, because I'm never sure if anyone else is going to love – or hate – the characters as much as I do.

The Family was a particularly difficult book for a variety of reasons. I work from home and spend a lot of time in solitude, so I didn't think lockdown would affect me as much as it did. That, and being a woman of a certain age, with all the joys *that* brings, threw me into a spiral of chronic insomnia and overwhelming brain fog. I had already struggled with the last few books, but it reached a peak when I started *The Family*, and there were times when I honestly didn't know if I could get it done. I took steps to sort myself out and am now able to think straight again, but that experience definitely made this book a challenge. But the pressure doesn't disappear when the book is finished, because

I then start the self-doubt process: convincing myself that my editor will tell me it's a pile of crap. That hasn't happened yet, thank God, but the fear is real!

You're a very seasoned writer. Looking back, what advice would you have given yourself when writing your first book?

The advice I would have given myself back then is the advice I give to aspiring writers who contact me now: to never think about who will eventually read your book while you're writing it. I was acutely conscious of what my mum would think of my first, and that massively inhibited me. I managed to shake it off, because I realised that the stories I wanted to tell would lose their power and realism if I didn't write them from the heart.

In the end, my mum was the first to read it, and she loved it so much she narrated it onto cassette tapes for my nana, who was in her nineties and blind by then. I would also have advised myself not to resist when – as very often happens – my stories start heading in different directions than I'd intended. It doesn't always lead to anything, in which case I scrap the changes and go back to the original version, but sometimes it can take me by surprise and reveal twists that even I didn't see coming.

In which ways is this book similar to and different from the books you've written before?

Each of my books are standalones, so the characters and situations are never the same. They are similar in tone, because I set them in rundown areas where ordinary people are often struggling to survive. I've lived in those places and have experienced some of the same hardships as my characters, so it's definitely a theme that is close to my heart. During those times, I also gained a great insight into the types of personalities I write about. I've known good people who were trying their hardest to get by but were sometimes forced to step outside the law in order to survive, and I've met bad people who committed horrendous crimes and thrived on instilling fear in their victims and wreaking havoc. One thing I learned very quickly is that no one is all good or all bad, and even the mildest-mannered of people are capable of doing unimaginable things when their lives or those of their loved ones are threatened. My books always have those elements, but I generally stick to one geographical area, where the characters live around each other, or at least know of each other. In *The Family*, there is a collision of three different worlds: the girl from the council estate meets the rich boy and gets whisked into a fairy tale life, only to discover a very dark secret behind the facade. Money can definitely buy happiness, but when the banknotes are soaked in somebody else's blood, sweat and tears, how long can it last?

When writing *The Family*, which were the easiest characters to write, and which were the hardest? Do you have any favourite or most disliked characters?

I get deeply involved with all my characters, so much so that I can hear their voices, see their faces, and even visualise the rooms they're in when I'm writing. I also feel their emotions, much to the amusement of my partner, who can tell at a glance what kind of scene I'm writing just by looking at my expression: I'll either be snarling, laughing or crying. I've also had people not recognise my voice on the phone, because they've rung when I'm in the middle of something nasty and I speak 'in character'. In *The Family*, I loved Cheryl, Bob, Agata, Sharon and Jakub, because they were the ones I was emotionally invested in; but I got a kick out of writing Dale, Sonia, Alfie and Estelle, because those type of characters allow me to unleash my twisted side.

Which scenes did you enjoy writing most?

I particularly enjoyed the scenes involving Bob and Cheryl; I just loved their relationship. Decades apart in age, they are more like family than neighbours, and the affection they have for each other moved me to tears at times. I also really enjoyed Jakub's scenes, because he's an extremely intense character with hidden depths. Scenes involving Sonia and Estelle gave me conflicting emotions, because I sometimes felt sorry for the latter, while despising her at others. One tiny scene I had fun with involved an elderly customer of Cheryl's at the café. In my mind's eye, as soon as the bell jangled over the door, I saw a tiny slip of a woman walk in who instantly reminded me of my great-aunt Nell. She always took salt in her tea, so my character had to have the same.

(Immediately after I finished answering this question, I felt guilty that I hadn't mentioned Anna – like she's real and would be offended that I left her out. Yikes! I did enjoy her snarky character – *and* how loyal she proved herself to be when push came to shove.)

Family is a key theme in this novel; how important is the concept of family to you? Did you draw on any of your own experience with family – your own or others – in any elements of the story?

My family is everything to me, but I purposefully avoid ever using any of their names in my books, and I never write their personal stories – or anyone else's. I have used some of my own past experiences, however; usually a memory of something unpleasant that happened to me when I was younger. I'll put a character into a similar situation, then allow them to work their way through it in a way I wish I'd been able to at the time. I mostly write from imagination rather than experience, but I have to be careful, because I have a habit of writing things that later come true. It's happened so many times it's not even funny anymore, and it's always too specific for it to be a coincidence. I'm also superstitious about putting the names of boyfriends and girlfriends together in my acknowledgements, after several couples split up within a year of the book coming out. Spooky!

There are some emotionally gut-wrenching scenes in this book. Which were the moments in the book you found it hardest to explore?

The sheer cruelty that some of the characters display towards others affected me deeply, mainly because I know that these things are actually happening the world over. We all know modern slavery exists; numerous news reports and documentaries have highlighted it. But we only ever see the aftermath, when the abusers are brought to justice. What we don't see is the horrendous torture they inflict on their victims before that – sometimes for many years. People assume that these things are hidden from view, but many victims are forced to work in plain sight, terrorised into keeping their mouths shut while earning money that will be snatched away from them the second they return to wherever they're being held. Sadly, it's happening everywhere. Maybe even in that house across the road from you right now...

What do you hope readers take away from *The Family*?

Apart from hoping that they enjoy it, I hope that it makes people aware that things are not always what they appear to be on the surface. That the people who smile a little too brightly when they're serving you in a shop, or the ones who never seem to look you in the eye as they strive to perform faster and better than everyone else, might just be living in terror behind closed doors.

Credits

Mandasue Heller and Orion Fiction would like to thank everyone at Orion who worked on the publication of *The Family* in the UK.

Editorial
Leodora Darlington
Sanah Ahmed

Copyeditor
Jade Craddock

Proofreader
Celia Killen

Marketing
Katie Sadler
Cait Davies

Contracts
Dan Herron
Ellie Bowker
Alyx Hurst

Audio
Paul Stark

Design
Tomas Almedia
Loveday May
Nick Shah

Editorial Management
Charlie Panayiotou
Jane Hughes
Bartley Shaw
Lucy Bilton

Finance
Jasdip Nandra
Nick Gibson
Sue Baker

Publicity
Sian Baldwin

Production
Ruth Sharvell

Operations
Jo Jacobs
Sharon Willis

Sales
Jen Wilson
Esther Waters
Victoria Laws
Toluwalope Ayo-Ajala
Rachael Hum
Anna Egelstaff
Sinead White
Georgina Cutler

If you loved *The Family*, don't miss
the next gripping page-turner
from the million-copy bestselling
Queen of Manchester crime!

THE CHILD

When Isla Hanson's husband, Jerry, dies, leaving his
entire estate to her, she knows she'll be set for life.
But contrary to the belief of his wealthy friends and
business associates, who all seem to think she was only
ever interested in him for the money, Isla truly loved
Jerry and struggles to imagine life without him.

With no children of her own, and no real family to
speak of, Isla is grateful for the support of her best
friend, Tia. But when a strange woman and child
appear at the funeral, Isla's entire world is turned
upside down, and she is shocked to learn that the
loving husband she dedicated fifteen years of her life
to might have been living a double-life all along...